Holding Back the Tide

Frank J. DeRuosi

The tide of change
brings new opportunity.
Hope you enjoy the book!
Frank DeRuosi

Black Rose Writing | Texas

ISBN: 978-1-68513-196-8
PUBLISHED BY BLACK ROSE WRITING
www.blackrosewriting.com

Printed in the United States of America
Suggested Retail Price (SRP) $24.95

Holding Back the Tide is printed in Baskerville

*As a planet-friendly publisher, Black Rose Writing does its best to eliminate unnecessary waste to reduce paper usage and energy costs, while never compromising the reading experience. As a result, the final word count vs. page count may not meet common expectations.

For Josh and Emma. Never stop pursuing your dreams.

Holding Back
the Tide

JUNE

"In early June the world of leaf and blade and flowers explodes, and every sunset is different."
-John Steinbeck

ONE

Charlie lay awake in bed watching the dust motes float freely in the beam of light that sliced through the tear in the window shade. Microscopic bits of skin, hair, clothing fiber, and dead bugs swirled in the sliver of sunshine like so many teenagers dancing with reckless abandon. The wound was made years ago when Charlie flung some random toy at his brother. Rather than connecting with his brother's head, as Charlie had intended, it hit the shade instead opening a gash.

His left hand was curled behind his head, aimlessly twisting his mane of thick, black hair. Casually, he rocked his head from side to side, allowing the light to fall onto his face and then onto the pillow. He was awake now only because his cell phone had been chirping for the last twenty minutes or so; friends wondering where he was; some SnapChat stories that begged for attention; other social media importance that only drained his battery. Charlie sat up and grabbed at the phone perched precariously on the end of the bedside table, but his jerky attempt only knocked it onto the floor. It disappeared into a sea of shorts, shirts, underwear, damp bathing suits, bath towels, and a myriad of footwear that lay scattered around the room. His mother had ridden him all day yesterday about the *unacceptable condition* of his room; marveling, in an irritated way, at how such a catastrophe of clothing could occur in the few days since their arrival at the beach house.

"It's my *side* of the room," he reminded her in a tone that was a bit too testy even for him. He wasn't sure why he answered the way he did, but he knew that lately his only mood seemed to be a dark one.

"Clean it," his mother snapped, which ended the conversation.

"Crap," he uttered as a quick glance at the floor did not reveal his cell phone.

Charlie sank back down into the hold of his bed, feeling defeated. He turned to where his younger brother slept. The bed was empty, and neatly made the way you would find a hotel bed made, right down to the stacked pillows. Not a stitch of clothing lay about. His bath towel hung on the peg next to the door with yesterday's bathing suit drying next to it. The top of his dresser was empty, except for a stick of deodorant, some Axe body spray, and a jar of hair sculpting wax. That was Carson, though, buttoned up. He was always a tidy kid, taking the time to put himself together. But when he turned thirteen recently, the interest in his outward appearance tripled: hence the products. Charlie looked at his own dresser; drawers in various open positions; a small metropolis of things cluttering the top–very few upright; and most without their caps. There were socks, a brush, hair gel, various deodorants, some cologne, and what looked like a couple of toothbrushes wedged in the spaces between.

"Crap," he uttered again, and sat up a second time.

He looked over at his brother's side of the room again. The pristine condition astounded him. It was as if there was a force field that parted the room in half, keeping Charlie's mess at bay. That's how stark the contrast was between the two boys. He could feel himself getting angry and wished he could just have his own space. He longed for a spot between four walls where he could disappear and be with himself without worrying when his privacy would be trodden upon by his annoying little brother. Carson's steadfast tidiness wasn't the only reason he was tired of sharing a room with his brother. Amongst other things, age was the driving factor.

Charlie was sixteen, soon to be seventeen. He didn't understand why he had to share a room with his freshly minted thirteen-year-old brother.

"Why can't he move into Sarah's room?" was how Charlie had always begun the conversation. "They're closer in age. They're both kids. They hang around together more. A lot of their friends are the same. They *like* each other."

"Charles, this conversation is old. Sarah is a girl. She needs her privacy. You and Carson are brothers. Biologically, it only makes sense that the two of you share a room. Besides, it's just during the summer. You'll survive." His parents always ended the conversation that way.

It struck Charlie as odd that he still thought of having *parents*; since now there was only one, and barely at that. His chest tightened as that thought registered in his head, mumbling the curse word that came instinctively after.

Grabbing at the closest bathing suit, somewhat stiff from yesterday's salt water, he tugged it on and made his way to the hall bathroom. He stopped mid-stride, spun, and began to kick his clothing aside, trying to find his cell phone.

"Aha. There you are," he said aloud as the iPhone dislodged from a jumble of beach towels and boxer briefs.

A sea of notifications littered his screen, mostly from his friend Jackson.

"Jesus, people, put your phones down," he said as he scrolled through his messages on his way to the bathroom.

Once inside, he glimpsed himself in the vanity mirror. Admittedly, he was a good-looking kid, but then immediately felt guilty for the indulgence. He had grown six inches this past school year and was no longer the tiny runt he was at the start of his sophomore year. Skinny, yes. But filling out.

His dark hair was tousled in a serious bout of bedhead. He could use to shear off the subtle stubble that grew above his lip and cradled his chin, and probably a shower. He sniffed at his armpit.

"Not bad," he muttered and reached for the deodorant. His phone went off again.

It's 10:30. Where are you?
I'm on the porch. WTF?

The text from Jackson read.

Charlie typed quickly and hit *SEND*.

Just got up. Be by soon.

He rubbed a dollop of sculpting wax between his two hands and tamed the beast that was his hair. After what seemed like a twenty-minute, powerful draining of his bladder, and a quick brush of his teeth, Charlie headed down the hallway to the living room. His brother and sister were sitting on the couch watching *Queer Eye*.

"Well, look who it is, Sleeping Beauty," his mother said as he passed through the kitchen. "Didn't think you were getting up today."

"Yeah. Me neither. Jackson's been texting. Woke me up."

"How is Jackson?" his mother asked as she poured herself a cup of coffee. "Haven't seen him much since we got here."

Here we go with the questions, Charlie thought.

"He's Jackson. Fine, I guess. You know." He grabbed a banana from the bowl on the counter that separated the kitchen from the living room.

Dropping himself into the recliner diagonal to the couch; he ripped off the peel.

Sensing his sister side-eyeing him, Charlie turned to face her and cocked an eyebrow.

"Ew," his sister Sarah said, looking at him. "Just, ew."

Knowing better, but taking the bait anyway, Charlie asked, "What?"

Sarah had undergone a transformation as well this past school year. A metamorphosis that, admittedly, Charlie was less than thrilled about. It seemed like overnight she went from being his sweet little sister to his biggest critic. She fancied herself a fashionista, as well as a life coach, and didn't pass up an opportunity to deliver some advice.

"Well, to start, that's the same bathing suit you had on yesterday. And I can tell by the waistband of your underwear and the fabric that is showing above the sagging board shorts that they're from yesterday, too. And I didn't hear the shower start up when you were in the bathroom…"

"Really?" his mom chimed in from the kitchen. "I could've sworn I heard water running for, like, twenty minutes. What was that?"

Charlie rolled his eyes and shook his head as his sister continued. "… which means you probably didn't bathe, just wiped new deodorant over the old–at least I hoped you did - which is gross. I mean, boys. You're just gross." Satisfied with her dressing down, Sarah cocked her head and smirked.

"Amen sister," Carson chimed in, "boys are gross," and he hi-fived Sarah.

Feeling his temper begin to rear its head, Charlie stood from the chair and headed for the front door. He narrowed his gaze at Carson. "Ya know you're a boy, right, nerd?"

"Don't pigeon hole my gender with your outdated labels, Charlie."

Charlie chortled and shook his head. His younger brother liked to think of himself as a champion of the cause. Whether that cause was gender identity, climate change, or ridding the world of plastic. "Carson, do you pee standing up?" Charlie asked as he neared the front door.

Both younger siblings' facial expressions portrayed a decent level of distaste for the question. "Not that it's any of your business, but yeah, I do."

"Welp, that makes you a boy," Charlie said as he pushed open the screen door and stepped onto the porch.

From behind, he heard his mother call out, "What are you going to do today?"

Charlie yelled back without turning, "Same thing I do every day, mom. Try to take over the world."

"Did you clean your room?" his mom yelled back, but Charlie didn't respond. Instead, he let the screen door slam shut behind him like a period on the conversation.

TWO

Stepping off of the porch and onto the sidewalk, the early morning sun fell over Charlie, warming his skin and brightening his mood. His disposition always lightened every time he left his house. It was an admission that further furrowed his brow.

He was happy to be back at the beach. It was a long school year, not without its own drama and disappointment. Now that he was back on the island, it seemed forever ago that he closed the door on his sophomore year. A year where everything changed, and, as far as Charlie was concerned, certainly not for the better.

The beach house had its perks, even though it meant rooming with his annoying little brother. His summer home brought carefree days of wandering the island, soaking up the sun, and being with his shore friends. Here, he could disappear all day. Not just from his mom and siblings, but sometimes, even from himself. The gladness he felt to be back at the shore pumped through him, almost causing him to smile. Almost.

The few blocks to Jackson's house were crowded with little kids carrying pails and various beach toys. Adults hauled colorful chairs and umbrellas as they made their way along the pavement, lugging coolers behind them. Teenagers sped by on bikes with surfboards, boogie boards, or skim boards tucked under their arms or nestled in racks. Cars slowed now and again, mistaking fire hydrants and drive-ways for parking spots. With each passing block, Charlie could feel himself loosen up. It was like getting out from under a weighted blanket. He could literally feel the ugliness inside of him just ooze away.

As he turned the corner onto Jackson's street, he could see his friend on the second-floor porch, digesting the news feed on his iPad. Jackson enjoyed his routine. His mornings began on the porch; news, or whatever passed as news these days scrolling on the iPad screen; coffee-iced or hot, depending on his mood. Spotify was always playing in the background running the gambit of ancient jazz favorites such as John Coltrane–inspired by and picked up from his dad- to the Indie Pop greats like Dua Lipa or Glass Animals. Once finished digesting the news flotsam on Twitter, Jackson would devour the social media sites, keeping up with the daily trappings of the twenty-first century teenager. Charlie always found Jackson's rituals a bit for show, but, again, that was Jackson. This morning was no different. Jackson was perched at the table in a Patagonia T-shirt and a blue and white pin-striped bathing suit, engrossed in the details of whatever played across the screen of the tablet settled between his crossed legs. 'Go Wrong,' by Hauskey, was pumping from the Bluetooth JBL speaker, floating out over the porch railing and falling down from above like sonic rain.

"Hey, Einstein," Charlie called up as he arrived at the front of the house. "Back door open?"

"Always." Jackson answered without breaking his gaze.

"Be right up," Charlie called back as he made his way down the side of the house to the rear entrance.

Jackson's house was a bit more than Charlie's. A three-story Victorian, it was rather impressive on a block of single-story bungalows and two-story homes. Modernized inside, it dated back to the early 1900's. It wasn't as *ostentatious* - a word Charlie's mother liked to use–as some of the new constructions, but still impressive. Years ago, the old lady underwent major renovations. The bedrooms had been moved to the first and third floors, and the living spaces on the second. Charlie entered the back door into a game room complete with a pool table flanked by two bedrooms and a full bath. He noticed Jackson's older brother Noah's door was closed, showing that he was probably in there, still sleeping. Charlie took care to pass quietly. As he walked by, he thought he heard a giggle, but dismissed it as some errant video feed leaching from some electronic device. Jackson's door was open, his room looking very similar to Carson's side of the room–everything was in its place.

At the far end of the room, a wide staircase led up to the second floor. Charlie took the steps two at a time and emerged into the light filled open kitchen, dining room, living room space that was in stark contrast to the Victorian exterior of the house. Jackson's Corgi, Keefer, greeted him as he made his way to the wall of sliders on the far side of the room. Pushing one aside, Charlie stepped out.

Glancing up from his iPad, then placing it on the table next to him, Jackson said, "Well, good morning, sunshine. I see your beauty rest did little for you," then added with a smirk, "clean your room yet?"

Charlie chuckled though his nose, "My *side* of the room. And, no. I've grown accustomed to the random chaos of the space. It mirrors my life these past few months."

Taking a deep breath and exhaling, Jackson said, "Yeah. That."

"Yeah. That," Charlie said. He could feel his throat closing and his chest tightening. He turned away from his friend as his eyes filled unexpectedly and looked out into the street. Off in the distance, he could see the sun bouncing off of the waves.

"Look, Charlie. Sorry about your parents, man. But lots of people's parents split up, you know? This isn't 1965 where you need to hang your head in shame or anything. Divorce is an acceptable part of life these days. Hell, it's almost trendy."

"Easy for you to say, Jackson. Your parents are still together. Shit. They're the shining examples of parents everywhere. They still hold hands, for Christ's sake."

Jackson considered Charlie's remark. "Yeah. They are kind of corny like that. Anyway…"

"Yeah, anyway. It is what it is. Guess I'll get used to it."

"You will. Give it time." Jackson offered.

But somewhere, deep inside of himself, Charlie didn't think he'd ever get used to it. His parents' divorce lurked in the background constantly: never really there, but never really not. It was the last thing he thought about before falling asleep, and the first thing that entered his mind when he woke up. He couldn't shake it. It was like a shadow in which he was forever cast. Every-time he looked at his mother, it reminded him of his dad's absence. The only time he escaped the ache was when he was asleep. There were days, heavy days where he was enshrouded by his own darkness, that he wished he could sleep forever.

Jackson broke his thoughts. "Anyway. Now that you're here, albeit unfashionably late, guess who I ran into last night?"

Jackson cocked one eyebrow in an expression meant to say, *go ahead, guess.* Charlie, not feeling playful, rolled his eyes and sighed.

"Jesus, Jackson, I don't know… Santa Claus?"

Picking up on Charlie's mood, Jackson didn't press the matter. He sat back in his chair and said matter-of-factly, "Madison Walker."

The mention of the name grabbed Charlie's attention, causing him to sit up a bit in his chair. Madison was a friend, someone they both had known for as long as they were coming to the island for the summer—which was all their lives. She was part of the group of friends Charlie and Jackson hung around with from June to the end of August every year. Then, through the marvel of social media and the wizardry of smart phones, hung with during the school year. Last summer, Charlie felt something change between Madison and him. Nothing bad, but different. He was drawn to her more. He found himself hanging on her words; seeking her company; and thinking of her as he lay awake in bed at night. Whenever they were together, there seemed to be something blossoming beyond the friendship they had enjoyed for so many years.

"Well, what about her?" Charlie asked. "I haven't really seen her yet. We just got here a few days ago, and I've been sorta lying low."

"I was out walking Keefer. She was with Kelsey, and Joey…"

"Joey? Joey Mastromani? God, he can be such a douche," Charlie groaned.

Joey Mastromani actually went to Charlie's high school back home. He was the only shore friend that Charlie saw frequently throughout the year. While Charlie and Jackson hung out occasionally during the school year, Joey was someone Charlie endured daily. While they weren't exactly enemies, they weren't exactly friends either, at least off the island.

"Let me guess, he told you all about what an awesome season he had in lacrosse, or maybe basketball, or was it track? Or maybe it was the 'slightly used' C300 daddy bought him because he got his driver's license? Or was it the mountain house his family has at Camelback? *Bro, you need to come hit the slopes,"* Charlie mimicked.

"Dial back the hating, my friend," Jackson answered. "Does he go on a bit about himself? Yeah. But that's just his obvious attempt to cover-up for the deep lack of attention he feels from his over-indulgent parents. And, not to come to his defense, he is actually a very talented athlete. You've seen him on the beach. He's a force. He's not so bad, really."

"Welp, you don't have to spend the entire year listening to him."

"Truth. Anyway. Back to Madison. I was out walking Keefer and as I passed Annie's the three of them tumbled out, laughing. Joey literally smashed right into me, dumping ice-cream all over my shirt. '*Dude! I am so, so sorry. I didn't even see you.*' Obviously, I said, '*Let me clean that up,*' Joey said and started to…"

"Jackson," Charlie broke in, "focus."

"Yeah. Sorry. So, anyway, after the usual '*How've you been? How was your school year? When did you guys get back down here?*' routine we all go through, Madison immediately asked if I had seen you yet."

"That's it? That doesn't mean anything. She knows we hang together. I mean, ten minutes ago my mom was asking about you because she hasn't seen you yet..."

"How is your mom? She doing alright..."

"Jackson! Bring it back."

Exhaling sharply, Jackson said, "Calm yourself, little boy. It was what followed that pricked up my ears. She turned to Kelsey and said, '*It will be so good to see Charlie. He's had a rough year and I hope he's doing alright. I wonder if he's gotten any taller? I mean, I haven't seen him, except in Snaps. God, I hope he hasn't cut his hair. He was letting it grow out. He has such magnificent hair, thick and wavy. The way it just tumbles around his face. And his eyelashes. Every girl's dream. Why is it that guys have such great eye-lashes? It isn't fair.*'" His pantomime of Madison was close to perfect. "So, you see buddy, methinks she has the hots for you," Jackson finished.

Charlie sat quietly for a second or two, haphazardly scratching at his earlobe. A small smile teased one corner of his mouth. The end of last summer flashed in his head. Was there something mutual there? Would he and Madison pick up where they left off? Did they leave off? He wasn't sure of anything.

Realizing that Jackson was staring at him, waiting, Charlie simply offered, "Hmmm."

"Hmmm?" Jackson repeated. "That's it? You got nothing more to say than *hmmmm?*"

"Yeah. I don't know...." Charlie trailed off, simultaneously shaking his head and shrugging his shoulders. "We'll see."

"We'll see? We'll see what?" Jackson asked.

"Just... we'll see. I don't know, Jackson. We'll see where it goes."

"Oh, I know where it's going, son," Jackson said insightfully. "Someone is finally going to become a man this summer. *That's* where it's going."

Charlie chuckled, "Yeah, well, I'm not holding my breath. I haven't even seen her yet, and a year is a long time. Lots can change." Charlie was an expert on the amount of change that can occur in just six months. "Anyway, what about Kelsey?"

Jackson seemed surprised by Charlie's question. "Kelsey? What about her?"

"Come on, Jackson. Don't play dumb. She's been after you for a couple of summers now. Everyone knows that. She practically falls all over you. She laughs at everything you say, and, by-the-way, you're not that funny. She stares at you, all mesmerized by your greatness. She follows you around like a lost puppy. You pick up any vibes?"

Jackson picked up the iPad and started scrolling again. "Kelsey. Honestly, I don't see it."

"Well then, you're blind, Jackson. Okay. Last year's Fourth of July party on the beach? Remember?"

"Vaguely."

"We were all hanging around. Me, you, Madison, Kelsey, Joey…"

Jackson interrupted, "Spare me the roster, Charlie. I am well versed in the names of our friends."

"Fine. Kelsey didn't move from your side all night. You walked to the water, she walked to the water. You went to the jetty, she went to the jetty. You left to get a slice, who went with you?"

"Well," Jackson said, returning the iPad to the table, "if I remember correctly, a few people went with me: Joey…"

"And Kelsey," Charlie supplied. "She practically was attached to your hip. In fact, she flirted with you for the rest of the summer. She went out of her way to talk to you, dropping compliments about your hair or your bathing suit, or some other stupid thing.

Constantly touching your hand or your leg. And what about the kiss at the end of our last night?"

Jackson pulled his eyebrows together. "That, my friend, amounts to nothing. The last night is always a slobber fest *'Oh, it's been such a great summer; Oh, I can't believe it's over; I'm going to miss you guys so much,* blah, blah, blah. And it was a kiss on the cheek. You can't count a kiss on the cheek as anything but that: a kiss on the cheek. As Freud is famous for saying, sometimes a cigar is just a cigar."

Charlie laughed through his nose. "Yeah. I'm not talking about cigars, Jackson. Look, everyone knows Kelsey wants you. Not sure why you don't know that. If anyone is going to become a man this summer, it's most likely gonna be you."

Certainly not with Kelsey, Jackson thought to himself.

The two friends sat in silence for a bit, taking in the morning. The sounds of traffic, both pedestrian and vehicular, played across the neighborhood like a movie soundtrack. Inside, the TV flared to life, signaling Jackson's brother Noah's emergence from his bedroom. It was Jackson who broke the quiet, returning attention to his and Charlie's conversation.

"Okay, Charles, you're right. I know Kelsey is interested. Hell, you'd have to be dense to miss the signals she was sending out. It's just…, I don't know. I've known her forever. I mean, she's fit and all, and she's a great friend." He paused for a second or two before adding, "I think I just want to keep it that way."

He turned away and looked back out over the neighborhood. Charlie noted Jackson's bouncing knee, something he did when he was anxious.

There was a sense of something in Jackson's voice. Charlie couldn't quite put his finger on it. It seemed to Charlie that his friend wanted to say more, but was holding back. With a sigh he said, "Look, I get it, I do. I feel the same way about Madison. But then, sometimes, most times lately, I don't. You know?"

Charlie and Jackson locked eyes.

With a smirk, Charlie added, "She really said all those things, huh? She talked about my eye-lashes?"

"Well," Jackson said with a sheepish tone and a shrug of one shoulder, "I may have embellished that part, but she was asking about you."

"Oh. So, *you* think I have nice eyelashes?" Charlie asked jokingly.

Jackson slowly shook his head. "Honestly, son. What am I going to do with you?"

The boys shared a smile as the screen door at the opposite end of the porch slid open. Noah walked out with Brooke Bower. Noah was wearing just a bathing suit. Brooke was in a white bikini that clung to her like paint. Charlie couldn't keep his eyes from tracing her every outline. Besides bathing suits, both wore smirks understood only by them. However, remembering the giggle he heard as he passed, Charlie immediately realized why Noah's door was closed and he felt his face flush.

"Good morning, lover boys," Noah called across the space, which elicited a small chuckle from his girlfriend. "What are you two up to this morning? Discussing plans for a romantic luncheon at Ove's?" Noah and Brooke plopped down in the pair of Adirondacks nestled in the corner. "Maybe a surf date? You could hold hands across the waves."

"Hey Noah. Hey Brooke," Charlie said. Then added without missing a beat, "Actually, we were thinking about some nude sunbathing up on the roof deck. Care to join us? Brooke, you can rub lotion on my back." Charlie winked at Brooke.

"I like that you try, Charlie," Brooke said, smiling warmly. "It shows courage. Confidence, even."

"Why thank you, Brooke," Charlie said with a slight dip of his head. "Noah, I'll let you smear my front," he continued, winking at Noah.

Noah laughed at that. "You'd enjoy that too much, nerd. Anyway, welcome back. It's good to see you. You seem, I don't know, taller, and a little more brooding."

Charlie shrugged, and turned his attention to Brooke, who was already lost in Noah's conversation. Turning to Jackson, Charlie said, "Now I know why his door was still closed."

Jackson rolled his eyes, "God. Those two. They're like rabbits."

"Lucky him," Charlie said, allowing his gaze to float back to Brooke from across the porch. In Charlie's limited life experience, Brook Bower was simply the most beautiful woman he had ever seen. He wasn't sure how long he was staring, but Jackson's voice snapped him back.

"Hey. Her eyes are a little higher."

Charlie felt his face flush again. "Shut up, Jackson."

THREE

"So, uhm… listen, Charlie," Jackson said, "there's something I've been wanting to talk to you about."

Charlie turned his attention back to Jackson. "If this is more shit about Madison, save it."

"No. It isn't," Jackson said. He turned away, looking out over the porch railing.

Charlie wasn't positive, but it seemed like his friend was nervous.

Jackson took a deep breath and let it out slowly. Turning back to Charlie, he said, "Look, uhm…"

At that moment, Darth Vader's theme song exploded from Charlie's cell phone. He didn't need to look at the screen to know that his mother was calling, as did his friend. His mother didn't know that the theme music for the evilest ruler known to the Galactic Republic was her calling card, and he thought it best that way. Sarah and Carson were privy to the tone, and they often threatened to let his mother know. But Charlie had enough dirt on the two of them to level the playing field. "*Go ahead, tell her,*" he'd taunt, "*but then you'll force me to mention…*" and the threat went away for a while.

"Mommy's looking for you," Jackson said, and grabbed at the iPad again.

The entire time Charlie and Jackson were talking, Charlie's phone was making itself known in his pocket. He ignored the rapid text pings that announced themselves every two to three minutes. Most likely, it was his siblings trying to track him down. Charlie had felt, for some time, that the most annoying thing about technology is that you were never truly by yourself. You could never actually 'get away' from anything. You were simply a text, or a call, or a SnapChat away.

"Better get that," Jackson said as his attention disappeared into the device he cradled in his hands.

Charlie dug the phone out of his thigh pocket and slid the button seconds before the call kicked to voice mail. "Hey Mom, what's up?"

"Where are you?" Charlie could hear the annoyance in his mother's voice. "Your brother and sister have been trying to reach you for an hour. What? You don't respond to texts anymore?"

Charlie looked at Jackson and rolled his eyes. "Okay, first," he said, trying to dull the edge in his voice, "I've only been gone for about twenty minutes, so I think they might be exaggerating a bit if they told you it's been an hour. And, second, I'm at Jackson's. Where else would I be at eleven in the morning?"

Jackson cocked his head to one side and said out loud to no one in particular, "Face down in a ditch, bound in the back of someone's panel van, held up at gunpoint at an ATM, washed up in the surf…"

Charlie laughed softly, but not softly enough for his mother not to hear, "Are you laughing? Do you think this is funny? What's funny about an older brother who ignores his younger siblings' text messages?"

"Nothing Mom. I, uh, I wasn't laughing. That was Noah. He's at the other end of the porch with Brooke. She must have said something funny." Charlie commended himself for his quick thinking and the deflection of yet another lecture from his mom. "Anyway. I'm sorry. Like I said. I'm at Jackson's. I'll check the messages when we hang up, okay?"

His mother's sigh signaled her acquiescence. "Well, I mean, that's fine. You can, but it's a little late now. They just want to go to the beach. I need you to cover until I can get down there, okay?" his mom asked.

It was Charlie's turn to sigh. "Seriously? Carson is thirteen and Sarah is eleven."

"I'm well aware, Charlie, you remind me at least five times a week. Look. I have some curriculum writing to do, and some lesson planning for next year. It's just for about two hours and then I'll join you guys. Please, Charlie."

It was Charlie's turn to yield, though begrudgingly. "Fine. I'll be home in five minutes. Can the prince and the princess wait that long?"

He pulled the phone away from his ear, slammed his thumb on the red button, and shoved the phone in his pocket before he heard the answer. His heart began to hammer in his chest as his left hand curled into a fist. He wasn't sure why he was so mad. There wasn't anything to be mad about. But here he was, building to a boil.

Turning to Jackson, he said, "I gotta go. Miriam needs me to take the royal highnesses to the beach. Jesus. It's like all I am lately is a built-in babysitter for her. She even made me take Carson for a fucking hair cut last week. It's like my only purpose right now is to take care of them. Oh, and mow the lawn. Honestly."

"You shouldn't call your mother by her first name, Charlie. That's not polite," Jackson said, trying some humor to deflate the pressure that was building in his friend.

"Spare me the lesson in etiquette, Jackson. Not in the mood," Charlie snapped.

Eyeballing his friend, Jackson proceeded. "Give your mom a break, Charlie. I'm sure the change hasn't been easy for her."

Sometimes in life, words spill out of your mouth a millisecond faster than your brain can stop them, leaving you to regret them immediately before the sound of those words even disappears on the wind. This was one of those instances. As soon as Jackson heard what popped out of his mouth, he winced.

Charlie turned his head from looking across the porch railing and met his friend's gaze with steely eyes.

"Give *her* a break," he said. "The change hasn't been easy for *her?*"

The rise in Charlie's volume caught the attention of Noah and Brooke, still in the Adirondacks on the opposite side of the porch. Jackson met their gaze and glanced back at his friend.

"Are you kidding me? What about me, Jackson? What about the effect the change has had on me? Huh, Jackson? What about that?" Charlie could hear his volume rising, but he couldn't stop himself. "I come home after practice one day and find my mother, my brother, and my sister crying hysterically on the couch. And between his sobs, because my mother couldn't get her shit together to tell me anything, between his sobs my little brother tells me that dad is gone. Gone. And I'm standing there, and it feels like I've just been hit in the gut with a bag of bricks, just staring at them crying on the couch. And I can't breathe, Jackson. I can't fucking breath. And I can't think of anything to say, because I'm, like, sixteen years old and what do you say? Then, finally, *finally*, my mother can squeak out something and says, 'He left us, Charlie. He left us,' in this broken, choked off whisper. So, like an idiot, I run upstairs and rip open his closet, right, like trying to prove they're wrong or something, and all of his stuff is just gone. All of it. It was like he never even existed. Not a trace of him. And the worst part is, he didn't even leave a fucking note. Not even a note. He knew what he was going to do when we all woke up that morning and he didn't say anything. Not even a god-damned text! Not to me. Not to anyone. He just vanished, disappeared. Do you know what that's like, Jackson? Do you?"

Charlie's heart was in his throat. He could feel his blood pounding in his temples, and his hands were shaking.

The color had drained from Jackson's face. He looked down at the table, shaking his head. Quietly he said, "No. No, I don't."

"No. *You don't!*" The words stuck in Charlie's throat.

He stood faster than he intended and knocked the chair he was sitting in over. Almost as abruptly as his anger washed over him, he immediately felt embarrassed for lashing out at his best friend. The boys met each other's gaze briefly and a thousand words passed between them, but neither said anything. Charlie turned towards the sliders. All Jackson could do was watch as he disappeared into the living room and headed for the stairs.

Noah and Jackson's gaze met again. "What the hell was that all about?" Noah asked.

"My stupid mouth," Jackson answered softly and looked out across the porch rail.

Brooke stood up and dashed inside, calling after him, "Charlie. Charlie, wait up."

Charlie pushed through the house, down the stairs, and into the common room. He was still so angry, so embarrassed. Jackson hadn't deserved that. Charlie was angrier now about how he treated his friend than he was angry about what Jackson said. Brooke, undaunted by Charlie's ignoring her, followed calling his name. When Charlie got to the door downstairs, he stopped and turned around as Brooke closed the distance between them. There she was. Standing right in front of him. Closer than she had ever been before. He could smell the sunscreen on her skin, the conditioner in her hair. For what seemed like forever, she just stood there, looking at him with the saddest of faces. Then she leaned in and gave him a hug. Not a quick, pat-on-the-back kind of hug, but a genuinely felt hug. She held him for a moment, rubbing his back. Unconsciously, his arms moved up and closed around her back and squeezed, as if he was holding on for his very life. Charlie's breath caught on the lump in his throat, and he could feel all the fury drain away. His shoulders actually sagged. Brooke broke the hug first. She stepped back, touched his cheek briefly, and then placed both hands on Charlie's shoulders. She didn't say anything. She just squeezed softly and smiled sincerely. Charlie nodded and smiled back. Quickly, he turned and made his way out into the sunshine. He didn't want Brooke to see the tears threatening to spill out.

FOUR

After Charlie left, Jackson wanted nothing more than to find a place and just be by himself. He grabbed his bike and headed over to The Beanery on Fifteenth Street. After a quick ride, he hopped off his bike and just let it fall to the sidewalk close enough to the building that people could still get by. He pulled open the heavy oak front door and stepped back in time. The building itself dated back to the 1920's, and little had changed since then. Café tables and chairs filled the room. Mahogany paneling covered just about every wall and the coffered ceiling. Vintage schoolhouse pendant lights hung from the ceiling. Behind the marble-topped counter, an enormous mirror took up the entire wall, foggy and crackled with age.

At the sound of the bell when the door opened, the man behind the counter looked up. "Ah. Well. Look what the cat dragged in."

"Hey, Pops," Jackson answered. John 'Pops' Bianchi was the proprietor of The Beanery. He was a congenial old man who knew everyone on the island. A year rounder, Pops had been running the Beanery since his father had stepped out thirty years ago. While the Shoebies sought out Starbucks or Ocean City Coffee for their daily dose of caffeine, those in the know came here. "How's things today in your little slice of heaven?"

"Eh, you know, cosi cosi," Pops answered.

Chuckling a bit, Jackson answered, "Yeah. I do know."

"The usual?"

"That would be great, Pops. Thank you." Jackson strode over to what he considered his table, tucked away in the bay of floor to ceiling windows that jutted off of the front of the building. He slid back a chair and took a seat. In the background, the ancient brass espresso machine came to life with a scream. It wasn't long before Pops walked over a steaming cup of cappuccino.

"Voila," Pops said as he set the cup down in front of Jackson.

The image of a pine tree floated on the frothy foam. Pops had been upping his game, keeping in step with the barista's back in the city. 'Evolve or die,' Pops said once a while back, when Jackson asked him about the design gracing the froth of his cappuccino. Jackson pulled a five-dollar bill out of his pocket and handed it to the man.

"Thanks, Pops. I like the tree. Give up on famous historical figures?"

Pops shrugged. "The noses were giving me a hard time. Mrs. Bianchi suggested I try nature. So…," he shrugged again.

Jackson smiled as the old man walked away. He sat for a moment, cradling the cup between his hands before taking a sip. The rich flavor was always a delight, and Jackson let a sigh out through his nose.

"Damn, that's good," he said to himself, and took another sip.

Outside, people went about their business. It was mostly Shoebies stocking up on souvenirs. The Beanery sat on the corner of Fifteenth Street and Asbury Avenue; the latter being lined with boutique shops that catered to the vacationers. From general beach items, to jewelry, to expensive knick-knacks, if it was invented to be purchased by someone on vacation, you could find it on Asbury Avenue. During the summer months, islanders rarely appeared on Asbury. This was another reason Jackson enjoyed coming to The Beanery. He could be alone amongst a sea of humanity who did not know who he was. The crowd on the promenade outside wasn't nearly as large as it would be as June slipped into July, but there were still a good number of people out and about.

The morning still weighed heavily on Jackson. How could he have been so stupid as to suggest to Charlie that the change must be hard on his mom? He shook his head in recognition of exactly how stupid his words were. Jackson knew Charlie was hurting. He remembered the frantic phone call he received that day back in January. He could still hear the utter loss reflected in his friend's voice. But what do you say to a person whose universe is unexpectedly ripped away? Certainly not, *I'm sure the change hasn't been easy for her,* Jackson thought and took another pull on his drink. He'd call Charlie later that day, or maybe find him on the beach. Right now, Jackson knew what Charlie needed was some space to cool down.

The door chime caught Jackson's attention, and he turned to see who had come in. "Shit," he said quietly aloud as Kelsey and Madison strode into the Beanery sharing a laugh.

Walking over to where he sat, they said simultaneously, "Hey Jackson." Though Kelsey's '*hey*' had far more of a sing-song tone to it than Madison's. If it was a text, the *hey* would have had an extra *y* or two.

"Hi guys. What brings you to the Beanery?" Jackson asked, knowing full well that his much-anticipated solitude was now history.

"Doing some shopping on Asbury. We saw you sitting in the window," Kelsey said. "You looked kinda sad, so we thought we'd come cheer you up. Is everything okay? That a new bathing suit?"

Jackson looked down at what he was wearing. "Uhm…, this? No. No, it's from last year. And I'm fine, thanks."

Deliberately tracing him with her eyes, Kelsey said, "Well. They sure look *good* on you, Jackson. But most everything does."

"Um, thanks?"

Flicking her hand in his direction, Kelsey answered, "You're welcome. Maybe we'll join you? Madison, honey, iced coffee? I'll be right back with two." Kelsey made her way over to Pops, who was already prepping the drinks he knew the girls would be ordering.

Jackson slid around the table, making room for his friends. Madison smiled and sat down in the chair that had once belonged to Jackson.

"So. Things going alright?" she asked.

"In-fact they are, Madison. How about you?"

"Alright, I guess. My folks are still on me about getting a job this summer. But, I mean, it's, like, summer. I'll have the rest of my life to work. Maybe I'll see if Pops needs some help a few hours here and there. I don't know."

"Yeah. What is it with our parents and them always wanting us to find jobs? It's not like we asked to be born. *They* wanted *us,* right? Next, they'll be asking us to pay rent," Jackson said.

"Who's paying rent?" Kelsey inquired, as she returned to the table. She placed a tall iced coffee in front of Madison and took a seat opposite Jackson. Delicately, she placed the straw in her glass, wrapped her full lips around the top, and took a long sip while looking up at Jackson from behind half raised eyes.

Madison chuckled, "No one. We were just talking about parents and their obsession with their kids' finding jobs."

"Ugh. Work, no way," Kelsey said, genuinely. "I never plan on working. I'm going to find myself a handsome, wealthy man, and just raise his children."

Jackson felt Kelsey's foot brush against his shin. Involuntarily, he pulled his leg back and took a sip of his coffee. When he looked at her, she was smiling at him. He smiled back, politely, if not awkwardly.

The door chimed again. This time, in walked Joey Mastromani. He was wearing a tank, exposing his already tanned, well-muscled shoulders and arms, and a pair of flowered board shorts. *So much for islanders not being on Asbury,* thought Jackson, as his solitude was further crowded aside. At first, Joey didn't see them sitting where they were, but Madison put an end to that.

"Hey, Joey. Over here," she called out.

Instinctively following the noise, Joey turned and tossed his head in their direction. *The Bro hello,* thought Jackson and smiled to himself.

"Be right over," Joey called.

"Anyway," Kelsey continued, "you'll never find me at a job."

"Honestly, Kelsey, I swear you were born in the wrong time period," Madison chastised. "You are perfectly suited to be a 1950's housewife, taking care of your husband and cooking his meals."

"Who ever said anything about cooking?" Kelsey said playfully.

Joey made his way over, clutching his coffee in a takeout cup, and squeezed behind Kelsey, sitting down right next to Jackson.

"New suit?" he asked. He took a cautious sip from the hot beverage, then said hello to the girls.

"No. Not new. Old. Had them last year, and maybe the year before that," Jackson said. He wondered why everyone was suddenly so interested in his bathing suit.

Shrugging, Joey said, "Oh. They look good on you, is all."

Lost for something to say, Jackson did a quick once over of Joey, and said, "New… uhm… new muscles?"

Joey smiled, looking down at both arms. "Yeah. Coach said I needed to hit the gym. Been about six months now. Thanks."

"Anyway," Jackson said.

He hated to admit it, but Joey looked good. He had the body just about every sixteen-year-old boy wanted. Not huge, like Arnold Schwarzenegger in his hay-day huge, but chiseled and tight. He watched Joey's bicep bulge as he lifted his coffee cup. It was like a baseball tucked under his skin. Looking at his own arms, Jackson toyed momentarily with the idea of hitting the gym himself, but then shook the thought away. Too hackneyed.

"Anyway," Joey repeated, still smiling at Jackson.

"Anyway, Jackson," Madison spoke, "like Kelsey said, we were walking by and saw you. Thought we'd say hello. Kinda surprised Charlie isn't with you."

Joey laughed, "Yeah. You two are inseparable. You dating yet?" he asked from behind a sly grin that conveyed the joke. Jackson smirked as if to say, 'so funny, ass-hat'.

Madison continued, "Have you seen Charlie at all? He's been a bit like a ghost–heard he exists but haven't seen him."

Oh yeah, I've seen him, Jackson thought to himself. *I've seen him bubble up in a fit of rage and explode all over my porch just a few minutes ago. I've seen him in a way I have never seen him before; red in the face; neck veins bugling; fists clenched into white knuckled little balls.* "Yeah. I just saw him this morning on my porch. We were hanging out, but he had to head home to watch his sibs. Think he might be going to the beach."

Madison's face brightened. "Oh. How is he?" she asked.

That's a loaded question, Jackson thought. "Uhm… he's uhm… he's… volatile," he answered, then took another sip from his cup.

Kelsey, Madison, and Joey exchanged quick glances. Seeing the confusion in their eyes, Jackson tried to, yet again, stuff words that carelessly spilled from his mouth back in.

He laughed weakly, "Kidding. Charlie is good. He seems good. He looks good too. His hair is longer than last summer, but not too long," Jackson babbled. "He's gotten taller, broader. He's filling out. I mean, you know, he turns seventeen in July, and all…" Realizing that he sounded like a proud grandmother babbling on, Jackson stopped talking and drank more coffee.

"Okay," Joey said, drawing out the word.

"Anyway," Jackson said, attempting to direct the conversation elsewhere. "What do you guys have planned for today?"

His three friends threw quick glances at one another. Then, as if scripted, all three shrugged simultaneously, and said in unison, "Don't know." The timing of their responses drew laughter from all four.

"Well, I was out for a bike ride and decided to head to 7th Street Surf Shop to grab a new pair of board shorts or two," Joey offered. Turning to Jackson, he said, "Want to come?"

Joey's invitation very much surprised and confused Jackson. Yeah, Joey was part of the group, but he was always part of the *group*. Jackson couldn't remember a time when he was with Joey without the rest of the entourage. Jackson stuttered a bit. He raised his hand and rubbed at the back of his head. "Um, yeah. Sure. I guess?"

Joey turned to Kelsey and Madison. "Guess we'll catch you guys later. Where are you going to be? Beach? Boardwalk? Porch? Pool?"

Madison and Kelsey looked at each other and shrugged. Jackson could pick up their sense of confusion as well.

Shrugging again, Kelsey said, "I don't know. Pool, probably."

"Just text us." Madison said.

Turning back to Jackson, Joey said, "Is that your bike outside?"

"Sure is."

"Great. I dropped mine on top of it. Let's go, then." Joey was up and out from behind the table before Jackson put his cup down. Sliding out of his own seat, he walked over to the counter and placed his empty cup on the top.

"Thanks, Pops," Jackson said absentmindedly.

He turned and followed Joey out of the coffee shop and onto the street. *Just what the hell is happening here?* he wondered.

FIVE

Charlie sat in his beach chair, stewing behind his pair of sunglasses. He couldn't shake the argument he had had with Jackson a few hours earlier. He and Jackson had had their share of disagreements over the years, but they tended to be minor squabbles over something ridiculous that never amounted to anything serious. This one was different. Jackson certainly didn't deserve the full onslaught of Charlie's rage. Charlie remembered the hurt in Jackson's eyes as he laid into him. Remnants of embarrassment, tinged with guilt, welled up again in Charlie's psyche. Deep down he knew it wasn't Jackson he was angry with. Unfortunately, it was Jackson who happened to be in the crosshairs when that anger sought a target.

He reached into the bag of snacks beside him and pulled out his cell phone. Nothing from Jackson. There were, however, a bunch from Kelsey and Madison asking where he was, if he wanted to meet up, or maybe hang by the pool at Kelsey's house. Ignoring the messages from the girls, he called up Jackson's contact and typed, *You alive?* but thought twice about it. He wasn't sure why, but he didn't feel like apologizing; not just yet, anyway. He let the phone fall back into the bag, adjusted his sunglasses, and sunk a little lower into the chair.

The beach was crowded, but certainly not as crowded as it would be, come the weekend. He could see Carson by the water's edge, tossing a football with his friend Ethan. The two of them were a weird set, Charlie thought. While scoring somewhat high on the dork scale–into Star Wars, Pokémon, and LEGOS-they were both remarkably un-nerd like at times. Watching them, it struck Charlie how gracefully athletic each was. Carson could throw a perfect spiral pass–daunting in the geek world - and Ethan never missed a catch. Even when Carson purposefully overthrew. Carson, too, was quite the receiver, snatching the ball out of the air with actual skill. There was something else Charlie noticed, possibly for the first time. His brother wasn't the pudgy little ball of geekiness he used to be. He thinned out. He was looking a little less like a kid, and a little more like a teenager. From where Charlie sat in the sand, Carson resembled him when he was thirteen, and he hated to admit it.

"Huh," Charlie grunted. "Guess you *can't* judge a book by its cover."

Amazed as Charlie was that Madison and Kelsey had not yet located him at the beach, that minor miracle did not apply to Sarah's attached-at-the-hip friend, Emily. As soon as they sat down hours before, Emily popped over to snag Sarah. They wandered off almost immediately, but the respite from the antics of two eleven-year-old girls ended abruptly.

"Boyfriend, leave the judging to us," Emily said as she and Sarah dropped in on Charlie's quiet.

Charlie forced a smile. "Welcome back. Where've you been?"

"Oh, you know," Sarah said. "Making the beach rounds. Any Twizzlers left?"

Charlie dug the candy out of the snack bag and tossed her the pack. "They're all yours."

Emily continued, "We were up on the boardwalk for a while, you know, people watching. But had to leave. The seagulls were crazy. Stupid Shoebies feeding them french fries and pizza crusts. Wish they'd all go home!"

Emily snapped off the end of a Twizzler like a shark snaps a seal. Charlie pictured her as a high-school senior. He was certain she would become that girl who sits on the sink in the girl's bathroom sucking on a cigarette as her friends beat the crap out of some hapless victim whose sense of style offended.

"Anyway. We thought we'd come see what you were up to. I see you haven't moved since we left. Charles, you might want to put a shirt on. Your shoulders are getting red."

"Thanks for the advice, Emily. I'll take it under advisement," Charlie said, looking past Emily at the ocean. The waves were kicking up. *Might be a good day to drag out the board. Once the lifeguards leave*, he thought to himself.

Looking around the beach, Sarah asked, "Have you seen Carson?"

"Oh, I see him!" Emily blurted. "He's at the water playing catch with Ethan. That Ethan is so cute. I could stare at him all day."

The comment dumbfounded Charlie, "Um, aren't you a little young to be talking about cute boys, Emily?"

"One is never too young to recognize true beauty," Emily said, and both girls laughed.

Charlie shook his head, "You're only eleven…"

Sarah piped up, "Charlie, everyone knows eleven is the new fifteen. And she's right. Ethan is cute. Nerdy, but cute."

"Carson is nothing to throw to the curb, either," Emily added. "He's like a mini-version of you, Charlie."

"Good God," Charlie said and dug his cell phone out of the snack bag.

"Well, we've lost him," Sarah said. "That's how you know he's done talking. He grabs his cell phone. Come on, let's dish tea with Carson and Ethan."

Both girls popped up like toast and ran to where the two boys were at the water's edge. Still nothing on Charlie's phone from Jackson. Charlie opened Instagram and scrolled aimlessly through the photos. Rolling across the screen were the digital diaries of everyone's perfectly bright, happy life. Nobody wanted to see the dark points of life. Who would be interested in that? There's enough drama and misery that happens live. A pictorial recollection of the dismay is hardly the escape social media provides. Charlie's own Instagram page was strangely silent these past months. *Nothing to see here, folks,* it seemed to say.

Charlie was just about to thumb open Snap Chat when he suddenly became aware of a chair dropping into the sand beside him.

"Hi hon. Thanks for watching your brother and sister. Is that them down by the water?"

"Yep," he said, his tone matching the length of the word. He could feel the anger that he felt with Jackson begin to simmer in his chest. He took a few deep breaths, trying to control the surge. His mom, ever astute, caught the tone and gave him a quick look.

"Well, thanks. I really appreciate it, Charlie. Hey, you might want to put a shirt on. Your shoulders are red."

Sometimes a pin prick is all it takes to topple a dam. Losing the battle with the surge of anger that was rising inside of him, Charlie couldn't help himself.

He turned to his mom and said sharply, "You said two hours. That was two hours ago. I've been sitting here for four hours, mom, watching your kids."

Charlie's mother recoiled from the remark, "They're your brother and sister, Charlie. It's not a lot to ask…"

Charlie cut her off before she could finish, "I'm not your built-in babysitter so you can have quality Miriam time. I'm not going to spend the summer looking after those two freaks. What's next? Me staying at home at night so you can troll Crabby Jack's looking for a hook-up?" A bit of a slap, he knew.

Charlie's mom sighed deeply, trying to quell her own anger. She approached him with kid gloves these days since the split with his father. She had watched her son slip into a dark place that he seemed only to be sinking into deeper. A hungry hatred that needed to be fed more and more, swallowing Charlie's carefree demeanor. She felt helpless watching her son be devoured by this insatiable monster, but was lost for a way to help him. "Charlie, can we not do this today? Give me a break, okay?"

Those words. There they were again. Charlie's anger surged.

"Give *you* a break, Mom?" Charlie hissed loudly. "You? Seriously? Give you a break? Jesus!" Charlie stood up, snatched his backpack, and stormed off.

Completely surprised by the vitriol billowing up out of her son, yet not surprised by it, she called after him. "Charlie. Charlie, what is wrong with you?"

Charlie continued walking. He didn't know the answer to that question.

With impeccable timing, Sarah showed up. She had caught the tail end of the conversation between her brother and mother. She watched as Charlie stormed off, red in the face, and hands clenched into fists. While only eleven, she was fairly astute, and she, too, was aware of the change taking place in her oldest brother. It made her uneasy.

"What was that all about?" she asked.

Miriam forced a smile meant to comfort, but did not quite nail the intent. She said "Nothing. He's just... he just needs some space, is all."

Sarah scoffed, "Well, he will not get that at the Jersey Shore in the summer, mom."

"Ain't that the truth, baby girl? Ain't that the truth?"

SIX

The 7th Street Surf Shop was a mob scene. The aisles were double stacked with people picking through merchandise. They were mostly Shoebs, vacation shopping for beach ware–flip flops, board shorts, T-shirts, Yeti mugs, hats. It was almost claustrophobic. Jackson followed Joey around the store. It seemed the hunt for new board shorts had turned into a full-blown shopping spree. Of course, this is what happens when mom and dad give you your own credit card without the burden of paying the bill. Joey was trying on board shorts. Jackson sat outside the changing room, lending his advice every time the curtain opened. He thought it odd that Joey had removed his shirt to try on the trunks.

"For the full effect," Joey answered when Jackson queried.

"I see," Jackson responded. "It has nothing to do with the new washer board abs?"

Joey smiled slyly. "That's the full effect."

That was Joey, full of himself, in a not-so overly conceited-that-you-want-to-strangle-him sort of way.

"I see," Jackson said again.

By Jackson's count, Joey was about to emerge with his eighth suit. As the curtains parted, Joey stood there shirtless in a pair of teal Rusty shorts. A streak of dark blue that ran up one thigh, across the back seat of the bathing suit, just below the small of your back, and down the other thigh.

"How 'bout these?" Joey prompted.

Jackson looked up from his phone. "Spin," he said, and watched as Joey did a complete three-sixty in front of the dressing room. "Again," Jackson said, and Joey did another turn, this time in the opposite direction. "Now, put your hands on your head."

Joey started to and then caught himself. "Real funny, ass hat," he said.

Jackson laughed, "I assume you are looking for my honest opinion, so I must say that in the myriad of board shorts you have tried on this morning, I think the current pair speaks the loudest."

Joey cocked his head. "Um, does that mean you like them?"

"Yeah. I like them. You look good in them." Jackson couldn't help but feel a little weirded out by his own words and quickly tried to cover. "I mean, they look good on you…" which didn't sound any better. "Just get them, for Christ's sake, will ya?" Feeling his cheeks redden, he glanced back at his phone.

Joey shrugged and disappeared back into the dressing room. He emerged moments later dressed as he was when they arrived forty minutes ago, Rusty shorts in hand, and headed for the register. Jackson stood and followed silently. After a quick transaction and exchange of pleasantries with the young lady behind the register, which resulted in Joey exchanging his Snap, the two boys were once again back on the street. Joey was quick to notice that Jackson's attention was fixed on his phone.

"Dude. You've been checking that phone, like, every two minutes this entire time."

Jackson, acutely aware that he was right, offered weakly, "Oh, yeah. Sorry. Uhm… just, I was just seeing if Charlie had texted or anything." He finished with, "He hasn't."

Both boys got on their bikes and began the trip back to their respective houses. At this time of day, biking was like an obstacle course—dodging traffic and pedestrians alike. The boys expertly weaved between the two.

"What's up with you two, anyway?" Joey asked, breaking the silence.

"Who two? Me and Charlie? What do you mean, up with us?" Jackson countered. "Nothing is up with us," he said, perhaps a bit too defensively.

"Relax, Jackson. I just meant, like, you guys are, like, always together and now you keep checking to see if he has texted you. Did you two get into a fight or something?"

"I wouldn't call it a fight. We, uhm, we had... I guess we had a bit of a disagreement this morning, and it ended kind of ugly. I was hoping he'd... I don't know. It's stupid," Jackson stammered. Truth was, he was genuinely concerned for his friend and worried about their friendship right now. Joey was right. He and Charlie were almost always in constant communication. It was disconcerting not to receive any messages from him over the past hour or so. Not even a stupid SnapChat of some inane thing he was doing.

"He's had a rough year, ya know? He's not the same kid he was in January, that's for sure. His dad bouncing kind of knocked the wind out of him. Kinda feel bad for him," Joey said.

Jackson was blown away by the words that tumbled out of Joey's mouth. He actually shook his head in confusion. He'd known Joey for some time. He always seemed like this superficial jock who cared more about sports and himself than anything else around him. He wasn't a complete ass, but he came close sometimes. His sudden awareness of Charlie and his struggle was, as far as Jackson was concerned, totally out of character.

"Wait. Are you actually concerned about Charlie?" Jackson asked, dumbfounded.

Joey scoffed, "I wouldn't call it concerned, more that I've just noticed a change. Especially around school, not that we hang around much or anything. Just that he's kinda pulled away from everyone, ya know? Sits alone at lunch a lot. Stuff like that. But I know you guys are tight. I guess I was just wondering..." his voice trailed off, "I don't know what I was wondering. Just wondering, I guess."

Jackson and Joey continued along in silence until they arrived in front of Jackson's house. Stopping by the steps, Jackson asked if Joey wanted anything to drink.

"Nah. Think I'm going to change into these new board shorts and hit the beach, but thanks," Joey said.

"Sure," Jackson replied. "You going to the beach alone?"

"Uhm…, I guess… unless you want to come too?"

First an invitation to go shopping, now an invitation to go hang at the beach. Jackson was thoroughly confused. He never did anything with Joey without the crew being a part of the activity, even if that activity was just hanging on the beach.

"Yeah. I think I'm going to just hang in the house today."

Joey shrugged, "Okay. Anyway. Thanks for hanging, Jackson. It was sorta fun. Guess I'll see you around." Having said that, Joey pedaled away.

"See ya, Joe."

Jackson stood there and watched as Joey disappeared down the street. It had been a crazy morning so far; one full of events that would undoubtedly play in Jackson's mind throughout the day, and perhaps days to come. He'd never been in a fight, to use Joey's term, with Charlie before, and he certainly had never spent as much time with Joey Mastromani on a one-to-one basis as he just did. The thing that confounded him the most was Joey's revelation of almost human qualities in asking about Charlie. That was something completely unexpected.

"WTF?" Jackson said aloud to no one in particular.

He pulled his phone out of his pocket and checked the display screen. Although crowded with notifications, the one he was looking for was disappointingly absent.

"Shit," he uttered as he walked his bike to the back of the house.

SEVEN

Charlie lay awake in bed, staring at the ceiling. The first light of dawn was creeping into the room, casting things in a strange glow. He could hear his brother breathing in the bed on the other side of the room. Carson stirred softly and mumbled something in his sleep. Charlie couldn't quite make it out, but whatever it was, it caused Carson to chuckle. Which, in turn, caused Charlie to chuckle.

Yesterday's events seemed like a week ago. After storming off of the beach, Charlie wandered aimlessly around town for a while. He didn't want to go home; he didn't feel like risking inevitable chit-chat with his friends should they stop by to see what he was up to. His mood was foul, and socializing was something he just didn't have the stomach for. As he walked, he found himself preoccupied with Madison Walker and what Jackson had said about her asking about him. He would be lying to himself if he didn't admit that he had had growing feelings for her at the end of last summer. It seemed to Charlie that as August leisurely slipped towards September, they had spent more and more time together alone. They found reasons to walk on the beach, or to meet up after dinner. His mother had even asked about it, inquiring if they were 'a thing', as she called it. But that was a year ago. While he thought of her often through the school year, and they stayed in touch through SnapChat and text messages, and other social media, he found it hard to believe that those feeling were still–if ever–mutual.

His directionless wandering led him to The Beanery. He shook the thoughts from his head as he stepped through the door. Pops greeted him with his usual "Hey Charlie," took his order and then told him that his friends had been in earlier that day. Charlie made his way to a back table, well out of sight from the window and the door. He drank his iced caramel latte. Interrupted only by his mother's text messages, Charlie spent the rest of the afternoon by himself wandering the streets. He arrived home well after seven, dodged a battalion of questions from his mom, and retreated to his room—well, his side of the room. He emerged a few hours later to take a shower. Afterwards, he holed back up in his room for the rest of the night. His mom texted a few times, alternatively asking if he was okay, if things were okay, and is everything okay? Charlie replied, 'yep' every time.

He grabbed his phone from the nightstand to check the time: seven-past-six in the morning. He kicked back the sheets, grabbed his board shorts, and quietly made his way to the bathroom. After a splash of water on his face to get the sleep out of his eyes and a quick brush of his teeth, Charlie thumbed the Surfline App on his phone: *two-to-three-foot swells*. Satisfied, he left the bathroom and scribbled a quick note on the house message board, 'went surfing'. While not on his list of favorite people right now, he didn't want his mother worrying when she woke and found him gone. Charlie headed outside and around to the back of the house. As quietly as he could, he grabbed his board from the garage, hopped on his bike, and rode the few short blocks to the beach.

The beach was always nice this early in the morning. Few people were out and about. As Charlie chained his bike to the boardwalk railing, he wondered why he didn't wake up early more often and get himself down to the beach. The boardwalk was a virtual ghost town with the errant biker or jogger going about their activity and offering a pleasant 'morning' as they passed by. Charlie picked up his board and walked onto the beach. Aside from a few other early morning surfers, the beach was deserted.

Holding his surfboard in front of him like a shield, Charlie dove into the shore break and paddled out to just beyond where the swells were forming. The June Atlantic was chilly but invigorating. Once deep enough, he spun around, so the nose of his board was pointing toward the shoreline. He pushed himself up into a seated position, straddling the board. *The surf report was a bit exaggerated*, he thought to himself, as the two-to- three-foot swells were more like one-to-two. He was glad he brought the seven-foot board. It was a waiting game now.

Bobbing with the motion of the waves, Charlie eyed his first swell. He laid back down on the board and watched as the wave grew. He paddled just as the rising water was at the back of his board. The board caught in the wave and he was on his feet. It wasn't a tremendous wave, certainly not the biggest he had ridden, but it provided a great ride. A smile settled onto his face as he maneuvered the board under his feet. There was no feeling quite like the one he got while surfing. In a way, it was as close to flying as a person could come. Nearing the shoreline, Charlie leaned backwards until gravity took hold of him and he fell into the water. The board continued forward, the leash tugging on Charlie's leg. Standing, he reeled his board back in, hopped on, and paddled back out.

The surf gods were gracious that morning, sending in rolling wave after rolling wave. Charlie rode just about everyone he tried for. He was so lost in the joy of surfing that he hadn't noticed that the lineup was becoming crowded. What caught his attention was a familiar voice from behind, calling his name. He turned to find Jackson paddling closer. Charlie smiled as Jackson pulled up alongside and straddled his board. The two boys rose and fell harmoniously with the tune of the sea.

"Hey," Jackson replied. "Pretty decent morning out here. You've had some great rides."

The sudden appearance of his friend took Charlie aback. He looked around and realized that more surfers were in the water than when he started. How'd he miss that?

"How long have you been here?" Charlie asked.

"About thirty minutes. You were absolutely lost in the waves. I dropped in on you and you didn't even notice. I thought maybe you were still pissed..." Jackson trailed off.

Charlie, suddenly feeling a combination of embarrassed, awkward, and remorseful, scratched the back of his head. "Yeah. That. Listen, Jackson. I'm sorry about..."

Jackson cut him off. "No. It's me who's sorry. I don't always think about what I'm saying. I shouldn't have said..."

"Don't worry about it. I... I don't know. I over-reacted. You didn't deserve that."

After watching a few other kids slightly older and younger than they were catch some pretty decent rides, Jackson said, "So. We're good?"

Charlie chortled, "Yeah. We're good, Jackson. Always."

Jackson smiled genuinely. "Alrighty then, son. Let's ride some of these bitches."

Maybe it was the fact that Charlie was in the water enjoying one of the best surf sessions he'd had in a long time. Or maybe it was the fact that things were once again normal between him and his best friend. Or maybe it was a combination of both, Charlie couldn't say. All he knew was that he was having a hard time keeping the smile from his face as he paddled into his next wave. The two boys spent the next couple of hours tearing up the surf. If not for the lifeguard's whistle breaking things up, they may have stayed out there all morning.

Jackson checked his watch when he heard the shrill sound. It read nine a.m.

"Right on time," he said to Charlie. "Gotta get the surfers out of the water so the Schoebs can enjoy the beach."

Charlie laughed, then dropped in on what would be his last ride of the morning. Jackson followed close behind. They were side by side as they neared the shore. Charlie looked at Jackson, grinning and nodding his head. He crouched and undid his leash.

"Don't you dare…" Jackson called out, but before he could finish his sentence, Charlie had already launched himself off of his board and was airborne. He grabbed Jackson around the waist mid-flight and the two boys careened into the shallow water.

"Ass-hat," Jackson said from behind a smile as he emerged from the ocean, shaking water from his right ear.

"Don't pretend like you don't love it when I wrap my arms around you," Charlie shot back.

Jackson just shook his head. Charlie dove under and swam to where his surfboard was being pushed to shore by the current. Jackson, with his board still secure to his leg, continued towards the sand. The lifeguard blew his whistle again to signify his dominance of all things aquatic, and to let the straggling surfers know they were not clearing his ocean fast enough.

"Ass-hat," Jackson said again as he picked up his board and walked to the beach entrance up by the dunes.

As he neared the opening, Madison Walker surprised him. She was coming down from the boardwalk.

Their eyes met and Madison said, "Oh. Hey, Jackson. Looks like some decent waves this morning."

"Hey, Madison. Yeah, it was a good time until Thor over there forced us out of the water," he said, motioning to the lifeguard.

Madison threw a glance at the lifeguard stand. "Ugh. Is Seth on today? He can be such a frickin tool sometimes."

"Yup. And Gunther. The two blond gods. Who the hell names their kid Gunther, anyway?" Jackson asked, which drew a laugh from Madison.

"I was hoping maybe you were with Charlie…" Madison began. As if on cue, Charlie appeared at the end of the split-rail fence, marking the way to and from the beach. His attention was back on the waves, which were building. He was mumbling to himself about the Shoebies ruining everything when he again heard his name being called. This time, it wasn't Jackson calling. It was Madison.

Turning his head towards the sound, his eyes locked on Madison. She was in a sports bra and a petite pair of shorts that caused all sorts of imaginative details to run wildly through Charlie's brain. The sun had already turned her a golden brown, and her hair was pulled back away from her face and secured in a ponytail. Charlie could feel his mouth fall ajar and his heart stop in his chest.

"There you are!" she said, closing the short distance between. She wrapped him in a hug, saying, "It's so good to see you."

The hug seemed longer than a 'hey-its-good-to-see-you hug' friends might share, and more like a '*hey*-it's-good-to-see-*you*' hug. Charlie couldn't be sure, because at the moment he was weak in the knees, a little short of breath, and his heart was trying to break free of his rib cage. Madison broke the embrace after what Charlie thought was a good twelve minutes, but still held him by both arms.

"I was beginning to think you ghosted me," she said and smiled.

"Yeah. No," was all Charlie could offer as the blood unhurriedly returned to his head. He tried again. "Uhm, it's uhm, it's good to see you too, Madison. You look, uhm, you look good."

Off to the side, Jackson shook his head and rolled his eyes.

"So do you, Charlie. You seem taller, more filled out." Charlie could feel his cheeks brighten, and he glanced at the ground.

"Yeah," Charlie squeaked. Jackson rubbed his forehead.

Madison continued, "Anyway, I was going for a jog. I popped by your house, Charlie, to see if you were there. Your mom said you were surfing. And here you are. You. And Jackson."

Charlie rubbed the back of his head. "Here we are."

Over Madison's shoulder, Charlie caught a glimpse of Jackson, who mouthed the words 'oh my God' at him, which caused Charlie to blush even deeper. He didn't know why he was having great difficulty sounding semi-intelligent or answering with more than mono-syllabic words and clipped sentences. Charlie was nervous standing there talking to Madison, and that was strange. He never struggled for conversation with her before. Maybe there was something more to the hug, he thought to himself.

Sensing the awkward silence settling around the three friends like a fog, Charlie attempted to break it.

"Anyway… uhm…" He failed.

Madison's attempt was far superior. "Okay. I'm going to get a jog in. Then I was hoping we could hang out? All of us–you, me, Jackson, Kelsey, Joey. It'll be the first time we're all together since last summer. I thought it would be nice to catch up on the beach. Maybe hit the boardwalk for lunch or something…"

Sensing another spasmodic episode of non-firing neurons building in his friend, Jackson stepped in to offer a coherent response that comprised more than a grunt, one word, or a fragmented sentence.

"Madison. That sounds great. I can't think of a better way to spend the day than all of us hanging out on the beach." He paused, thinking Charlie might chime in.

However, his friend still appeared somewhat catatonic in his slack jawed gaze, so he continued.

"We'll meet you guys back here around noon. Right, Charlie?" Jackson hoped that using Charlie's name would somehow be a subtle sign that he should say something.

Startled by his own name, Charlie said, "Huh? Oh. Yeah, sounds good."

Jackson raised an eyebrow and slowly shook his head as if to say, 'you sad, sorry little man.'

"All right," Madison said cheerfully. "This'll be fun. Noon it is."

She spun in a manner that made her ponytail whip and ran up to the boardwalk. Charlie couldn't help but stare at her ass as she moved away from him. As she got to the top, she stopped as if something had just occurred to her. Charlie, immediately worried that she might sense the heat from his eyes on her bottom, broke his stare.

Turning back, she called, "It's great to see you, Charlie." She lingered for a moment, smiled again, and took off down the boardwalk.

Charlie watched her from a distance–taking in all of her this time - until she disappeared amongst the other people crowding the boardwalk. While most joggers wore a pained expression and slogged along, Madison paced down the boardwalk gracefully, like a swimmer. She appeared to be gliding, her stride was so smooth. The only sign of her running was the bounce of her ponytail behind her. Charlie drew in his breath and exhaled gradually.

Jackson began snapping at him and broke the trance. "What the hell was that?" he asked.

Charlie drew his eyebrows together. "What?"

"Uhm, it's uhm, it's good to see you too, Madison. You look, uhm, you look good," Jackson repeated in a voice meant to convey buffoonery. "Dude, you seriously need to work on your game. You sounded like Lenny in Of Mice and Men. *Tell me how I seem taller and have filled out again, Madison,*" Jackson mocked. He was well read, and Charlie hated when he started using characters and quotes from god-awful high school reading list classics that Charlie either didn't read or couldn't remember what the hell happened in the book. "I'm at a loss." Jackson finished, shaking his head.

"What are you talking about, Jackson?"

"Charlie. Tell me you didn't pick up the vibe that was hanging out there? I mean, seriously, you could literally reach out and pick up that vibe as if it were a giant ball of congealed hormones lying in the sand. The sexuality wafting off of Madison directed at you was palpable, Charlie. And then, *and then*, she actually stopped to make a point of telling you how great it was to see *you* again. Not *us.* You. She wants you, Charlie. A fucking blind man could see that."

"You think?" Charlie asked in a tone that was a mix of disbelief and optimism rolled into one.

Jackson moved closer to Charlie and put his hand on Charlie's shoulder. "Yeah. I think," he said, looking Charlie square in the eye. "Question now is, what are you going to do about it, son?"

Charlie pondered his question. Truth of the matter was, Charlie had little experience with girls, dating, or the nuances involved in navigating this new, sexually charged road he found himself thrust upon with the blitzkrieg of puberty. That's not to say he had been single and dateless these past years, but the rate at which he 'dated' probably fell second to continental drift. Even when he found himself in a relationship, they never lasted long: a few months, maybe more. He answered Jackson's question with a shrug.

"Lordy, Lordy. You are a hot mess, Charlie McIntyre."

Charlie nodded his head in agreement. "I don't know. Girls make me... nervous, I guess. I never know what to say, or how to act, or even where to put my hands, for Christ's sake."

Jackson just shook his head and turned toward the boardwalk, and walked away.

Charlie followed, and after a while, Jackson spoke up. "Here's what I know, Charlie. Madison started dropping hints last August that she was into you. She just deposited a few dozen more at your feet, which means after months away, she still, for some reason I cannot begin to fathom, thinks about you *in that way*. If you don't start picking up those hints, she's going to think you are not interested in her *in that way* and find someone else at which to throw hints."

"Yeah, but..."

Jackson held up a finger. "I'm not finished. As for not knowing what to say, or how to act, just be you, Charlie. It pains me greatly to say this, and if you ever repeat this to anyone, I will first, deny it, and second, I will kill you, but you are a good-looking guy, actually, very handsome. And you can be clever and funny. Don't over think shit. Say what comes to mind. Relax. And as for not knowing where to put your hands, well, I'm fairly certain we can find you a book that details all the places to put your hands when you are with a girl."

"Can't I just watch something on YouTube?" Charlie asked. "You know I hate to read."

"Oh, I'm pretty certain you watch a lot of stuff on YouTube and other less acceptable websites that stream countless hours of debauchery directly to your bedroom or bathroom or the backseat of your car or wherever you have special Charlie time. But, Charlie, remember, that is not reality. It's fantasy."

"Well, isn't it the bizarre that makes for the most interest?" Charlie said.

Jackson stopped walking and turned to his friend. "Wow, that was fairly coherent. Proud of you. And, speaking of bizarre, let me tell you about the day I had yesterday with Joey.

"Joey?" Charlie asked incredulously.

"Yeah. Joey."

Jackson spent the remaining time it took for the boys to walk the few short blocks to their respective houses, detailing the events of the day before. He started with the Beanery, the conversation there, and the invitation to go board shorts slash rash guard shopping. He wove in the time at 7th Street Surf Shop as he followed Joey around the store, the shirtless modeling of all eight bathing suits, and the curious comment Joey made about them going to the beach together.

Jackson finished just as the boys reached the point where they had to break off in different directions to head for their houses.

Charlie stood for a moment, speechless. Then said, "What the hell?"

"Exactly," Jackson said. "See you back at the beach in a few."

EIGHT

Charlie arrived back at his house to find his mother sitting on the porch swing, clutching a steaming cup of coffee. Amy Winehouse drifted softly out of the Bluetooth speaker that sat on the table under the window. His mom was quietly singing along to *Valerie.* Charlie could feel his mood change almost immediately. If he were a mood ring, the bright blue color of calm, content, and lovable, which reflected his time surfing with Jackson, was rapidly being replaced by anxious and stressed black. He laughed to himself as he thought of another Amy Winehouse song that so wonderfully described his demeanor any-time he approached his house. He tried to shake the mood from himself, but very much like a piece of tape stuck to your finger, it was difficult to lose. When his mom saw him walking up the sidewalk, he faked a smile.

Smiling back, she said, "Hey there, surfer man," a nomenclature of which Charlie was not a fan, "there you are. How were the waves this morning? Catch any good rides?"

Charlie swallowed the upsurge of annoyance that was swelling from deep within. He resented the fact that his mother had made him feel this way lately. He resented this new brooding, angst ridden stereotype of a teenager he had become. He resented being constantly heated whenever he was around his family. He just couldn't help himself. Since his mom split with his dad, Charlie struggled with being civil–to his mom, to his brother, and to his sister. He didn't know about his dad because he hadn't heard from him since he left–which piled more anger onto the already heaping pile of resentment and hostility Charlie had become whenever he was home. He quickly became aware that his free hand was clenched tightly into a fist. He took a deep breath and told himself to relax.

"Hey mom," he began, impressed with how un-confrontational his tone actually sounded. "Waves were pretty good. Jackson was there. We had a good time until the guards had to clear the water so the Shoebies could swim without danger of being taken out by a crazed surfer. But it is what it is," he finished with a shrug.

He lifted his board over the railing and let it rest on the floor. As he stepped onto the porch, his mom slid in the swing, making room for him.

"Come sit. Sarah and Carson aren't up yet. Enjoy the quiet before the storm with me." She patted the space next to her. Swinging with his mom was not high on Charlie's list of things-to-do-at-this-moment, but he walked over and plopped down next to her. Around them, the street was coming alive as the morning grew old. Neighbors were emerging from homes to mimic the action that was taking place right now on Charlie's front porch. The odd conversation drifted from open windows, married here and there to clips of news anchors reading from teleprompters.

Silence always made Charlie uncomfortable. Never the conversationalist, he didn't know how to strike up a dialog. Jesus, he thought to himself, she's your mom. You've lived with her for almost seventeen years. Speak up.

"So…." he said, and let it hang out there. Nervously, he began bouncing his leg, a habit that drove his mother crazy.

Placing a steadying hand on Charlie's knee, she said, "So. Jackson is good? He hasn't been around much since we arrived."

"Yeah. He's good."

"Did you guys plan on meeting at the beach this morning to surf?" One of his mother's classic loaded questions. She didn't like him surfing alone in the morning, or ever. Charlie knew if he told her the truth, he'd find himself in a world of shit he simply did not have the time or the patience to visit right now.

"Yeah. We texted each other last night."

"Good. You know I don't like you going surfing alone. And thanks for the note letting me know where you were."

Charlie nodded, "You're welcome."

To a passerby, the scene would resemble nothing more than a mother and son chatting in the morning air. To Charlie, however, it felt like two adversaries powdering the tension between them with pleasantries.

The silence resumed shortly thereafter, as did Charlie's bouncing leg. The first of the vacationers were making their way past the house and down to the beach. There was one enthusiastic boy, probably six or seven years old, lagging a few steps behind his family, carrying a bucket and pail while singing to himself. He already had his inflatable water wings wedged on each arm. He looked like a miniature bodybuilder as he swaggered down the street, unable to put his arms down by his sides. The Shoebs and his mom exchanged morning pleasantries as they passed the house.

"Isn't he adorable, Charlie?" his mother asked as the smallest Shoeb replete with customary beach possessions, waved a 'hello'.

Charlie furrowed his brow. "I guess. I mean, he looks kind of funny with the water wings already on, his eyes are oddly spaced, and you can tell he's a Shoebie 'cause of the sneakers and socks…"

His mother shut him down with a stare. Charlie turned his gaze to the floorboards of the porch. Silence. Knee bouncing.

"Oh, hey. Did Madison meet up with you guys? She stopped by on her jog and was asking if you were here. I told her you were surfing."

"Umm, yeah. We saw her as we were leaving. Jackson and I are going to meet her back at the beach in a couple of hours."

"She is such a nice girl, Charlie. If memory serves, you guys had sort of a thing going at the end of last summer, didn't you?"

A thing? *A thing?* Charlie could never understand the words adults used. A thing. A thing was an object that defies the senses, an object that didn't quite have a designation. As in '*what is that thing on the end of your nose?*' or '*did you see that thing that crawled out of the wall?*' or '*what was that thing in the Upside Down, anyway?*' It occurred to him then that his mother was waiting for an answer.

"Oh, umm… I don't think we had a *thing* going last summer, mom."

"I don't know, Charlie…" his mother said playfully. "I saw the way she followed you around and how you looked at her with puppy dog eyes."

Puppy dog eyes. *Puppy dog eyes*? *What the fuck does that even mean*? "Mom, really?"

"Well, she seemed awfully enthusiastic when she asked about you. Said she's been looking for you for days, and that she was worried you wraithed her, or was it poltergeisted her…"

Rolling his eyes, Charlie said, "Ghosted, Mom. The term is *ghosted.*"

"Well, whatever the word is, it doesn't sound like a nice thing to do. Have you… ghosted her? What does that even mean, Charlie?"

"It means when you just stop communicating with someone– you don't return texts or calls or anything. You just stop interacting with them," *you know, like dad,* his mind said. "And no, I didn't ghost her. I just didn't want to talk to anyone, I guess. Wanted a few days to myself to… I don't know, sort things out."

He regretted the last few words a millisecond after they spilled out of his mouth. He knew they would serve as an opening at the head of a path which his mother would love to stroll down. The level of discomfort in Charlie was growing ever so slowly. Similar to the way the drip eventually filled a coffee pot.

"Sort things out? Like with Madison? So, you do have feelings for her?"

"Mom, please…"

"Charlie, it's very healthy for a boy your age to have those feelings for a girl."

Those feelings. Those feelings like when I see her, my throat tightens, and my mouth dries up? Those feelings? Or maybe it's those feelings I get when she stands close to me, and my stomach does that roller coaster thing, and my cheeks heat? Or how about those feelings I get when she places her hand on my knee or my thigh, or her hand brushes against mine? Those feelings?

"You've been so sullen for such a long time now. I think it might help if you… I don't know, connected with someone, if you know what I mean."

Charlie groaned, "Mom. I am *not* having this conversation with you."

"What's wrong with a mom having a conversation with her soon to be seventeen-year-old son about dating? You're a handsome young man, Charlie. Girls, and maybe some boys… *Ohmygod, she did not just say that…* are going to find you attractive and want to get to know you. I just think Madison Walker is one of those girls. Ask her out. What could it hurt?"

Charlie's leg bouncing was so frenzied that the swing on which they sat was bouncing up and down as well.

"Jesus, Mom, you sound like Jackson right now." Again, regrettable words spoken too soon, spilling from the mouth of a flustered teenager.

His mom perked up. "Jackson thinks Madison has the hots for you too, huh? Well, there you go Charlie. Even your best friend thinks you guys should hook up."

The patience cork popped. Charlie jumped up from the swing and took a few steps across the porch. "Oh my God, Mom. I am not having this conversation with you. And before you go using that term again, you might want to check Urban Dictionary."

Just as he picked up his surfboard, the screen door opened, and his brother Carson walked out. He did a quick scan of the porch.

"Hey, Charlie, did you go surfing this morning?" he asked as Charlie jogged down the steps, surfboard under one arm.

"Yep," he said without looking back.

"You said you would take me with you."

"Next time," Charlie shot back.

"But you said that the last time, Charlie," Carson replied with slight frustration in his tone.

"Yep," Charlie said as he disappeared around the side of the house, heading to the yard.

Carson looked at his mom. "What bug crawled up his ass?" he asked.

"Carson. Watch your mouth. And I don't know. We were talking about Madison and how maybe he should ask her out."

"Oh yeah, she definitely is interested in him. Has been since, like, last August or so. Everyone knows that," Carson replied.

"Right?" his mom shot back, "Anyway, I just suggested that maybe they hook up or something and he got all uppity like he does."

Carson sighed disapprovingly and clucked. "Oh, Miriam. Please tell me that you did not just tell your hormonally charged teenage son in the throes of puberty to 'hook up' with a girl."

"Well. Yeah. I did."

Shaking his head reproachfully, Carson said, "Mother, you basically just told him to go have sex with her."

"What? No. Hook up means, you know, hang out, maybe kiss... doesn't it? Oh, my God!"

Carson sat down next to her on the swing and patted her on the knee. "It's okay, mom. Happens all the time. Why don't you compile a list of what you consider to be 'hip teenage jargon' and I'll decipher them for you, okay?"

"Shit Carson. No wonder he got angry."

"Nah. He's just angry all the time. You could have said 'Hi Charlie, what a beautiful day it is today', and he would have told you to piss off. I know from experience."

Miriam McIntyre considered her second born for a second. "Is Charlie mean to you, Carson? I mean, like, beyond the usual-siblings-aggravating-each-other, mean?"

Carson sighed, "Mom. He's mean to everyone lately. And yes, beyond the usual-siblings-aggravating-each-other, mean."

"What is wrong with that boy?" Miriam said aloud.

"Just about everything," Carson replied.

NINE

After Jackson parted company with Charlie on the corner of Fourth and Atlantic, it was a half block walk to his house. He was stoked about the surf session with Charlie, and he smiled at the thought of how great it was to be surfing with his friend after a long winter. Even more so, he was glad that things were okay between them. Of all his friends at the shore, and at home, Jackson enjoyed hanging around with Charlie the most. As far back as he could remember, he and Charlie just seemed to click. Jackson's grin broadened as he walked down the side alley to the back of the house and dropped his surfboard into the rack.

Walking over to the clothesline, he grabbed a towel and headed to the outdoor shower. He turned the water on and waited the few seconds it took for it to heat up. Stepping out of his bathing suit and underwear, he closed the door behind him stood in the cascade of warm water. He loved the outdoor shower. While there were 3 full bathrooms in the house, Jackson only ever showered outside. Even in the rain. There was something about being naked outside that sat well with Jackson. He stood in the hot cascade and let the water fall onto him. Briefly, his inner voice toyed with the idea of a quick bout of special Jackson time, but decided against it. After about fifteen minutes, he turned the water off, dried, wrapped the towel around his waist, and went inside.

Joey was sitting on the sofa in the game room watching TV, much to Jackson's surprise, which paused him in his tracks. The slam of the screen door caused Joey to look in Jackson's direction.

"Oh. Hey, Jackson," he said. "Your brother said it was alright if I waited here for you. Hope you don't mind."

He wasn't positive, but he could have sworn that Joey's eyes darted south, then popped back up to meet Jackson's eyes again. Feeling exposed in nothing but a bath towel, Jackson made his way past Joey to the other side of the pool table.

"Uhm, yeah, no problem. Do you... do you want something to drink or something?" Jackson stammered. "There's soda and shit in the fridge over there." He tossed his head in the direction of the refrigerator up against the far wall. While polite on the outside, Jackson was wondering just what the hell Joey was doing in his house, waiting for him to come home.

Joey didn't look at the fridge. "Nah, Bro. I'm good." Awkward silence filled the space between the two boys. Riverdale played unwatched on the television as Archie lamented some wrongdoing and Jughead plotted to avenge it. "Hey," Joey said, throwing his chin at Jackson. "You been working out?"

Jackson reflexively looked down at his mostly naked body and then back at Joey. "Umm... no, not really. The occasional jog here and there to avoid the Dad Bod, but... yeah. No."

"Oh," was all Joey said. There was the eye dip again.

Another round of awkward silence crept into the room. Jackson moved towards his bedroom door, which was partly open. He could have sworn he closed it when he left this morning. Scratching his head, he said, "Is there something you want, Joey? I mean, not to be rude, or anything, but why are you sitting on my sofa watching Riverdale on Netflix?"

"Just wanted to see what you were up to today, is all. Thought maybe we could hang out."

"Okay. Yeah. Sure... well, Charlie, Madison and I are going to meet at the beach around noon to hang out.... you're, you're welcome to join us if you'd like."

Joey's attention never left Jackson, which was making Jackson increasingly uncomfortable. All he could think about was that this whole situation was like some B-mafia movie and any second now some pistol toting thug was going to emerge from his bedroom and pump two slugs into his forehead. Jackson replayed the shopping trip in his mind, trying to figure out if he committed some mafia based faux pas wherein Joey would need to exact retribution by terminating Jackson's life.

"Sure, that sounds cool. We could just hangout here until then, or maybe hit The Beanery, or something," Joey said.

Comfortable that this wasn't a hit but still uncertain about the whole situation, Jackson said, "Well, okay. I, uhm... I'm just going to throw on a bathing suit." He turned and began walking into his room.

"You look fine in just that towel," Joey chuckled as he finally turned his attention back to the glowing box affixed to the wall.

Jackson stepped into his room, closed the door, and let the towel fall to the floor. He smiled a small smile and shook his head. "What the hell is happening?" he said out loud to himself.

TEN

Noon at the beach was probably the absolute worst time to arrive. By the lunch hour, what seemed like all of humanity crowded the shoreline. It was hard to see the sand between the sheer number of people jockeying for their own tiny sliver of oceanfront property. A sea of umbrellas and beach tents stretched as far as you could see and dozens of Bluetooth speakers were cranking out various Pandora/Apple Play/Spotify stations forming a constant thrum that filled the air. Conversations mixed with crying babies and laughing kids filled the space in between.

Charlie stood on the boardwalk at the head of the access ramp, taking it all in. It was near impossible to find anyone from this distance, but he and his friends had their spot–just to the left of the lifeguard stand, and at the high tide mark. He chained his bike to the boardwalk railing and made his way to the beach.

"Do you have a tag?" the kid sitting in the chair under a clip-on umbrella asked. Judging from the squeak in his voice and the hairless nature of his legs, Charlie guessed he couldn't have been more than thirteen or fourteen. Charlie had seen him sitting there occasionally but didn't know his name. He thought it was Ted, or Fred, or Steve, or something.

Charlie nodded, spun slightly so Ted, or Fred, or Steve, could see the beach tag pinned to the pocket of Charlie's backpack and made his way into the throngs of people gathered on the beach like ants on a sugar pile.

Behind him Ted, or Fred, or Steve said, "Thanks. Enjoy the day."

To which Charlie, without turning around, acknowledged by raising his hand in a wave that could be interpreted as either 'thanks, you too' or 'whatever'.

As he wove through the clustered assemblies of families, friends, lovers, and others, he couldn't keep from thinking about Madison. In fact, he hadn't stopped thinking about her since seeing her jog off. Next to Brooke, Madison was the most beautiful girl Charlie knew. It was more than just her appearance though, which was stellar, make no mistake. She was fun to be around. She was a genuine person and a great friend. He loved how she listened when you talked, making a point to actually put her phone down and make eye contact—who the hell does that? Or how she was always willing to help. She was the type of person who chased the little kid's beach ball to catch it and give it back; she always found a spot where no one was sitting and faced away from the wind when she shook out her beach towel so sand wouldn't fly on anyone; she held doors open for people behind her; and stepped aside to let people out before she went in. She smiled at everyone. Everyone. And her laugh. Charlie smiled when he thought of Madison laughing. Madison's laugh was like that favorite song you've been waiting all day to hear; it was like a small breeze blowing through wind chimes on a summer's day.

It hit him then. Charlie realized the explanation for the turmoil rolling in his stomach at the moment: he did have a thing—to use his mother's phrase—for Madison. He stopped walking and let the idea of being attracted to Madison settle over him. His heart picked up a beat in his chest. If Jackson, his mom, and evidently everyone else he knew, were right, Madison was attracted to him as well. That thought sent his heart into absolute defib. Why was he so nervous? He had known Madison forever. They were friends. They got along incredibly well. Which was precisely why dating Madison was the prefect recipe for screwing all of that up. Charlie quickly took up residence in his own head, spinning doomsday prophesies for their future. What if things didn't work out? What if they were a horrible couple? What if she was clingy or demanding? Texting and calling every second to find out what he was doing and where he was? Worse, what if he became a loser asshole, like some boys at school who treated their girlfriends like toys they were only interested in when they wanted to play? He hated those guys and swore he would never be one. The hamster running on a wheel in his mind was ramping up its speed, threatening to spin 'what-if' scenarios faster than Tasty Cakes falling off an assembly line.

"Jesus, Charlie. Get a grip," he said to himself out loud.

"Get a grip on what?" Jackson asked as he walked up behind him, followed closely by a shirtless Joey.

Charlie actually jumped. "Damn-it, Jackson. You scared the shit out of me. Don't sneak up on people."

Jackson smirked, "Uhm… sorry? What are you doing? You're just standing here. You lost or something?"

"Nah, just looking to see if Madison and Kelsey were here. Hey Joey," Charlie threw a weak wave at Joey. Looking him over, he added, "You, ah… you been hitting the weights?"

Joey flexed as a response. "How you doing, Charlie? Long time, no see."

"I saw you on the last day of school, Joey. We have homeroom together," Charlie said.

"Yeah, but that was like, I don't know, days ago. Whatcha been up to?"

"Different day. Same shit," Charlie said.

"I hear ya, bro. Hey, I see Kelsey," Joey walked towards Kelsey, leaving Jackson and Charlie standing in the sand.

"Did he just 'bro' me?" Charlie asked.

Jackson laughed through his nose, "Yeah. You got 'bro-ed'. It's just Joey, you know? Perpetual jock. He can't help it."

"Dude drives me crazy. I don't know what it is. Probably his giant ego, but he drives me crazy." He paused briefly, then added, "Man, he grew some serious muscles, didn't he?"

Jackson, tracking Joey with his eyes as he walked away, said, "He's alright. And yes, he did. Anyway, what are you getting a grip on?"

Charlie furrowed his brow. "Huh? What do you mean?"

"Charlie. When I walked up, I heard you say '*Jesus, Charlie. Get a grip.*' What are you gripping and is it appropriate to be gripping it in public?"

"Welp, get your mind out of the gutter. I was just… it was… I mean, I was just…" Charlie stammered.

Jackson narrowed his eyes at his friend. "How long you were standing in the sun, Charlie? Should I call a lifeguard over?"

Charlie pondered telling Jackson the epiphany he had while walking over to find his friends down by the shoreline. On the one hand, Jackson had already been haranguing Charlie about why he needed to ask Madison out. Pointing out, repeatedly and without mercy, that the astronauts on the international space station two-hundred-fifty-one miles above the Earth could pick up on the signals Madison was sending out. Bottom line, Charlie was apprehensive, though he didn't want to admit it. All along, he had been brushing aside Jackson's theory as if it were a pesky mosquito. It would be hard to swallow now if he admitted to Jackson that he was, in fact, attracted to Madison, and had been since the end of last summer. On the other hand, why should he not tell Jackson? Jackson was his best friend. Each knew details about the other that presumably no one else knew. They spent many a long night sitting on porches, or biking through town, talking about the things teenage boys talk about. Hell, he talked more to Jackson than he did to anyone else, including members of his own family. If he couldn't trust telling his feelings to his best friend, then who could he trust? *Therein lies the rub*, Charlie thought. These days, he didn't trust anyone anymore. How do you ever trust anyone ever again when the one person you trusted the most drops an atomic bomb and obliterates the village that is you? Charlie looked at his friend. He could feel a wall go up in the sand between where he and Jackson stood.

Charlie chose to lay on some mortar. "It was nothing."

Jackson looked him over for a second. Slowly nodding his head, he said, "Oh. Okay." He walked towards the lifeguard stand, then stopped and turned around. "You know, if you need to talk, or tell me something…" Jackson caught the irony of his words, as he desperately needed do that very thing with Charlie.

Charlie cut him off a bit more sharply than he intended, "I'm fine, Jackson. Jesus. It was nothing, okay? Forget it." And he too started out for the lifeguard stand. As he pushed past Jackson, the sand shifted beneath his feet and their shoulders bumped. It was an accident but came off rather aggressively. To soften the blow, Charlie added, "But, thanks," without looking at his friend.

He didn't want to be angry, especially at Jackson. What better way to avoid it all than just walking away? he thought to himself. On that sun scorched beach, Charlie could feel the shadow settling over him again. One so big, it was near impossible to walk out from under it.

Jackson watched as Charlie walked away. It annoyed him that Charlie gave him the brush off. He could tell there was something on Charlie's mind. The shoulder slug was hard-hitting, and it confused Jackson. But like he had said earlier, Charlie was somewhat volatile these days. They'd been friends for too long not to know each other's moods or to not understand each other's body language. Charlie's abrupt departure told Jackson that a nerve had been struck. Then again, Charlie had been a bundle of exposed nerves since his father had disappeared from his life. Jackson thought back to their conversation of a few days ago, and how quickly it became ugly. Charlie was right. Jackson did not know how it would feel to have his dad suddenly decide he no longer wanted anything to do with him. Just thinking about that made Jackson's stomach knot up. He swallowed hard. How could anyone move past that? he wondered. Do you ever move past that? A wave of sadness washed over Jackson at the realization of what, exactly, his friend must be going through. As much as he wanted to help Charlie, he just didn't know how.

Then there was the matter about which Jackson still needed to talk to his friend. He had been carrying it around for some time now, waiting for an opportune time to open up. To let it out. But seeing how Charlie was dealing with some serious shit, he thought it best to wait. The longer he waited, though, the more troubled he felt.

"Damn," he said aloud and went to join his friends.

ELEVEN

The lifeguards on duty that day were two of the beach's finest, if not most authoritarian, boys. Griffin Bennet sat alongside Shane Coleman in the lifeguard stand. Griffin was proudly wearing his OCBP tank top. Shane preferred to be shirtless. Both were wearing their standard blue city issued guard shorts, the waist bands turned over twice to hike up the shorts' legs.

Both eighteen years of age, and more than just somewhat full of themselves, Griffin and Shane were what you would picture in your mind if asked to conjure the perfect image of a beach lifeguard. They sat on the stand, one leg on the footrest, one foot on the seat, looking like something out of an Abercrombie & Fitch catalogue with their square jaws, impeccable hair, and movie-star bodies.

Griffin, standing at six feet and three inches, was shredded and devoid of both body fat and body hair. While not naturally hairy, a trait inherited from his father, he fastidiously removed every outcropping that appeared on his lean, toned frame. Except for his sandy brown eyebrows and his close-cropped mane, he was as hairless as a naked mole-rat. Amazingly, he never tanned, and his skin was the color of vanilla ice cream. No one was quite sure how this was possible, as Griffin Bennet spent most of his week out in the sun. There was talk of him being a vampire, as, if you caught him at the right angle, he seemed to shimmer in the sun. His eyes were topaz, which only served to further the vampire rumor. To look at him, one would wonder if the boy ate anything at all except for protein shakes to keep from dying, or perhaps human blood.

Shane Coleman, just shy of Griffin's height by two inches, stood in stark contrast to his life saving compatriot. His skin reflected his daytime office hours and was the color of coffee with a splash of cream. He wore his jet-black hair cut short on the sides, but full and wavy on top. Shane's eyes were the stuff of legends, and at any given time on any given day of the week, there were at least three dozen conversations taking place somewhere on the island between middle-aged women about Shane's eyes. Unlike Griffin, Shane embraced his secondary male characteristics. While not overtly hairy, Shane did not remove the hair that sprouted out under his arms, below his knees, or leading from the bottom of his belly button and disappearing beneath the curled waistband of his shorts. It was that very trail of dark, coarse hair that was the topic of conversation as Charlie plopped down in the sand beside his friends.

"… and his happy trail is just so sexy," he heard Kelsey say. "I mean, not just Shane's, his is hot. But any guy's, even Jackson's brother. He has a great one, too. I saw Brooke twirling Noah's between her fingers once, and it just looked so, I don't know, intimate, you know?"

"What are you guys talking about?" Charlie asked as he was late to the conversation and struggled to believe Kelsey was actually talking about happy trails, Brooke, and or Jackson's brother.

"Happy trails," Joey said, the boredom evident in his voice. "Can you believe it?"

"Uh," Charlie responded, pulling off his shirt and looking down at his own hairless stomach. "None here."

He could have sworn Madison was watching him as he wiggled out of his shirt.

"Me neither," Joey quipped back.

Madison chuckled.

Kelsey continued, "Well, that's part of the reason why I need to admire Shane's, and Noah's, and every other guy who walks by. You two are still prepubescent. You two barely have hair on your legs, for Christ's sake."

Charlie looked down at his own legs and then at Joey's. Kelsey was right, he thought, for pushing seventeen their legs still resembled those of a fourteen-year-old.

"Why are you talking about my brother, Kelsey?" Jackson asked as he arrived on the scene.

He sloughed off his backpack and dug out a towel. He looked over at Charlie, but Charlie seemed to be staring at Joey's legs.

Joey craned his neck to take Jackson in.

"She's in love with his happy trail. She just loves the way Brooke twirls it between her fingers. It's so, I don't know," Joey raised his voice an octave to imitate female vocals, "*intimate*." Joey looked at Kelsey and smirked, which prompted Kelsey to flip Joey off.

Jackson stripped off his shirt and sat down across from Charlie and Madison. Arranged in a semi-circle, his friends sat facing the ocean. He briefly made eye contact with Charlie, who dropped his eyes to the sand.

Jackson looked down at his flat, freckled belly, ran a hand over it and jokingly said, "Smooth as a baby's ass," eliciting a burst of laughter from the group.

Charlie looked at Jackson and smiled. The cloud was passing, and he once again felt a little embarrassed for snipping at his friend.

"At the risk of sounding like a creepy, incestuous, voyeur, pervert, I have to admit that I sorta admire Noah's happy trail, too. As happy trails go, it's a nice one. Not too thick, not too wide. And I've seen him twirling it between his fingers too," Jackson offered.

"T.M. fucking I. Jackson," Joey said. "Next thing you'll be telling us is that you admire his perky little ass as you watch him in the shower." Jackson raised an eyebrow.

"Joey, that's just gross," Madison said. "Only you would think that Jackson watches his brother shower. And why, in God's name, would you call Noah's ass 'perky'?"

"It kinda is," Kelsey said longingly. "It just pops out like a bubble, and stands out in everything he wears. Put him in a pair of clingy gray sweats and girl..." Her eyes glazed over as she disappeared into some hormone laced fantasy about her friends' older brother's ass.

Jackson, always one to play along and push the envelope, said, "Well, I mean, we did used to take baths together. Like, there are pictures. Brotherly love, and all that."

"Oymygod, Jackson," Madison laughed.

"Whatcha looking at Charlie?"

The sound of Kelsey's voice snapped Charlie back. Suddenly, aware that he was staring at his own smooth stomach, he looked up. He didn't know just how long he was staring at his belly button, but long enough, evidently, to attract attention.

"Find anything?" Kelsey asked. Both girls chuckled.

"Yeah, Charlie. Something pop up that you're not sure what to do with?" Joey kidded. Jackson shot Joey a cautious stare.

"Funny, Joey." Charlie hesitated before he continued, "I was just, I don't know. I wouldn't mind having a happy trail. They're, uh, they're kinda manly."

"Hells yeah, they are!" Kelsey affirmed. "I think you'd look pretty hot with a happy trail, Charlie. What do you think, Madison?" Kelsey baited her friend. Simultaneously, Jackson and Joey turned to look at Madison.

Charlie felt his cheeks redden. He glanced furtively at Madison, whose cheeks were also turning crimson.

Madison smiled and looked down at the sand briefly. "I, uh, I think Charlie looks pretty hot just the way he is."

Madison's eyes darted around for a few seconds before settling on Charlie's. They held each other's gaze, albeit briefly. In those seconds, Charlie's heart threatened atrial fibrillation. His breath came in quick puffs, and whatever food was in his stomach threatened to reemerge. Not knowing what to say, Charlie just smiled, though weakly, rubbed the back of his head with his hand and cast his gaze to the sand. A very brief silence settled over the friends.

Joey shattered the moment, "Screw that shit!" he said. "I hope I remain the smooth, hairless, sexy beast that I am now. Hair don't grow on steel, you know." Like an exclamation point on his words, Joey flexed to prove his argument. His body rippled as his burgeoning muscles were called into duty. "Any hair grows on this temple, I'm shaving it off."

Jackson, trying hard not to be impressed with Joey's muscled physique, said, "Well, far-be-it-from-me to contradict you, but you have armpit hair, Joey. And, based upon that fact, it follows that you also have, well, pubic hair, if I may be so clinical. So that ruins your 'hair don't grow on steel' theory."

Joey dragged the back of his left hand across his jawline, then deliberately wet his lips with the tip of his tongue. He leveled his gaze at Jackson and cocked his head ever so slightly. Then he smiled that Joey smile. That half smile you smile when you are part of an inside joke or know a secret. "I like my armpit hair", he said. "I like the way the hair curls when I'm sweaty. Not to quote Charlie, but I think it's kinda manly." He placed both his hands behind his head as if to add a visual to his statement. "As for my pubes, well, maybe I do, and maybe I don't."

He let his words just hang out there. Joey held his pose, hands behind his head, reclined on his backpack, legs bent at the knee and spread. He stared right at Jackson. It was almost like he was challenging Jackson, Charlie thought. Then, Jackson did something Charlie had never seen Jackson do before. He blushed. And not slightly. Jackson's cheeks turned crimson, causing Charlie to cock an eyebrow.

Kelsey, raging inferno of estrogen that she was, sensed a new topic of conversation. Like a shark circling a struggling, bleeding swimmer, she seized the opportunity.

"Shaved pubes on guys is also so hot," she said, looking right at Jackson.

Jackson was still looking at Joey in a quizzical, amused way one might have when watching a baby struggle with putting a block in the corresponding hole. His cheeks were still the color of a fire truck.

"Really, Kelsey?" Joey asked, breaking his and Jackson's staring contest. "Eleven-year-old boys don't have pubes; you think they're hot? I'll bet ya Charlie's brother doesn't have pubes." The friends looked at Charlie as if silently looking for confirmation.

Charlie shrugged and shook his head in an *I-don't-know* gesture. "Well," Charlie began, "Carson is actually thirteen, so... I mean... I would think... maybe?" He let his comment trail off. He shrugged again.

"You think Carson is hot, Kelsey?"

"Again, Joey, gross," Madison offered. "He's just a kid. Honestly. What dark and disturbing things grow in that mind of yours?"

"Hey, don't get mad at me. Kelsey is the one who thinks guys without pubes are hot. Just trying to establish a baseline," Joey countered. "And Kelsey, just how many guys have you seen without pubes?"

"Wouldn't you like to know, Joseph?" Kelsey said playfully.

Having had enough talk of the hair that grows on bodies during puberty, Charlie rose to his feet.

"Okay," he said, "I'm going in the water. You guys enjoy your conversation about Joey's pubic hair." He strode towards the shoreline.

Madison popped up. "I'll come with you, Charlie. Wait up."

"Me too!" Kelsey said.

Jackson reached over and grabbed her by the wrist. "No. You're not. Stay here and talk to Joey about his pubic hair, or the lack thereof. Figure it out."

Kelsey looked at Jackson the way a lion sizes up its prey before pouncing. She may have actually licked her lips. Lowering her voice, she leaned into Jackson so that her face was just inches from his and whispered, "I'd rather talk about yours."

Jackson swallowed hard. "Um, yeah. Okay."

Charlie turned and stopped, giving Madison time to catch up. He took her in. Wearing a white and blue striped bikini that fit like plastic wrap, she demanded your attention. Her auburn hair pulled back into a ponytail. It was obvious that she was an athlete as she moved gracefully through the sand. Her long legs rippled as she closed the distance. Her breasts, barely contained in her spaghetti string top, bounced in time to her step. Charlie's heart was fluttering, and he hoped he wouldn't pass out right in the sand or, perhaps more embarrassing, rise up in his swimsuit. The latter struggle was real at the moment.

"Thanks," Madison said.

"No trouble," Charlie responded, and the two walked side by side the rest of the way to the water. Madison's hand occasionally brushed against Charlie's sending shock waves through his system.

The ocean was chilly that day, but not so cold that you couldn't venture in. As the two walked deeper, the waves crashing against their bare stomachs felt like little pins stabbing at them. They stopped when they were about thigh deep. Around them, people reveled in summer. Kids tossed balls and rode boogie boards. Teenagers wrestled one another in fake WWE matches. Couples coupled, holding onto each other as the water washed over them. Charlie's heart was still racing. He struggled with something to say. Which came as a surprise because he never had trouble talking with Madison before. Thankfully, Madison saved him.

She stepped out a foot or two in front of Charlie, turned so that they were facing each other, and said, "That Kelsey. She can be a bit much, don't you think?"

"Yeah. I mean, happy trails and pubic hair? Welcome to casual beach banter amongst high-school students, right?" The mention of pubic hair in Madison's presence sent a lightning bolt through Charlie's body. He moved deeper into the ocean. Madison followed.

"And Joey. Jesus. Do you think he shaves, you know, down there?" Madison asked. She pointed with her index finger to Charlie's crotch when she said 'down there'. This, of course, caused further reason for concern in Charlie.

"Honestly, Madison, what Joey does in his pants doesn't ever cross my mind." Madison laughed musically, which caused Charlie to join her. They stood for a moment or two as the waves swelled and broke around them.

Charlie cautiously turned the conversation back to Madison and himself. "So, uhm… that thing you said, you know, when we were talking about happy trails. About me looking hot just the way I am. Did you… did you mean that, Madison?"

Madison's cheeks flushed, and she looked down at the water. She smiled then and looked back up at Charlie. Softly, just barely above a whisper, she said, "Yeah, Charlie. I did." Then added carefully, "I've thought that for a while now."

Charlie smiled. He suddenly felt triumphant, like he won a raffle, or found twenty dollars lying in the street.

"Oh. Um. I'm glad. I uh… I uh think you're hot too." He cringed inwardly as soon as the words popped out of his mouth. "No. wait. That's not true. I mean, Jesus, that's not what I want to say." Charlie took a deep breath, trying to squelch some of the adrenaline that was now coursing through his body, threatening to shut down his brain. "I think you are absolutely beautiful, Madison. So beautiful. And so smart, and so kind, and so… perfect. And lately, lately you make me so nervous when you're near me. My throat closes and my heart races and I feel so stupid because I never know what to say and I just end up grunting or answering you with one word and that just makes me feel like a loser and all. It's just. It's just…" He trailed off and looked away.

Maddison stepped closer to him, closing the distance. "What, Charlie?" she asked, touching his forearm.

Shivers ran up Charlie's spine, and it wasn't because the water was chilly. Charlie scratched the back of his neck. *What would Jackson do?* he thought to himself. Which, he acknowledged inwardly, was a weird thing to think of at this very moment in time, face to face with a girl, in a somewhat romantic moment. *Jackson was always calm and confident. He always knew the right words to say and he would just say them*, Charlie decided of his friend.

"Charlie?" Madison probed, inching closer.

"It's just that…. well… I ahh… I like you, Madison. You know? In that way. And I was just, you know, wondering if maybe, you know…?" Charlie looked away again, embarrassed by his less than articulate confession of romantic interest. *Jackson was right*, he thought. *I am a monosyllabic moron.*

Madison smiled warmly. Her eyes kept bouncing from the water to Charlie's face and back again. She held her bottom lip with her teeth. "I like you too, Charlie. In that way."

Charlie turned back and looked at Madison, his full attention on her face. Neither saw the wave building, growing larger and larger as it closed the distance to the shoreline. It crested and broke right behind Madison, throwing her forward into Charlie's chest. They both struggled against the force of the current, which pushed Madison into Charlie. Charlie dug the balls of his feet into the sand to keep them from being knocked over. When the wave passed, Madison was pressed right against Charlie. Chest to chest. Stomach to stomach. Skin touching. His hands gripping her arms at the elbows, holding her steady. Her hands clasped on the small of his back. Her fingers slipped just below the waistband of his bathing suit, just at the base of his spine, gripping him. Charlie let his hands slip down from Madison's arms, slowly tracing her body, coming to a rest on her waist. Their hips pressed into each other. Madison raised hers, pressing ever so slightly forward, and, completely overwhelmed, Charlie succumbed to his hormones.

Feeling what little space there was left between them rapidly fill up, Madison looked down, and then back up at Charlie. She smiled and whispered, "Oh. Hello."

Charlie, somewhere between utter elation and total and complete embarrassment, just as quietly said "Hi." They stood that way, locked together, neither moving, as the world disappeared around them.

From the shore, the shrill whistle of either Griffin Bennet or Shane Coleman pierced the day and disappeared on the breeze. Normally, Charlie would have turned to see what offense the rulers of the surf were calling out. But not today. Not then.

TWELVE

Up in the sand, Jackson sat on his towel, listening to the conversation that continued between Kelsey and Joey. Much to his dismay, that conversation hadn't strayed too far from body hair. After some probing, Kelsey got Joey to admit that he did indeed shave off the small amount—Joey's words—of hair that grew on his nether region. *Thank God,* Jackson thought, *for the light shed upon that mystery.* What followed was the two of them trying to find out if Jackson was a member of the club, too. Jackson deflected the inquiries.

At the moment, the two were discussing whether men should shave their armpits. Griffin Bennet, of course, was the example that Kelsey was holding up against all of mankind. According to Kelsey, Griffin was a true feminist. In shaving off all of his body hair, he stood in solidarity with women all over the world forced to do the same because of societal expectations. Joey, ever the jock, felt that armpit hair, evidently unlike pubic hair, was what made a man, a man. Jackson thought about inserting himself into the conversation with a brief anatomy lesson in what physical characteristics separate the male species from the female species, but decided against it. They were talking to each other, and Jackson was enjoying not being a part of the conversation. He had a lot on his mind anyway: foremost, Charlie. His friend for many years was simply not himself. To Jackson, the situation with Charlie was like when an actor in a TV show or a movie sequel is replaced by a new actor, but the character remains the same. Charlie still looked like Charlie, but inside—something was different; something was off. He thought back to that night in January when Charlie called him to tell him that his father had left; how Charlie's voice was thick and choked with the threat of tears; and how helpless Jackson felt when Charlie finally broke down. His breathless sobs on the other end of the phone for what seemed like hours. Jackson felt utterly useless, up in his room, sitting on his bed in another city, listening to his friend unravel over AT&T's network. His stomach knotted remembering that night. This newness in Charlie had begun shortly after. The few times during the winter and spring that Jackson and Charlie had gotten together to hang out, Jackson could see the difference. Normally upbeat and goofy, Charlie had become quieter and more serious. It wasn't a quick transformation, but a slower one. It was more like a shadow that makes its way across a room filling it with night. These last few days, it seemed to Jackson that maybe night was taking Charlie over.

Off in the distance, the shrill screech of a lifeguard whistle pierced the air, penetrating Jackson's thoughts. Jackson, Joey, Kelsey, and every other sunscreen slicked beach goer turned to the shore as the sound of the whistle faded around them. As the three friends scanned the water line to see what great offense caused the Gods of the Stand to sound off authoritatively, their eyes laser locked on the young couple clinging to each other in the surf. A couple whose resemblance to Charlie and Madison was uncanny. Kelsey's jaw slackened at the realization.

"Sonofabitch. Will you look at that?" Joey said.

A smile spread across Jackson's face when he recognized his best friend clinging rather intimately to Madison Walker in the chilly New Jersey Sea. He was happy for Charlie. He needed something good to happen to him. Something that might pull away, if even for a moment, the backpack of misery he had been carrying around with him. "Well, it's about frickin time," he said aloud.

"Hells yeah," Kelsey said. "It *is* about frickin time. Madison has been chasing that boy since the middle of last summer. The Snap Chat courting over the school year must have eaten up tens of thousands of gigabytes alone. I was beginning to think he might be gay."

Joey laughed, "Charlie? Gay? Ain't no way."

Jackson turned his head to look at Joey. "Oh, and what? You can tell someone is gay by just looking at them?" he tossed across the sand challengingly.

Joey, his head slowly pivoting, turned his full attention towards Jackson. "As a matter of fact, I can," he said, his eyes never leaving Jackson's. Jackson could feel his face swiftly flush again.

"Ohmygod!" Kelsey said. The sudden outburst causing both boys to return their attention to Madison and Charlie lingering in the surf. "Kiss her for fuck's sake."

Soft-spoken is not a phrase that has ever been applied to Kelsey's expression. She was the person who embodied a Broadway actor's projection. If you walked into a party thrumming with people, you could pick out Kelsey's voice above the rest. So, in either an expression of compliance or complete coincidence, at the precise moment of Kelsey's demand of a kiss, Charlie did precisely that, though somewhat awkwardly.

"I'll be damned," Joey said.

"Sonofabitch," Jackson muttered.

"Yes," Kelsey chimed in.

THIRTEEN

The moments in the surf that followed Charlie's kiss were an eternity of inner dialogue bouncing off the inside of Charlie's skull and reverberating around his head like a Superball in a clothes dryer. Charlie wasn't sure if they should hold hands, stand facing each other, or stand side by side. Should he put his arm around her waist or across her shoulder? Should he be touching her at all? He grew rapidly aware of his hands and what they were or were not doing. He scanned the ocean with his eyes, hoping to catch a glimpse of other couples, to gain some insight as to what to do next. His limited experience in the world of courtships only added to an abundance of self-doubt that already existed. His mind flashed to his high-school hallways, cafeteria, and other public spaces. He'd seen kids his age interact with their significant others on more than one occasion, hadn't he?

Charlie's mind jumped to Noah and Brooke, the only couple he knew well. They often sat beside one another on the beach, hands rested on knees, or walking, holding hands, and laughing. *Hands, again. What do I do with my hands?* They always seemed so natural together, like an extension of one another. Their PDAs were never vulgar or crass, but they have had years of practice. Charlie was all of five minutes swimming in the relationship pool and he was already foundering, looking for a floatie to save his life. It was times like this that he wished he had an older brother.

In the days pre-kiss, he and Madison would be throwing a ball, or body surfing, or playfully wrestling with each other. Considering Charlie's unpredictable reactions that were occurring below his belt line, he thought it best not to wrestle with Madison at the moment. But the kiss had changed everything, of that he was certain, and it all happened so unexpectedly. He dismissed the notion of getting together with Madison only a few days ago, almost laughing it off. Then, today, seconds ago, he kissed her. The spectators in the stadium that was his mind were doing The Wave. *He had just kissed Madison Walker.* He hoped he had done it reasonably well and didn't come across like some slobbering puppy hungrily licking the peanut butter and jelly sandwich crumbs from the face of its owner. Perhaps the use of tongue was presumptuous? Maybe he should have stuck with just an open-mouthed kiss? Should he have opened his mouth at all?

He was vaguely aware of Madison talking, but all he could focus on was her lips. Charlie wanted to kiss her again. He didn't want to stop kissing her. Was it too forward of him to lean in and plant another on her? Was he being foolish not to? How does anyone decide when the right time to kiss someone is? *Is* there a right time to kiss someone? Dating, Charlie thought, needs a 'How-To' manual, or at least an App that he could download.

"So, what do you say?" Madison asked.

"Huh?"

Madison smiled. "You haven't heard a word I've said, have you?"

Charlie blushed, "Well," Charlie started, letting his eyes bounced back and forth between Madison and the waves. "I *was* watching your lips, if that counts for anything?"

"Oh? Watching my lips, huh?" Madison said, moving a little closer.

Charlie was still watching her lips. He smiled and shrugged. Suddenly, he felt awkward, like in-that-manner-you-feel-awkward-when-the-doctor-asks-you-to-drop-your-underwear-

and- turn-and-cough, manner of feeling awkward. He felt as if everyone on the beach was watching them, waiting to see what his next dorky move would be. He actually started to sweat.

Madison was face to face with him now. Charlie's heart slipped into an epic drum solo as he felt her fingers playfully touch his obliques, tracing the muscle.

"I said, maybe we should head up to the sand. My feet are getting numb."

"Oh. Um… sure. Yeah. Yeah, that's a good idea. Sure." Charlie turned and headed back to the shore.

As he did, Madison caught his dangling right hand with hers, pulling him back to face her. She leaned in and gently kissed him. It was hesitant, the way one might touch an iron to see if it was hot. Charlie returned the kiss, drawing her in closely and holding her against him.

Parting, she looked at him. "Are you okay with this, Charlie? I mean, you know, are we dating now?"

There was that word again. Dating. *What does that even mean?* Charlie thought. In late elementary school, it meant you hung out together at recess. In middle school, it meant you sat together at lunch and courted via text messages. But this was high school. Dating. Do you hold hands as you walk down the halls? Do you sit side by side in the classes you may have together? Does she attend your sports practices, watching from the bleachers? Do you carry her books? Do you hang out together after school at some local coffeeshop staring adoringly into each other's eyes while wistfully discussing college and the future? Do you FaceTime instead of Snap Chatting?

"Yeah, I guess we are. I mean, if that's okay with you?"

"I guess we are then," Madison said.

An unabashed smile spread across Charlie's face; a smile which he could barely contain.

FOURTEEN

A day at the beach has a way of sinking into your soul and healing all that ails you. It can wash away the doubt that stains your consciousness and silence the self-deprecating talk that is often the loudest voice in your head. A day at the beach has a way of rebuilding all that has crumbled. The breeze brings with it a sense of calm, of clarity. The sun heating your body bakes away your anxiety, you can feel your disquiet sloughing off like so much sunburned skin. It was one reason Charlie loved being at the beach. One of his earliest memories is of laying beneath a tent made of towels, listening to the surf and the muted conversations of the surrounding crowd mixed with the smell of salt air and seaweed, feeling completely at ease. People speak so nonchalantly of their 'happy place', as if some coffee shop, or a comfortable sofa by a sunny window could ever fulfill that role. For Charlie, Third Street beach was as good as it gets and today, it didn't get much better.

The most awkward part of the day, after the semi-embarrassment of his raging hormones introducing themselves to Madison, and the first kiss, was sitting back down amongst his friends. It was obvious that they had all seen what transpired in the waist deep surf. The darting eyes and the tongue-tied conversation upon their return made it incredibly apparent. The strangled banter ranged from small talk about the water temperature, to who had better donuts—Ove's or Browns. A topic decided upon when they were all nine years old: Charlie, Jackson, Kelsey, for Browns; Joey and Madison, for Ove's. The fact that they had had that tired conversation yet again spoke to the change in dynamics that had just taken place in the chilly surf. To Charlie, it seemed that Jackson's facial expressions ranged from total elation to a deep envy, or maybe sadness. He couldn't quite place it. Charlie noticed Kelsey was practically sitting on top of Jackson. Though each on their own towel, the space between them was barely perceptible. Occasionally, Kelsey would touch Jackson on the knee, which seemed to elicit an adverse reaction from Jackson. Joey was strangely silent, sitting back and taking it all in. Finally, Kelsey, in her 'in-your-face, no-holds-barred' manner, said what everyone else was thinking.

She looked right at Madison and Charlie and said, "So. You two dating now? I mean, you were all over each other in the water. And might I add, if you are dating, it's about fucking time."

"There ya go, Kelsey. Ever so subtle," Joey said, raising his water bottle in a mock toast. He paused, took in both Charlie and Madison, then added, "So. Are ya?"

Charlie could feel his cheeks flush. There was that word yet again, dating. While he knew precisely what it implied, he had still no idea what it meant. He looked at Madison, who was equally flushed. This was one of those moments his dad told him about; when a man needs to be a man and speak up, be truthful. The thought of his dad charging into his head threw him off. The fist in his stomach returned and his breath caught in his throat. He looked down at the sand, unable to form words, as the tears threatened his eyes.

"Guys," Charlie heard the familiar sound of his best friend's voice rising about the rest. "I think it's great that Charlie and Madison have finally realized that which we have all known since last summer. They like each other. I'm happy for you. Everyone deserves someone in their life that matters. Mazeltov!"

Charlie looked up from the sand as Madison took his hand in hers. This was a strange new reality, a terrain yet traversed. Despite his words, Jackson looked somber: not quite sad, but not quite happy. Something was up with him, but Charlie couldn't quite place it. Kelsey stared warmly at Jackson, almost longingly. Clutching his words that faded on the air as if by some slight chance they were meant for her, and her alone. Joey looked past everyone, staring beyond his friends, beyond the crowd of people, out over the ocean, yet seeing nothing at all. He looked… uncomfortable. Charlie glanced at Madison; someone he had known all of his life. Someone who was now much more than just a friend. She smiled, and squeezed his hand, shrugging as if to say, 'what does this all mean?' Glancing back at his friends, he could sense a feeling of detachment. As always, they were all together, but somehow, they each seemed all alone. For a brief instance, Charlie had a sense of dread, like this was the beginning of the end of everything he had ever known. He felt that from this point forward, somehow, things would be forever changed. Anxiety's fingers clamped tightly around his throat and squeezed it shut. His stomach tumbled as his chest tightened, forcing out the air. There had been enough change in his life these past six months, enough for a lifetime. He struggled against the sudden wave of sadness that bore down upon him, threatening to sweep him away. Charlie, taking a slow, deep, purposeful breath, closed his eyes and disappeared into the calming cacophony of the beach.

FIFTEEN

As the day progressed, the number of people basking like so many seals on the rocks, dwindled. The sun dipped behind the houses and the boardwalk, casting longer and longer shadows onto the sand. The lifeguards had left a while ago and all that remained were the die-hard beach goers. It was Jackson's favorite time of the day. The loud conversations of mid-day were all but gone and it was easier to just get lost in the wind and the waves. Charlie grabbed his board and ventured out about thirty minutes ago, after Joey, Madison, and Kelsey called it a day. Jackson sat now, in the sand, watching his best friend catch a wave here and there.

He and Charlie began surfing at the same time, having progressed through the obligatory boogie-board and skim-board phase of childhood, and admittedly, Charlie was a better surfer. Yeah, Jackson could hold his own on a wave, but Charlie was graceful in a way rarely seen at the Jersey Shore. It was like Charlie disappeared when he was surfing and simply became one with his board, one with the wave. Jackson mentally laughed at the small twinge of jealousy that crept into his head and then pushed it away.

Reaching to his right, he pulled his cell phone out of his backpack and checked the time: six forty-five. Sighing, he stood and gathered up his stuff. From within the backpack in the sand next to him, Darth Vader's theme song played softly. It had been going off roughly every five to ten minutes for the entire time Charlie was surfing. Charlie was most likely going to get an earful when he got home.

As if psychically connected, Jackson turned to the ocean, just as his friend sat up on his board and looked at him from across the water. Jackson smiled, raised his arm up over his head and drew circles in the air with his finger, signaling to Charlie that it was time to wrap it up. Charlie caught one last wave and rode it into the shore. Jackson, realizing that he was staring, transfixed by his friend's ride, shook himself out of his trance. He reached into Charlie's backpack and pulled out his towel just as Charlie arrived on the scene.

"Nice session," he said, tossing it to his friend. "You looked good out there today."

"Thanks. You should've come out. It would have saved me from that annoying nine-year-old who kept trying to talk to me and get pointers."

Jackson laughed, "Yeah, I saw that. I don't know, just wasn't feeling it today, I guess. And you know, you could've talked to him. We were that age once and I remember us always pestering Reese, Noah, and those older guys for tips."

"I remember that." Then cocking his head to one side, Charlie said, "Oh, hells, does that make us the older guys now?"

Jackson turned to Charlie and hesitated a second. Cocking his head to one side, he said, "Yeah. I guess it does. Weird, huh? I mean, growing up. It can be weird."

It was Charlie's turn to hesitate. He looked at his friend; someone he had known since diapers; someone who had always been by his side. "Yeah. A little." Charlie hesitated again, finished drying himself off and folded up his towel. "Hey, Jackson," he began haltingly, "you, okay? I mean, is everything all right?" The two boys were looking right at each other now, and Charlie knew the answer to the question before Jackson even told the lie.

"Of course, Charles. I'm good. Just a little tired, I guess. Nothing an après-beach nap can't take care of."

"Okay." But they both knew it wasn't.

Charlie had known Jackson long enough to understand that Jackson talked when Jackson was ready to talk. Whatever was brewing hadn't completely percolated yet. When it did, Jackson would reach out.

Suddenly, and well timed to break the thick air that was settling between them, Darth Vader's theme bled out of Charlie's backpack and both boys laughed.

"Oh yeah, I meant to tell you that your mom has been calling for the last thirty minutes. Charlie-boy is in some deep shit, methinks."

"Frick. You know what? I'm not even going to answer it. It was a good day today, and I will not let her chew me out right now for some imaginary offence and ruin it. Christ, I'm starting to understand why my dad left." Charlie's last sentence hung out there as the last bars of music playing from his phone ended. Jackson tossed a worried look his way. "Anyway," Charlie said, and he slugged on his backpack and picked up his board.

Jackson did the same, and they headed towards the boardwalk.

"Anyway. It was a good day for you. And speaking of weird, I have to admit that seeing you and Madison together, in that kind of boyfriend and girlfriend way, is a little weird. Good. But weird."

"Yeah. Uhm, it is actually a lot weird. Good, but weird. I guess it'll take a little getting used."

"How so?"

Charlie laughed and shook his head. "You know, Jackson, I'm not sure. I don't have a lot of experience dating. And now, I'm here for the rest of the summer, and we all hang out together every day, and I guess I just don't know how to play it, you know? Like, do I always have to sit next to her? Do we hold hands? Do we have to hang out together at night now too? Can we still wrestle in the water, because I gotta tell you now that I think of her as my girlfriend every time I touch her, I have to think about baseball, if you know what I mean? And what about you? Can I not just hang out with you now like we always do? Is that going to piss her off? I just… I just don't know."

"Charlie, methinks you think too much."

"Yeah, I do."

Inwardly, though, Jackson was feeling some of the same things as his friend. This was new, and Jackson wasn't sure where all of this was heading or how it would all play out. They had all been friends for so long. This sudden shift in dynamics left him feeling uncertain and confused, like when you wake up from a dream and, for an instant, you don't recognize your room or know where you are. Everything looks familiar, but you just can't place it.

They walked down Third Street towards each other's houses. The same street they had been walking for sixteen years, but tonight, the air felt different and the sounds somehow weren't the same. Jackson looked over at his friend and took him in. The summer had always belonged to the two of them. People joked about just how inseparable they were. Even when they were with their friends, it was the two of them, and everyone else. This thing with Madison was going to change that, and while Jackson was happy for Charlie, he was a little afraid for tomorrow. *Growing up is weird,* he thought again. *One day you're playing with buckets and pails, and the next day you're filled with thoughts, and feelings, and emotions, and desires that seemingly come from nowhere. It's as if you go to bed one night and a hole opens in your head and all this adult shit gets poured in. Shit, you're just not quite ready to process or handle.*

Jackson was percolating. Actually, was getting close to boiling over. It was just him and Charlie right now. They were getting closer to Atlantic Avenue, where they would break off and head to their own houses. Now is a good time, Jackson thought, to get this off my chest. His mouth dried up and his heart pounded. He took a deep breath to keep himself from throwing up and blew it out. "Hey, Charlie, there is actually something that I wanted to talk to you about."

Charlie stopped and looked at his friend, who, oddly enough, looked as if he were going to throw up. "I know, Jackson," Charlie said matter-of-factly.

Surprised, Jackson stammered, "You know? You know what, Charlie?" There was a hint of panic in his voice that Charlie picked up.

Charlie side-eyed his friend, perplexed by his reaction that seemed a bit extra. "Uhm, that something is bothering you. I've kind of sensed it all day. That's why I asked if you were all right. What's going on?"

Jackson fell silent for a few seconds, scratching awkwardly at the back of his neck. "Okay, well, it's not that something is bothering me so much as it is that I just have to tell you something, and that I haven't told you this thing is actually what's bothering me, not necessarily the thing that I have to tell you because I'm not bothered by that. Concerned a little, I guess, but not really bothered by it, because it is what it is, and I can't be bothered by it because there would be no point in that. I think, now, I'm actually okay with it, and…"

Charlie cut in, "Jackson. Focus. What's going on?"

Jackson nodded his head in agreement. "Okay. You're right," Jackson took a deep breath, and blew it out, "Charlie, I um…"

Abruptly, the familiar sound of Carson's cracking voice calling Charlie's name filled the street. Both boys turned in the direction from which it was coming and saw Charlie's brother on his bike heading towards them.

He fishtailed to a stop in front of them. "Hey, Jackson." Then turning to Charlie he said, "Mom is pissed at you. She's been trying to call you for like forty-five minutes. She sent me and Sarah out to find you. Why didn't you answer your phone?"

"Mom was calling?" Charlie feigned. "Oh, I guess my phone is on vibrate."

Just then, the symphony in Charlie's backpack started up. He and Jackson tossed amused looks at one another.

"Vibrate, huh? She's pissed, Charlie. You better come home now." Carson pedaled away. "I'm going to let her know you haven't drowned. But boy, she is going to kill you when you get home," he called back.

Charlie sighed, trying to push down his own anger. The familiar knot in his stomach had returned, but he was trying not to let it get the better of him. Unaware, his left hand had curled into a fist. Turning back to Jackson, he said, "Sorry. What were you going to say, Jackson?"

Jackson half smiled and shook his head. "Don't worry about it, Charlie. You need to get home."

"You sure? I mean, at this point, I'm already dead. What's another few minutes?"

"Nah, man. It's okay. It can wait."

Charlie looked his friend up and down. Something was up. He could see it in Jackson's face. He looked… worried, maybe even a little scared. Maybe a little sad.

Charlie shrugged, "Okay. Guess I better get going."

"You think you'll be around tonight, or do you think you'll be under house arrest?"

Charlie smiled at his friend. "Probably house arrest, but I'll text you. See ya, Jackson." With a toss of his chin, Charlie pivoted and continued the short distance to his house.

"See ya, Charlie." Jackson stood on the sidewalk watching his friend walk away. He pulled in a few deep breaths in an attempt to get his heart to stop hammering his rib cage.

SIXTEEN

Charlie wondered how many times he had been in this position, on his back in bed, staring at the ceiling. One hundred? A thousand? Ten thousand? How many moments in life are spent doing the same thing in the same place? When you add them all up and string them all together, how many years does that add up to? Charlie remembered his dad saying once that the average person spends twenty-six years of their life sleeping. Charlie frowned at the memory.

"That's ten more years than I am old," he said to himself.

As expected, Miriam lit into him with a wrath unseen for a stretch. The last time his mom was that angry was the day he and a friend moved Carson's entire bedroom onto the sidewalk with a 'free' sign taped to everything. Miriam was not happy, but the stunt was well worth the stint in solitary Charlie had to endure thereafter.

The tirade began before the screen door slammed shut behind him. He knew he was in trouble when Sarah got up off of the couch and left the room. She usually reveled in her oldest brother being dressed down publicly. Somehow, even she knew that today was going to be a doozy. After about fifteen minutes of being bombarded by words like selfish, irresponsible, moody, and disappointing, Charlie stopped listening. He stood motionless by the kitchen sink, and absorbed the verbal punches, one after another, landing squarely. His eyes leveled, staring through his mom, through the wall, beyond the island, and searching for something that just wasn't there. The Cliff Notes version of the rant was that Charlie is self-involved, uncommunicative, cares little about spending time with his family, needs to start pulling his weight around the house, and spend less time with his friends. Typical.

The unexpected silence pulled Charlie back into the kitchen. His mom was staring at him, as if waiting for something.

"Well?" Miriam said. "Anything to say for yourself?"

Charlie thought. He had a lot to say. It had been building up since the divorce, since his dad just decided that none of them were worth it anymore and walked away. Suddenly, Charlie, at sixteen years old, was supposed to take over for a father who decided to just leave everything behind and disappear. Overnight, Charlie had become the man of the family, at least in his mom's eyes, and was expected to pick up the slack left by her partner. Expected to be home for his siblings. Expected to fix things that break; leaky pipes, garage door openers, the fucking modem when the internet goes down. Expected to babysit when his mom went out on her girls' nights, and there were a lot of girls' nights. Expected to pick up her slack as well and just keep swimming through his life as if there wasn't a twenty-pound weight in his stomach every day he woke up. Expected to keep being the same cheery Charlie that he used to be. Except that old version of Charlie was dead and buried beneath a mountain of hate and resentment.

Charlie remembered a meme he once saw that read: *A smart man knows what to say. A wise man knows whether or not to say it.* While advice taken from a meme isn't always the best idea, this one seemed to suit the situation nicely.

Shrugging, he said, "I got nothing, Miriam." He knew using her name would piss her off, and it did not disappoint.

"What? We're on a first name basis now?" his mother volleyed. "I am your mother, Charles."

"Yeah. Well, maybe when you act like it again, instead of some high school sophomore who has just discovered wine, I'll go back to calling you mom." He stared her down for a few tense seconds. Cocking an eyebrow, he added, "Are we done here, *Mom*?"

Charlie's words and sarcastic tone landed heavily and seemed to knock the wind out of his mother. She took a step backwards and put her hand to her mouth. Their eyes met and Charlie held her gaze, challengingly.

"Are we done here?" he asked again, calmly, slowly.

"Just go to you room. You're grounded," his mom said.

"Whatever. And don't you mean my side of the room?" He pushed past her, walked the short distance to his room, and threw the door shut behind him.

That was three hours ago. Charlie lay on his bed since, staring at the ceiling. His anger boiled away to a mild annoyance. The fist in his stomach remained, the weight on his chest constricting every breath. The threat of tears, right behind his eyes. He wondered if they would ever go away.

His phone vibrated in his pocket. It was Jackson.

You alive?

Yep. Been holed up in my room for the last 3 hours.

Miriam go nuclear on you?

LOL. Yep. Haven't seen her that fired up since I moved Carson's room onto the sidewalk.

HAHAHA! That was a good one. You were grounded for like a week, weren't you?

Haha. Yep. Good times at the McIntyre house.

So… are you under house arrest tonight? Meeting everyone at Annie's and then we're probably going to hang on the beach.

Oh yeah. Probably for the rest of my life. She can be such a pain in the ass, you know? She's disappointed in me. Says I'm self-involved. Problem is she just wants me to be the other adult in the house.

It'll blow over. You know that. Not the first time you've been in Miriam's dog house. Anyway. Just wanted to make sure you weren't dead.

LOL. Thanks. Guess I'll catch up with you tomorrow. Tell everyone I said 'hey' from Eastern State Penitentiary.

HAHA, will do. See ya tomorrow.

Charlie put his phone on his chest. Then, remembering something, picked it back up and typed,

Oh, hey, Jackson. What was it you wanted to tell me today?

He watched as the small ellipses appeared in the corner of his screen. Then stopped. They appeared again after a few seconds and stopped one more time. Odd, Charlie thought. Jackson was usually quick with a comeback., but things with Jackson seemed to be off lately. At last, Jackson's response popped on the screen.

Nothing. Never mind.

I'll tell you when I see you.

Okay

Charlie could sense that things with Jackson weren't okay. He let it go. Funny, he thought, how days change. This afternoon he and Madison got together; everything was wonderful. A few hours later, he was alone in his room, facing an evening of Netflix by himself. He reached onto the floor to retrieve his laptop and booted Netflix. Tonight seemed as good a night as any to re-watch *Big Mouth*.

Carson appeared in the doorway. He lingered for a second or two, uncertain if he should enter, say something, or just go away.

He chose the second. "Want some company?" he asked hesitantly.

"Nope. I don't." Charlie responded too quickly and way too coldly.

In his periphery, he could see Carson linger for a few seconds in the threshold, then turn and head back down the hallway. Guilt welled in Charlie. The fist in his stomach moved up to his throat, and the tears pushed at his lids. True to form, he choked it all down. Swallowed it. He stuffed it all back into his tidy little jar where he kept all of his pain, all of his anxiety, all of his emotion, and screwed the fucking lid down. Tightly. *Boys don't cry, right? They don't feel.*

Sighing deeply, he pushed his ear buds into his ears. Focusing his attention on his laptop, he allowed himself to disappear into the glowing screen, blocking out his room, his family, and himself.

SEVENTEEN

The house on the corner of First and Ocean was a throwback to a time when beach houses were squat and demure. While not quite two stories, it sat elegantly on its plot, surrounded by white stones and river rock where grass and flowers beds previously reigned. Decorative grasses popped up here and there to add some texture to the otherwise stone landscape. The obligatory beach paraphernalia hung on porch walls and above the door. Signs like "What happens on the porch, stays on the porch"; wooden logos shaped like surf boards that read, "Welcome to the Beach" or "It's Wine O' Clock Somewhere".

Bright red awnings shaded the porch and the upstairs windows. Nestled between the modern three- and four-story homes that litter the town, Madison Walker's house might seem like a dinosaur. The only hint of showiness was the classic 1965 hunter green Triumph TR4 convertible parked in the driveway; a trinket with which her dad would never part.

Madison sat on the porch sipping an Americano she picked up at Berenato's Café on the corner. The sun was freshly up and the street was quiet, except for the occasional jogger or early morning bike rider. She enjoyed this time of the day. While she loved summers at the beach, the days became crammed with day trippers and vacationers alike. By ten a.m., there would be a steady stream of people flowing up and down the street until the sun shrank from the sky and dark descended upon the town. It didn't bother her, but some days it made her feel claustrophobic.

She thought of how things were when she was younger, still in elementary school. The neighborhood was different then. Most of the houses still resembled hers. Modest homes that didn't cast shadows or block the breeze. Things change, though, and as the value of the modest homes increased, it was hard not to sell to developers who envisioned a different First Street. As neighbors sold and moved out, more vacationers moved in; coming for a week or two and clearing out for the next band of wide eyed Shoebies intent on soaking up a vacation's worth of sand, sun, and fun. They parked their cars in driveways, cluttered the sidewalks with their wagons full of beach supplies, and clogged up the restaurants, delis, and coffee shops. Which is why Madison rose with the sun. She glanced to her left at the giant, four-story foam green monstrosity that loomed over her garage. She used to be able to see the ocean from her bedroom window. Now, all that graced her view was a side deck and a sliding glass door.

She took a pull from her coffee and refocused her attention to the slight breeze and the chatter of early morning birds. She closed her eyes and let the calm of the morning wash over her. A shrill, but familiar, voice broke the serenity.

"Um, like, why don't you have your phone?"

Madison didn't have to open her eyes to know that Kelsey was standing on the sidewalk in front of her house.

"The larger question at hand, Kels, is what are you doing up so early?" Madison replied.

By now, Kelsey had made her way onto the porch and took up residence in the Adirondack next to her friend.

"I'm up because my mom thought Saturday morning at seven-thirty was a good time to have the A/C units serviced. And while I am not opposed to watching hot young mechanics putter and bang around, I would prefer it to happen a bit later in the day. I've been texting you for like an hour."

Kelsey's parents, years ago, decided to keep up with the flavor of the neighborhood. They had their bungalow razed and replaced it with a four-story home more fitting for the new and improved beach town. The house had enough A/C units to cool a small city.

Madison took another sip of her coffee. She loved her friend, but Kelsey's flair for the dramatic did sometimes wear on her.

"First world problems, huh?"

"Um… yeah, Mads. Anyway, since you weren't answering your phone, and I was awake and all, I thought I'd walk over to see if you were up and just ignoring me. And, BTW, the mechanics are not young, and they are most certainly not hot. Double disappointment. And it would appear that based upon your cell phone face down on the table next to you, that you were ignoring me!"

Madison smiled warmly. Sometimes, it was best not to engage with Kelsey. To just let her run out the rant and then hope to move on. Kelsey had always been a bit boy crazy. But since around seventh grade, boys seemed to occupy her every thought. The past couple of summers she had fixated on landing Jackson, and she wasn't subtle about it. Madison had talked with Kelsey a few times about playing it a bit more coolly with Jackson, to not be so in-his-face about her intentions. He was less the typical hormone crazed teen boy, and a more laid back-introspective young man. But Kelsey was anything but demure. It seemed to Madison that the more Kelsey chased Jackson -who, in Madison's opinion, was a good-looking guy and worthy of the pursuit–the more he ran away. Maybe Jackson had cold feet, or maybe he didn't feel the same way about Kelsey. But there was no mistaking how Kelsey felt about Jackson.

"So. Charlie…" Kelsey's voice trailed off, not completing the sentence.

Here we go, thought Madison. "So. Charlie," she replied, "yeah."

What exactly was she supposed to think about Charlie? She'd be kidding herself if she didn't admit that she thought Charlie was cute, and the extra height and broadening physique added to her attraction. The spur-of-the-moment romp in the waves yesterday afternoon sure was fun, she thought, and he kissed well—exceptionally well–which surprised her. Then she felt him pressed up against her. Madison could feel her cheeks flush. She smiled a knowing smile that did not go unnoticed by her estrogen charged friend.

Kelsey pointed an accusatory finger at Madison, exclaiming, "Yep! There it is. You're love struck. I can see it in your eyes, and your red cheeks. You're hot for Charlie, aren't you?"

"Kelsey, don't make anything more out of this than it is. I mean, yeah, I like Charlie. That's no surprise. I've been talking about him to you for almost three summers now. And yesterday was fun and exciting. But now it seems almost weird, you know?"

"You lost me, Mads. What is weird about finally getting together with a guy you've been crushing on? Lord knows I would love to get with Jackson. That fish is hard to reel in."

Madison took another pull on her coffee as she thought about her feelings. She went to bed last night, practically jumping out of her skin. She was so happy about what had happened between her and Charlie, but when she woke this morning, there was doubt.

"It's just that, well, we've all grown up together. We've known each other since we were little kids. And now, now we're these hormone crazed teenagers trying to sort out feelings and emotions that wreak havoc with our minds. I know I like Charlie. I've always liked Charlie. But I'm trying to figure out when my liking Charlie became me *liking* Charlie," she said.

"I can tell you, Madison. It was when he turned thirteen, started growing armpit hair, and filling out his shorts. You talked about him all summer long. He was all you could talk about."

Madison rolled her eyes. She remembered that summer. Charlie, Jackson, Joey. They changed. They swore more. They bragged more. Their talk leaned towards what their parents would call socially inappropriate. Charlie and Jackson seemed to have an inside joke, or a knowing look, for just about everything. She changed as well. She noticed Charlie more; how he looked, what he was wearing; the way his hair fell around his face. She noticed his body more too; how he had grown taller and leaner; how suddenly he had the beginnings of muscles; how his abs showed when he laughed; how faint hair appeared on his lower legs; how his voice deepened. Kelsey was right. It was that year. She shook off the memory.

"It's just that we're all great friends, and I don't want to risk losing his friendship. I mean… I don't know what I mean."

The two girls were quiet for a few seconds.

"Look, Mads. It's not like you two are gonna get married. Jesus. You've only been a couple, for what, fifteen hours? Charlie is a nice guy. Well, at least he used to be. He seems a little dark this summer, but I guess that's understandable. See where it goes. If you still feel weird about it after a while, talk to him. Who knows, maybe he feels weird about it too? Hell, I wish Jackson and I would find some time to suck face in the surf. I'm thinking that boy is never gonna bite. Maybe I'll switch my focus to Joey. Now there's a boy that puberty has been good to," both girls laughed.

"Joey. Yeah, he is looking good," Madison said. "But I think Joey is too into Joey to find the time to be into anyone else."

"Truth, girl," Kelsey said. "Truth."

As the girls recovered from their laughter, a black Mercedes-Benz S560 slowed to a crawl as it rounded the corner onto First Street. Obviously, the driver was looking for house numbers. The sleek, low-slung vehicle continued its unhurried trek past Madison's house, and pulled into the driveway of the sea foam eyesore next door. As if by a wave of a magic wand, the garage opened. It wasn't unusual for cars to be pulling into driveways on a Saturday morning during the summer. Turn-over was a commonplace thing. New vacationers arrived as the old vacationers left. However, two things were unusual. First, the time. Mornings on turn-over days were for leaving, not arriving. Second, was the large moving van that pulled up behind the Mercedes.

Madison knew the house in proximity to hers was for sale. Most of the larger, newer houses were. Perhaps it had sold. The idea of new neighbors wasn't unpleasant. Owner-occupied houses brought an end to the parade of people who came and went from Memorial Day to Labor Day each year.

The back doors of the Mercedes swung open and out stepped two boys. Probably Madison and Kelsey's age. Maybe one a few years older than the other. Both boys were impeccably dressed, very much looking the part of old New England money. The Versace slides alone would buy an Americano a day, all summer long, with money left over.

As the boys stepped out of the car, each raised their Maui Jim aviators from their eyes and did a quick look around the neighborhood. Even from where the girls were sitting, the blueness of the boys' eyes was noticeable. The color reminded Madison of a glacier. Dropping his sunglasses back into position, the older looking boy said something to the other, but neither girl could hear. Whatever was said it elicited a laugh from both boys. Without closing his car door, the older boy stepped onto the driveway, and disappeared into the house, following, the girls guessed, his father. An older woman moved from her side of the car around to the younger boy and stopped to talk with him. He smiled at whatever she said. When she walked away, he turned to take in the neighborhood. His eyes met Kelsey and Madison's. He smiled again and tossed his chin in their direction. The two girls waved back. He mouthed the word "hey", lingered for a second, and joined the others in the house. Three refrigerator sized men began unloading furniture from the truck now blocking the street.

"Well, well, well. What have we here?" Kelsey said. "New neighbors. Very hot, and seemingly wealthy, neighbors to boot. I think maybe it is time for me to move on from Jackson and pursue new options."

"You don't even know them, Kels. Looks aren't everything."

Even though Madison knew that to be true, it was hard not to linger on how attractive both boys were. They were magazine handsome. Perfect hair. Perfect jawline. Perfect smile. But something about the entire scene didn't play right with Madison; something about the boys' laugh. It wasn't a laugh that would indicate something funny. It was more mocking and judgmental; the laugh frat boys share when the nerd shows up at the party. Out of nowhere, an uneasy feeling settled over Madison, like a cloud casting a shadow on a sunny day. A shiver tracked up her spine despite the warmness of the morning.

EIGHTEEN

The day dawned gray and gloomy. Low-hanging clouds spread out across the sky and did their best to block out the sun. It wasn't going to rain, but blue sky was not promising. Jackson found himself at The Beanery, slumped over and staring mournfully into the top of his half-finished cappuccino. His mood matched the day. Pop's frothy creation today was something resembling a seagull, though what remained of the bird was little more than milky film stuck to the side of the cup. He kept replaying his conversation of the day before with Charlie. Why hadn't he just said it? he wondered to himself. He could have just let the words fall out of his mouth. It was Charlie, right? So why didn't he?

Then later that day, Charlie had given the perfect opportunity. He brought it up in a text;

Oh, hey, Jackson. What was it you wanted to tell me today?

Jackson was staring at the text illuminated on his phone. His reply was right beneath.

Nothing. Never mind.
I'll tell you when I see you.

Had he just told Charlie, then maybe things would be different; maybe he wouldn't feel so gloomy right now; maybe he would feel relieved; maybe they both would be talking about it; or maybe they wouldn't. That right there was what scared Jackson the most; maybe they wouldn't be talking. The other morning when Charlie stormed off of the porch, there was a strange feeling in Jackson's stomach. One he'd never experienced before. It was a cross between that feeling you get on the downhill drop of a rollercoaster and being kicked in the balls. Charlie had never walked away from him like that before: furious, red faced, and fists clenched angrily. Charlie was angry with him, or at least at what he had said. No friendship is without quarrel, and his friendship with Charlie was no exception, but never like that. Jackson shook away the thought.

"What's going on, Jackson?" Jackson was so lost in his thoughts that he hadn't noticed Pops standing beside him.

Pulled from his head, Jackson replied, "Huh? Oh, hi Pops. Nothing."

The old man eyed Jackson for a bit, taking him in. "Hmmm. Are you sure, son? You've been slouched over that cup for a while."

Jackson quickly became very self-conscious. "Yeah, Pops. I'm good. Guess it's just the weather."

"Could be. Weather tends to affect people." The old man paused a bit, then continued. "But here's the way I see it, Jackson. I've owned this coffee shop for a very long time. In all those years, from time to time, I've seen people stare into their cups the way you are right now. Generally, one of two things causes it. One: a loss—a girlfriend, a spouse, someone special. A hole opens up in their life that's hard to plug, and they're not sure how to close that hole. Two: a dilemma. A choice that needs to be made, but the person just can't bring themselves to make the choice. Even though, in their hearts, they know exactly what they need to do." He paused again, looking at Jackson. "So, which is it?"

Jackson wondered for a minute if the old man was psychic. He sighed, straightened himself up, and pushed his cup away. "The second, Pops. There's something I need to tell someone, something important. But I'm just not sure how to tell it, or how this person is going to react to what I have to tell them. I, um, I don't want to upset this person, because this person means a lot to me, and has been going through some tough stuff. But I also need to tell them this thing. Because this thing… this thing is getting harder not to tell, and heavier to carry. And… well…" His voice trailed off as his eyes filled up. Jackson turned his head away so Pops wouldn't see.

"Jackson," Pops began, "you're a good kid. Probably as good as they come these days. And Charlie is a good kid too. I've been watching you guys for years. Watching you grow together. You are the best, best friends I know. I don't think there is anything that can come between you two. Just tell him what you need to tell him. He'll understand."

Jackson's breath caught in his throat. "Pops, how do you know I'm talking about Charlie?"

The old man smiled and tapped his forefinger on the side of his head. He gave Jackson's shoulder a squeeze as he walked away. At that moment, Jackson's phone buzzed on the table, startling him.

Hey Jackson. What's up?

It was Joey. Jackson stared at the phone for a long minute before picking it up. What could Joey possibly want? He texted back:

Nothing. What's up?

Just hanging. Up for doing something?

Jackson found that same confusion settling over him. Any time he and Joey had texted, it was always part of a group text between the gang. They never actually communicated directly to one another. It struck Jackson for a moment how strange that was. He'd known Joey just about as long as he'd known Charlie, and yet, Jackson always seemed to hold Joey at arm's length. He wasn't quite sure how to respond. He dipped his toe in that pool.

What'd ya have in mind?

Don't know. I'm home. Come on over. We'll figure something out.

Unconsciously, Jackson scratched at his head as he read and re-read the exchange on his phone. This was weird, he thought to himself. If it was Charlie, he would already be on his way over, no hesitation. But it was Joey. Not that he didn't enjoy hanging with Joey, but it was always with other people. Except for the other day, Jackson remembered, when they hit up the surf shops. At first, it was a little strange and uncomfortable to be one on one with Joey, even awkward as they jostled about through snippets of small talk. But as the day progressed, and Jackson relaxed, he found he was enjoying being out with him. Joey was funny, in a slightly stuck-up, semi-self-involved sort of way. He was easy to be around. Jackson's phone pinged again.

Well...

What the hell, why not? Jackson's thumbs punched at the screen.

Sure. I'll be right over.

He pushed back his chair, stuffed his phone into his pocket, and headed for the front of the coffee shop.

"Thanks, Pops," Jackson called as he walked through the front door. Pop's waved from behind the counter. Though the day was still gray, Jackson's mood had swiftly, and inexplicably, brightened.

NINETEEN

A couple of days had passed since Charlie's incarceration. As with all things, there was a process following Charlie's transgressions that led to 'Major Miriam Meltdowns'; first came *The Grounding*. In this most recent incident, he had been relegated to his room for the evening with a complete shutdown of communication from his mother—save for, perhaps, a half-hearted, steely, 'good night', as she made her way to bed. The morning immediately following the grounding came what Charlie liked to call, *The Reckoning*. During this stage, Miriam began limited, albeit terse, communication. These quipped interactions allowed Charlie the opportunity to gauge the level of hostility that remained within her. Simple interactions that could pass as pleasantries: "Good morning." "What are your plans?" "How was your day?" Little, everyday exchanges that seemed genuine but still dripped with anger or frustration. The untrained eye, or ear, would never pick it up, but Charlie and his mom had been down this road before, more so since the divorce. The Reckoning could last anywhere from twelve to twenty-four hours, depending on the severity of the incident that caused The Grounding in the first place, and always ended with an actual pleasantry from his mom. She had a host of non-verbal indicators that informed Charlie that the tensions between the two were over: a hand on the shoulder, or the forearm; a rub on the back as he passed her; a smile and a hug. Charlie liked to think of this stage as *The Cease-Fire*. He never thought of it as a reconciliation, because he knew it was just a matter of time before another battle began that would have them both back at The Grounding. It was all very circular. The Cease-Fire came a day ago, and Charlie was doing his best to avoid any type of conflict. It was difficult, because it was precisely his walking on eggshells at home that added to his frustrations about being at home. His heightened awareness of everything he said led him to find ways to never be at home. Miriam's favorite thing to harp upon was his never being home as it gelled nicely with her second favorite 'Charlie's Shortcomings': spending more time with his friends than he does with his own siblings. Which is exactly what he was doing at this moment. Though this particular friend had recently become something more, and Charlie was still trying to wrap his head around that.

Charlie had been thinking about Madison every second, or so it seemed to Charlie, since they parted ways at Third Street Beach a few days before. All day, she was there. Not necessarily in his head the way a television with the volume way too loud would be. More like the sound of a dripping faucet in an upstairs bathroom; present for a moment, then drifting off into the background for a while, until it catches your attention and holds your focus until it drifts off again.

Currently, Charlie's attention was laser focused on Madison's eyes as she sat across from him on her front porch. It's funny, he thought, how you could know someone for so many years and never notice little details about them, like the color of a person's eyes. Madison's eyes were mostly brown, but circling her pupils was a faint sunburst of orange. It reminded him of where the petals of a Black-Eyed Susan meet the center of the blossom. He wondered what other things he simply had not been paying attention to about Madison, or anyone, for that matter. How many little clues to life, the universe, and everything appeared right in front of his face that he had failed to notice?

His stomach was swirling, but not in the way it had been swirling since he came home that day to discover his dad had left for good. That was a distinct feeling. That was weighty and burdening, almost like he had swallowed a heavy stone that now sat lodged in his throat, partially obscuring his airway.

This was more like the feeling you get right before you had to give an oral presentation in front of the class, or when you were about to do something that didn't scare you, but didn't comfort you either; a little anxious, a little unsure; and a bit more damp than usual under the arms.

Charlie slowly realized that Madison had stopped talking. A momentary bout of panic washed over him, as he was unsure why she stopped talking. Did she ask him a question? If so, what was it? Was she waiting for an answer? Or was this just a natural pause in the conversation? This happened a lot when his mom was lecturing him. She would pause and look at him, head tilted, like some android processing data. In these instances, Charlie had tuned his mother out approximately fifteen seconds into the diatribe of why he was not measuring up to her expectations, or why he was letting his siblings down, or why he needed to do better, he was often unaware of what his response should be. He had learned these past months that 'okay' seemed to always suffice, but Madison wasn't lecturing, and for the life of him, he actually did not know what she had been saying.

Those eyes, he thought, as she smiled at him. He felt his body warm as his thoughts drifted; thoughts that caused his cheeks to flush. From the street, an unfamiliar voice, at least unfamiliar to Charlie, shattered the moment.

"Hey Madison, what's up?"

Making his way up the stairs onto the porch was someone Charlie had never seen before. Not unusual in the summer, but unusual that this person knew Madison's name. *Damn, he's handsome,* Charlie's brain flashed. He felt his defensive systems come on-line. Charlie noticed Madison flashed a genuine smile, and not just a friendly 'hey-how-you-doing-Shoebie-who-has-rented-the-house-next-to-mine-for-a-week' kind of polite smile.

"Oh. Hi, Asher. How's everything? Getting used to the island? I would think it's different from Martha's Vineyard."

Asher, what kind of name is Asher? Charlie could feel his pulse quicken and his defenses ticked up to Def-Con Four. Asher chuckled, a perfect chuckle that matched his perfect looks.

"Yeah. Definitely not the Vineyard," he said as he looked around the street, "but it's kinda nice." *Kinda nice?* Charlie repeated in his head. Def-Con Three. "Anyway, I saw you sitting here, and I thought I'd come over and say hello. See what you were up to today. Maybe we could grab an iced-coffee or hit the beach or something. I mean, if you're not busy." Asher turned to look at Charlie as he said, 'if you're not busy.' Def-Con Two.

Charlie's breath was coming now, shallow and quick. He had no reason to be angry. He didn't know this kid, but he couldn't shut his adrenaline down. Something about Asher just didn't sit right with Charlie.

Madison looked over at Charlie as it seemed she suddenly remembered he was sitting there. "Oh. Yeah. Asher, this is Charlie. He has a cute little house a few blocks over." *Cute? Little?* Charlie's mind clung to the adjectives. The boys exchanged steely looks. "Asher. Charlie. Charlie. Asher," Madison said, pointing to each boy with her palm facing up as she said each boy's names, respectively.

Both boys smiled tightly and raised their chins at each-other in a universal silent hello that came across more like an invitation to throw down. Asher held Charlie in his gaze long enough to tick up Charlie's weapons systems. *Is he sizing me up?*

"Asher's family just bought the house next door," Madison said, jerking her thumb toward the four-story goliath next door. "It's their new summer house. Asher's dad got transferred to Manhattan from Boston and the Jersey Shore's a closer commute in the summer than Martha's Vineyard. There you have it."

There you have it. Poor little rich boy.

Asher held Charlie's gaze for a second or two longer before turning back to Madison. "So. Are you guys, like, dating? Or just lifelong island friends?"

Def-Con One. Charlie's fists closed into tight balls. His heart was pounding in his ears. The sudden rage that was about to consume him scared the crap out of him, but he couldn't shut it down. All he wanted to do was pound Asher into a little pile of pulp, and he didn't know why.

"Both," Charlie said, perhaps too aggressively. A long, tense silence popped up and joined them on the porch. Charlie unclenched his fists and breathed a little.

Asher chuckled his perfect chuckle again. "Relax, bro. It's all good." Then, turning to Madison and tossing his head towards Charlie, he said, "He's a feisty one, isn't he?"

Madison, concerned about Charlie's reaction, smiled awkwardly.

"Anyway, I guess you're busy. I'll catch up with you later." He turned to leave and then added, "Oh, hey, Madison. You should come check out the house sometime. I'll show you my room. I think it faces yours."

There was a smirk on his face that Charlie wanted to erase with a baseball bat. As he descended the porch stairs, Asher made a point of meeting Charlie's gaze one more time. It felt like a challenge.

"Nice meeting you, Chuck," he said as he walked away.

Charlie's pulse was still thrumming in his ears. He drilled holes in the newcomer's back with his eyes as walked away.

"When did he move in?" Charlie asked.

Madison could tell Charlie was upset. Hell, his annoyance wafted off him like stink, but she didn't know why. Maybe this is what Jackson meant when he said that Charlie was... what was the word he used? Volatile.

"Uhm, couple days ago, maybe a week. Not long. Why?"

"I don't know. I just don't like him."

"Are you okay, Charlie? I mean, you seem… upset or something."

Charlie wasn't okay. He was mad, not just mad, but angry; so angry that he just wanted to lash out at someone, or throw something, or break something. His stomach was twisting, wringing itself out like you would a damp towel. The crazy thing was, he didn't quite know why. All he knew was that he wanted to beat the shit out of Asher.

Feeling unable to quell the volcano rising from within, Charlie stammered an excuse to leave. "I… I gotta go, Madison. Sorry. I remembered my mom wants me home to watch Sarah and Carson." He stood, once again pushing the chair back a bit too forcefully. "I'll text you later," he said and was down the stairs in a flash.

Head down, he pushed toward the corner. Once clear of Madison's view, he began to run. His thighs pumping like pistons, he ran as fast as he could, as if he were running for his life.

Back on the porch, Madison sat, confused by what happened. She'd never seen Charlie like that before, and it troubled her. Charlie was always light, relaxed, and easygoing. That was one reason she found him so attractive, but what she just saw… he looked like he was going to strangle Asher. A thought registered in her head just then: she needed to talk to Jackson.

TWENTY

Madison walked over to the kitchen table to retrieve her phone. She pulled up Jackson's number, then hesitated. Was she crossing a line, she wondered, texting Jackson about Charlie? If anyone knew what was up with Charlie, it would be Jackson, she rationalized. She was concerned about how angry Charlie seemed to get; it wasn't just that, though. Charlie had seemed off lately, distant, quiet, and brooding. It wasn't obvious behavior, more like just below the surface. If you didn't know Charlie well, you wouldn't notice. To Madison, it was obvious that something just wasn't right. She needed answers.

"Screw it." She fired off a text.

Hey Jackson...

Hey Madison. What's up?

Got a minute? I wanted to pick your brain.

Haha. Sounds gross. What can I do for you?

It's about Charlie. I'm worried.

Everything okay? You guys break up already? LOL JK. What's up?

He just seems, I don't know. Different.

Well, you said that he grew a little and filled out. Maybe that's it ☺

I don't mean different physically. I mean, yeah, he has grown, and it looks good on him and all, but… he seems dark, moody.

Did something happen?

Well, we were just sitting on my porch when Asher stopped by. We were all talking, but Charlie seemed to get upset. He like totally bolted. Said he would text me later.

Asher? Is that the kid who moved in next door to you? He seems okay.

Yeah. He's alright. It's just. I mean, I remember at the Beanery you said that Charlie was volatile. And like, based on how angry he became over nothing… I guess I was just hoping you knew what was going on.

Yeah. He seems to get angry real fast these days. His dad walking out hit him hard. I'm worried about him too.

Is there anything we can do?

I guess just give him his space and try to let him know we're here to help if he needs it… when he needs it.

Okay. I guess that makes sense. I knew his parents' divorce was hard, but that was like months ago. Guess it isn't easy to just put it behind you.

I guess it's not.

Thanks, Jackson. You're a good friend.

Anytime. You too, Madison. And Madison. It's not you, right now, with Charlie, it's Charlie.

Madison stared at Jackson's response. She honestly didn't know how to respond or if she even should. What did Jackson mean, exactly? She put her phone back in her pocket and made her way up to her room.

■   ■   ■

"Who was that?" Joey asked.

Jackson was still holding his phone, but looking beyond it, beyond the walls of the room.

"Huh? Oh. It was Madison."

"What'd she want?" Joey asked.

Jackson took a deep breath and shook away the anxiety that settled over him like a fog. "Um, she's worried about Charlie, is all. It's nothing."

Joey took in Jackson. Secretly, he wished he had a friend he cared so deeply for; someone who he could talk to the way Charlie and Jackson talked to each other. Someone.

"Yeah. He's not been the same. He's usually a goof in a funny sort of way, not a moron sort of way, ya know? Chatty, always talking or doing something that makes you laugh. Now, not so much. Thought maybe being back at the beach would change that for him. Guess not. I feel bad sometimes. He's struggling with his dad being gone."

Jackson turned his head to look at Joey with the kind of narrow eyes and furrowed brow you get when you stumble across something on the street or along a path in the woods and you just can't figure out what the hell it is.

"What?" Joey asked, almost defensively.

Jackson smiled. "Wow. You actually noticed someone other than yourself and felt their pain. You showed signs of empathy and compassion. I think this is a breakthrough, Joey."

Joey chuckled, "Fuck you, Jackson."

Jackson smiled, but didn't say anything in return. He just sat on the edge of the bed, taking Joey in as he sat perched up against the headboard.

TWENTY-ONE

Everyone has their favorite time of day at the beach. Charlie's was early morning, before the Shoebies crowded the beach and the lifeguards showed up. He loved to surf then; the beach belonged to the few early risers who welcomed the day.

Carson's was around five o'clock in the afternoon when Ove's would give away whatever donuts were left from the day. The beach thinned then. Carson and his friends would break out their skim boards without the risk of slamming into anyone.

Sarah's favorite time of the day was high noon. The beach was alive with people, and she surrounded herself with her friends. To them, the beach was their private talk show where they hosted a myriad of conversations, mostly about the Shoebies, or who had a crush on who, what boy was so hot, or the latest TikTok trend. Typical preteen banter.

To Charlie's mom, her favorite time of the day was the small hours of the morning; the middle of the night; coming in off of the porch having finished a glass of wine or a gin and tonic or a cold beer. Everyone was in bed and the house was quiet. She would go from room to room and peek in on her sleeping kids. When they were awake and talking–or arguing–it was hard to see them as the babies they once were. It was easier to see the days gone by in their quiet, restful faces, as she watched from thresholds.

It was where she was now, standing in the doorway of Charlie and Carson's room. A door she quietly pushed open moments before. The absurdity of the room caused her to smile. It truly was as if a force field divided the space in half; a transparent shield keeping the chaos of Charlie's side away from the quiet calm of Carson's. Both boys were asleep, but it was Charlie she was gazing upon. He lay on his back, shirtless, with his head turned in her direction. One leg was outside of the covers, the other tucked in. Gone were the soft features of a face that belonged to a boy. The slight baby fat that once clung to his stomach had melted away, revealing the beginnings of a six-pack. She marveled at how grown up he looked so suddenly. His jaw squared, his cheek bones sharper, and his muscles popping here and there. Melancholy accompanied her as she softly made her way across the room and sat down carefully on the edge of his bed. Charlie stirred a bit as her weight shifted the mattress, but he didn't wake up.

The divorce had been hardest on Charlie. It was hard on all of them, but Charlie revered his dad; held him up on a pedestal. Though for the life of her, Miriam McIntyre did not know why. Charlie's dad was a decent enough dad, but not one who showered the kids with attention, or even affection, for that matter. He spent most of his days and nights holed up at the law firm, working. When he was home, he was usually holed up in his office. Charlie would compete for his dad's attention, coming up with hair brained reasons why they should spend time together. She knew why Charlie had become sullen, angry, hating everything and everyone. She just didn't know how to fix it.

Gently, she reached out and tucked an errant lock of hair behind Charlie's ear. Leaning in to kiss him on his forehead–something he would never allow awake–she noticed something sticking out from between the mattress and the box spring. She pulled at it to reveal a picture of Charlie and his dad. Charlie was about twelve and he looked so happy. His face beaming as they both smiled into the camera. A wave of sadness crashed into her, threatening to drown her in the undertow.

"Oh, Charlie," she said, placing a hand softly on her son's head and stroking his hair.

"Mom?"

She quickly wiped at her eyes and turned her head to the other side of the room. Forcing a smile, she said, "Hey. Carson. I'm sorry, did I wake you up?"

Moving across the room silently like a ghost, she took up residence on the side of Carson's bed that faced his brother's. She noticed the beginnings of adulthood creeping into his face too, the length of his body, the size of his hands.

"You okay, babe?"

Carson sat up a bit, rubbing at his eyes. "Yeah. What are you doing? Is Charlie, okay?"

"Sure, he is. I was just checking in on you guys before I turned in myself."

"Oh. Okay." Carson slid back down and turned on his side. "Good night, Mom."

"G'night, Carson."

She leaned in and kissed him on his head. Something he still allowed during awake hours, but for how much longer she wondered. She rose and made her way to the door, swinging it shut behind her. A thought popped into her head before the latch clicked.

Turning back into the room with just her upper body, Miriam called softly into the darkness, "Hey, Carson?"

"Yeah?"

"The other day, you mentioned Charlie has been mean to you. Meaner than the usual brother-annoying-brother kind of stuff."

"Yeah," Carson replied sleepily.

"He, uhm. He isn't hitting you or anything like that, is he? I mean, like being aggressive towards you at all?"

Carson sat up again. Looking at his mom, he said, "No. Nothing like that. I wish, though."

"You wish? You wish what? That he would hit you?" Miriam asked, concerned for her younger son's safety or sanity.

Carson hesitated briefly. "No. It's just that, well, at least then, he would be interacting with me, you know? Paying attention to me. Like he used to." Carson pivoted his head to take in his brother, asleep in his own bed. "Now, I don't know. It's like I don't even exist. He doesn't even talk to me anymore except to tell me to fuck off." Carson glanced at his mother. "Sorry."

Miriam's eyes brimmed. "It's okay, Carson. Sometimes the word fuck just sums everything up, you know?"

Carson's face lit up briefly, but then just as rapidly faded as a shadowy thought crept into his head.

"Is he ever gonna come back?" he asked in a tone that fell somewhere between sorrowful and quizzical.

"Who? Your dad?" Miriam asked, her breath catching in her throat.

Carson shook his head, then looked back across the room at his sleeping brother. "No. Charlie. Is Charlie ever going to come back?"

A single tear slipped over Miriam's lid, and she was glad for the dim light of the room. "I hope so, baby", she said through a thick, emotion laden voice. "I hope so. Get some sleep."

Carson slipped back down under the sheet, turning his face to the wall. "Good night, Mom."

When the door latched shut, Charlie spun to face his wall as well. His breaths came in slow pulls. He struggled to keep the anger that was surging inside of him from exploding all over the room.

TWENTY-TWO

The familiar voices of his family floating down the hallway from the living room woke Charlie. He had a fitful night's sleep, which was firmly established by his entanglement in his bedsheets. He had dreamed of his dad. They were on the sidewalk in front of his house, back home, and his dad was walking away. Charlie kept running after him, calling out, but no matter how fast he ran, he couldn't close the distance between them. No matter how loud he called, his dad seemed not to hear. Then Carson appeared. He was looking at Charlie in a confused way.

"He's never coming back, Charlie. Don't you get that? He doesn't care."

He hated dreaming about his dad. He always woke up so raw. It was like when you pull a bandage off a wound, only to end up reopening it.

Charlie kicked himself loose from the tentacles of his sheets and lay uncovered on his mattress. He hadn't brushed his teeth last night and the consequence of that played out in his mouth at the moment. Had Sarah been correct? Are boys gross, as she observed days prior? He replayed himself and Madison sitting on her porch in his head. Why did he get so upset? What was it about Asher that pissed him off so much, other than that annoying Boston accent? Did he overreact?

"Yeah, you did," he said to himself out loud.

There was just something about that kid that set Charlie on edge. Asher didn't show up as just a friend. There was more to his intention, Charlie was certain of it, and then there was his parting remark–*Nice meeting you, Chuck.* It was iced with sarcasm and he used 'Chuck'. Charlie hated that nickname. It was as if Asher knew. Charlie could feel himself getting tweaked again and shook it off.

He yawned, rubbed the sleep out of his eyes, ran a hand through his hair, and sat up. The voices down the hall rose and fell in conversation, interrupted by moments of laughter; though there was something not quite right about it. There was an unfamiliar voice, and Charlie wondered what his siblings were streaming on Netflix this morning. More *Queer Eye*? Perhaps *Derry Girls?*

Charlie grabbed at his phone to check the time: eleven-fifteen. His screen was an epic novel of text messages and SnapChat notifications. Sighing heavily, he scrolled through the refuse of social media announcements and SMS bytes that clogged his screen. As he strolled into the living room, he was still in the posture of most teens–head down, focused on the tiny screen in his hand. The sudden ceasing of all conversation caught his attention and caused him to look up, but not instantly. When he dragged his face from his phone, he saw his mom, Sarah, and Carson sitting on the couch, each wearing an amused smirk. Carson's eyes were wide, and Sarah lifted her hand to her face to stifle a laugh. It was then that Charlie noticed Madison sitting in the recliner. For a second, the room did that weird stretching backwards effect you see in movies when something terrible was about to happen. That thing, that terrible thing that caused the room to stretch and elongate, was Charlie realizing he had left his bedroom in just his boxer briefs and was now standing in the living room in nothing but his white Calvin Klein's in front of Madison. Who, at the moment, was smiling in a not-so-much- embarrassed-but-more-of-a-humorous-pity-kind-of-smile, but, he noticed, not averting her eyes. Charlie was momentarily paralyzed as the humiliation of the situation settled over him.

"Were you camping last night?" Carson asked, shattering the silence.

"Huh? What?" Charlie stammered, confused by the moment and the sudden question.

"Were you camping? I'm just asking, 'cause it looks like you're still pitching a tent." Carson said, barely able to contain his laughter.

Charlie reflexively covered his crotch with both of his hands. "Jesus, Carson!"

Sarah, in a surprise exhibition of street knowledge, chimed in. "Nah. I just think his one-eyed trouser snake is hungry this morning."

Both Carson and Sarah broke down into fits of hysterical laughter. Even Charlie's mom struggled to maintain her composure, raising her hand to her face to cover her smirk.

"Kids," she offered weakly.

Horrified, Charlie shot back, "Really, Sarah?"

He turned his attention to Madison. "I am so sorry. I didn't know you were here. I'll um, get dressed. God. I am so sorry." Then, turning to his mother, said, "Mom, why didn't you text me or come get me or something other than letting me walk out here in my underwear?"

"I did text, honey. You must have still been asleep. Honestly, I don't know what you are so upset about. I mean, Madison has seen you in a bathing suit for years. And, well, we all know you have a penis. It's not a big secret."

Charlie could feel his cheeks light up. "Ohmygod, Mom! Jesus. You did not just say that!"

Charlie looked apologetically at Madison, who had yet to turn away. In fact, she seemed focused rather intently on Charlie standing there in his underwear. Which, for some reason, sent a wave of blood rushing in a direction that was not prudent.

"Well, it's definitely not a secret anymore," Sarah said, pointing.

"That's for sure," Carson followed, "but it does look pretty big. What do you think, Madison?"

Charlie wanted to rip his brother's head off to stop him from speaking.

Madison, breaking her gaze momentarily to look at Carson, shook her head and said, "I. I, um…" and trailed off, smiling.

Charlie, currently a mixture of being appalled, exasperated, embarrassed, and flustered, spun on his heels and jogged down the hallway back to his bedroom; both hands still covering everyone's topic of conversation.

Carson called out, "There he goes, in all of his morning glory." Sarah and Carson erupted into laughter again.

Charlie shot back, "Fuck off, Cason!" and slammed his bedroom door.

"See. Told ya, Mom," Carson smirked.

Turning to Madison, Miriam said, "Sorry about that, Madison. It was nice seeing you and catching up. I'd better go see if he's okay. And you two," she said, turning to her younger children, "enough."

Sarah and Carson shrugged. "Whatevs," Sarah said.

Miriam pushed open Charlie's bedroom door just as he was stepping into a clean pair of underwear.

"Jesus, Mom! Can you knock? I'm almost seventeen years old. You can't just come barging into my room anymore." Charlie tugged up his underwear and dove into a pair of basketball shorts.

Miriam knew he was right, and she immediately felt badly. Hard as it was for her to admit, Charlie was turning into a young man. He needed his privacy. She glanced at Carson's bed. Hard, she thought, when you have to share a room with your younger brother. She was beginning to understand Charlie's adamancy about having his own room. Maybe she could convert the attic space?

"You're right, Charlie. I'm sorry. I'll knock from now on."

Charlie was rummaging for a shirt to throw on. "What do you want, anyway?" he growled. His anger radiated off of him and heated the room.

Miriam could sense that Charlie's hackles were up. A situation she was becoming accustomed to. She measured her words. "I just wanted to apologize. It certainly wasn't my intent to embarrass…"

Charlie spun. Adrenaline pumped through his veins like gas through a fuel injector igniting the engine. "Embarrass? Why should I be embarrassed, Mom?" he said in a tone that mixed anger and sarcasm into a venomous tenor. "I mean, I was only standing there in front of Madison in my underwear for what, like five minutes? All the while my younger brother and sister ripped boner jokes, and you did nothing to stop them. Embarrassed? Nah, not at all, mom. It's every day that your little sister refers to your dick as a hungry one-eyed-trouser-snake, in front of your girlfriend, right?"

"Charlie, it was all…"

"No, Mom. No. How could you let me just walk into the living room in my underwear with Madison sitting there? Why didn't you come to my room? I mean, Jesus, it's not like you're afraid to come to my room, right? You just barged in on me naked, like ten seconds ago. Or at the very least, when you saw me come out of my room, you could've said something before I made it all the way into the living room. Last time I checked, there's a clear sight line from the sofa down the hallway. I don't know, maybe shout out a warning or something? What the hell, Miriam?"

The last few sentences of Charlie's rant certainly were heard by his mother, as sound is just a displacement of air vibrating on your eardrum, and Charlie's verbose tirade certainly moved a good amount of air in the room. Sometimes, though, just because you hear something, doesn't mean you're listening, as was the case with Miriam. Her brain was processing a few sentences behind.

"Wait, did you say your girlfriend…?"

"God! This is why I hate being in this house. I fucking hate it. Sarah is forever riding me about my clothes or how I look or how I frickin smell. She takes pot shots about my arm pit hair or the hair on my legs and how gross it is, or she's making some snide comments about a zit, or a blackhead, or some other ridiculous thing that I have no control over. And Carson, he can't leave me alone for a hot second, always asking if I want company like I'm some lonely old lady in a nursing home desperate for attention. Or riding me to take him surfing, or to hang out with me and Jackson, or to play catch with him at the beach. I mean, Jesus, I'm not his fucking nurse maid. Or his dropping of hints that my side of the room needs to be cleaned up. There are days, I swear, that I just want to rip his goddamned bed apart and throw his shit everywhere. And then there's you…"

Charlie's outburst came to a screeching halt, as if someone had paused him with a remote control. His chest was heaving. He stood there, fists clenched, panting, swirling in his own cyclone of raw anger. For a moment, everything was still. It all just stopped. His mom snapped the world back into motion by taking a hesitant step towards him. As she reached out to touch him, to just lay a steadying hand on his shoulder, Charlie recoiled. Caught off guard by Charlie's cold reaction, she dropped her hand to her side. Charlie could see the hurt in her eyes.

"What about me, Charlie?" she asked.

Charlie eyeballed her, knowing full well what he wanted to say, but uncertain if he should. For months now, he'd been keeping everything down, swallowing his words, burying his feelings. His chest was so tight he worried his ribs might shatter. He wanted to throw up. *Just tell her,* the voice inside his head screamed. *Tell her exactly how you feel. Tell her everything that you have squelched since that day in January, when he disappeared. Tell her.* He took a quick breath, the kind you take when you prick your finger with a pin, fighting to keep his insides from exploding all over the room.

"Nothing," he said curtly. "Just leave me alone." Pushing past her towards his door, he added one last stab of the knife. "And stay the fuck out of my room at night."

Paralyzed, Miriam watched Charlie from behind as he stormed out of the room. Her first born had successfully sucked all of the air out of her lungs, and she struggled to catch her breath.

■　　■　　■

The route to the boardwalk was awkward and tense, Charlie thought. Once clothed, he and Madison departed the McIntyre residence and just started walking; whether out of habit or a subconscious desire to be on the beach, Charlie automatically turned in the shoreline's direction. For a block or so, he was a few steps ahead of Madison, head forward, shoulders squared, as he tried to screw down the lid on everything that had boiled out in his bedroom. A task that was becoming not only more frequent, but more difficult to do. Maybe she sensed his tension, or maybe she could read body language, or maybe she knew to just hang back for a while. Whatever the reason, Charlie appreciated the space. His breathing was returning to normal, but his heart was still pumping faster than it should (maybe his brisk pace, he thought), and the boulder in his stomach that didn't ever seem to go away weighed on him.

By the second block, Madison had fallen in step beside Charlie. Charlie had slowed his pace to a more casual stroll than a sprint, and the two walked side by side for a bit. He could feel his ire begin to subside. At one point, Madison asked Charlie if he was okay, to which he quipped, "Yep. I'm good," but they continued on in silence. When they reached the bottom of the ramp leading up to the boardwalk, Madison slipped the fingers of her right hand between the fingers of Charlie's left hand, and the two hands closed together.

Lightning surged through Charlie's body at Madison's touch, coursing through every one of his nerve endings, setting his insides alight. He hoped Madison was feeling the same way. That simple act, taking his hand, caused the remaining anger and frustration and humiliation that weighed on Charlie to wash away like sidewalk chalk in a downpour. He turned and smiled, and she smiled back.

They held hands as they made their way down the boardwalk, avoiding the occasional bike rider and weaving through the throngs of people that already crowded together along the walk. They didn't let go when they ordered water ice at Brown's, or when they walked a bit further to an open bench. They only let go to manage their spoons. They sat, shoulder to shoulder, mostly in silence, enjoying the mango and blue raspberry water ice that a few years ago, neither of their parents would have allowed them to have at eleven forty-five in the morning. When finished, Madison rested her left hand on Charlie's right leg, right above his knee. Lightning.

"Charlie. I'm so sorry about this morning. I thought I'd come over and say hello. I was out walking. I figured you'd be up. I, uhm, I certainly didn't mean for that to happen."

Charlie scratched at the back of his head. "It's all right. I know you didn't. I'm not upset with you."

Seeing an opening in the conversation, Madison tested the water. "Who are you upset with, Charlie? I mean, you just seem upset a lot, and the other day, when Asher showed up, you seemed upset then too. Is everything... I don't know, is everything okay? Are you okay?"

The question caught Charlie off guard. He hesitated before answering, trying to figure exactly what to say. "Yeah, I'm okay. Everything is okay. Guess I'm just trying to figure a lot of things out right now."

"What are you trying to figure out, Charlie?" she pushed.

So many things, he thought. "Well, for one, I guess I'm trying to figure out us, you know?" He hesitated again before continuing. "And the other day, with Asher, I'm sorry about that. I don't know what that was all about. I mean, like, I was angry, but I don't know why I was angry." The voice in the back of his head said, *yeah, you do*, but Charlie ignored it. "I guess I thought... I don't know what I thought. I'm sorry."

"It's okay, Charlie. I was just worried. Mostly about you."

Charlie smiled. "And this morning. I wasn't angry with you. Mostly my mom. I mean, Jesus, I was standing there in my underwear, ya know? Yeah, sure, my family has seen me in my underwear before. But, like, well… you haven't. And then all that bullshit from my brother and sister, which, like, damn Sarah, where'd you learn that stuff? And Carson, I just wanted to punch him in the face, you know?" The familiar tightening in Charlie's chest returned. He took a deep breath and exhaled, running a hand through his hair. "Anyway, I was more embarrassed than mad."

They sat in silence for a moment or two, processing what was said, and maybe what wasn't said; leisurely spooning water-ice onto their taste buds.

Madison spoke up, hesitantly, "Not to side with your mom, or anything, but she was kinda right."

"Wait, what?" Charlie said, somewhat in shock.

"I've seen you in your bathing suit with your shirt off since you were three years old. You and Jackson and Joey, you always have your shirts off. It's a guy thing, always showing off the abs. So, there's no surprise there, right?"

Charlie smirked and shook his head. "Yeah, but there's a difference between being on the beach in a bathing suit and standing in the middle of the living room in your underwear, Madison. It's just embarrassing, is all."

Madison took Charlie's hand again. "Well, Charlie, from what I saw, I'd say that you have nothing to be embarrassed about."

Much to Charlie's surprise, Madison leaned in and kissed him, right there, on the boardwalk, in broad daylight, with dozens of people walking by. It wasn't the type of kiss your mom or your aunt might give you; it was the type of kiss your girlfriend would give you. She tasted like mangos.

Lightning, again. Explosive, super charged, lighting.

TWENTY-THREE

Later in the day, Charlie and Madison joined their friends in the sand. Like most summer days, the itinerary wasn't packed. Wake up. Check the phone. Meet up at the beach. After water-ice on the boardwalk, Charlie and Madison went their separate ways for a time. Charlie, much to his dismay, had to return to his house. When he left, he wasn't ready for a day in the sand. He needed a suit, his backpack to carry the necessities needed to spend the day under the sun and fooling around in the surf. He also wanted to grab some cash from the hoard he kept rolled up and tucked beneath his underwear in his bureau. Money that he squirreled away during the winter to help carry him through the summer at the shore. The supply was dwindling, and it wasn't yet July.

Carson and Sarah were sitting on the porch swing when he arrived at his front door. Still angry with them from the morning, Charlie took the front steps two at a time, not even looking at his siblings. He hoped his body language and his icy demeanor telegraphed how pissed he still was with them. As he grabbed at the handle of the screen door, Sarah called his name, causing him to stop. Sighing heavily, he turned to face his siblings. He didn't speak, just raised his eyebrows and shrugged slightly in the international gesture meant to convey *'What?'*

"Aren't you even going to say hello?" his little sister asked condescendingly.

Charlie scoffed, "Why? So, you can mock me? Maybe tell me something snide about the clothes I'm wearing? Sling some other condescending comment my way?"

He pulled on the door again and was just about inside the house when Carson asked him a question he didn't quite hear.

Charlie stepped back onto the porch. "What did you say, Carson?" Charlie leveled his gaze at his younger brother. Something was off. Carson looked angry, but in a way with which Charlie wasn't familiar. He wasn't sure, but there seemed to be hatred lurking behind Carson's eyes. Charlie asked again, "What, Carson?"

"What did you say to her, Charlie?" His tone chilled the air.

Charlie furrowed his brow in confusion. "What are you talking about, Carson? What did I say to who?"

"To whom," Sarah tossed. Charlie shot daggers in her direction that pinned her to the wooden swing.

Carson's voice raised a notch, "To mom, Charlie. What did you say to her when you were in our room?"

Sarah, sensing that maybe things were about to do down, got up off of the swing. She squeezed past Charlie and disappeared into the house. She mumbled something under her breath as she passed, but Charlie couldn't quite make out what it was. His attention focused on his brother. He was certain it was some affront towards his character, but he didn't give a flying one.

Charlie scoffed again. "I don't know," he said dismissively. "A lot of stuff. What does it matter anyway?"

Carson's face was turning red, and he was welling up. "It matters because after you left, she was crying. Sarah and I could hear her, Charlie. Mom was in our room crying. And not just sniffling back tears. Crying. Struggling to catch her breath, crying. So, what did you say, huh, Charlie? What did you say?" Carson's anger bubble over. He wiped quickly at his right eye.

Charlie paused. For a brief instant, he felt bad about what he said to his mom, but just as readily as the feeling manifested itself, he squashed it away. *Good. She deserves to cry. This was all her fault,* he thought to himself. *Everything is her fault.*

"Carson, I don't have time for this."

Carson stood up and took a threatening step towards his older brother.

"Yeah. That's the problem, Charlie. You don't have time for anything or any of us. Just you. It's all about you, Charlie. Isn't it?"

Charlie's left hand curled into a fist. "Don't push me, Carson. Just don't."

"Or what, Charlie? Huh? What are you gonna do?" Carson's gaze fell to his brother's clenched fist. He laughed mockingly, "Hit me? Is that where we are now, brother? Or maybe not talk to me? Pretend that I don't exist? That none of us do? Maybe you'll tell me to fuck off, or something? How will it be any different, Charlie, than what it is now?"

Now it was Charlie's turn to get angry. That familiar sensation, growing in his stomach and radiating outward, spreading like a virus. *Beat the little shit to a pulp, Charlie. Beat him unconscious. Go on. Do it.* The thought startled Charlie.

"Don't," was all he managed, in a voice thick with malice.

Charlie spun, made his way into the house, and headed directly to his room. He was swallowing hard, trying to clear his heart from his throat.

Above the noise of his pulse pounding in his ears, he heard his brother yell from behind, "You're not the only one he left, asshole!"

Charlie pushed away the tears that threatened to come in a tidal wave. Forced them down and locked them away. He'd become skilled these past months at shutting down his tears. His anger, however, wasn't as easily caged. It wasn't until the fourth or fifth punch to the wall that he managed to tamp down the lid on that beast. By then, the knuckles on Charlie's left hand were bloody, and the plaster dimpled and cracked. Another wound in the room to match the torn window shade.

Behind him, the floorboards creaked, and he turned. Sarah was standing there in the doorway. She looked scared, as if she were watching some crazy stranger screaming at the lettuce in the grocery store. She backed away slowly, leaving Charlie with blood welling between his knuckles, and the familiar weight dragging him down.

It was Joey's voice that snapped him back from the memory. He'd been replaying that scene in his head for most of the afternoon and, while the beach was always like a spa day for Charlie, today's sojourn brought brief respite.

"Huh?"

Joey pointed to Charlie's left hand. "Your hand. Looks like you had a bit of a fistfight."

Charlie covered up his knuckles self-consciously. "Oh, that. Uhm, it's nothing. I scraped it on the side of the house carrying my surfboard."

Joey looked skeptical. "Okay. It's just that, well, I've been in a few fist fights before. And that's usually what my knuckles look like afterwards. Carson's compulsive neatness finally get the best of you and you had to smack him down?"

You have no idea how much I'd like to, Charlie thought to himself.

"Where's the surfboard?" Jackson asked.

"What?"

"You said you were carrying your surfboard. Where is it?" Jackson asked again, looking around.

"I left it at home. I changed my mind about bringing it."

Madison was sitting cross-legged in the sand next to Charlie. She was talking to Kelsey about some Instagram story or other such banality. Truth be told, he wasn't too sure about anything that had passed since he got to the beach to join his friends. He was there, but he wasn't. It was like watching a TV show that you're not quite paying attention to or being in pre-calculus class: you're there, you hear it, but it isn't quite registering.

Madison placed her hand on his shin and played with the hair that was there. The touch of her warm fingers against his skin made him pay attention. In that moment, he took in his surroundings; his friends; the ocean; the blue sky. Normally, he would be content. This time last year, he would have been utterly in love with this moment; the sun; the sand; his best friend; his squad. It should be perfect, but it wasn't last year, and things weren't perfect. Charlie closed his eyes against it all. If only he could travel in time.

The sand shifted next to him as Jackson moved in closer. "Hey."

"Hey," he said, opening his eyes.

Jackson spoke softly so only Charlie could hear, "What do you say we hit the boardwalk for some fries or maybe a shake? The conversation here has stalled, and I could use to step away from Kelsey's advances for a bit."

Charlie pondered the offer for a second or two. Hitting the boardwalk at midday was his and Jackson's thing. Sometimes it was just to get away from the group for a while. Others it was to scope out the girls strutting along the weathered walkway. Some days it was for some fries or a shake. Today, though, Charlie's mood was just not having it.

"I don't know, Jackson. Not right now. I think, maybe, I just want to stay here."

Jackson nodded. "Does your desire to stay perched on your butt have something to do with the fact that Madison is currently stroking your lower leg as if it were a cat?"

Charlie laughed through his nose, "Yeah. Maybe. That and the fact that I'm not so sure I should stand up in public right now."

Jackson chuckled, "Dude. Get that in control."

Charlie laughed as well, picking up what Jackson was dropping. "Easier said than done, my friend."

"Ain't that the truth?" Jackson paused, shifting the topic. "Things going okay with you two?"

Charlie thought again for a second or two. "Yeah. I guess. I mean, it hasn't been that long. It's weird though, you know?"

Jackson shook his head, silently communicating his confusion. Charlie continued uncertainly, "I don't know, just sometimes it feels awkward. Almost like we're pretending. And then others, like this morning on the boardwalk, it feels so right. Even so, under it all, there's this feeling, like, I don't know…" Charlie trailed off.

"Is it a bad feeling?" Jackson pressed.

Shaking his head, Charlie said, "No. Not bad. It's just like… I feel like maybe this is a mistake. Like maybe we're just better off being friends. You know?"

Jackson nodded slowly, "Yeah. I know."

"I guess… I just don't want to screw things up. She's a good friend, always has been, and now…" Charlie shrugged and trailed off, "Anyway."

Jackson thought he understood. Dating a friend doesn't always end gracefully, or so he'd heard.

"Anyway," Jackson repeated, "boardwalk?"

Charlie just smiled and shook his head. It felt good to be talking to Jackson. They hadn't seen much of each other the last few days, and it was nice to not be communicating through text messages or SnapChats.

"You okay, Charlie?" Jackson asked.

And there it was. The ubiquitous inquiry of health, sanity, and overall well-being. *How many fucking times have I heard that question asked since January? A thousand? Ten thousand?* And always the same answer: *yeah, I'm good.*

Charlie sighed, "Are any of us, Jackson?" he said. It was dark, and it drew a concerned look from his friend. So, he covered, "Kidding, man. Yeah. I'm good."

Jackson took him in for a long while, a stretch of time that made Charlie uncomfortable. Jackson finally smiled a half smile and nodded. The two boys sat there in a way that only lifelong friends could, speaking volumes to one another without words, saying everything that needed to be said with just a look. Jackson knew Charlie wasn't okay. Charlie knew that Jackson knew that he was wrestling with demons. Neither one of them fully knowing when the grapple would be lost.

Out of nowhere, a soccer ball crashed into the encampment. It landed squarely between Madison and Kelsey. Jackson and Charlie both looked simultaneously. An errant ball breaking into your day was not anything unusual at the beach. This particular soccer ball, however, may not have been so haphazardly kicked.

"Oh, hey Madison. Hey, Kelsey. Sorry about that," Asher said as he walked up to retrieve the ball. His brother Logan was in short step behind. Both boys were already tanned, and Charlie wondered if they were sprayed on. "You guys know my brother Logan, right? Well, Kelsey, I know you do, seeing how you and he seem to spend a good deal of morning porch time together." Logan smiled at Kelsey, who blushed. She got up and walked over to Asher's older, though somewhat less handsome, brother. Asher continued, "Logan, you know Madison. This is… Jackson, right?" Jackson nodded, "And that is Joey, and over there is Chuck."

"It's Charlie."

Jackson could hear the poison in his friend's voice.

Asher smirked that smirk that Charlie wanted to wipe off of his face with an ax.

He turned to face his brother, "It's Charlie." Then turning back to Charlie, he said, "Sorry Chuck." Peripherally, Charlie could see both Joey and Jackson pivot their heads and look at him. Charlie just stared straight ahead, but Jackson noticed his friends' fingers balling themselves up into a tight fist. "Anyway, sorry about the ball. Hope it didn't kick sand up on you, Mads. If so, you know, I'd be happy to brush it off."

Madison, now wearing a worried expression as an accessory to her bikini, glanced over at Charlie. Then, turning back to Asher, she said, "No. It didn't. I'm fine."

There was something about the way Asher looked at her that made Madison uneasy. She wasn't scared or threatened in any way, more anxious. She suspected Asher was the type of kid who always got what he wanted, no matter what the shiny object or expensive trinket may be. Madison thought perhaps she was the next shiny object. She looked at Charlie again and could feel the chill coming off of him. His eyes tracked Asher as he moved, not blinking, the way large cats track their prey before pouncing. A shiver skated up her spine.

Logan and Kelsey had moved off towards the shoreline. They were shoulder to shoulder. Logan stood about a foot taller than Kelsey and was about twice as wide. It was hard to see from where Charlie was sitting, but it looked like they might have been holding hands.

"Those two," Asher said, jerking his thumb toward his brother and Kelsey.

"What about them?" Joey asked.

Asher looked at Joey, signature smirk playing across his face, "Let's just say that Kelsey spends an awful lot of time up in Logan's room, and leave it at that."

Joey shook his head. He looked at Jackson, tossed his head in Asher's direction and said, "This guy."

Asher began knocking the soccer ball back and forth in a well-intended display of superb footwork. His athletic prowess meant to impress Madison specifically, and to challenge Joey, Jackson, and Charlie peripherally.

"Impressive," Joey said in his best bored-Joey-tone, "you can kick a ball with your feet." Joey slow clapped.

Jackson raised his eyebrows and smirked. Asher chuckled and turned towards Joey. As he did, he caught Charlie's icy gaze. Placing his foot on the soccer ball to stop it, Asher leveled his gaze at Charlie.

"What's up Chuck? Hey, I made a pun," Asher chuckled at his own cleverness, but no one else joined him. "You look a little pale."

Charlie counted to ten in his head. He knew Asher was poking, trying to see how far he could push things. In a sense, Asher was pissing in corners, the way an animal marks its territory, but Asher was a newcomer here, and Charlie and his friends had been pissing on this beach for a very long time, literally. *Keep it together in front of Madison,* the little voice in his head sounded.

"Is there something you want, Asser?" Charlie asked, purposely dropping the 'h' from his name.

Asher's smirk stretched into a full-blown smile. "Yeah. There is something I want…" His voice trailed off as he turned to look at Madison. Turning back to Charlie, he said, "But, uhm… I think it's going to be a little harder to get than I thought."

Charlie, who had been sitting with his arms resting on his thighs, straightened his back the way a cobra does before it strikes. The hair on the back of his neck stood up.

Jackson, sensing the tension like electricity in the air, whose eyes had not left his friend since Asher appeared, was quick to intervene. Popping up from where he sat, he moved in front of Charlie, blocking his friend's view of his intended target.

"Hey, Charlie, how about those fries, huh? I'm getting hungry and could use to stretch my legs some. Let's hit the boardwalk. Come on."

Charlie could feel himself losing the battle to the dark side.

"Charlie? Let's go," his friend spoke softly, looking squarely into Charlie's eyes, almost pleadingly.

Charlie nodded and stood up. He grabbed his backpack and shirked it on. Jackson did the same, and the two boys made their way off of the beach.

"We'll be back," was all Jackson said to his friends left sitting in the sand.

Joey shook his head. Turning to Asher, he said, "Dude. Do not poke that bear."

Asher puffed up his chest, "Don't know what you're talking about, dude." He drew out the word *dude*, long and slowly.

Joey laughed mockingly and shook his head again. Standing up, he took a step towards Asher.

"Why don't you take your ball and go play your little foot game with your big brother?"

Asher lifted the ball from the sand with his foot and caught it. He squared himself to Joey and smirked. The two boys stood that way, a foot or so apart, chest to chest. It was a montage played out on countless school yards, in thousands of gymnasiums, and high school playing fields around the world. Boys, about to throw down over something trivial and stupid that somehow or some way threatened their masculinity. Testosterone charged showmanship, neither willing to deescalate.

Madison splashed cold water on the display. "Hey. Enough, you two. What are you both, twelve?" she said condescendingly. "Back off Asher. And you," she said, pointing at Joey, "sit back down." The two boys didn't move for a few seconds, prompting Madison to chastise them again. "I said, enough."

Asher smiled, not taking his eyes off of Joey, "Sure, Mads. It's all good. Guess I'll catch up with you later." He took two steps backwards before turning and tossed his head in Madison's direction, "See ya, Mads." He headed down to the shoreline.

Madison leveled her gaze at Joey. "What the hell was that, Joey?" she asked.

"You tell me, Mads," Joey said, using Asher's nickname in an attempt at mockery. Surprised, Madison furrowed her brow. He read her confusion and continued. "Oh, come on, Madison. He was totally macking on you. In front of Charlie. I know ya'll have only been dating for a bit, but damn. That Asher is one cocky son-of-a-bitch." Joey crossed his ankles and sunk to his towel without the use of his hands. "That boy is trouble, Madison. He keeps playing with you the way he is, and he and Charlie are gonna go, and go hard. Thank God for Jackson. He's a better person than I am. I would have just let it play out." He reached into his backpack, pulled out his Air Pods and popped them in.

Inside, Madison knew Joey was right. She had felt something about Asher from the very first time he stepped out of his parent's car. Maybe it was the way he conducted himself, as if everything was owed to him. Maybe it was his 'in-your-face' manner. She couldn't quite put her finger on it, but she knew one thing for certain. Asher was trouble. She just didn't yet realize the extent.

■   ■   ■

On the boardwalk, Charlie and Jackson wove their way through the crowds of people enjoying the sun, as they headed towards Chickie's-N-Pete's, intent on some curly fries. Neither was talking at the moment. To the casual on-looker, it would be hard to determine if the two boys were actually walking together, or just happened to be in proximity to one another. Charlie was just a step or two out ahead, while Jackson was giving his friend some time to cool off. He knew when he was ready, Charlie would slow his pace and start up a conversation.

As they walked, Jackson couldn't help but notice how many girls tracked them both as they passed by. Some were boldly making eye contact and smiling, some throwing a quick wave in their direction. There were a few that plain out cat called. He wasn't quite sure which of them was being looked at more, but his guess was Charlie. It had always been that way, Jackson thought. He considered himself a good-looking guy, but there was something about Charlie that just drew you in. From the earliest age, Charlie was the center of everyone's attention without him even knowing. He gave off an energy that you just wanted to be around. He wasn't gregarious, or showy, and certainly not conceited; nor was he the type of person who demanded you pay him mind through extroverted showmanship behavior. Charlie was just genuine. That kid who somehow was friends with everyone, no matter the circle in which they revolved. Though, admittedly, Jackson thought, the energy Charlie was giving off these days was more inclined to drive you away than to draw you in.

"Those girls were checking you out," Jackson said matter-of-factly.

Without turning or breaking stride, Charlie said, "No. They weren't. They were checking you out."

"I don't think so, son. The one in the red bikini said 'nice legs.' My friend, my legs are, at best, skinny sticks, lacking any type of muscular definition. Which is in direct contrast to your well-proportioned thighs and sculpted calves, though not in a gross, overly veiny body builder sort of way. Just in a sort of bike-rider, perhaps dedicated jogger, or accomplished tap-dancer, sort of way."

Charlie shook his head and slowed his pace to allow Jackson to fall in step. His friend certainly had a way with words.

"True, but the one in the white bikini said something about pretty blue eyes. And that, my friend, would not be me. You have the pretty blue eyes."

Both boys stopped and laughed, struck by the absurdity of the conversation they were having with one another. They turned to give the last gaggle of young ladies that passed them a parting glance. As if there was some telekinetic connection beckoning to the girls, they too turned to survey the young men they had just passed. The girls giggled and waved. Both boys smiled and threw an awkward wave back in the girl's direction. Turning away, they continued down the boardwalk towards their destination. Things felt right again, like summers past.

After a few moments, Charlie said, "You think I have nice legs?"

"You think I have pretty blue eyes?" Jackson retorted.

Charlie stopped and looked at Jackson. He titled his head from side to side, then raised a single eyebrow.

He nodded and said, "Yeah. I guess you do. Hadn't really looked before. They're like the sky." Jackson felt his cheeks flush. Charlie smirked. "This is getting weird, Jackson."

"Yeah. A little." Both boys continued on their way. Seeing a conversational door open, Jackson pressed on, "Speaking of weird.

What was going on back there in the sand, Charlie? I mean, you looked like you were going to rip out that DB's throat."

Charlie scratched at his head. "I don't know. That Asher just rubs me the wrong way, you know? He's so arrogant, and smug," *And fucking perfect,* his brain added, "I just want to erase his face with my fist."

"I could tell." Jackson noticed a shift in his friend's demeanor. His face changed, grew more somber; in the same way a storm cloud gradually rolls in off of the ocean and blots out the sun, Jackson could sense a change in Charlie's mood. Instantly, he regretted bringing up the topic.

"And what's his thing with Madison? Huh?" Charlie continued, his brooding deepening. "He was like that with her when the two of us were sitting on her porch. He just walks up and starts in, you know? Like hitting on her right in front of me, like I'm not even sitting there. I mean, who the hell does that? He treats her like she's some prize he has to have. Like she's some treasure in a claw machine and he won't stop feeding it dollars until it's in his clutches."

"I noticed that too." Jackson, ever the diplomat, continued, "So, like, you and Madison have only been dating–if that's what we're calling it–for a week? Maybe a little more?"

"Yeah? So?" there was a hint of aggravation hidden in Charlie's voice.

"So, if this was three weeks ago, or maybe last summer, would it make a difference? Would Asher piss you off so much? I mean, other boys have come-on to Madison in all the years we've known her. You weren't bothered by that, like you are now. So, is it that you and Madison are sucking face, and his obvious attempts to gain her favor piss you off? Or is it that Asher is just an entitled dick? Because if it's the former, then I guess you're right to be upset. But if it's the latter, then maybe you need to dial it back some?"

Charlie stopped abruptly, his back stiffened. Jackson knew he just crossed a line. For the first time in their friendship, Jackson felt uneasy around his best friend. The two of them could talk about anything and everything all day without fear of upsetting the other. Now it felt like all Jackson did was walk on eggshells when he and Charlie were together.

"What? I need to dial it back? Don't tell me you actually like that guy or something?"

"I'm not saying I like him, or don't like him. It's just…"

Charlie cut him off, more sharply than the conversation warranted, "It's just, what, Jackson? What? What tidbit of Jacksonian advice do you have to offer me now? Huh?" Charlie's voice was rising. "What little token of observational Jackson-isms will you drop on me this time?"

Jackson grew aware of everyone around him and how this looked. Charlie's legs, planted firmly on the wood with his left hand balled up, his arm bent at the elbow and his left shoulder dropped slightly below his right.

Jackson swallowed, thought of his words, and proceeded cautiously, "It's just that I know I don't like what he does to you."

Charlie took a step forward, narrowing his eyes. He cocked his head and leaned into Jackson's face. "And what's that Jackson? What does that ass do to me?" Charlie was breathing hard.

Jackson swallowed again; his adrenaline amped up. "This," he said softly. "Look at you. You're ready to punch me, Charlie. I can see it in your face, in your body. This is what he does to you. He makes you angry. And lately, that's all you are, Charlie. Angry. Angry at me. Angry at your mom. Angry at everyone. And I don't know why."

Jackson's gaze dropped to Charlie's left hand, causing Charlie to look as well. As if waking from a dream, Charlie noticed his clenched fist and the crusted blood still between his knuckles. His arm pulled back, winding up. He looked up at his friend. Jackson watched as the color drained from Charlie's face, as the gravity of the situation settled upon him.

Like a drunk, Charlie staggered back two steps, "Shit, Jackson. Shit."

He let out a breath as he drew the hair back from his forehead with both hands. He let them drop onto the back of his neck, and held them there, fingers interlocked. Charlie saw the same look in Jackson that he had seen in his sister earlier in the day. Fear. What was wrong with him? Panic took over like an automatic pilot. He was about to throw down with his best friend. Over what? Asher? *What the hell?*

"I uh… I gotta go, Jackson. I gotta go." Charlie spun on his heels and disappeared into the crowded boardwalk.

"Charlie, wait," Jackson called. "Charlie, talk to me. What the hell is going on with you?"

But either Charlie didn't hear, or he ignored the plea. He turned onto the Tenth Street ramp, heading out to the street, and bolted.

TWENTY-FOUR

Behind the small bungalow that served as the McIntyre family's summer home sat a small one-car garage. As old as the house, it hadn't sheltered a vehicle for quite a few decades. Unfinished inside, it was a testimony to years of summer life at the beach. Rain-stained clapboards behind studs served as the ceiling and walls. The cement floor cracked and pitted with age. A single bare light bulb hung from the ceiling, suspended from knob and tube wiring.

Around the interior were the various necessities of beach life: surf boards and beach chairs; boogie boards that now just gathered dust; a small collection of skim boards in various sizes detailing the growth of their owners over the years; bicycles, rusted chains, and beach towels. Old tools that may have once enjoyed some use, but now just laid around abandoned in haphazard positions, an old washing machine, and an even more ancient refrigerator. Charlie sat in the middle of all of this, sprawled in a frayed and tattered beach chair that had seen better days, sipping at a beer he pulled from the fridge that currently wheezed away in the corner, struggling to cool against the day's heat. The beach was his absolute favorite place to be, for sure, but being alone in the garage was next on the list. Something about the smell of old wood mixed with the salt air comforted him. Swiping beers from the fridge was a bonus.

He tilted the bottle back and drained what remained. Rising from the chair, he dropped the empty bottle in the recycle bin, pulled a fresh one from the fridge, expertly popped the top against the edge of the workbench and dropped back into his seat. He looked around, taking in everything. His whole life could be catalogued in this space, he thought to himself. Almost seventeen summers. He wished he could just live here.

Taking another pull from the bottle, he looked at his phone. The text conversation with Madison was still up when he unlocked the screen. It was shitty of him to not go back to the beach after he raced away from Jackson, but he felt he explained it away well enough. *Not feeling well, too much sun, catch up later,* was the gist of the digital conversation. Madison seemed okay with it, saying she hoped he felt better. Funny, the person he was thinking about the most as he sat alone in the musty shade of the garage wasn't Madison. It was Jackson. Charlie was feeling guilty. These past weeks, he had unloaded a couple times on Jackson for no reason, other than he simply couldn't control his rage. Jackson didn't deserve that. Charlie checked his phone again, hoping there was a text or a Snap from his friend, but nothing was there. Maybe Jackson was giving him some space, Charlie thought. Maybe Jackson was pissed. That concerned him more than how Madison might feel.

Things used to be so easy. He and Jackson never fought. They were together all the time, hanging out, sucking the day out of the day; surfing when they wanted, roaming the island, just being stupid the way teenage boys are. A few hours ago, Charlie was ready to pummel him; to beat the shit out of him, and for what? Suggesting that Charlie needed to reel things in? He hated himself for that right now.

Then there was Madison. Suddenly, he had a girlfriend–if that's what she even was - to work into plans, and to worry about offending, or explaining away why suddenly you went home. He wasn't even sure if he wanted a girlfriend. He knew he wanted the fringe benefits that go along with having a girlfriend, those beautifully enticing dalliances that constantly danced through his head these days. But a girlfriend?

The icing on the 'things-aren't-how -they-used-to-be' cake was his parent's divorce. They used to be married and now they weren't. Charlie's dad used to live with them and now he didn't. Charlie's dad used to ask about his day, send a text message, call him on the phone… and now he didn't. There was an entire cargo container of emotions churning around that topic like so much debris swirling inside a twister that Charlie was trying to keep locked up inside, but the lock was giving.

When you're a kid, you can't wait to be a teenager, Charlie thought. It all just looks like so much fun. Here he was, just past the middle of his teenage years and what he wouldn't give to go back to being ten. He dropped the phone into his lap and pulled again from the beer as Carson walked into the garage. He stopped momentarily, surprised to see his brother sitting in a beach chair in the middle of the floor, drinking a beer. Carson, not acknowledging his brother, walked over to the fridge, opened it up, and pulled out two beers. He turned and started out. Charlie smiled approvingly.

"Hey, Carson. Mom know you're drinking beer?"

Carson stopped. Turning around, he took a few steps back into the garage. "Does mom know *you're* drinking beer?" he countered.

"Touché, little brother," Charlie said, then drained the last of the contents. "Where you going with those?" he asked, tossing his chin at the beer bottles in Carson's hand.

Carson looked down at the beer, then back to his brother. "Oh, what? You're talking to me now, Charlie? That's nice, so you actually do see me. Wow, and you haven't told me to fuck off yet. It's a record."

Charlie could feel his adrenaline amp, he settled it as best he could. He didn't want a fight with Carson. Not now. Not after today.

Truth be told, he deserved Carson's sarcasm. Time to make amends.

"Yeah. Look, Carson. I uhm… I'm sorry, you know? It's just… I've been going through a lot…" Charlie's voice trailed off, and he turned his face away from his brother.

Carson's demeanor softened, but not much. "We're all going through a lot, Charlie. You're not alone in this."

Words of wisdom from his younger brother. Charlie nodded his head. "Yeah. Anyway, where *are* you going with those?"

"Inside. Ethan is here. We're gonna hang out, maybe watch something dumb on Netflix."

"You and Ethan drink?" Charlie asked, dumbfounded. "How long have you been sneaking beer, bro?"

It was Carson's turn to smile. "A while now. You gotta pay attention, Charlie, otherwise things go unnoticed. If you don't stop and look around occasionally, you miss things. Any other questions before I head in?"

Yet again, Charlie was struck by how much his little brother resembled a teenager. It was a transformation that occurred overnight. Maybe Carson was right. *Maybe I* do *need to pay a little more attention,* Charlie thought to himself. He was about Carson's age, maybe younger, when he and Jackson had begun to sneak beer out of refrigerators and get a quick buzz on.

"Just one. Where is mom, that you and Ethan can hang out in the living room getting drunk?"

Carson shook his head in a chastising way. "Dude. It's Beach Happy Hour Night. All the parents are sitting on the beach, drinking wine and eating cheese. This house will be empty 'til at least nine o'clock. Gotta open the door to opportunity when it comes knocking, big bro," Carson said with a smile. He turned, left the garage, and disappeared into the house.

Charlie ran a hand through his hair. As he did, he caught a whiff of himself and made a face. When was the last time he took a shower? This morning? Last night? He couldn't remember. Rising from the chair, he stepped out of his bathing suit and underwear, walked across the small yard to the outdoor shower and stepped in. The water felt good against his warm skin. He'd shower. Change. And track down Jackson. He owed his friend an apology. One that was long overdue.

◼   ◼   ◼

Emerged from his room, fresh and dressed, Charlie made his way down the hall towards the living room and front door. It was amazing what a shower can do to improve your mood, he thought to himself. Marry that to showering outside, naked, and it becomes the perfect experience. There was something gratifying about looking up and seeing blue sky and clouds as you bathed. He sometimes wondered if the surrounding houses could see into the shower from their second floors, but he didn't care if they could. Deep down, he hoped they did. Somehow, that made the shower even more enjoyable.

Ethan and Carson were sitting on the couch, a bowl of popcorn between them. Two empty beer bottles were on each of the end tables. Both boys clutched a half empty one in their hand. The TV was on, but the boys were focused on Ethan's iPhone. When Charlie entered the room, Ethan looked up and then dropped the phone onto the cushion. He self-consciously pushed down on the front of his bathing suit with his free hand as he adjusted his position on the couch.

Charlie chuckled, "What are you two watching?" though Charlie was sure he knew the answer to that question.

"Um, nothing. Just some dumb YouTube videos," Carson said.

Charlie laughed, "Okay, but it looks like you've been doing some camping. You too, Ethan."

Both boys' cheeks flushed, and they dropped a hand to their shorts. Charlie moved towards the front door.

Pausing, he turned and said, "Back off the beer, guys. The last thing you're gonna want is to be trashed when mom shows up. Ethan, you know your mom will ground you, like, forever. And where is Sarah, anyway?"

"She's at the beach with everyone," Carson responded, cheeks still red.

Charlie nodded and made his way through the front door onto the porch. "Have fun, you two." Carson stood and followed him onto the sidewalk.

"Hey, Charlie," he called. Charlie stopped and turned to face his brother. When Carson didn't immediately respond, Charlie raised both palms to the sky in the universal gesture for 'what'. Sheepishly, Carson finally said, "Don't tell mom, okay?"

Charlie shook his head. "There's nothing to tell, Carson. You're thirteen. Just be careful with the beer. It can sneak up on you. And go easy with the 'YouTube' videos," Charlie raised his hands and made air quotes. "You'll rot your brain."

His little brother nodded. Carson and Charlie stood on the sidewalk for a moment and exchanged a small smile. It was the most civil, almost friendly exchange each had had with one another in God only knew how long. It was almost the way things used to be between them, before Charlie shut everything and everyone out and disappeared behind a stone wall. He felt good, almost happy, inside. It had been so long that the feeling caught him off guard and he thought maybe he might be having a heart attack.

"Go inside. Have some fun."

Carson nodded appreciatively. "Thanks, Charlie. You too."

Carson spun and bounded back up the stairs and into the house. As the door closed, Charlie could hear Ethan exclaim, '*ohmygawd,*' from within the living room. Charlie shook his head and set off for Jackson's.

Beach Happy Hour Night had gone on for just about as long as Charlie could remember. Once a week, his friends' parents would meet up on the beach around five p.m. Once the lifeguards were gone, the beer, wine, cheese, and other schniblies would emerge from bags and coolers. The adults would spend the next four hours catching up, laughing, and trying to reclaim some nugget of a time when they had fewer responsibilities. When Charlie was younger, he'd tool around in the surf with his friends, maybe venture out onto the jetty–strictly forbidden when the lifeguards were on duty–and hang out. As he and his friends turned into teenagers, they realized Beach Happy Hour Night could also be their happy hour night back home. It was a few hours, unsupervised, and they took full advantage of that.

Charlie walked down the small alley to the back door of Jackson's house. The door was locked, which was weird, but Charlie knew the code. He keyed the numbers and listened to the mechanical whine as the deadbolt slid back. Upon entering, he went right to Jackson's room to see if his friend was there. Jackson's door was open, but his room was empty. Upstairs, Charlie could hear music playing, so he made his way up to the living room. Someone was up there. He could hear shuffling and muffled noises. Charlie emerged into the living room and froze where he stood, one foot on the landing, the other still on the last step. He felt like someone kicked him in the stomach. His knees buckled, and he grabbed for the wall as he felt all the air in his lungs being sucked away.

"What the fuck?" was all he said.

Jackson was in the kitchen, locked in an embrace, kissing Joey. He spun when he heard Charlie's voice, and Joey looked over his shoulder. Both boys' faces went pale. Jackson swiftly broke free from Joey and made his way hurriedly around the kitchen island. Joey took two steps away from Jackson, trying to conceal what had risen below.

Jackson and Charlie stood, staring at each other in horrified silence. Slowly shaking his head, as if trying to convince himself that what he just saw didn't actually happen, Charlie backed down the stairs. His hands raised and disappeared into his hair, clutching his head. The room was spinning, and he thought he might throw up.

"What the fuck, Jackson?" he said, his voice thick. "What the fuck?"

Jackson, his stomach rolling, walked cautiously towards his friend. "Charlie. Charlie, just wait a minute, okay?" But Charlie was still moving unsteadily down the stairs. "Charlie, please, just wait. Let's talk. Please."

Charlie clutched at the railing to steady himself, feeling as if someone had obliterated the last remnants of his recognizable world. He could feel himself losing it. His stomach was swimming. His head was reeling. The jar's lid was loosening. Frantically, he looked between Jackson and Joey, who was still standing in the kitchen, confused as all hell. Finally, the jumbled puzzle pieces flying around Charlie's brain fell into place and what he witnessed came together.

"Jackson, are you gay?" Hearing the question, he realized how stupid it was. "Oh my God, you *are* gay. Oh my God. Oh my God, Jackson? How did I... why didn't you... fucking, Joey?" he asked incredulously. The room tilted and swayed. Charlie thought he was going to throw up. "I gotta go, Jackson."

Jackson took a step in Charlie's direction. As he did, Charlie put up both hands and backed away.

"Charlie," he said in almost a whisper, his eyes brimmed with tears. "Charlie. Please, just wait. Don't go. Talk to me right now, Charlie. Please."

Charlie took a deep breath that caught in his throat and shook his head. What the fuck was happening?

Feeling the need to come to Jackson's aide, Joey spoke up, "Charlie..."

Charlie looked past Jackson at Joey. Pointing a finger at him, he snapped in a voice, teaming with anger, "Shut the fuck up, Joey. Right now, just shut the fuck up." Uncharacteristically, Joey just nodded and backed down, throwing a worried look in Jackson's direction.

Jackson remained motionless, frozen in fear, staring at Charlie with pleading eyes. "Charlie."

"No, Jackson. No," Charlie took a bunch of breaths. Nothing made sense at that moment. "What the fuck?" he said, sounding so broken. He looked back and forth between Jackson and Joey. Raising a closed hand to his mouth, Charlie muttered breathlessly, "I can't breathe right now, Jackson. I can't." He stood there, disbelief dripping off of him like so much water, staring at his friend as if he were an utter stranger. Shaking his head, Charlie said, "I can't do this. I can't." He staggered backwards down a few steps before spinning around to take the remaining steps two at a time.

Jackson surged forward to catch his friend, but Charlie disappeared down the stairwell.

"Shit…, shit, shit," Jackson slammed his hand down on the banister. He turned and walked back to where Joey was still standing in the kitchen and began to pace the floor. "This is bad. This is terrible, Joey. Not the way I wanted him to find out. Shit!" Jackson punched a cabinet and then shook the pain out of his knuckles. "Shit."

Joey and Jackson stood in the kitchen, neither knowing what to say. The gravity of the situation weighing them down. Jackson walked over to the fridge and pulled out two beers. He handed one to Joey, and then went and sat down on the couch, draining the bottle in one pull. Joey pulled another beer out of the fridge and sat down next to Jackson. Twisting off the top, he held out the bottle.

"Thanks," Jackson said, taking it.

Joey ran a hand across his chin a couple times, obviously wanting to say something, but uncertain as to what. Never being one for tact, he vocalized what was on his mind. "So. You think he's going to tell?"

Jackson let a weak laugh escape him. "Jesus, Joey. My very best friend, who I have known my entire life, who means the absolute world to me, just walked in on us swallowing each other's tongues, and all you're worried about is whether he's going to tell or not?" Jackson took another pull from the bottle. "Charlie was right. You are a douche."

Joey shrugged and took a hit from his beer. "I guess we're out now?" He turned to look at Jackson.

Jackson met his gaze. "Guess we are."

He turned back and stared at the staircase. The image of Charlie's stunned, and stricken face emblazoned on his mind. Where did he go? Jackson wondered. More importantly, was he okay? Was their friendship okay? Despondently, he ran a hand through his hair and down the back of his neck. "Fuck."

■　　■　　■

Charlie yanked open Jackson's back door and raced down the alley. As if he were fleeing something threatening his very life, he hit the sidewalk in a full-blown sprint. He didn't know why he was running; he just knew he needed to run. He ran for blocks, arms pumping, thighs burning. He ran until he thought his lungs were going to burst through his chest. When he could no longer adequately suck in enough air to keep him going, he stopped.

He sank down onto a curb, gasping for breath. Chest heaving, Charlie dropped his head between his knees. Try as he might, there was no containing the geyser of emotion building inside. Fending it off at this point was like trying to cap a ruptured water main with a band-aid. The tears just came in silent sobs, splashing onto the street. He was confused and overwhelmed. He was angry and hurt. What the hell had just happened? He replayed what he saw over and over in his head. Perhaps, his mind grasped, he had mistaken what was happening? Maybe it wasn't what he thought.

How could it be? But the image was burned into his memory: Jackson standing in the kitchen, his back to Charlie, head tilted, one of Joey's hands resting on Jackson's hip, and the other cupping the back of Jackson's head. There was no mistaking that scene. His best friend, someone he thought he knew as well as the back of his own hand, someone he trusted, and confided in, and had known his whole life, was making out with another guy. It wasn't just another guy; it was Joey, of all people. Charlie's gut tightened and churned. The world began to spin again, and Charlie returned his head to his knees. He needed someone to talk to, someone to help him sort through this, someone he could just unload on, but that someone had always been Jackson. Sitting there on the curb feeling completely and utterly alone, a sudden thought occurred to him. After wiping his nose and eyes, Charlie reached into his pocket and pulled out his phone.

Hey, you home?

On the porch. Just me. Wanna hang?

Yeah. I'll be right over.

Charlie shoved the phone back in his pocket, willed himself to get up off of the curb, and ran.

TWENTY-FIVE

Charlie covered the ten blocks or so to Madison's house on First Street in an amount of time that would command the attention of any high school track coach. Two cars almost hit him and he had to dodge and weave his way through a family on an ice cream adventure that had spread out across the sidewalk like some herd of grazing Shoebies. He collided with one twelve-year-old or so, knocking him off of his bicycle and onto the sidewalk. Charlie tossed a quick apology and continued on. Charlie was sent off with some very colorful, and extremely demeaning, adjectives hurled down the street after him by one very upset, but not truly injured, pre-teen. Charlie marveled at the boy's vibrant vocabulary.

He arrived at Madison's house, short of breath, lightheaded, and looking like he had just stepped out of the shower. His hair, plastered to his head, and his shirt soaked. He stood at the bottom of the porch steps, clutching the railing, and sucking in air. His appearance must have evoked either great concern or wondrous curiosity from Madison, as she simply stood up from the Adirondack in which she had been sitting, and quizzically moved to the porch railing. She stared at him in a way that was not dissimilar to the manner one might stare at a piece of modern art as you try to determine its meaning and or its significance.

Charlie, feeling like he had oxygenated his blood enough to manage words, looked up, and quietly said, "Hey."

He took the few steps up to the porch level unhurriedly and stood for a second or so in front of Madison. He took a halting step forward. Hesitantly, he reached out, taking hold of Madison's arm, and gently pulled her into a hug. He buried his face in her neck and just relaxed into her grip. The knot between his shoulder blades faded away, and the rock that had nestled in his stomach gradually dissolved to dust, thankfully replaced by those swarming butterflies, fluttering, warming him. Without breaking the embrace, Charlie picked his head up from Madison's shoulder so he could see her face. She looked so beautiful, smiling, but obviously concerned. Madison asked if Charlie was okay. *That's a loaded question,* Charlie thought to himself. He most definitely was not okay. He couldn't remember the last time he felt okay. He hated his home life. He resented his mother. Animosity towards his dad was slowly taking hold. He was purposefully driving a wedge between himself and just about everyone else, and he didn't know why. He just found out his best friend was gay in the worst possible way imaginable. The feelings for the girl he now held were a swirling mess of uncertainty, and the familiar calm he thought the shore would bring, the normalcy he so desperately needed in his life right now, was just not materializing. Standing there on the porch clinging to Madison, he wondered if he would ever again feel like the Charlie McIntyre of days gone by. *I'm so not okay*, he said in his head. *I am probably the farthest thing from okay that one could be.* The tears were right behind his eyes. *Jackson,* his mind said.

"Right now, right here, yeah. I am."

Madison's smile broadened a bit, though her eyes still reflected worry. "Uhm, I don't mean to sound forward or anything, but would you mind taking off your shirt? I'm assuming it's soaked with sweat, and uhm… well, that's just kind of… gross."

Suddenly self-conscious, Charlie stammered, "Ohmygosh, yeah, sure. I'm sorry."

As he pealed the sweaty t-shirt from his torso and tossed it on a chair, Madison did a quick once over of Charlie's bare chest and flat stomach. Charlie thought her gaze lingered for a bit at the exposed band of his boxer-briefs, but then her eyes bounced up and met his, her cheeks flushed. This time, it was Madison who stepped forward, closing the distance between them. She placed her hands on Charlie's hips and stepped into him. She allowed her hands to trace him from the small of his back to the breadth of his shoulders and then casually back down, across his chest, to his stomach. Charlie let the sensation wash over him like a cooling wave. *What the hell, Jackson? Why didn't you tell me?* His mind poked again.

"You sure you're, okay? I mean, you came tearing up the street like you were being chased by someone. Something going on?"

More like I was chasing something, Charlie thought to himself. *Racing to catch up to a life that somehow bolted. Trying to catch something that maybe just didn't exist anymore.* He texted Madison because he needed to talk through things, to make sense of things, but now, he just didn't want to get into it. He shut down the image of Jackson and Joey in each other's arms. Forced it, at least for a bit, into a dark room and closed the door.

"Yeah… uhm. No. Nothing," he said, shaking his head. "Everything is just…" shrugging, he let his words trail off. A strange feeling settled over him. An awkward sensation, as if he were an eighth grader trying to muster the courage to ask a girl to dance. It made Charlie chuckle a little. He knew what his body was telling him. *Just say it, Charlie,* his internal voice implored. *Say it.*

"I really want to kiss you right now, Madison. Would that be okay?" He hoped he didn't sound stupid, but right then, there on the porch, all he could hear in his head was his health teacher going on about consent. Madison smiled and nodded.

Neither was sure how long they remained there, locked in an embrace, kissing, on Madison's front porch. It could've been hours. It could've been seconds. It's like that in perfect moments. Time seems to just stop, and you exist in the center of that moment as if the moment itself were a spotlight, and you are bathed in its brilliance. You don't want to step out of the center of that light, because you know the second that you do, the moment is over. It's terrifying and exhilarating all at the same time. It was like that, standing there on the porch with Madison; terrifying and exhilarating.

As all moments end, the shrill blast of a car horn, followed by someone, the driver, or passenger perhaps, recommending loudly that they should get a room, intruded upon theirs. Charlie and Madison laughed and broke their embrace. Self-consciously, Charlie tugged at his shorts and looked around. They made their way over to the Adirondacks by the front door and sat down, side by side. Leaning in, Madison brushed Charlie's hair back from his forehead. She kissed him again, then dropped a hand onto his knee. A shiver ran up Charlie's leg and settled in his abdomen.

Charlie was glad to have taken his shirt off, as the night air was heavy. The sky was just turning that purple- blue it gets as the sun slips lower on the horizon. The neighborhood was quiet, as were he and Madison. He was glad for the silence. It wasn't an uncomfortable silence, there on the porch, just silence. Charlie was happy to just sit and let the slight breeze play across his exposed skin, raising small goose bumps as it did. He closed his eyes and tried to stave off the onslaught of the day's events from stampeding through his mind. *What the hell, Jackson?* But it was hard. *For once, Charlie,* his mind chastised, *stay in the fucking moment.* Shutting the movie in his head down, he opened his eyes and found Madison staring back at him.

Without thinking, he leaned across his chair, and they began kissing again, more intensely than before, more intimately. Charlie's breaths were coming quicker as Madison pulled him in closer and tighter. His adrenaline pumped as their hands traced each other's outlines. It was the slam of a screen door from somewhere in the neighborhood that interrupted the moment this time. Breathing hard, Charlie sat back in the chair, this time not concerned about his shorts. Charlie caught Madison stealing a quick look. He smiled. She placed her hand in his, and they locked fingers.

"So…" Charlie said.

"So…" Madison echoed.

That comfortable silence settled around them again, as each tried to sort through the feelings that were building inside. Madison watched Charlie intently, her eyes traced him. She noted the rise and fall of his smooth stomach. She marveled at the definition of his chest, and the two-dime sized darker regions spaced so evenly apart. She found herself staring at his legs, wanting to touch the fine hair that grew there.

"Charlie. Can I ask you something?"

"Sure. Anything."

"Okay. So, Uhm. I was wondering if…" Madison trailed off, obviously unsure how to ask what it was she wanted to ask. Charlie thought he caught some embarrassment play across her face. "I mean, I was wondering… are you… um… have you ever…?"

Swiftly understanding where the question was heading, Charlie interjected, "No. Um… no. Not yet. Have you?"

Madison blushed and looked away. "No. Not yet."

Charlie smiled, "No, but I mean… I think about it… a lot, you know? Probably more than I should." A sudden wave of his own embarrassment swept over him at his revelation. He could feel his cheeks burning.

Madison bit her lower lip and nodded, "Me too, Charlie."

That struck Charlie as odd. He didn't think girls thought about stuff like this, but then realized how dumb that thought was. *Of course she does. She's going through the same changes I'm going through. Puberty isn't just for boys, dumb ass.* Madison squeezed his hand, drawing his attention back to her.

"I think about it a lot, you know. I mean, it's this thing that almost follows you around, like some stranger stalking you. And sometimes I think that maybe it's best to just turn around and face that stranger, you know? Well, not a stranger, but more like this right-of-passage, like getting your driver's license, almost. When you're fifteen it's out there in your future and you think about it, and how you'll do, and you worry about passing, and you think about what it'll be like to drive, you know?" Charlie nodded, following along, "It's like that. It's out there and we wonder when it'll happen, and who it will be with, and what it'll be like, and like, I mean, sometimes it just keeps you awake at night, you know?" Charlie nodded again, but said nothing, as he was unsure where the conversation was going, or if Madison had finished.

Madison looked out over the porch railing for what seemed like an eternity to Charlie, but was probably more like five seconds. Charlie could feel the pulse in his wrists.

Self-consciously, Madison turned back and said almost apologetically, "Is it cool that I said all that?"

Charlie nodded again, still not saying anything, but not looking away either. Madison met his eyes and stared into Charlie like no one had ever before. She wet her lips, holding the corner of the bottom one under her front teeth for a second.

Shyly, almost imperceptibly, she said, "I think I'm ready, Charlie."

Charlie's eyes widened. He wasn't sure, at the moment, precisely what she said. He worried that something may have been lost in translation. He was famous for slipping off in a conversation and not knowing what the hell had been said. So, like any sixteen-year-old in his uncertain position, one wherein he thought he knew what the topic of conversation was but was decidedly not one hundred percent convinced, he asked for clarification, "What?" Then stammered, "Not like, what are you ready for, what? Like are you ready for ice cream or a walk or something, what. But, I mean, like, more like, what did you say, what, or actually, not what did you say, but more of a what, as in what did you mean?"

Madison laughed and tugged at her ear; her cheeks tinged with red, "I've been doing a lot of thinking, Charlie. And I think I'm ready. For that. And I'd like it to be you. Charlie. Is that okay? Are you ready?"

It was decidedly one hundred percent what he thought she said, and in context, too. Charlie took a second to let the situation settle over him, envelop him. His pulse and breathing quickened. He tried to catalogue every detail in his mind; the porch; the sky; the clothes Madison was wearing; the surrounding sounds; the music spilling from the car that just drove down the street; the sounds of the last birds of the day; and the children playing. He wanted to take a screenshot of the moment and save it to memory. Then, certain the instant was emblazoned upon his mind, he nodded yes. *Jesus God! This is definitely going to happen,* his mind silently screamed.

Smiling, Madison stood. Taking him by the hand, she led him inside and up the stairs to her bedroom. With each step, Charlie swore his heart beat faster and louder. He was a lot nervous. He was a lot scared. He was terrified that his knees would give out. He wondered if Madison felt the same way. He was worried that his desert dry mouth would give him bad breath, or if it would make it hard to kiss. He was unstable on his feet, and he hoped Madison couldn't feel the tremor in his hand. They reached the second floor and walked the short distance down the upstairs hallway to her bedroom and stepped inside. Closing the door behind her, she guided him over to the bed. Charlie, still shirtless, stood with his hands on Madison's hips. The only sound in the room, aside from Charlie's heart beating like a bass drum, was their breathing. Reaching up, Charlie cupped Madison's face and kissed her gently. He let his fingers brush through her hair, and then down her back, resting them at her waist.

"Is it too soon to do this yet?" he asked, hoping to God for the answer that was already in his head.

Madison, never turning away from his gaze, softly said, "No. Do you think it is?"

Charlie just shook his head. "Are you nervous?" he asked.

She nodded, saying "a little." Charlie nodded and then kissed her again.

"Are you?"

Charlie nodded again. "Yeah. A lot."

They stood there, tracing each other's curves with their hands.

"What about your parents?"

Madison smiled, "Beach Happy Hour Night."

Charlie's heart threatened to burst through his chest as Madison's fingers found the button on his shorts and she pulled him down onto her bed.

■　　■　　■

After Charlie bolted from Jackson's house, and Joey had thought it best that he head home himself, Jackson sat alone on the porch. He had graduated from beer and moved onto his father's Woodford Reserve. Bourbon had a way of making everything better, he remembered hearing somewhere, sometime. He was cradling his second glass in the palm of his hand. The sky was just turning that purple- blue it gets as the sun slips lower on the horizon. The night air was heavy, and the neighborhood was quiet. Jackson was glad for the silence. He needed to think, but the building presence of alcohol in his bloodstream dulled that sense. In its place, emboldened by the deleterious effects of the warm amber liquid, self-doubt and melancholy were taking hold. *Why hadn't he just told Charlie? Why did he wait so long? It's not like I just found out myself.* Tears waited like so many Visigoths outside the walls of Rome. He sucked in some more bourbon and grimaced as he swallowed. *Now what?* Jackson thumbed the speech bubble on his iPhone, though his aim was a bit off. His screen lit up to a host of one-way text messages:

Charlie?
Hey, Charlie?

Come on, man. Text back.
Where are you?
You okay?
Charlie? Give me a chance to explain.
Call me.
Come on Charlie, pick up.
Jesus, Charlie, please hit me back.
Charlie, I'm starting to worry. Talk to me.
Charlie? Please?

The two FaceTime's went unanswered as well, as did the Snaps. The knot in Jackson's stomach grew, and he thought he was going to throw up. He lifted the glass and drained it just as the screen door slid open. His brother Noah emerged onto the porch. Jackson, wiping quickly at his eyes, did his best to pretend that he wasn't upset or drunk.

"Hey little bro. You out here all alone? Where's Charlie?" The mention of his best friend's name was all it took. The Visigoths stormed and the walls of the city fell.

Jackson straightened up and ran his hands through his hair. "Fuck, Noah," was all he could manage before the tears came.

Startled by his brother's reaction, Noah rapidly closed the distance on the porch between the two of them. "Hey Jackson. Jackson, buddy. What's wrong? You okay? Is Charlie okay?" Noah asked, immediately concerned.

Wiping at his eyes and nose, Jackson said, "I don't know. I fucked up, Noah. I fucked up."

"Jackson. What are you talking about? What's going on?"

Jackson took a breath and let it out, "I was here… in the kitchen, and I was with a guy…. and my back was to the stairs… and I thought I locked the door, I know I locked the door, but Charlie knows the code… he knows the fucking code because he's like family, you know… and I didn't hear him come up. I didn't hear him, Noah… and he saw me, you know… he saw me… he fucking saw me with a guy, Noah... and then he bolted... he said he couldn't breathe, and he just bolted. And that was like an hour ago... and he won't return my texts, and he won't take my calls.... and I don't know if he's okay, and I think... I think I just fucked everything up, you know? I fucked everything up. Everything."

"Shit, Jackson," Noah said, shaking his head. "You haven't told Charlie yet?"

"I tried, Noah. I tried a couple times. He's just been going through so much lately, you know? I didn't want to complicate his life anymore. And yet, here we are. I'm such a fucking idiot."

Noah took a deep breath and let it escape him. He reached down to where his brother had slumped back down into a chair and lifted him up. Grasping him by the shoulders, Noah looked him square in the eye. Firmly, but softly, he said, "Hey. Look at me, Jackson." Jackson sheepishly complied. "You are not a fucking idiot, and you have not fucked anything up. You are an awesome kid, and your sexuality doesn't change that, or define that. True, not the best way to let Charlie know that you're gay. But he *is* your best friend, and I know you guys are tight. This will be okay. Alright? Another bomb was dropped on him tonight. Not that being gay is like a bomb going off, but you know what I mean. Just give him some time."

Jackson nodded and then buried his head in his brother's shoulder. He couldn't remember the last time he and his brother had hugged. Noah was a 'stand-off, don't touch me, stay out of my personal space' kind of guy. Man-to-man PDAs were definitely not a part of his wheelhouse. Jackson wasn't sure how Noah would react. He just knew that he needed to feel safe, the way he did when he was a kid and in the presence of his big brother. Jackson let out an enormous sigh as he felt his brother's arms close around his back and squeeze.

"It'll be alright, bro. I promise," Noah said, rubbing a hand up and down Jackson's back. Then, in classic Noah form, he added, "If you tell anyone about this hug, I'll cut your balls off in your sleep," eliciting a much-needed belly laugh from Jackson. "Now. Before mom and dad get back, why don't we head up to the roof deck and have a little more of that bourbon you dipped into?"

"That'd be great, Noah," Jackson said, releasing his brother.

The two boys went inside. Noah moved over to the bar. He poured two fingers of bourbon into the glasses. Handing one back to his brother, they made their way up to the third floor towards the circular stairs at the end of the hall that led to the roof deck. They exited the door into the growing darkness.

Looking out over the railing, the view of the island was spectacular. The lights of the Ferris wheel that loomed above the rooftops had just blinked on and the boardwalk was alight with neon signs that splashed a rainbow of color into the darkening night. The ocean was to their left, and off in the distance to the right, the bay lay like a mirror, the remnants of sun burning on it. Despite what had happened, the night itself was perfect.

Still looking out across the railing, Noah said, "So. This guy you were with tonight. Do I know him? Please tell me he ain't some fucking Shoebie."

"No, he isn't a Shoebie. And, yeah, you know him."

Noah tipped the rocks glass to his lips and took a pull. Nodding, he said, "This non-Shoebie, was he waiting for you on the couch a while back?"

"Yeah. He was."

"Damn, Jackson. Joey Mastromani, huh?" Noah raised the cut crystal glass to his lips and took another sip. "Guess he's a decent enough looking guy, I mean, as guys go and all. He can be a bit of a douche, but not too much. Don't take any shit from him." Noah paused for a second, then added, "Is he the first guy you've, you know, made out with?" Noah asked.

"Yeah. I mean, there have been guys that I've wanted to be with. But none that I went after. If I'm being honest, Joey made the move. It was nice, until it wasn't, you know?"

Noah turned to look at his brother. "Wow. First kiss, and it happened during summer, at the beach. It could almost be an original Netflix show."

Jackson laughed, "Yeah, a pretty bad one. Hey, you're not going to tell anyone that Joey and I were..." Jackson said.

"What? Muggin down?" Noah took a sip from the drink in his hand. "Nah. Ain't my place, little bro. I haven't told anyone about you, not even Brooke, because that's not my place either. But I'm glad you told me, though. I figure, when you're ready, you'll tell the people who need to know. Until then, people don't need to know. That's your decision to make. Not mine. I mean, Jesus, it's not like I have to go around telling everyone that I'm straight, you know?"

Jackson stood on the deck, taking in his brother, who had returned to looking out across the town. Unexpectedly, his chest seemed to swell with something that was close to awe, mixed with a bit of admiration, and wrapped in some love. Noah was the quintessential jock. Three season athlete in high school, captain of every team, and popular amongst his peers. He was a *guy*, in every sense of the word. Now, here he was having a frank and open conversation about a topic he probably didn't fully understand or even know how to approach: his brother's homosexuality. That profoundly moved Jackson.

"Thanks, Noah."

Noah turned to face his brother; a confused look played across his face. "For what?"

"For this. For not being weirded out by my being gay. For being able to talk to me about my life and shit."

"Welp, to be sure, I am weirded out by you, but it has nothing to do with you being gay," Noah paused. "Look, you're my brother, Jackson. The type of person you're attracted to will never change that. You, being okay with you, your life, and the decisions you make, is what's important. Now, finish your drink before the 'rents get home. And for fucks' sake, don't get all mushy on me. You know I hate that shit."

Noah play slapped the side of Jackson's head and went back to looking at the night settle over the town. Jackson joined him. He felt better, but not by much. Try as he might, he couldn't shake his worry for Charlie. It was there, in the back of his mind, like a mosquito bite you can't reach to scratch. He couldn't shake the idea that tonight was the beginning of the end of his friendship. A thought that sickened him and rocked him to his core.

As if sensing a disturbance in the force, Noah laid a reassuring hand on his brother's shoulder and with a soft but firm squeeze said, "It'll be alright, Jackson. Trust me."

Through a heavy sigh and a trembling voice, Jackson said, "I do."

TWENTY-SIX

Charlie walked the short distance from Madison's house to his own by himself. The night certainly changed in a manner that was both unexpected and momentous. He played it out in his head over and over, from Jackson's house, to his curbside meltdown, to Madison's porch, and all that came after that. It brought a flurry of feelings: pride, accomplishment, betrayal, elation, and sorrow. He wondered how an evening that started out so horribly could end so magnificently.

He smiled to himself as the evening's finale played across his mind. Unexpectedly, his mind churned. What did this mean for him and Madison moving forward? How had this impacted his friendship with Jackson? Was it at all? How was everything that happened that night going to change Charlie's life?

There it was again: change. Everything seemed to be changing, everything had changed. Nothing would ever be the same. It was an ongoing theme in Charlie's life since that January day he came home from school and was beaten upside the head by the realization that nothing is certain, and everything can go to shit on the drop of a dime. Things at home will never be the same. Things with Madison will never be the same. Things with Jackson... he stopped mid-stride and pulled his phone out of his pocket. He punched the text icon and then opened Jackson's thread.

Charlie?
Hey, Charlie?
Come on, man. Text back.
Where are you?
You okay?
Charlie? Give me a chance to explain.
Call me.
Come on Charlie, pick up.
Jesus, Charlie, please hit me back.
Charlie, I'm starting to worry. Talk to me.
Charlie? Please?

Charlie began to type something back, but stopped. Try as he might, he still had no words. He had nothing to offer Jackson at the moment. The feelings that swirled around what he had seen were still a matted knot of confusion with which Charlie still grappled to untie.

Now, though, when it was in the rearview mirror, he felt badly for reacting the way he did, but could anyone blame him? Still, Jackson was his best friend, and somehow, Charlie knew he had let him down. Disappointed him. Hurt him. But Charlie was hurt, too.

Shoving his phone back in his pocket, he sauntered down the half block to his house. His mood souring. He knew he had to make things right with Jackson. He worried if things with Jackson would ever be right again; which was stupid because if he had walked in on Jackson making out with a girl, they would have been sitting in the sand, high-fiving and fist-bumping about it right now. So why should it matter? Why should it matter that it wasn't a girl? *But it does matter, doesn't it?* That pesky, irritable voice inside his head said loudly, which only bolstered Charlie's disappointment in himself. He needed to sort that out before he said anything to Jackson. Did it matter that it was a boy? Or that it was Joey? Or did it matter that Jackson didn't feel comfortable enough to tell him? That Jackson has probably known, no, has known, about his sexuality for years now, and said nothing. The fact that Jackson didn't confide in him made Charlie a little angry, which he knew was ridiculous. Maybe that's what mattered? But he couldn't help but be mad that his best friend would keep something so important to himself, could he?

Then another thought rushed through Charlie's head. He wondered if maybe it was his fault that Jackson never confided in him. Charlie tossed that word 'gay' around in a derogatory, critical way all the time. Everyone did, right? It doesn't mean anything, does it? When you call something you don't like, or think is stupid, gay? It doesn't matter. Does it? Try as he might, he couldn't recall Jackson using the word gay in that way. Maybe when they were younger. But recently? Charlie couldn't remember.

As thoughts go when your mind is reeling, another one came crashing through his brain like a rock shattering a window, halting him dead in his tracks. *Joey knew*. Somehow, Joey knew, and Charlie didn't. How could Joey see something that he completely missed? How could Joey, a peripheral friend at best, pick up on... what? Body language? Side comments? Other subtle tells that went completely unnoticed by one of Jackson's closest friends? Charlie wondered maybe it was because Joey was looking? Or was it that Charlie simply refused to see?

His mind ricocheted off of that thought and banged into a new one: *It doesn't matter to Jackson that I'm attracted to girls. Why should it matter to me that he's attracted to guys?* And that's the way it went as Charlie walked home in the dark. His thoughts playing off of one another as if in a game of wall-ball. The one he kept coming back to was the one he seemed to be so hung up on. *Why didn't he tell me?*

"This fucking blows," Charlie said aloud as he closed the few dozen feet to his house. He didn't notice his brother Carson sitting on the porch swing.

"What fucking blows?" his little brother asked.

Surprised, Charlie looked to his right. Carson was gently rocking the swing with the ball of his foot. Charlie remembered when Carson's legs dangled, not able to touch the porch floor. It didn't seem that long ago. Change.

"Hey. Nothing. What are you doing out here? Where's Ethan?" A millisecond later, Charlie inquired, "You sober?"

Carson chuckled, "Yep. Ethan went home about a half hour ago. Mom and Sarah are at Annie's grabbing some sundaes. Where are you coming from? Where's Jackson?"

Charlie's stomach tensed. He stood on the porch for a minute, just letting the night settle around him. There was so much to process, so many things to wrap his head around. So many feelings.

"Uhm… I was at Madison's. Don't know where Jackson is." He followed with, "We're not married, you know?" maybe a bit too harshly.

Carson shrugged, a little confused by his brother's response. "How was your night?" he asked, hoping to cash in on Charlie's lighter mood from earlier in the night.

Damn, that's a loaded question, Charlie thought. How was his night? How does one wrap up the events of the last few hours in a simple word that encapsulates everything that went down between the time he left the house and that very second? What word?

"Startling, Carson. My night was startling."

Carson cocked his head in a way that showcased his confusion with his brother's choice of words. "What's up Charlie? You seem… I don't know, different."

Charlie laughed in his head at the question. Leave it to Carson to find the word that exactly described Charlie's night, and how he was feeling. The last few hours differed from any other night Charlie had ever experienced, and tomorrow would be a different day, unlike any other. As would every day that followed. Charlie was different now, in many ways. Jackson was different now, too. His thinking about Jackson was different. Madison, too, was different, changed. His relationship with each of them was different, and now... what? Complicated? Everything was different now. Everything had changed.

A deep sigh escaped him as Charlie pulled open the screen door and headed inside. "I'm going to bed, Carson."

The screen door slammed behind him as he stepped into the living room. For the first time since he arrived at the beach house, the walls didn't feel entombing. He didn't feel like he was going to crawl out of his skin, or worse, explode. Maybe it was because, at this moment, what he needed was something familiar, something to be the same. Maybe he just needed things to be the way they always were. Maybe. Whatever the reason, he wrapped himself in the sentiment, let it wash over him. Cleansing him.

As he passed into the kitchen, he let his hand drag along the top of the half wall that separated it from the living room. Charlie walked down the hallway and took notice of the pictures that had hung in the same places for as long as he could remember. Family shots, beach days, and lifetimes forever frozen in full color and reduced to eight by ten stills, and five by seven-inch snapshots.

Turning into his bedroom, he traversed the short distance to his bed on the far wall. He tossed his phone onto the side table, stripped off his shirt, stepped out of his shorts, and fell into bed. Before settling, there was one last thing he thought to do. Reaching over, he grabbed his phone and turned it off for the first time since he turned it on. He let it drop to the floor. Tugging the sheet up around his waist, Charlie turned to face the wall and welcomed the blackness of sleep.

TWENTY-SEVEN

The café wasn't overly crowded, but still contained enough people to keep Pops busy behind the counter. A tanned mixture of the vacationing populace chatted and sipped at their early morning dose of caffeine. Some were cradling the cup as if gleaning the energy found inside through osmosis. The teenage Karens blended almost seamlessly with the middle-aged Karens; the future versions of themselves were somehow available as a hint of what's coming. A few twenty-something guys guffawed as they recounted the conquests of the night before; the categories of which were most likely limited to various drinking exploits, or carnal conquests that added to the body count. All in all, a usual summer morning scene played out.

Jackson felt as if there were a host of tiny little people inside his head trying to break through his skull with sledgehammers and pickaxes. Each clattering of silverware, burst of laughter, or even the thud of a cup being placed too heavily onto a tabletop sent a shockwave of white light careening through his head, causing him to wince. He had awoken in the middle of the night by both the pounding in his head and the sloshing of his stomach. After laying on his back trying his best not to acquiesce to the sudden call for freedom by the contents of his gut, he dashed to the bathroom across from his bedroom and granted its release. He popped two ibuprofens, which, upon swallowing, he immediately threw up. He splashed some cold water on his face, cautiously took two more ibuprofens—which he kept inside him—and went back to bed.

That was six hours ago, and while his nausea had passed, the thrumming in his head had only diminished slightly. The sun light splashing and bouncing across his table at The Beanery stung his eyes so much so that he had returned his sunglasses to his face even though he was indoors—a look he would rail against on any other day.

He'd been sitting at his table for about thirty-five minutes now. When he could bring himself to rise from his bed, the first thing he did was check his phone. The memories of the night before were cloudy, but not so murky that he didn't remember what had taken place. They weren't so hazy as to block out the look on his friend's face. The one thing he was hoping most to see on his phone wasn't there. Nothing from Charlie. He thought about Face Timing, or texting, or Snapping Charlie, but didn't want to seem desperate. Nothing worse than someone blowing up your phone because you haven't responded to them, right? That would just be frantic.

Jackson couldn't help but feel frantic, though. It had been well over fifteen hours without a word from Charlie. Even in the dead of winter, amid school and sports and their respective non-beach lives, the two boys always found a reason to be in touch with each other. Even if that communication was some dumbass SnapChat about the tater-tots that accompanied some nasty school lunch.

The churning in Jackson's stomach returned. This time, he knew it wasn't caused by the alcohol he had consumed the previous night. This time, it was anxiety. In his head he could hear his words to Noah: *I fucked everything up, everything* playing repeatedly in a horrible sound loop.

Jackson was so engrossed by treading water in his own personal pool of despondency that he didn't notice the chair across from him pivot; nor did he notice the body that quietly sat down. It was the familiar voice that pulled him back from the deep end.

"I knew I'd find you here." Looking up, Jackson was glad he was wearing sunglasses because his eyes immediately brimmed. "What's with the sunglasses? You hate it when people wear their sunglasses inside. What is it you call it? Pretentious? You look pretentious."

Jackson realized he was holding his breath and let it escape him. "Charlie."

Charlie smiled, uncomfortably, remorsefully maybe, and said, "Jackson."

The two boys sat staring at each other in silence for a bit, a worry between them that one could palpate. Jackson removed his sunglasses and set them on the table just in front of his cup. Charlie sat tapping his fingers on the sides of his lemonade. He drew some of it through the straw as he cast furtive glances in his friend's direction. Jackson pushed down the urge to puke as the little men in his head began to bang again with renewed vigor.

It was Charlie who spoke first. "Well, now that we've got the introductions out of the way, you look like shit. Bus hit you or something?"

Jackson half laughed and glanced sideways out the window. "Something like that, yeah."

Charlie did a slow nod, taking in his friend. It was Jackson sitting in front of him, same as he always was, same hair, same eyes, though bloodshot and baggy, same face. Charlie lay awake for a good portion of the small hours of the morning wondering what this exact moment would be like; how it would feel and what he would say. Like some eight-year-old with an overactive imagination, Charlie envisioned some strange new version of Jackson that Charlie couldn't quite explain. As if Jackson would be replaced with an exact duplicate of himself who acted and said things like his friend, but wasn't his friend and he would have to spend the rest of the summer trying to convince his other friends that Jackson wasn't Jackson. However, right now, right there, sitting across from him, was Jackson in real time.

Again, Charlie broke the silence that was growing larger than the elephant in the room. "Listen, um… about last night…"

Jackson cut him off. Leaning into the table, he said, "Charlie, wait. I am so sorry. You have no idea how sorry I am right now. I didn't mean for you…"

Charlie was having none of it. He shut Jackson down. Picking up his hand and placing it palm up, Charlie said, "Jackson. Shut up. Okay? I know it's hard for you to stop talking, but just stop talking and listen." Jackson swallowed hard and stopped talking. He slumped against the back of his chair. A feeling of uneasiness wrapped itself around him, squeezing off his air. His first thought was *I have fucked everything up.* His second thought was *God, I'm going to throw up.* He dropped his gaze to the table, unable to meet his friend's eyes for fear of what he was about to say. Charlie looked away, out the window, as if his words were there, splayed across a sandwich board on the sidewalk like cue cards from which all he had to do was read. He rubbed a hand through his hair, the way he did when he was worried or upset, or anxious, and that only made Jackson more nervous. For a second, he thought he might hurl right there on the table.

Charlie exhaled and started talking, deliberately, purposefully. "Jackson, you have nothing to apologize for. Nothing. It's me who's sorry. I owe *you* an apology. Hell, I owe you a lot of apologies these past weeks. But last night… I shouldn't have reacted the way that I did. It was… I don't know, foolish and childish, and not cool. Not at all cool. I'm sorry about that. It's just that it caught me off guard, surprised me, you know?" He stopped talking and shook his head remorsefully. "I didn't know, Jackson. I don't know how I didn't know. Maybe I just wasn't paying attention to you, to clues, and I'm sorry about that too. I thought I knew you, Jesus, like I know the back of my hand, but I guess none of us knows each other one hundred percent, you know?"

Jackson tried to break in. "Charlie…"

But Charlie cut him off again, "I'm not done Jackson," Charlie jumped in. "Just listen, because this isn't easy for me to say, and I need to say it, okay?"

Jackson nodded. His chest felt like it was in a vice that was being cranked down, tighter and tighter. There was something heavy inside his gut right now, kicking and rolling and threatening to claw its way out. He dropped a hand to his stomach, as if to hold it in.

Charlie pulled in a deep breath, held it for a second, and then blew it out. "I was awake most of the night thinking about what I saw. What you were doing. What upsets me isn't that you're gay, or even that the guy you were making out with was Joey—which, to be honest, is surprising. But, as I was staring at the ceiling in my room, I realized what upsets me the most, Jackson, is that I didn't know. And I'm not upset at you, honestly. I was, at first. At first, I was so angry with you. So angry… but that was wrong. I'm not angry at you anymore. Right now, I'm angry at myself." Charlie paused, as if he were uncertain of what to say next. Jackson just sat, holding his breath, still waiting for the shoe to fall. "You're my best friend. You've always been my best friend. How I acted last night… I failed you, Jackson. I am beyond sorry that I didn't see this. That I didn't see you for… I don't know, for who you are, I guess. But now, right now, I see you, Jackson. I'm so sorry I didn't before." Charlie scratched the back of his neck and glanced down at the table. He had rehearsed a version of his speech most of the night, and each time he did, he teared up a little. He was proud of himself for getting through what he had to say without becoming an emotional basket-case in front of his friend. Raising his eyes to meet Jackson's he said, "There. You can talk now."

That was not the direction Jackson had expected Charlie's soliloquy going. He had fully expected that this would be the end of their friendship, that Charlie was going to say something like he never wanted to see him again, or that there was no way they could be friends anymore. It took a minute for Jackson to regain his composure before he could manage words without his voice cracking.

Even then, all he said was, "I don't know what to say," which made both boys laugh.

"Well, there's a first."

"Right?" Jackson quipped, and both boys laughed again.

Jackson was abundantly relieved that Charlie was sitting across from him right now. And though the laughter took the edge off of the moment, it wasn't quite natural. There still seemed to be something hanging between them. Charlie still looked uneasy, guarded almost. Which, in turn, made Jackson feel unsure. *Give him time* he heard his brother's advice from the night before echo in his head.

"Can I ask you something, Jackson?" Jackson nodded from behind his cup of cappuccino. "As I was thinking about you last night, about this, I kept coming back to the same question, like I said. Why didn't you tell me? I mean, you have to have known for a long time now. Why didn't you ever say anything to me?"

Charlie's inquiry elicited a shrug from Jackson. "Shit, Charlie. I've wanted to, for a while. A long while. I tried a couple times over the past few weeks. But…" He stopped and looked hesitantly at his friend, then turned to look out the window.

"What, Jackson?"

Jackson exhaled loudly, emotion already filling his throat, "Charlie, a lot has gone down with you recently and you've not been you. You've been stuck in this dark place these past months and I didn't want to add to that, you know? I didn't want to heave anymore shit onto your pile…" He trailed off.

Charlie nodded. He had been in a dark place; he could agree to that. He still was in a dark place. To be honest, this added to his angst. But that wasn't fair, was it?

"Appreciate that, Jackson, but I think I could've handled this. This is important to you, and so it's important to me, too. You know you can always talk to me, right? I mean, have I done anything or said anything that maybe upset you or made you think you couldn't tell me this?" Jackson bit the edge of his upper lip and just shook his head no. His right leg began to bounce rapidly, and he again turned away from his friend and looked out the window. "What aren't you telling me, Jackson?"

Damn-it Charlie, Jackson thought. He picked at his fingers. He knew the reason he had waited so long to tell Charlie about his sexuality. It weighed on him every day. It was the reason he'd lost plenty of nights' sleeps.

Charlie pressed, "Jackson, what is it?"

With a sigh, Jackson said, "Okay. Truth? I never told you because I was afraid…" Jackson broke off and looked out the window again. The speed with which he bounced his leg increased.

Charlie gave his friend a minute before he prodded, "Afraid of what?"

Just tell him. Jackson turned back. He looked Charlie dead in the eye. "I was afraid that I would lose you as my friend, Charlie. I was scared to lose you." Jackson could feel his throat tighten, but he pushed on, "And when you said last night that you couldn't do this, that you couldn't breathe, and you bolted, I thought that's exactly what I had done," Jackson's gaze faltered. He took a deep breath. Held it for a second or two and let it out. "I thought I lost you."

Silence settled at the table. The two boys processing all that was said and heard. In all the years that Charlie had known Jackson, never did he imagine that this was a conversation they would ever have. In all the years that Jackson had known Charlie, this was a conversation that he played out so many times.

Charlie nodded slowly. As he lay awake last night in his bed processing all of this, that thought had entered his mind. Would Jackson's sexuality be the thing that came between them? The wedge that pierced their cohesiveness and gradually drove them apart, ending their friendship? Then, Charlie realized that for something to come between two people, someone has to let it. He wasn't going to be that person. He decided then that Jackson's sexuality wasn't going to be a wedge and that his friendship was more important than what gender he was attracted to.

Charlie scratched at his cheek and leaned across the table. "My truth, Jackson, is that I don't think there is anything you could do that would ever cause me to stop being your friend. Even sucking face with Joey Mastromani." Jackson laughed out loud, and Charlie sat back in his chair and shrugged, "So. You're gay."

"Yeah, Charlie. I'm gay."

With a sly smile, Charlie quipped, "Well, Jackson, there's something I've been meaning to tell you. I've been meaning to tell you this thing for a long time now, and I hope this doesn't affect our friendship. So here goes. I'm straight. You're the only person I've ever told. I hope you're okay with my sexuality because I value your friendship more than most anything else in this world. And I hope the fact that I'm heterosexual doesn't come between us. Because I can't, for the life of me, imagine a me, without a you. We're like... the salt and the sea, ya know?"

Charlie's words caused Jackson's heart to swell, and if they weren't sitting in the middle of the Beanery, Jackson thought he might slide back his chair and give Charlie a hug. Instead, Jackson fought back the onslaught of emotions he was feeling in that divinely perfect moment and shook his head. "You're an idiot."

Charlie laughed. "I've been called worse. There is one more thing before we put the period on this conversation for today," Charlie added. "So... like, when I'm sleeping over, or you're sleeping over, I don't need to... you know, worry about you putting the moves on me or anything, do I?" he asked, obviously being playful.

Again, shaking his head, Jackson replied, "Dude, don't flatter yourself. You are so not my type." Then after a pause, he added, "Besides, I don't think of you that way. I never have. You're like a brother to me. You always have been."

Jackson's last words caught Charlie by surprise. A lump popped into his throat that he struggled to swallow, and he could feel his eyes well up. Shaking off the feeling and wiping at his eyes in a quick I'm-not-crying-you-are sort of way, he added, "Same."

This was unfamiliar territory for both boys, but navigating the terrain went much smoother than Charlie thought. Why shouldn't it have, though? He and Jackson had a lifetime of history that cemented them together like the mortar between bricks. They all had history: Charlie, Jackson, Madison, Joey, and Kelsey. That history would always be a part of their lives and a part of them. Thing about history is, you can't change it. It exists unaltered for all of time. It is what it is.

The future, however, well, the future is as fluid as the ocean itself. Neither boy knew, at that moment, what the future would bring, or the strain that future would cause on their friendship.

"Okay. Can I ask you another question?" Charlie said. Jackson nodded. From behind a furrowed brow, Charlie asked, "How long have you known?" It sounded dumb as soon as he heard it, sort of like asking *how long have you known your hair is brown?* Still, it was another question that kept popping into Charlie's head as he searched his bedroom ceiling for answers the night before.

Jackson chuckled quietly and nodded. "Yeah. That's a good question, Charles." He took a sip of his drink and looked past Charlie for a second or two, trying to find an answer. He hated when gay characters in movies and books spouted forth the hackneyed, *I've always known,* response to that question, as much as the question itself bothered him.

"Well, if this were a movie, or if I were a character in a book, I guess I would say that I've always known, but I'm not sure that's true." Jackson paused, his eyes looking towards the ceiling as if for guidance. He returned his gaze to his friend and continued, "I mean, when you're a kid you don't think 'hey, I'm straight', or 'hey I'm gay'. You don't think anything at all. You just go about being you. So, I can't say that I've always known because I haven't. Though I guess it was always there." Jackson picked up his cup and took another swallow. Setting in gently down on the table with both hands, he pressed on, "I remember being nine or ten and you, and my friends back home, started talking about girls and who had a crush on who, and how this one or that one was pretty, and stuff like that. And I remember noticing those things, but that was just it. It was like appreciating a nice car, you know? Yeah, I could see how awesome it was, and I could appreciate the beauty of it, but beyond that… nothing. And then around sixth or seventh grade, I grabbed Noah's laptop to do something and when I open it up, porn was on the screen. So, I hit play, and as I was watching, I realized I was more interested in the guys than the girls. As I got older, I remember looking at certain guys and feeling something… desire or want… I don't know, and then, one day, it hit me like a bag of bricks. This realization finally that this is what my friends felt when they were talking about girls, only for me, it wasn't girls. So, yeah, definitely at least since I was eleven or twelve or so…" He trailed off, his face darkened, and his volume dropped, "And I remember… Jesus, I remember hating myself." His brows furrowed as he continued, "Just hating myself so much, for so long, just not wanting to be me, to be gay. Just wanting to be like every other guy I knew. God, I hated what I was. But try as I might to be someone else, pretend as I could, I just wasn't that guy. I wasn't straight. Finally, I accepted I wasn't like every other guy. I was more like every fourth or fifth guy. And that's okay. I'm okay. Now."

The gravity of what Jackson had just dropped weighed heavily for a moment on Charlie. He felt so stupid for not being aware of any of this, for being a part of Jackson's life through all of that and not knowing. Jackson never once let on that he was hurting, or struggling, or confused. Charlie thought of his own struggle and how it weighed on him daily.

"Jesus, Jackson. I'm sorry you had to go through that alone. I wish you had said something…"

Jackson shook his head and said, "I wasn't alone, Charlie. I told Noah pretty early on, and he's been so supportive in his walled-off-non-emotional-stand-offish- sort of way. Hell, he helped me out last night, a lot. And I couldn't tell you until I was okay with me. And even then, well, like I said, I was just afraid it would be this wedge that came between us, and I hope it won't."

Charlie had to laugh to himself at Jackson's choice of words. "It won't. I got you Jackson, always."

At that moment, Pops appeared at the side of their table. Like always, he was wearing a white apron, and carrying a once white rag that he used to wipe tables. Clean silverware jangled in one pocket of the apron, and napkins peeked out of the top of the other like baby kangaroos glimpsing the world.

"Well, if it isn't my two favorite islanders," he said. "First time I've seen you both in here together this season. Nice to see you boys." Then, looking directly at Jackson, he said, "I trust everything is okay between you two, yes?" Which struck Charlie a bit cryptically.

Jackson beamed, "Yeah Pops. Everything is great."

Pops nodded a few times, smiling back at the boys. Turning back to Jackson, he said, "Good. I'm glad." Then to both, "I like you two. You're good people, good friends. Take care of each other, as best you can. Now, if you'll excuse me, I gotta go clean up that mess those Shoebies left. Hope to see you again soon, you two."

"See ya, Pops," the boys called in unison.

Jackson turned to Charlie and said, "Okay. Can I ask you a question?" He said it cautiously. Knowing what he was about to ask, worried Jackson. The two boys had just cleared a giant hurdle in their relationship and here he was, poised to erect another. Lately, Jackson never knew what was going to set Charlie off, but sometimes you have to walk through landmines to save your friend.

With a shrug, Charlie offered, "Of course."

Jackson thought of couching his words to ease into his question with some bush beating. However, he figured the best way to find out where a landmine lay was to just fling a brick into the field. "Why are you so angry all the time?"

Surprised by the question, Charlie actually sat back in his chair as if the force of Jackson's words blew him backwards. Did he even know the answer to that question? Was he angry with his dad? Was he angry with his mom? Was he mostly angry with himself and how he's been acting? How he's spent the last six months just pushing everyone away? Charlie shook his head, which confused Jackson.

"So... no, you're not angry? Or no, you don't know why you're angry? Or no, you don't want to talk about it?" Jackson inquired.

"The last two," Charlie said weakly.

Jackson nodded his head. "Okay. But, when you figure out the second one, will you promise me you'll do the third one? Will you talk to me?" Charlie nodded. "Fair enough, Charles."

While Jackson was hoping to have a frank conversation with Charlie about his volatility of late, he was happy that he didn't experience any of that volatility by asking the question. Charlie would talk when Charlie figured things out. Admittedly, Jackson was disappointed that Charlie would not let Jackson walk with him down that path. *It's not like you opened the gate to your own path, right?* Baby steps, Jackson thought to himself.

"What do you say we get out of here and hit the surf?" Charlie asked.

Jackson nodded. Both boys pushed their chairs back. Jackson picked up his sunglasses as Charlie grabbed their cups and dropped them on the counter for Pops. As they climbed onto their bikes outside, Jackson turned to Charlie and said, "Hey, can I ask you one more question?"

Charlie laughed, "Is this how it's going to be from now on? Asking permission to ask questions? Fire away, Jackson."

Jackson laughed. "Do anything interesting last night? I mean, if anything last night could have been more interesting than what you walked in on?" He peddled down the sidewalk away from the coffee shop. Charlie pulled his bike up alongside Jackson and the boys fell in sequence together.

"Welp," Charlie said, "you have no idea. Let me tell you about last night…"

JULY

"Do what we can, summer will have its flies."
-Ralph Waldo Emmerson

ONE

One day seeped into the next, as days do in the summer. Morning to night seamlessly meshed together like links in a chain. June quietly and effortlessly gave way to July. The remaining days in June were spent as usual: days and nights being among friends, punctuated with laughter, and making memories in a way that only teenagers can. However, much like a well-worn comfortable T-shirt versus a brand new one, the feel of the days, at first, was different in so many ways.

In their new reality, Charlie and Jackson found some cohesion. It had taken a few awkward hours over a few awkward days, but the flavor of what their relationship had been before Charlie knew Jackson was gay gradually returned. Their groove settled back to the days when there wasn't that difference between them. That's not to say that Charlie felt any differently about his best friend. He didn't. But now and again, out of nowhere, the fact that Jackson was into guys just popped up. It wasn't a problem; it was just there. When cruising the boardwalk or sitting in the sand and some fit girls walked by, Charlie would call Jackson's attention to them, only to remember that Jackson was probably more into the guys the girls were with. Jackson always went along, and Charlie appreciated that, but somehow, knowing now what Charlie knew, it just wasn't the same. He often wondered if Jackson felt that way. He wondered if, somehow, Charlie's sexuality got in the way now and again. Though it hadn't yet happened, Charlie wondered if Jackson wanted to point out fit guys to him, but kept himself from doing so because Charlie just wasn't into that. This caused Charlie to wonder if Jackson was being himself around Charlie or if he was still holding back.

In the days that followed Charlie's walking in on two of his friends, Jackson and Joey came out to Madison and Kelsey. In a surprise show of confidence, both Joey and Jackson had shown up at Charlie's house a day or so after Charlie and Jackson met at The Beanery. They came, they said, because they needed his advice on whether they should tell Madison and Kelsey, and, if so, how. The three of them spent a good portion of the afternoon sitting on a bench down at the skate park–a place no one would ever look for them–talking about navigating the waters in which they now found themselves afloat. It was the first time Charlie had ever talked to Joey beyond a greeting in a school hallway, or casual back-and-forth banter on the beach. It was the first time Charlie had seen Joey as anything more than an accessory to a group of friends or an overconfident jock. It was the first time Charlie had actually seen Joey. He was chagrinned to discover that Jackson had been right. Joey wasn't so bad. He was kind of funny, in a not so overly sarcastic sort of way. He was way smarter than Charlie had ever given him credit for, and while he could still be a bit of a douche, he was someone that his best friend wanted to spend time with. Joey was someone that made Jackson feel good. That fact, Charlie came to realize that afternoon, was more important than any predisposed notion of Joey, to which Charlie may or may not still subscribe.

"You have to tell at least Kelsey and Madison," Charlie had said with an air of certainty he didn't know he possessed. "We're with them just about every single day, and that just wouldn't be fair to them. But, more importantly, if you two are going to have a relationship, it's not fair to you guys to keep it a secret. That wouldn't be right either." Charlie's logic even surprised by him.

Joey and Jackson had turned to face each other. Joey put his hand on Jackson's knee, which didn't go unnoticed by Charlie.

"Kelsey is going to shit," Joey said.

"Yeah. She absolutely is," Charlie said, looking at Jackson, now understanding why Kelsey's two summers of advances had gone unrequited.

So, they decided Charlie would text the group, suggesting they hang out that night, maybe grab an ice-cream and then head over to the Gardens to hang by the lagoon. As the sun touched the rim of the bay, setting the water ablaze, Jackson and Joey told two of their oldest friends about themselves and how they felt for one another. The conversation ended with the five of them group hugging on the dock. A new reality was settling over them, and now, days after that night, which would remain forever emblazoned on Charlie's mind, that new reality between them seemed to take hold.

It was awkward and uncertain at first, to be sure. If Charlie had to be honest, those first times he watched Jackson and Joey together were difficult for him. He often found himself turning away, embarrassed and uncomfortable, he wasn't sure which. But Jackson had never turned away from Charlie and Madison, and Lord knows there was opportunity for him to do so. Charlie owed his friends that level of acceptance. To Charlie it was like that scratchy, brand-new T-shirt: the more you put it on, the more comfortable it became.

Things with Madison and Charlie also seemed to find a groove. There was no denying what had happened between them. That was something they would share for the rest of their lives. Charlie thought of that night, pretty much all the time. He was glad about it and wouldn't change what happened, but somehow that night changed him, changed them, in a way for which he wasn't yet ready. He had told no one other than Jackson, and he was pretty sure that Madison had at least told Kelsey. When he looked at her now, it was like they shared a secret. They knew each other in a way that no one else did. Sometimes, that puffed Charlie up, but sometimes, that scared the shit out of him, and sometimes it confused him.

"What the hell are you scared about?" he remembered Jackson asking on an ever increasingly rare day that the two of them were together without everyone else. They were sitting up on the roof deck of Jackson's house, one cloudy day, sneaking beers and just hanging out.

"Welp, if I knew, I wouldn't be scared, now, would I?" Charlie fired back.

"Maybe, son, just maybe, what scares you is the enormity of the act, you know?" Jackson offered in a typical Jackson way as he tugged on the beer bottle. Charlie scrunched up his face and cocked his head in confusion. "Charlie, this wasn't some random hook up with some random girl in the bathroom at some random party after which we'd be fist bumping on the walk home. It's Madison. Someone you've known your whole life. Someone you have feelings for. And it was the first time for both of you. That's kind of enormous, man. You can't get out from under the canopy of that. It will always be with you." He took another pull from the bottle, pleased with himself.

"I guess," Charlie offered weakly as he took a sip of beer.

"Now, what are you confused about? I have a little experience in being confused about things. Let me help," Jackson said.

Charlie let his gaze drift up to the billowing gray clouds that lazily drifted by above their heads. What was he confused about?

"I don't know. It's just that sometimes I wonder if we should have waited, like maybe we went a bit too fast. And as much as I wanted to do it, sometimes I'm not sure that we should have." Charlie turned to look at his friend, a slight smirk on his face. "Does that make me gay?" he said jokingly.

Jackson laughed at the attempted comedy. "No, idiot, that makes you introspective. And that's not a bad thing. Honestly, you and Madison moved fast, but you can't take back what's been done. You just gotta figure out how you move forward." Jackson paused for a second, then sitting up and turning to Charlie he said, "Listen, if you're not sure about what you're doing, or you even slightly regret what's been done, then you should stop, and talk to Madison, you know?"

Charlie nodded and marveled at how insightful his friend could be. One night, as he and Madison were wandering around the island, fingers entwined, Charlie did talk. He told her how he was feeling, and about what he thought. Turns out that Madison felt similar, and while they were together again since that first night, they spent more time talking and getting to know each other in their new roles. Much like his relationship with Jackson, Charlie found a new reality with Madison.

While the feel of the last days of June, now the first days of July, weren't exactly the same as they had been in years past - Charlie wondered if anything ever would feel the same again, which padded his ever-present melancholy - there was a new sense of normal growing. Like watching the first seedlings of a garden sprout from the ground, Charlie was hopeful.

TWO

The waves lapped lazily at the smooth sand of the shoreline. Encouraged by the wind, fist sized puffs of foam skated up the slope of the beach, before coming to a rest and melting away. Other than the occasional sea gull, Charlie was alone on the beach. The sun wasn't quite up yet, but it threatened the horizon with its light. The sky, a calming blue-gray that only comes in the early hours of dawn, began to reveal the billowy clouds that were hidden by the dark not so long ago.

Charlie plopped onto the sand when it was still dark. He had lain awake listening to his brother breathing and the nighttime groanings of the house since about three-thirty in the morning. Around four, he climbed out of bed and into shorts and a hoodie, and quietly left the house. He had become quite skilled at sneaking out of the house in the middle of the night. His weekly spraying of door hinges with the can of WD40 he found in the garage aided his efforts.

It was chilly sitting there in the sand on the edge of the ocean before the warming sun, and Charlie was glad for the hoodie he slipped into. With the cold sand chilling his feet, he sat shrouded by the cowl, hunched over, watching the ocean. There was something almost magical about being the only person on a beach. To Charlie, it felt like being perched on the edge of the world. He wondered to himself why he didn't do this more often, probably because he had to get up too early. That, and if Miriam ever found out he was sitting alone, in the dark, on the beach, she'd have his balls. No, Charlie thought, moments like this one don't need to come often. They just need to be enjoyed when they happen, he concluded. Charlie was enjoying being alone in his moment.

About fifty yards offshore, a pod of dolphins breached the surface, spouting water into the air. Gracefully, they arced in and out of the water as they moved along parallel to the shoreline. Charlie wondered what that must be like; to spend your days swimming through life, not being weighed down by the entanglements which seemed to accumulate more and more, the older one became, winding in tangled knots around your ankles, making it even more difficult to move forward. For just a second, Charlie thought about swimming out and joining them, and to just keep swimming until he couldn't swim anymore. He shook that thought from his head.

He just couldn't seem to get out from under the weight of the last six months, no matter how hard he tried. His parents' divorce still troubled him. He kept waiting to get used to it, as if one morning he would wake up and the knot in his stomach would just be gone. As if, one day, like magic, his old self–the one where he wasn't suffocating beneath his anxiety or on the verge of tears at any given moment or just a hair's thickness away from exploding in anger–would come back and say '*Hey, I'm back. Off with you now, twisted up, angry, resentful Charlie. I've gotten used to it.*' Isn't that what people always say, *you'll get used to it?* That's what his guidance counselor said way back in February when Miriam forced a meeting on him. That's what his lacrosse coach said that day in the locker room when he felt obligated to have a heart to heart with Charlie, again, most likely spurred on by his mother. Over and over Charlie had been told *he'd get used to it,* but here Charlie sat, still not used to it. There were days he was just angry; angry with his mom for sucking at marriage; angry with his dad for walking away and disappearing from his life; angry with his siblings for being his siblings; and angry with himself for being such a baby about it, for not putting it behind him and moving on. Like Jackson said, weeks ago, divorce was almost trendy these days. Why did he care so much that his dad left? His dad didn't seem to care at all. Why should he?

And, Charlie thought to himself, *why should I care?* He hadn't heard from his father in just about six months, which was like an open wound that someone kept pouring rubbing alcohol into. In the early days of the divorce, Charlie had texted his dad frantically seeking information, asking for some reason, or some answer as to why things went to hell. *It's complicated* was the standard answer. Charlie wanted to scream *Calculus is complicated, dad, nuclear physics is complicated, the first time you put on a jockstrap is complicated! Telling me why you left seems to be a straightforward answer!* For a while, his dad wouldn't even tell him where he was or if he was with anyone. After a dozen days or so of pleading, Charlie found out that his dad was in Florida. He'd transferred to his firm's Miami office, and no, there was no plan for him to come back. That was a knife to his gut. Charlie had stopped texting after that. His dad did as well. That was mid-February, and Charlie hadn't received a single call or text since. His birthday was in a few weeks: seventeen years old. He wondered if his dad would remember, as it seemed he had done a bang-up job of forgetting everything else: him, Carson and Sarah; the life he had in Pennsylvania with a woman named Miriam. A softball sized lump materialized in Charlie's throat, one so big, he almost choked as he tried to swallow it down.

Then there was Miriam. These past few weeks, Charlie and his mom could barely be in the same room together. Wednesday nights became hers so she could socialize with other adults–translation, get lit with the ladies -and she needed him to be around the house– interpretation, baby-sit. There was always a host of questions about his friends, his plans, where he was, where he was going, and his relationship with Madison. There were always allegations of misconduct, or activities she'd hoped he wouldn't involve himself in.

If not being bombarded by the constant stream of queries, Charlie was met with a list of disappointing things, or a list of things he'd forgotten to do, or a list of things she needed him to take care of.

The latest eruption occurred two days ago when Miriam handed Charlie a grocery list and asked -no, told - him to head over to Acme to pick the items up so desperately needed for their survival. He'd done grocery runs before and was glad to help. After all, it got him out of the house, but when he returned and she lit into him about forgetting a few of the items on the list, he lost it. What ensued was a shouting match, the likes of which he was sure could be heard on the boardwalk, swirling around how he'd become so unreliable, so self-involved, and how she needed him to be more present. It ended with Charlie hurling at his mom a hateful *"I'm not your goddamned husband. He left, remember?"* and storming out of the house. He hadn't spoken a word to any family member since. Miriam's number one on her Top Ten Things Wrong with Charlie Playlist was the much-harangued frequency with which he was absent from the family home. How she didn't understand why he was never around escaped Charlie. Charlie didn't see *The Reckoning* coming anytime soon, let alone *The Cease Fire.*

Charlie closed his eyes against the lightening sky and let the sounds and the wind wash over him. He reminded himself that he was sitting there to escape, and he allowed himself to do that. The sky wasn't yet blue, but it was far from black. Charlie leaned back on his elbows and tried to find some peace within himself. Down by the jetty, way off to Charlie's left, the first jogger of the day appeared. The person stopped, pulled something out of a pocket to look at—a cell phone maybe, shoved it back in and began to run again. Charlie paid no attention, trying to just let the moment cradle him. As the person closed the distance, their trajectory changed, and the runner headed for where Charlie was sitting. After a second, he recognized the ponytail bobbing in time to her footfalls.

"Hi Charlie. I thought I recognized that handsome young man beneath the hood," Madison said, catching her breath. "What are you doing here so early? Surf is kinda flat," she said as she looked out over the ocean.

Charlie was equally surprised to see Madison. He knew she was an early morning runner, but, if recalled correctly, she preferred the even surface of the boardwalk to the pitted and shifting shoreline. While he missed being alone in his bubble, he was happy to see her.

With a shrug, he said, "Couldn't sleep. Thought I'd catch a sunrise... do some thinking."

Madison smiled warmly, "It's summer, Charlie. Save the thinking for the school year." She leaned down and placed a kiss on his lips. "Hope you were thinking about us?"

Charlie laughed. That was the one thing he wasn't thinking about. "Always," he lied. "Anyway, what are you doing jogging along the beach? Thought you were a boardwalk runner?" All the while, Madison's attention kept being pulled back to the beach beyond Charlie, as if she were looking for something, or someone. Instinctively, Charlie looked around to see if anyone else had appeared.

"Oh, yeah. I still do. It gets old, though, you know? I mean, how many times can you run along the same stretch? Besides, I've been reading that jogging in the sand is a better workout. Burns more calories. Helps shape your legs."

Charlie took in Madison's lean body. A body with which he had become very familiar these past few weeks. He still marveled at how beautiful she was. Even in workout clothes, there was no denying the curves that graced her. Another familiar feeling began to spread through Charlie's body as he sat there taking in his girlfriend–a term that he still wasn't quite used to.

"You're perfect just the way you are, Madison."

"Aww, thanks Charlie. You're pretty perfect yourself."

That's when Charlie saw it. Madison's eyes locked on a position further up the beach. Charlie turned to see another runner coming down the Fourth Street entrance ramp. He jogged to the shoreline and stopped. Charlie could see his head turning, as if he too were looking for something, or someone.

"Anyway, Charles McIntyre, I'll leave you to your thinking. Glad I ran into you—no pun intended. Do something later?" Charlie just nodded.

He watched as Madison continued down the beach towards Fourth Street. As she did, the second runner moved as well. As Madison closed the distance, the second jogger picked up his pace, matching Madison's steps as she passed. Together, they jogged on. *That's weird*, Charlie thought. From this distance, he couldn't be positive, but he was pretty sure that the second jogger was Asher.

Charlie turned back to face the ocean, very aware of the new monkey that menacingly clawed its way up his back and found a comfortable spot to perch on his shoulders.

THREE

Asher sat perched against the headboard of his bed, hands clasped behind his neck. He was still sweaty from his run, and if his mother saw him stretched out, unbathed, on the 1,000 count Egyptian cotton sheets of his bed, she'd be none too happy. She was irritable these days as they had yet to find a housekeeper, and his mom was unaccustomed to having to perform the day-to-day chores required to maintain a household. They interfered with her mid-day martinis, her gym time, and golf. She could often be heard on the phone complaining to her friends back in Boston about how this tired island pales in comparison to what she had become accustomed to on Martha's Vineyard. She couldn't understand why they settled on this house, on this beach, rather than something in Avalon or Stone Harbor. Asher wondered if there was anything that pleased his mom, other than the more than ample earnings of her husband. She wasn't a horrible person, just maybe over indulged.

From his vantage point, Asher had a clear view through the sliding door that led to his small, but comfortable, balcony directly into Madison's bedroom, across the short space between the houses. He couldn't see much, her door, a bureau, a lamp, but he peered, nevertheless, hoping to gain more insight into his next-door neighbor. Occasionally, he would catch glimpses of Madison as she entered the room or moved about the space. Sometimes he felt just a small twang of guilt and, perhaps, perversity, as he sat in the shadows of his room, staring into Madison's private space. He recalled the night a few weeks ago that he spied Madison enter her room with Charlie in tow. He remembered being jealous at first, and then angry that it wasn't him.

Also accustomed to being over indulged, Asher struggled with understanding why Madison had shown no interest in him. Never, in his life, had he had the frustration of having to work for a girl's attention. They'd be crazy not to pay attention to him. He was handsome, and not in your average guy handsome sort of way. Asher grew up hearing words like *stunning, breath-taking,* and *gorgeous,* used to describe his appearance. Guys envied his body type and girls wanted to touch it. He'd worked hard at developing the perfect balance of a spoiled rich kid mixed with a good amount of, but not too much, humility. The American Express Centurion with his name on it didn't hurt either.

Just what did she see in Charlie? he wondered. From what he had gleaned through asking around, Charlie was just some kid from some town in Pennsylvania just outside Philadelphia. Sure, his dad was a partner in one of the more prestigious Philadelphia law-firms, but he bailed on the family a few months back and headed south. His mom was a public-school teacher. Asher's dad probably made in a month, twice what Charlie's mom made in a year. The house they called a summer home a few blocks away was his grandparents, and while it was nice, it couldn't compare to Asher's four-story, six-bedroom home. Charlie wasn't a bad-looking kid, either, but he paled compared to Asher's chiseled looks: most did. So just what was it about Charlie…

Sometimes in life, aha moments hit you upside the head with the intensity of a pillowcase laden with rolls of quarters. It was like that when Asher finally figured it all out. History. Madison had history with Charlie. They all had history together. Every summer, for their entire lives, they had come to this beach and woven the separate threads of their existence together. He couldn't compete

with that. His history was in Boston. Parties in brownstones on
Commonwealth Avenue; school years spent away at Phillips
Academy with trust fund babies; and summers on Martha's
Vineyard, day tripping to the compound on Hyannis Port to hang
out with the descendants of dead presidents and senators. It didn't
matter to Madison that his inner circle comprised the progeny of
Wall Street moguls, bankers, and congressmen. He had no history
with *her*, with any of them. Not that he cared to have a history with
them, just the one. In that moment, Asher knew he had to build his
own history with Madison. He decided he would begin to stitch
together their own tapestry, one in which he wasn't just the new
rich kid, an outsider, but someone you could relate to, hang out
with; someone with similar interest, a friend, maybe more.

Asher's attention was drawn back to the present by movement
from the house next door. Madison had walked into her room,
wrapped in a towel, with her hair wet. She stood for a moment in
front of her bureau, brushing out tangles from her hair. Putting
down the brush, she rummaged through a few drawers, pulling out
a few articles of clothing. She crossed over to the other side of the
room and out of Asher's sight line. That feeling of guilt, married to
perversity, washed over him briefly and he turned away. Grabbing
the cell phone off his night stand he stabbed out a message with his
thumbs.

**Hey Logan, you still getting together with Kelsey this
afternoon?**

Yep. Why?

Mind if I tag along? Got nothing to do.

I guess, sure.

Would you do me a favor? Would you ask Kelsey to invite Madison?

I could. What are you up to Asher?

What makes you think I'm up to something, bro?

Haha. Because you always are...

Haha. Just trying to get to know her better, is all. She is our neighbor. So, will you?

Anything for my baby brother.

Thanks.

Quite pleased with himself, Asher dropped his phone back onto the bedside table. Hopping up off of his bed, he stripped off his running shorts. Purposely, he crossed in front of the sliders a few times before heading to his on-suite shower.

FOUR

Charlie managed to get back in the house, shower, and change before anyone else had stirred from their slumber. He was more than impressed with his newfound level of stealth. In a moment of kindness or weakness, he brewed a pot of coffee. He didn't drink it except occasionally in its iced fashion, but Miriam did, and he hoped that perhaps the fresh pot ready upon her waking might move things towards The Reckoning. Loath to admit it, Charlie didn't like the tension that crowded the house these past few days.

It was a few minutes shy of eight o'clock and the day was shaping up to be a beautiful one: sunny, cloudless blue sky, low humidity and a soft breeze. He was alone on the porch, gently rocking in the swing, basking in the experience, when the screen door pushed open. Sarah padded out in her bare feet, already in a bathing suit. She clutched a cup of coffee, which struck Charlie as something between odd and exaggerated. She paused for a beat, surprised by Charlie sitting there, then gestured with her free hand to the empty spot next to him. Charlie nodded and patted the swing. Sarah sank down next to him. Charlie caught himself looking to see if her feet had yet touched the porch floor. The tips or her toes were just about there.

With a raised eyebrow, he inquired of his sister, "Since when do you drink coffee?"

"Since we got here. Mom and I have coffee time in the morning. Sometimes Carson joins us. Actually, Carson usually joins us."

As if waiting in the wings, Carson appeared on the front porch with a cup of coffee in his hand. Charlie's presence startled Carson as well. Seeing no room on the swing, he pulled one of the high-back rockers over and joined his siblings.

Charlie cast confused glances at each. "So, let me get this straight. You guys *and* mom, have coffee time in the mornings? On the porch. Together. Every day." Both siblings nodded. "How have I missed this?" Charlie queried with a furrowed brow.

Carson just shook his head in an oh-you-sad-sorry-little-man sort of way. Sarah provided the answer in her typical bothered tone. "Charlie, you aren't up until, at the earliest, eleven o'clock in the morning. There's lots that goes on around here that you miss daily."

Ain't that the truth? Charlie thought to himself. It seems there was a lot in Charlie's life lately that he had failed to notice. "Maybe I should get up early more often," Charlie posed.

"Maybe you should," Carson responded. Charlie looked at his brother to see if his remarks were meant as a challenge, but only sincerity played across Carson's face, which only called up that familiar lump in Charlie's throat.

Charlie nodded in agreement. "Yeah. Maybe I should." Sarah patted Charlie on his thigh and smiled. She took a sip of her coffee and grimaced. "Need more sugar?" Charlie asked.

Sarah scoffed, "Sugar is for amateurs. Besides, I'm sweet enough."

All three turned as the screen door popped open again to reveal their mom, in a tank and sweat shorts, stepping out onto the porch. Like Sarah and Carson before her, she was surprised by Charlie's presence. Caught off guard, all she managed was, "Oh." Charlie wasn't sure if he should be concerned that his presence startled his family members, or if he should bask in that accomplishment and wear it like a medal. Miriam grabbed the remaining rocker and dragged it over, positioning it across from Carson, by the porch railing. She smiled at her two younger children and took a sip from her cup.

Swallowing, she said, "Mmm, this is fantastic. Carson, did you make this?"

Carson just shook his head. "It was ready when I got up. I thought you made it, Mom."

She looked at Sarah, who just shook her head, silently echoing the sentence just iterated by her brother. Confused, it took a few seconds to arrive at the only remaining conclusion as to who made the coffee. Miriam looked at Charlie skeptically. "You?" she asked.

Charlie nodded. "Yeah, Mom. It was me," Charlie said, trying not to be offended by his mom's disbelief that he could actually do something for someone other than himself. "I was, uh… up early today for a change."

"But you don't drink coffee, Charlie."

Charlie shrugged. "Not hot anyway. But I know you do." Looking around, he added, "And evidently, so does everyone else."

Miriam smiled warmly at her firstborn. From within the house, her cell phone made itself known. Rising to answer the call, she reached over and ran a hand through Charlie's unruly hair. "Thanks, Charlie. That was sweet of you," she said and disappeared inside to fetch the phone.

Sarah looked at her two siblings, paused with the timing of a skilled comedian, and said with a sly grin, "The Cease Fire."

"Without the Reckoning," Carson added.

Standing in the living room, the noise coming from outside which she couldn't quite place, surprised Miriam. It took her a full ten seconds to realize that the sound was that of her children laughing together as one: belly laughing. She couldn't remember the last time that joyous sound had graced her ears. She let the call bump to voicemail.

FIVE

To Charlie, the day's feel had taken an uptick. When he awoke earlier that morning, he was feeling as he always did: shadowy, brooding, morose. Sitting in the sand in the dark, he questioned whether he was even going to make it through. It seemed the weight he had been carrying was pushing him down, forcing him into the sand. But now, he wasn't quite sure what he felt as he pedaled towards the boardwalk. He knew it wasn't happiness, or at least he didn't think it was. It had been so long since he was genuinely happy; Charlie wasn't exactly sure what that felt like anymore. These past weeks, he'd come close. His days spent with Jackson and his nights with Madison brought a level of comfort and familiarity that eased his anxiety and almost erased his sullenness. Some remained, like a pencil mark after you clear away the eraser's rubber shavings.

On the other hand, he knew with certainty that he wasn't despondent, because despondency was as familiar to him as was the route he took to school. The feeling that swam around inside Charlie at the moment was definitely not hopelessness. The best he could describe it as was a brightness, not like the sun or a searchlight, but more similar to the early morning sky stealing through the rip in the shade in his room and seeping in from around its edges; slivers of light that were not necessarily bright enough to light up the room, but just enough to give some shape and clarity to things. Charlie wondered if the openly pleasant interaction between his family on the porch had something to do with it. He hated to admit it to himself, but the short time he spent chatting and laughing with his mom, and brother and sister, felt good. Being on the porch talking as a family harkened back to the days before–before the divorce, before the weight heaved on him, before the wall went up. Was he finally getting over it? Maybe, he thought to himself, getting over it didn't happen overnight. Perhaps it was a process?

In any event, or for whatever reason, Charlie felt better, lighter. All the time he was on the porch with his family, his phone had been blowing up in his pocket. Normally, he would have disengaged from whatever conversation was taking place and disappear into the tiny glowing hand-held box. It was a sticking point for his mom. She'd go on about how it was rude, or telegraphed the wrong message, or showed people he didn't care to be where he was, or something along the lines that somehow made Charlie the one at fault. There was something so right about listening to Carson go on about his exploits with Ethan, and Sarah's running commentary on the chosen beach wear of passers-by, or this game his two younger siblings had called Shoeb, or Non-Shoeb where they guessed which category people walking by fell into, and how his mom's face just seemed to glow as she listened to her children, and soaked up everything, that he let his phone take a back seat for a change. He thought that life behind the wall he erected maybe worked the opposite of his intention. Rather than keep people away, it sealed him inside.

Around the sixteenth or seventeenth ping his mom smiled at him and said, "Go ahead, Charlie. Someone is obviously in need of your attention."

"Probably his boyfriend," Sarah shot across his bow. Charlie let it pass.

"Or maybe his girlfriend," Carson volleyed, to which Miriam raised an eyebrow.

Charlie dug his phone out of his pocket. All the texts were from Jackson. The second to last simply said **donuts.** The last was:
At Browns, where are you? Almost all gone!

Charlie smiled, a simple gesture, but when Charlie raised his head from his phone, he matched eyes with his mom. Miriam's eyes were wide, and her free hand covering her mouth as if she had just seen something awe-inspiring.

Sarah quick slapped Charlie's thigh, saying, "Let me guess. Jackson. He wants donuts."

Taken by Sarah's accuracy, Charlie shook his head in disbelief. "Yeah. How'd you know?"

Smugly shrugging her shoulders, Charlie's little sister said, "It's a talent," which caused his mother to chuckle.

"Go ahead, Charlie," his mom said. "You know how Jackson gets when he's hungry."

He did know how Jackson got when he was hungry, and it wasn't pretty. A hungry Jackson was a cross between a sullen twelve-year-old and an angry beaver. "You sure? I mean, Jackson will be fine without me." *What just popped out of my mouth?* he thought. Was he dehydrated, he wondered? Perhaps that was why he didn't bolt given the opportunity? He'd read somewhere that dehydrated people often talk gibberish, or was that something Jackson had said? Regardless, his own willingness to stay on the porch with his family surprised him. He thought, for a hot second, that perhaps he was on the verge of a stroke.

Miriam nodded her approval. Charlie smiled and nodded in agreement. He stepped out of the swing and disappeared inside the house. A minute or so later, he walked his bike from behind the house and paused on the sidewalk in front of the McIntyre residence.

"Okay. Uhm… I guess I'll see everyone later?" *What the hell is happening*? his mind screamed at him. *Are you actually making plans with your family?* it queried. *What is wrong with you?* Charlie shook his shoulders the way you do when a shiver runs up your spine.

Catching the action, Miriam cocked her head. "Everything alright, Charlie?"

"Huh? Oh, yeah. Just the breeze, I guess. So, uhm, yeah. See ya." Charlie hopped on his bike and peddled off towards the boardwalk.

It wasn't long before he nosed his bike towards the Second Street ramp onto the boardwalk. He leaned the bike left and continued the short distance to Brown's. A short way down the boardwalk from where he was, he could see Jackson sitting on a bench with a box of donuts in his lap. He wasn't prepared for Jackson to be with Joey, and the sight of him caused some pause in Charlie. To see them both sitting there, an outsider wouldn't think that they were together, in that way, just two guys, sitting on a bench, shoving donuts into their faces. Nothing unusual there, but on closer inspection, little things came to light that hinted at the fact that these two boys were more than just friends. The closeness with which they sat to each other, one boy's thigh resting on the other's, hand glancing a knee, shoulders brushing. Charlie wasn't quite yet used to Jackson and Joey being a couple. Admittedly, while he seemed to come to terms with his best friend being gay, he wasn't quite comfortable yet with Jackson actually acting on his feelings. Also, when Charlie saw them together, there was a splinter of resentment festering just under the skin. Charlie grappled with that feeling many nights as he lay awake, staring at his ceiling, trying to figure it all out. The best he could come up with was Jackson had begun to spend more time with Joey than with him. Then Charlie would think, *haven't I begun to spend more time with Madison? How is it different?* The jury still hadn't returned a verdict.

Charlie slowed his bike and hopped off beside of the bench. He leaned his bike against the rail and said, "Hope you saved one for me."

Scoffing, as if hearing the most ridiculous statement in the world, Jackson replied, "Of course. Cinnamon. Your favorite."

Charlie tossed his head at Joey as he reached into the box. "Hey Joey, what's up?" He ripped off a good portion of the donut and popped it in his mouth. *How could anyone think Ove's had better donuts?* he wondered to himself as his taste buds exploded and did a happy dance. He polished off the rest of that donut and reached in for another. Mouth still full, he mumbled at Jackson, "What do I owe you? I'll Venmo you."

"Forget about it, son. Consider it part of your birthday present."

Joey nodded. "Yeah, that's right. Someone turns seventeen in a week or so." It struck Charlie as odd that Joey would remember his birthday was in July. Granted, he had known Joey for a good many years, but never did Charlie think that Joey would remember anyone's birthday but his own. "Having been seventeen since the end of May, I can say with all certainty that there doesn't seem to be a big difference in my life." Then, as if realizing he had just put his foot in his mouth, turned to Jackson and added, "Well, except for you."

"Nice save, ass."

"Yeah, well, it's just a number," Charlie replied, mouth still full of donut.

Jackson placed his hand on Joey's thigh, and Charlie cringed mentally, then felt bad about it. Looking up at Charlie, he said, "So, hey, I thought you may have ghosted me. Was your phone dead?"

"Nah. Was just sitting on the porch with the family. Evidently, my mom and siblings have coffee hour every day. Seems I've been sleeping through it all summer. Go figure."

Jackson choked on his donut upon hearing Charlie's statement. Raising an eyebrow, he said, "You mean, you had Miriam time without getting into a fight?"

Charlie laughed, "Yeah. Right? More so, Sarah didn't hurl any insults my way. And Carson was actually entertaining. The whole experience was…" Charlie paused and scratched his chin in search of a word to describe the time spent with his family.

"Surreal?" Joey provided, which prompted both Charlie and Jackson to turn and stare at him as if he had just taken the Lord's name in vain in the common room of the Villa Maria by the Sea convent. "What?" Joey scoffed, obviously offended, "Don't let the fabulous physique and jock status fool you. I held down a three-point-five last year," he said, trying to dispel that which was assumed. "Jesus Christ," he said, half insulted, half for effect.

"Surreal," Charlie finished.

Joey placed his hand on top of Jackson's hand, that was already on Joey's thigh. Charlie looked away, unexpectedly and inexplicably, uncomfortable.

"Speaking of surreal," Jackson said, "I was out walking Keefer this morning, down on Beach Street, over by Gardens Road heading back to my house, when I thought I saw Kelsey, Logan, Madison, and Asher in line at The Sand House Kitchen. But by the time I got close enough, they must have been seated." Charlie could feel his stomach tense at the mention of Asher's name.

"Wait. What?" Charlie asked. "You saw who?" his voice rising a bit. Jackson could see his jaw grinding.

Suddenly reminded of the tenuous relationship his best friend shared with Asher, Jackson spoke markedly, trying to back-pedal away from any unintentional angst he may have just caused his best-friend. "Well… I, uhm, thought I saw Madison with Kelsey, Logan, and Asher at The Sand House Kitchen. But, um… I couldn't be sure, because, like I said, I was on Beach by Garden, and that's a good distance away. I mean, it's July, you know? The island is full of Shoebies. Could've been doppelgangers," Jackson trailed off.

Charlie flashed back to the runner on the beach early that morning. His stomach tightened.

"Anyway," Jackson continued, "couldn't be one-hundred percent sure." He turned to Joey and said with his eyes, *a little help here.*

Joey, surprisingly in tune with Jackson, piped up, "So, hey. The Fourth is coming up." Jackson smiled, thankful for the change of subject.

"Yeah. Kelsey is still planning on a party at her house. We have nothing else to do. Should be fun. The beach will be packed. Might as well hang at her place. She has a pool and all," Jackson said, sounding very much like Captain Obvious.

Taking a deep breath, Charlie said, "Yeah. I mean, I guess. Sure. That could be fun. Kelsey's pool parties usually are."

The image of Madison and an unknown jogger running down the beach still played in his mind, which morphed into Madison and Asher walking together down the street. A flick of motion caught his eye. Instinctively looking towards it, Charlie caught Joey curling his fingers into Jackson's. Charlie's anxiety spiked. His abdominals felt like he had just done three sets of eighty sit-ups. *Why was this bothering him so much?* Jackson, noticing Charlie's gaze intently fixated on his and Joey's hands, and the pained expression on his face, uncurled his fingers and placed his hand on his leg. He adjusted his position on the bench so there was a bit more room between himself and Joey. Charlie looked at Jackson and could feel his cheeks burn. He'd hoped he didn't make Jackson feel uncomfortable, knowing full well he did. He shot Jackson an 'I'm sorry' look. Jackson nodded, feeling a bit disheartened. Charlie felt like he was crawling out of his skin.

"So, hey. I... uhm, guess I'll leave you two to it," Charlie said, grabbing his bike by the handles. He spun it around so it faced in the opposite direction and hopped on.

"What's up? Where are you going?" Jackson said.

"I, um, I gotta clean my side of the room. I, uhm... figure I'll capitalize on the good vibes from this morning and make Miriam happy. Catch up later, okay?"

Pushing off of the boardwalk, Charlie pedaled away. Jackson couldn't help but feel a little deflated. Charlie was never a good liar, nor was he good at masking his feelings. He could see how uncomfortable Charlie was, being there, talking with him and Joey. A cloud of worry settled over Jackson, darkening the day.

"What's his problem?" Joey asked as Charlie grew smaller with distance.

Jackson knew precisely what Charlie's problem was. As much as it pained him to say it aloud, he did, "Us."

"Huh?" Joey asked. "What did we do? I was nice."

Smiling weakly, Jackson said, "I don't think it's what we did. More so, it's what we are." Jackson watched as his best friend pedaled down the boardwalk, growing smaller each second. Jackson's hope was that Charlie's ideology, his thinking of him as his friend, wasn't growing smaller as well.

■   ■   ■

Down by the Gardens Plaza Condominiums that stretched above the beach casting its shadow on the boardwalk, Charlie dug his cell phone out of his pocket. With single handed expertise, he pumped out a text:

Hey. Whacha ya doin?

Nothing much, you?

On my bike. Just left Jackson and Joey. Donuts at Browns.

Sounds like fun. Though you know Ove's has better donuts ☺

Haha. Old argument. Same outcome.
You with anyone?

Kelsey. Having lunch.

Just the two of you?

Ellipses filled Charlie's screen, then stopped. It was a few seconds before they appeared again, heralding the arrival of a response.

Yep.

Where are you?
Want company?

Another hesitation. Then…

You know I always do, but
It's kind of a girl's day.
Maybe later? Beach?

Sure. Cya.

Okay. Cya.

Charlie shoved the phone back into his pocket. He banked his bike to the right and headed down the Fifth Street ramp off of the boardwalk. Hitting the street, he dropped his head and pedaled. Leaning into the turn onto Atlantic, he let loose. He wove through the streets, gaining speed and momentum with each block. When he picked his head back up, certain his lungs were about to give out, he found himself at Eighteenth Street and Bay. He slowed to a crawl and hopped off. Letting his bike drop onto the sidewalk, he grabbed some curb and waited for his breath to catch up to him. He wanted to believe Madison; he did, but what he saw on the beach, gelled with what Jackson said, made him certain Madison had lied to him.

Sensing, perhaps, that it had overstayed its welcome, the lightness of the day that had visited Charlie, promptly headed to the front desk and checked out.

■   ■   ■

Madison placed her phone face down on the table at which she sat with Kelsey, Asher, and Logan. The waitress had just dropped their lunch onto the picnic table. Her iPhone jockeyed for space amidst the oversized plates of breakfast omelets, French toast, lobster burgers, and tuna poke bowls. She felt guilty for telling Charlie a lie. Though, she rationalized, it wasn't exactly a lie, was it? She was with Kelsey, that much was truth and she was having lunch. Knowing Charlie's inexplicable issue with Asher, though, she thought it best not to mention anyone beyond Kelsey. What does the Catholic church call that? she wondered. A sin of omission? Maybe that's why she felt a little culpable.

"Who was that?" Kelsey asked, turning her attention away from Logan. The two of them had become quite the item over the past few weeks.

Madison met her eyes. "Charlie. He was wondering where I was, what I was up to."

Asher leveled his gaze at her. "Oh really? Did you tell him where you were?" he asked.

"I told him I was with Kelsey."

Asher smirked, "Just Kelsey? 'Cause I'm counting two more people sitting at this table, Mads. You tell him I was here, too?" his tone suggesting more of a challenge than a question.

Logan spoke up, tugging on Asher's leash, "Back off, Ash."

Asher turned to face his brother. "What?" he said with a shrug. "It's a legit question, Logan. I mean, we're both here too." Then, turning back to face Madison, he said, "So, Mads. What'd you tell him?"

Madison looked at Kelsey. In the back of her head, the reason Kelsey called and invited her to this luncheon was beginning to materialize. It was becoming clear to Madison, too, that maybe the morning jogs may not be as friendly as she once thought. Kelsey smiled weakly; the sudden tension spilled like so much salt on the table, apparent on her face. "It's just that…" Madison began.

"It's just that, what? You don't want him to know that we're together?" Asher jumped in. "That you're here with me and Logan. The Interlopers. Or is it that you don't want him to know you're with me?" Asher smirked that smirk.

Madison could feel her guard go up, "No, Asher" she said tersely. "Well, not exactly. You're right. I didn't want him to know I was here with you. You do something to him." She regretted her words almost immediately. She felt like she had just let slip to Thanos the exact location of an Infinity Stone. Asher pounced.

"What do I do to him, Mads?"

Logan tried to deflect once again. "Ash, dial it back, bro. I mean it."

Asher scoffed at his older brother's attempt at authority. He turned back to Madison and waited for an answer. Kelsey began nervously playing with the paper sleeve from her straw, ripping off pieces and rolling tiny balls. Finally, with a shoulder shrug meant to dismiss the entire conversation, he said, "whatever."

"You're right, Asher. I should've told Charlie the whole truth. I just didn't want to get into it over text messaging. He's just been…" she hesitated, then changed direction, "I'll tell him when I see him. I mean, we're just having lunch, right?" She asked in a way that seemed like she was trying to convince herself.

"Sure," Kelsey chimed in. "Lunch with friends. Perfectly harmless." She laughed and patted Logan on the forearm.

"Yeah. Lunch with friends," Asher repeated. "Anyway. Not sure what you see in Chuck. But if ever you grow tired of his brooding moodiness, I'm pretty sure there are plenty of guys who would want to get with you, Mads. Plenty. In fact, some are probably closer than you think." Asher let his last sentence hang in the air. He began stuffing fries into his mouth.

Kelsey did her best to steer the conversation in a new direction by bringing up her Fourth of July pool party. Logan and Asher were keen to attend. Logan commenting that the in-ground pool was the thing he missed the most about the Vineyard house. Asher added his dad had been talking about sinking one in the yard for the next season. Madison, only half listening, tried to process what had just happened. How an outwardly innocent invitation to lunch seemed to harbor a secret intention that was somehow lost in translation.

SIX

Lunch ended around one-fifteen or so. The boys had a three o'clock tee-time and wanted to shower and change into something more 'golf appropriate', because board shorts and tanks are not permitted at Harbor Pines. They said their 'so-longs' at Kelsey's house, and the boys continued on their way to First Street. Things were left that maybe they would see each other later, though Madison had no doubt that Kelsey and Logan would most definitely do just that. Madison was also fairly certain that Asher would find a way to be somewhere she was. She hated to admit it, but once the mood lightened after they abandoned the Charlie conversation and her lie of omission, the time went well. It was actually enjoyable. Logan could be quite charming and funny. Even Asher, when he put his ego in the back seat, was pleasant to be around. He also wasn't too bad to look at either. In fact, Madison thought Asher was probably one of the most handsome boys she'd ever met, which certainly added to his already engorged ego.

Her mind then drifted to Charlie. He was certainly handsome as well, not like Asher's model good looks, but in a down-to-earth-boy-next-door kind of way. What made Charlie more attractive was the fact that Charlie didn't realize how attractive he was. She always liked that about him. Charlie was genuinely surprised if you complimented him or told him he looked good. He'd blush, say thanks, cast his eyes quickly to the ground, and smile that charming smile revealing his one dimple on his right cheek. Charlie was the opposite of Asher. Asher knew he was beautiful. He projected that understanding–which, in a bad-boy-sort-of-way, worked for him.

Sitting with her legs dangling in the cool, crystal, chlorine laced water that filled Kelsey's pool, she still felt conflicted. Asher's intentions were obvious. If she stopped to think about it, he telegraphed his intentions quite clearly pretty much from shortly after their first hello. Marry that to the early morning jogs, and Madison chastised herself for being so blind, then checked herself. Maybe she wasn't blind to his macking on her, so much as she chose not to see the forest for the trees. Maybe she liked the attention? If that was the case, she wasn't being fair to Charlie or Asher, though she didn't ask for Asher's attention. He's freely giving it. As far as she could tell, she hadn't led him to believe anything other than they were friends. Was it so wrong to bask in his notice?

Kelsey emerged from the house carrying two iced teas and a bag of Twizzlers. She padded over on bare feet to where Madison was sitting on the edge of the deep end of the kidney-shaped pool and handed a drink to Madison. She sat down next to her friend and dropped her legs into the water.

"Wow. I'm surprised it's still so cool. Usually by the beginning of July it's like bath water." Turning to Madison, she asked, "You looked lost in thought. Everything alright?"

Was everything alright? Madison thought. "Oh. Yeah… yeah, everything is great. I was just thinking about lunch, is all." She plunged her hand into the bag of Twizzlers and ripped off two strands.

Kelsey swallowed some iced tea. "Yeah. That was a lot of fun. Honestly, I don't know how boys can eat so much, and never gain weight. Hate them!" Kelsey said in mock loathing. "It's kind of nice to get to know Asher a little better, too. I mean, at first, I thought *'what a stuck-up little DB'*, but once you get to know him, he's not too bad."

Madison laughed. "I was thinking the same thing. And, damn, if he's not easy on the eyes."

Kelsey raised her glass, gesturing a toast, and Madison clicked hers against the side of Kelsey's, "I'll drink to that, Mads."

Madison leaned back onto her forearms and reclined against the hardscape of the pool deck. She drew her hair back away from her face with her right hand and looped it around the right side of her neck. Sipping from her tea, she idly kicked her legs in the water, turning up waves that meandered across the pool width. "Can I ask you something, Kels?"

"Sure, Mads. You know that."

She took a breath, hesitated for a moment, and said, "Is it me, or is Asher wanting to be more than just my friend?"

Kelsey laughed amusingly. "Girl, it is not you. That boy is totally macking on you. And he's not being subtle about it either. Logan tells me that Asher is trying his best to get you to kick Charlie to the curb…"

"What? So, you knew? I mean, you know Asher is trying to get between me and Charlie? And you still invited me to lunch? What the hell, Kelsey?" Madison's voice rose an octave.

Kelsey, perhaps realizing she had said a bit too much, tried to deflect. "Well, Madison. I mean, yeah, I knew Asher was hot for you. But I didn't think his coming to lunch was a ploy to get you to dump Charlie."

"Why didn't you say something?"

"Like what? *Oh, by the way, Asher is hot for you and he's trying to break you and Charlie up?* You're a big girl, Madison. Surely you can see that he likes you. If you don't, you're just not paying attention, or you refuse to see it. Either way, Asher isn't being shy about it. Even Charlie has it figured out."

Madison turned to face her friend. Incredulously, she asked, "You think?"

Shaking her head in disbelief, Kelsey said simply, "Mads, Charlie practically goes postal every time Asher is around. Why do you think that is?"

Madison considered her response. She was right; it was fairly obvious that Charlie did not, in any way, shape, or form like Asher. She thought it was just a clash of personalities, but now that she thought about it... "I would think that Charlie is secure in our relationship, and that he has nothing to worry about. That's what I think."

"Oh girlfriend," Kelsey said sardonically, "that's because you are thinking like the intelligent woman that you are. In matters such as these, you need to think like the testosterone laced, territorial, corner-pissing teen-age boys of which we happen to call our friends. In their hormone spiked brains, this is medieval times, and they're knights jousting for your attention."

Both girls laughed at Kelsey's overly dramatic, albeit accurate, explanation. "Honestly, Kelsey, where do you come up with this shit?"

Shrugging, Kelsey responded, "Sometimes I surprise myself. Anyway, I think we're all set for the Fourth..."

Madison's thoughts trailed off midway through her friend's recounting of the Fourth of July pool party she was going to throw. She couldn't help but be preoccupied by the new dilemma dropped in her lap. The realization that Asher wanted to be more than just friends weighed on her, as she was already way more than just friends with Charlie. There was still a lot of summer left, and the likelihood of the two boys not running into each other was slim to none. Her best friend was dating Asher's older brother. Kelsey was a part of their circle of friends that shared days and nights from June to the end of August for as long as Madison could remember. Logan was destined to become a part of that circle, if even peripherally. Which meant so too would Asher. She'd have to talk to Asher and explain to him that all they could be were friends. Deep down, she suspected Asher was the type of guy that no matter how much talking you did, he found ways not to hear what was being said. A chilly uneasiness settled over Madison there beneath the heat of the July sun.

SEVEN

Charlie maneuvered his bike up the brick walkway between his house and the next-door neighbor's and pulled it into the garage. He hopped off and let it fall to the floor. His sweat drenched T-shirt clung to his skin, and he struggled to get himself out of it. Once finally free, he let that drop to the floor as well and made his way over to the clothesline at the back of the yard, where he pulled off a towel. Walking over to the shower, he wiggled out of his remaining clothes and stepped inside.

The cool water falling over him rinsed the grime of his marathon bike ride away, but didn't do much to wash away his mood. He stood under the showerhead for a few minutes, letting the water fall on him like rain before he lathered. In the back of his mind, he just couldn't shake the idea that Madison was sneaking around with Asher. He knew it was ridiculous to allow himself to travel down this avenue of thought, but he just couldn't keep himself from hopping on that trolley. Madison wasn't the type of person who would do something like that, he told himself. She and he were dating, and he needed to believe that she respected that. Still, the streetcar of suspicious doubt chugged along with him onboard. "Jesus, Charlie," he said aloud as the water ran down his shoulders and back, "you're overreacting, again."

"Overreacting to what?" he heard his mother's voice from beyond the shower wall. "Is that you in there, Charlie?"

Great, he thought to himself, just great, "Who else would it be, Mom?" He answered in what he hoped was a pleasant enough tone.

"Honestly, Charlie. You and Carson sound the same these days. It's hard to tell who is talking sometimes. My little boys, both becoming men." Charlie was glad that a white plastic wall separated him from his mother's line of sight, not because he was in the shower wearing just his birthday suit, but because the eye-roll he just threw at her would certainly have been cause for a lecture. "What are you doing, anyway?" his mom asked.

Another eye-roll. "Um… showering?" Charlie answered, unable to curb the sarcasm in his tone.

"No kidding, Charles. I meant, what are you doing home in the middle of the day? I thought you'd be at the beach with Jackson."

"Yeah, I was, then I took a bike ride," *Oh*, his mind said, *is that what we're calling the anger induced, paranoid laced Tour de France you just took across half the island and back? A bike ride?* "Was sweaty and a little ripe when I got home, so I thought I'd shower."

"Oh, okay. I walked into the house from the front and could hear the shower. Just making sure it wasn't left running again. I'll be on the porch if you need me."

"What could I possibly need?" Charlie said beneath the noise of the running water. He swore parents everywhere must think that their kids can't manage without some sort of parental involvement. His mom was famous for Location and Aid Updates: *I'll be on the beach if you need me; I'll be in my room if you need me; I'll be at grandma's if you need me.*

Above the noise of the shower, he said, "Righty-o, Mom." Running his hands through his hair, he rinsed out any conditioner that might remain. To himself, he said, "You're imagining things with Madison and Asher, Charlie. Get a grip." He turned off the water, wrapped a towel around his waist, and went inside.

Once in the kitchen, he pulled a Coke out of the refrigerator, popped the tab, and headed out to the front porch, where he could hear his mother talking to someone. Pushing the screen door with his foot, he stepped out onto the porch, and was by surprise by the back of a man sitting in one of the rockers. For a second, he thought it was his dad, and his heart skipped a beat. Then he realized that the hair wasn't the right color, and neither was the posture. Stopping in mid-stride, at mid-porch, door slamming shut behind him, Charlie just managed an, "Oh, um…" before his mom jumped in a bit too effervescently.

"Oh, hey Charlie. This is Dan. He's a friend from work." The man who Charlie ever so briefly thought was his father shifted his position so he could turn and look at Charlie. Charlie, remembering he was in nothing but a bath towel, clutching a can of Coke, became very self-conscious. Reflexively, he dropped his free hand down in front of himself. Dan stood to shake Charlie's hand, which he had just dropped down in front of himself. In Charlie's mind, a real quandary materialized.

"Hey Charlie. It's nice to meet you," Dan said, right hand outstretched, stepping towards Charlie. "I've heard a lot about you."

You've heard a lot about me? *Funny, I haven't heard anything about you.* Charlie was motionless on the porch, eye-balling Dan the way a father might scrutinize his daughters' date when he showed up at the door. *Dan.* He was about his mom's age, maybe a little younger, with a white polo, khaki shorts, ubiquitous stubble, a haircut specifically quaffed to reflect a wind-tossed style, boat shoes, socks - definitely a Shoebie - and no wedding ring. Finally, Charlie took Dan's hand and pumped it slowly. He glanced at his mom, and then back at Dan, and then back at his mom.

"So…" Charlie asked, drawing out the *so* in a tone one might use when trying to size-up a situation, "is this a date?"

Dan let go of Charlie's hand and arced his eyebrows.

"Charlie!" his mother said in a fake amused tone that actually meant *wait until I get you alone, young man.* "Dan is renting a place over on St. Charles. We had lunch and then I invited him over for a drink."

Charlie's eyes darted to the small table between the rockers, noting the half-filled wine glasses. He also took note that neither his mother nor Dan denied it was a date. In fact, Charlie took particular notice of the way Dan cast a hopeful glance at his mother when Charlie asked if it was a date, and the ever so slight smile that played across his mother's face when her eyes and Dan's met briefly.

For no real reason, Charlie grew resentful. Who was this guy who had heard so much about him, anyway? What was he trying to do? "So. It's a date. I mean, wine in the middle of the afternoon says a little more than beer in the middle of the afternoon, don't you think, *Dan*?" Realizing that he might be caught in the middle of something he definitely did not want to be caught in the middle of, Dan just smiled awkwardly and somewhat sheepishly and sat back down.

From her seat, Miriam drew in a slow, purposeful breath, the way you would before you jumped off of the pool deck into the deep end. She leaned forward in her rocker and, in an almost a threating manner, rested her elbows on her thighs.

Through a smile that more resembled gritted teeth, she said pointedly, "Charlie, Dan's a friend. We're having some wine. We're adults. We can do that. I think maybe you should go put some clothes on now. Don't you?" Which was less of a question and more a statement of dismissal. "Or do you plan on standing on the front porch wrapped only in a towel for the rest of the afternoon?"

For a hot second, Charlie thought about plopping himself down on the swing on the opposite side of the porch. But, being clad in a towel that barely came to mid-thigh, which would provide to his mom, Dan, and any passerby, ample viewing of the family jewels, he decided against it. Instead, he threw one more suspicious look at his mother and turned to head inside. Half-way between the living room and the porch, Charlie hesitated. There are times in life when in a mere second you formulate something to say, realize you shouldn't say it, envision all the consequences that will come from saying it, know it's best left unsaid, but say it anyway. Charlie was in the middle of that second, and he chose poorly.

Turning over his shoulder, he volleyed a grenade into the space between Dan and his mother. "I'm not calling you dad," and then casually stepped inside. He didn't need to wait to see if the projectile landed, or if it even hit it's intended target. He knew it did.

Charlie, now in his bedroom, had barely yanked on a pair of shorts when there was a knock at his bedroom door, though to call it a knock would be somewhat inaccurate. This was more of a thump, two quick thumps to be precise, the kind produced when you use the side of your fist rather than your knuckles. Without waiting for an invitation to enter, the door swung open, and Charlie's mom stormed into his room. *At least she knocked this time,* he thought. Charlie squared himself, meeting his mother's gaze, ready for the fight.

"What was that all about, Charlie?" she asked in pinched, hushed tones. "Your behavior was unacceptable, young man." *I got the 'young man,'* Charlie thought. *Reserved only for the most egregious behaviors. Score.* "You embarrassed me, and you embarrassed Dan. You need to apologize to him."

Reaching for a T-shirt from the 'clean' pile on the floor, Charlie scoffed. As he wiggled himself into it, he said, "Apologize? For what? Dan's a big boy. He can take a little friendly banter." Charlie paused, thought, and then chose poorly for a second time, "Or did I hurt his feelings?" he said in a mock baby voice.

Miriam drew in another deep breath and took a step towards her son, dropping her voice a level. "You need to apologize for the 'date' comment, and you need to apologize for the last thing you said before you came into the house. Honestly, what were you thinking? You were rude and out of line."

His mother's remark stung. His heart rate increased tenfold. *I'm out of line. I'm out of line? Here we are six months since dad left and you're sitting on the front porch in the middle of the day tossing back wine like some amped up teenager hoping for a hook-up, and I'm out of line? Here we are six months since dad left and every morning I wake up with a knife in my gut because I just can't seem to move past this no matter how many times I tell myself I have to, and you're having lunch and cocktails with some dude from work, and I'm out of line? Here we are six months since dad left and all I do is hurt and you don't seem to notice, or care, and you're already with some other guy, and I'm out of line? Here we are six months since dad disappeared, and every day I struggle just to breathe. And I'm out of line?*

Charlie shook his head in stunned disbelief. "I'm not apologizing to anyone, Miriam. Not to you, and certainly not to some guy you're hoping to hook up with. Oh, and you should probably do some research on that term if you're planning on using it."

They stood for a long moment, as he and his mom seemed too often do these days, eye to eye, shoulder to shoulder, looking into each other, but not seeing. Charlie turned and picked up his iPhone from the end of the bed and slipped into his flip-flops. His comments were building in his head, pushing against the sides of his skull, screaming for release: mean, ugly comments he knew he'd regret if he said them. He moved past his mother to the bedroom door, hoping against all hope that he could make it out before he chose poorly for the third time, but the thing with angry words is they tend to be a force not easily reckoned with. Like a tidal wave, there isn't much one can do to stop the surge. Charlie paused in the doorway. Without turning, he pulled the pin and lobbed another grenade, "Hopefully, you won't drive him away like you did, dad."

The sound of his mother's sharp inhale was all the confirmation Charlie needed to know that he hit the target once again.

■   ■   ■

"And she's sitting there on the porch all googly eyed and gushy like some crushing eighth grader introducing her boyfriend to her posse for the first time, '*Oh, hey, this is Dan, isn't he wonderful?*' Charlie said in an exaggerated falsetto, meant to mimic an adolescent girl. *'Just look at us drinking wine in the middle of the day, trying to pretend it's not a date, but we both hope that it is.'* I mean, Jesus, for real? Is she going to start dating men? 'Cause that is messed up. I hope to Christ that I never drown or get run over, or some other horrible tragedy that kills me because, obviously, Miriam has no trouble moving on. She'd probably wait for what she thinks to be an acceptable amount of time, like, I don't know, thirty days, and then just adopt a teenage boy from Russia or somewhere to replace me. If she does that, don't you be his friend, Jackson, because I will haunt you. For real…"

Jackson had been listening to his friend rant for about fifteen minutes now. He knew it was best to just wait until the rant ran out of steam, which it seemed to be doing. Charlie stepped out onto the second-floor porch minutes after the text arrived asking where Jackson was, already with a full head of steam about him. If Charlie were a cartoon, white clouds would have been billowing out of his ears. He dropped into the chair next to Jackson and just started talking. It took Jackson a minute or so to figure out just what the hell his friend was raving about, but he got the gist of it. The rest of the time Jackson spent trying to figure out why Charlie was all hype.

After a pause where no more words came from Charlie, Jackson took the opportunity to speak, albeit in measured words. "So, uhm… what if, and just hear me out, what if this Dan guy is just a friend? I mean, it's not unusual for our parents to have a few drinks in the middle of the day with friends, right? So, maybe there is truth to what Miriam said… he's renting a house, they had lunch, and then some drinks… mid-day… you know teachers, they were probably talking about how awful administrators are, or some godawful pain in the ass kid from the school year, or something like that…" Jackson trailed off waiting to gauge his friend's reaction before he continued, but Charlie just stared out across the railing. "… and I don't think Miriam would replace you with a Russian orphan should you die, which I hope you don't because that would break me, like forever. And rest assured, if she did, you know, replace you with a Russian orphan, which again, I don't think that she would, but if she did, I would never be his friend, ever..." Jackson paused again hoping his attempt at some humor would soften some of the space between them right now. He absentmindedly thrummed his fingers on the arm of the chair in which he was sitting as he watched his friend for some response.

Shaking his head and turning to face Jackson, Charlie said, "I just can't believe it, is all." He shrugged his shoulders and rested his chin in his hand. "I just can't believe it."

Jackson knew Charlie's statement opened a door for some honest dialogue about his parent's divorce. He knew its weight bore down on his best friend every single day, and he knew Charlie was beginning to suffocate under it. He also knew from firsthand experience how easily Charlie flew off the handle these days, but Charlie was his friend, and sometimes being a friend means you have to play the bad cop role. Cautiously, Jackson pushed, "What can't you believe, Charlie?"

Charlie looked a bit incredulously at his friend. "What do you mean, Jackson?"

"What can't you believe, Charlie? That your mom was drinking in the middle of the day with a friend? Or that your mom may have been drinking with someone she hopes to begin a relationship with?" Proud of himself for putting it out there, Jackson braced against the coming explosion, literally gripping the arms of his chair.

Much to his surprise, it didn't come. Instead, Jackson watched as his friend's eyes teared up, then just as quickly cleared. Softly, in almost a hurt tone, Charlie said, "It's only been six months, Jackson." He shrugged, "I don't know, it just doesn't seem long enough, you know?"

Jackson spoke markedly as he slowly nodded. "I don't know, Charlie. I can't begin to know what you or your family are feeling, or what you're going through." He paused and looked up at the porch ceiling as if the words he was going to say were somehow there. "But, you're right. It's been six months. Maybe," Jackson paused again. He knew what he had to say, what Charlie needed to hear. He weighed the consequences of the words he was about to say, but, Jackson decided, a hard slap of honesty is sometimes needed to knock some sense into you. "Maybe your mom has realized *it is* time to move on, to adjust to this new normal, to live with it as best she can, you know? Maybe, Charlie, it's time for you to do the same."

Jackson watched his friend intently, hoping he hadn't said too much or pushed too far. He still gripped the arms of his chair. Charlie swallowed hard and took a deep breath. He turned again to look at his friend and said in clipped words, "I know, Jackson. Don't you think that I've..." Charlie's knee began to bounce frantically, as he stopped in mid-sentence, "I've tried, I have, but every day I wake up, and it's there..." Charlie's voice broke. He stopped again and looked away, pinching his lower lip between his thumb and forefinger. A small lump appeared in Jackson's throat. Regaining some composure, Charlie tried to continue. Exhaling slowly, he said, "Every day. Every day... I wake up, and I'm just... I'm just filled with..." but he couldn't finish the sentence. Instead, he bit his lower lip and just shook his head.

Jackson sat silently for a bit. Whatever Charlie was going through, it was painful for him, and Jackson didn't want to push him too hard. He knew Charlie. He knew when he was ready, he'd talk. Jackson just hoped that his friend became ready before he broke under the weight of what he was carrying with him.

"Remember when we were kids?" Jackson asked. Charlie let out a single breath laugh and nodded. "We'd build sandcastles down in the wet sand. We'd spend hours just piling up sand and shaping and sculpting until we created these giant, elaborate builds, with ramparts, and towers, and stairs. We'd build whole kingdoms out of sand."

Charlie smiled in agreement; his eyes glossed with memories. "Yeah, I remember that. Seems so long ago now, doesn't it?"

It was Jackson's turn to nod in agreement. "Then, as the tide came in, we'd dig trenches to divert the creeping ocean around them, prop up boogie boards, and pile mud walls up in V shapes to deflect the ocean. We tried our damnedest to stop the crumble, to keep at bay what we knew we couldn't. In the end, no matter how hard we tried, we couldn't hold back the tide, and everything that was there, everything we built, was swallowed by the sea. Erased. But it was okay, because we knew we would just start again the next day, fresh." Jackson paused, and Charlie wondered where he was going with this sudden burst of nostalgia. Continuing softly and with heartfelt words, Jackson said, "Regarding your dad leaving, Charlie, maybe you're just holding back the tide. And we both know how that ends."

Charlie's breath caught in his throat. Jackson could wax philosophical with the best of them, throwing down BS like a pro, but now and again, his insight was spot on impressive. With a small chuckle, Charlie said, "It all ends in tears, anyway."

Jackson pulled his eyebrows together in confusion.

"Jack Kerouac?" Charlie smiled at his friend, impressed with himself for providing a quote his well-read friend did not know. "The Dharma Bums. For some reason, that line stuck with me."

"Color me impressed."

"What? Don't let the fabulous physique and jock status fool you. I held down a three-point five last year," Charlie said, causing both boys to break out into hearty laughter. Unexpectedly feeling an overwhelming fondness for this moment, Charlie said, "Thanks, Jackson. For this. I mean, just the two of us, like it used to be. I miss this. A lot sometimes."

Jackson looked long and hard at his friend. He knew exactly what Charlie was talking about. Since Madison and Joey entered their lives, the occasions of just the two of them hanging out grew fewer and fewer. While Jackson enjoyed his time with Joey, nothing compared to his time with Charlie. "Yeah. Me too, Charlie."

"You thinking what I'm thinking?" Charlie asked his friend.

Jackson laughed, "If you're thinking some Crunchik'n, I am."

"Hells yeah!" Charlie replied.

In seconds, both boys were off the porch, on the street, and heading for the boardwalk. The sun beat down, baking everything in its heat. Shimmering bands of light rose from the cement and macadam. The sky stretched endlessly on towards the horizon, painfully blue, and without a single cloud. *On days like this,* Charlie thought as he and Jackson walked on, *the sun just hits different.*

EIGHT

The ambient glow from the streetlights and houses tried their best to blot out the starlight from the sky, but the night was clear and without a moon. Charlie marveled at how many stars still littered the sky despite the surrounding illumination. He was lying next to Madison in the middle of the tennis courts across the street from the high school. The clay of the court was still warm from the daytime sun, and it felt good on the backs of his thighs and arms. Shoulder to shoulder, left hand entwined in her right, Charlie drank in the moment. They weren't talking much, or barely at all, and surprisingly, their phones were just as silent. A cool breeze swept lazily across them in stark contrast to the warmth beneath them. Sounds of traffic, people talking, and the occasional skateboard wafted with the breeze. It was a perfect summer night.

The nights had been ending this way more and more as the summer progressed. Charlie and his friends would meet up somewhere—the boardwalk, the beach, Annie's, someone's porch—but as the night grew late, people broke off with their person of interest and stole away into the evening. Admittedly, it was still hard for Charlie to watch as Jackson and Joey bade their goodnights to everyone and walked off. Sometimes they held hands and walked shoulder to shoulder. Sometimes they just appeared as friends. But Charlie knew they were more than just friends, another new reality he would just need to get used to. He missed hanging out with Jackson, just Jackson, especially at night. He missed the conversations that, much like a winding, slow-moving river, lazily flowed from topic to topic. He missed the laughter. Those times with Jackson were not just fun, but deeply personal, as they shared with one another those things they shared with no one else. Dreams, ambitions, and insecurities, that passed only between the best of friends.

Madison squeezed his hand, returning him to the moment. As much as he missed the way his friendship was with Jackson, he liked this as well. Being with Madison often hushed his inner scream. Being alone with her helped silence the dialogue he had with himself, helped quiet the angst. Even now, in silence, the feel of her fingers interlocked with his, the pressure of her thigh against his thigh, the smell of her conditioner that teased his nose now and again as it caught on the wind, kept him and his mind in the moment. This moment, lying next to Madison, staring up at the stars, heart fluttering ever so slightly for reasons unrelated to the ones that these days caused his pulse to quicken. This moment was perfect. He wished he could just lie there all night and let the world pass him by.

"Have you ever thought that each one of those stars is a sun, maybe like ours? And that each one of those suns could be at the center of its own solar system, and that each one of those solar systems could have a planet capable of supporting life?" Charlie said softly and thoughtfully, "And have you ever wondered that if that was the case, are there life forms, people, maybe like us, or maybe completely different, lying on their backs staring out into the night sky of their planet, wondering whether each one of those stars is a sun, maybe like theirs. And that each one of those suns could be at the center of its own solar system, and that each one of those solar systems could have a planet capable of supporting life?"

Madison turned her head to look at Charlie. "Funny. I was about to ask you what you were thinking about, now I know." She paused and looked back up at the sky, "I guess it would be arrogant of us," she continued quietly, "to assume that we are the only life in all the universe. But, if there is one thing at which humans excel, it's arrogance," she finished.

"Truth," Charlie said, never taking his eyes from the sky. Madison rolled to face him and propped up on an elbow. Gently, she ran her fingers through his hair, lovingly sweeping it off of his forehead. Charlie turned his head to meet her gaze and smiled. There was something electric about Madison running her hands through his hair, something intimate about the simple act that Charlie enjoyed, and his body warmed to her touch. Madison leaned in and kissed him.

"What was that for?" he asked, smiling.

Madison shrugged. "You're cute, I guess," she said, cupping his chin in her hand.

"You guess?" Charlie said with a chuckle and then returned the kiss with a longer one.

"That was nice," Madison said.

"Thanks," Charlie said, "I've been practicing with Jackson." A year ago, a few weeks ago even, that statement would have been met with the jest with which it was meant. But this wasn't a year ago, or even a few weeks ago. Remembering the new reality with Jackson, Charlie felt compelled to clarify. He stuttered clumsily. "Oh, uhm... yeah. I mean, Jackson and I aren't actually, you know...?

Madison reached over and placed a finger on Charlie's mouth. "Relax Captain Hetero. I know you were just kidding." Charlie nodded and looked away, somewhat embarrassed. A year ago, or even a few weeks ago, he wouldn't have tried to explain it away, or defend himself. Why now? he wondered. "Can I ask you something, Charlie?" Madison continued.

"Of course."

"Well, you and Jackson. Are you guys okay?" Madison asked quietly.

Charlie sat up, confused a little. "What do you mean?"

Sitting up as well, Madison tried to clarify, "I guess I'm asking if you're okay with Jackson being gay? I know how close you guys have always been, and you must have been blindsided by his coming out. I mean, we all were, in a way, I guess. But, well… are you okay?"

That is an excellent question, Madison. For the most part, Charlie was okay with Jackson being gay, except when Jackson was with Joey. Then Charlie struggled, and he wasn't sure why. He knew he shouldn't. He knew that Jackson and Joey were acting the same way he and Madison did, the same way Kelsey and Logan did, but for some reason… he shook the thought away.

"Yeah. Yeah, of course. Why do you ask?" Suddenly worried, Charlie added, "Am I giving off a vibe or something?"

Madison laughed, "No, not really. But…" she broke off.

"But what?" Charlie poked.

Hesitantly, Madison said, "It's just that sometimes, when Jackson and Joey are together, you know–*together*, you look, I don't know…" Madison looked up to the sky, searching for the right word. "… uncomfortable, I guess is a good word."

He must have been giving off a vibe. Truth was, whenever Jackson acted on his affection for Joey, Charlie was uncomfortable. When he saw Jackson and Joey kiss, or hold hands, or any intimate contact between them, no matter how small or fleeting, it was as if Charlie didn't know who Jackson was. It still surprised him, and yeah, it did make him uncomfortable, he admitted to himself. He just didn't know why. Smirking like he was just caught doing something bad, Charlie said, "So I am giving off a vibe. Cuff me, officer."

"Oh, you'd like that too much, Charles McIntyre," Madison said with a laugh. "You're not giving off a vibe, it's just something I've noticed because you're so damned cute I'm always looking at you." She planted another kiss on Charlie's face.

So, if Madison could pick up Charlie's uneasiness, that meant that Jackson probably can too. Suddenly, Charlie felt badly about that.

"Yeah, I guess, sometimes it makes me uncomfortable, and I hate myself for feeling that way. It's just that... I don't know," he shrugged. Charlie searched himself for a reason. "It's just that I've always thought of him as being straight, you know? I mean, growing up, that's just the way Jackson was in my head. It's just the way all my friends are in my head, you know?" Madison nodded. "We always talked about girls, and who was hot, and who had a great body, and..."

Madison broke in, "Oh? Who *is* hot? Who *has* a great body?" she said with a smile. "Tell me, Charles McIntyre."

"Oh stop. Like you and Kelsey don't do the same thing with boys? I mean, Jesus, every time Shane is sitting in the lifeguard stand, Kelsey works herself into a lather," Charlie retorted.

"Guilty. Cuff me, officer," Madison said, still smiling, holding both arms out with her wrists together.

Charlie smiled back, "Anyway, I guess in my head, Jackson is still that kid and when I see him holding hands with Joey, or kissing Joey, it still just catches me off guard." He shrugged again, ending his sentence.

Nodding, Madison said, "Yeah. I get that. But, you know, Jackson is still that kid, Charlie. That kid you've grown up with. That kid who is your best friend. That kid who probably knows more about you than I do, or your mother does, or anyone else does. He loves you. And you love him."

The mention of the word 'love' caused Charlie to shift his position on the tennis court ground. Feeling his cheeks flush, and not wanting to explore his unresolved issues with Jackson's sexuality, Charlie attempted to deflect with humor, "Well, isn't this romantic? Me and my girlfriend, sitting alone under a starlit sky, talking about my gay best friend and how much he loves me. How tender."

Madison leaned in again and kissed him. Charlie met and returned the kiss. The two held that embrace for an amount of time that caused, in Charlie, some rerouting of blood.

"So," Madison said, breaking the embrace, "new topic." Charlie rolled his eyes jokingly. "Don't you roll your eyes at me, Charlie McIntyre, especially when the new topic just so happens to be your birthday."

"Well, then. I take my eye roll back," Charlie apologized.

Madison pushed some of Charlie's hair away from his face. She loved the way his thick hair felt as it slipped through her fingers. "Someone I know turns seventeen soon. Have you given any thought about what you might want for this grand occasion?"

Another excellent question, Charlie thought. He had indeed given a significant amount of thought to his upcoming birthday and what he would like. He had lain awake at night thinking about this. It had occupied his mind during many given activities–surfing, sitting on the beach, streaming crap on his laptop, hanging out with his friends. It was crawling around right now, in the back of his mind. But how do you tell anyone, particularly your girlfriend, that the one thing you truly want for your seventeenth birthday is to hear from your dad? To actually know that at the very least, there was one day in the year that your dad was thinking about you. How do you tell anyone that the best gift you could get for your birthday was just a sliver of recognition from one of your parents? How?

"I have," Charlie said. "There's nothing more I would like for my seventeenth birthday than to have a bacon cheeseburger and fries from Brown's on your front porch with you."

Madison laughed and kissed him, "Your wish, then, shall be granted." Slyly, she added, "And perhaps just a bit more."

"I like the sound of that," Charlie said, wrapping his arms around Madison and pulling her in close. The street noise had fallen off, and the island was settling in for the night. Charlie buried his head in Madison's neck and let the smell of her hair envelop him. He wished he could freeze time so this moment would last forever, but the laws of physics are static, and there exists an age-old adage that states *all good things must come to an end*, and this particular moment fell prey to both. From Charlie's backpack, the familiar notes of Darth Vader's entrance march sounded, shattering the stillness that had surrounded them.

"Uh-oh," Madison said, letting go of Charlie, letting her hands trace his back down to his waist.

Reaching into his backpack, Charlie retrieved his phone and raised it to his ear. "Shit, Madison. It's twelve-fifteen."

He was officially forty-five minutes past his curfew. Bracing himself for the reprimand, he slid the button to the right and held the phone to his ear. Madison did not need the phone to be on speaker to follow along with the conversation.

"At the tennis courts... Madison... God Mom... sorry, I lost track of time... you're right, I should have texted, but I wasn't ... yes... yes... I know how late it is now... alright... *alright*, I'll be right home... I'm leaving now... bye."

"Jesus..." Charlie began, but before he could finish his sentence, Madison's phone rang.

"Seems like our mom's share the same sleep cycle." They both laughed as Madison answered her phone. After assuring her mom that she wasn't dead or kidnapped, Madison slipped the phone back into her pocket.

Charlie held out his hand, "Shall we?" he asked.

Taking his hand in hers, Madison replied, "We must," and the two headed toward the gate and on down Atlantic Avenue towards their homes. Charlie's came up first, but he already decided he would walk Madison home, and then backtrack to the McIntyre residence. A delay, he was sure, that would only serve to bite him in the ass.

"You in trouble with Miriam?" she asked.

"Most assuredly, I am. The question you should ask is which lecture will I get? I'm placing my money on the oldie but goody *You're too old to lose track of time, have a cell phone for a reason, and a curfew*. But who knows? She may go with another old favorite titled *How Irresponsible of You Charlie*. It's a catchy tune, a real toe-tapper. What about you?"

"Oh yeah. Helen was not happy. I'm placing my bet on the usual *The Perils of Staying Out After Eleven-Thirty P.M.* lecture. She is fond of that one. You know, Charlie, after eleven-thirty, there is nothing to do except get into trouble."

"Yeah, I've heard that before. Maybe someday we'll get to test the theory? I mean, shit, here it is twelve-fifteen, and we haven't gotten into any trouble yet. Maybe the real trouble sleeps until one a.m.?"

"You're such a dork sometimes, Charlie," Madison said, squeezing his hand. They both continued on towards the inevitable reprimand that awaited in their immediate future.

"Well," Charlie said after a time, "guess we wouldn't be very good teenagers if we weren't always in trouble with our parents. Personally, I'm kicking ass in that department."

They walked the rest of the way in silence, enjoying each other's company and the stillness of the night. It wasn't long before the well-lit porch of Madison's house loomed before them. They said goodbye at the foot of the stairs, in the way a teenage couple says goodbye. Charlie held onto Madison's hand as she climbed the steps until the distance grew to great, and, arms stretched to their limit, he let go. She turned before going in, waved, and disappeared inside. An upstairs light flicked on, signaling the stirring of a parent. Charlie did not envy Madison in that moment, but knew full well, his moment was awaiting at home. He began the couple of blocks journey back to his own house, delighting in every second of the past few hours with Madison. It was, he thought to himself as he walked back along the deserted, dark streets, a perfect night.

From his porch, hidden in the shadows, Asher watched the entire scene play out in front of him. Much like a thunderstorm rolling in off of the water, his resentment towards Charlie grew ominous and dark.

NINE

It was the riotous cacophony of Charlie's phone buzzing on the bed-side table that roused him from sleep. He had had that dream again about his father; the one he hated having.

His bed sheets were damp with sweat, and his hair clung to his forehead. Sitting up, the imagery of the dream faded from his mind, but the feelings remained. A hollow emptiness served up on a platter of melancholy. Surprisingly, when he arrived home the night before, so egregiously late, Miriam's only offensive assault was to try to wilt him with a glaring look that missed its mark. Rising from her perch on the sofa, she simply said, "We'll talk about this tomorrow," and disappeared down the hall to her bedroom, leaving Charlie alone in the darkened living room feeling somewhat relieved.

His phone buzzed again, vibrating loudly against the wood tabletop. No doubt his group of friends putting together plans for the Fourth of July. His dream, married to the fact that as un-American as it sounded, Charlie was not a fan of the hoop-la that surrounded Independence Day, only soured his mood. For the time being, he was just going to leave his phone where it was. The digital clock atop Carson's bureau across the room broadcast the time: eleven thirty-five. Charlie rubbed his head and yawned greatly, releasing what slumber remained.

Swinging his legs around, he hopped out of bed. Grabbing for the nearest pair of shorts, he stepped into them and out into the hallway. The house was quiet. There were some subtle echoes of conversation, that sounded like Sarah and Carson, floating in from the backyard, but the TV was off, and the kitchen empty. Charlie tugged open the refrigerator, poured a glass of lemonade, padded out onto the porch, and was greeted by his mother.

"Well, good morning, Charles." Charlie noted his formal birth name being used and realized immediately that the reprimand he had escaped last night was forth coming. He drew in a deep breath of air as if to steel himself against the salvo.

"Sit down. Let's have a conversation." Miriam motioned to the high-back rocker next to hers.

Dutifully, if not begrudgingly, Charlie moved across the porch and dropped into the seat. He smiled weakly, arching his eyebrows at his mom before turning his attention to the street beyond the railing.

"Listen, I am trying to give you your space, trying to loosen the reins a bit because I realize you are getting older and need a little more freedom. I am." Clearly, Miriam had been rehearsing this. "But you were forty-five minutes past your curfew last night, without a text or a call to let me know why. Parents worry. It's innate, and it is very unsettling to do a bed check and see that one of your kids is missing when they should have been home."

Charlie watched as a contingent of Shoebie's poured out of the house across the street, a sizeable amount of beach gear in tow. The thirty-something man, whom Charlie assumed was the dad, already looked frustrated. The woman in his company, whom Charlie took as the mom in the entourage, seemed exhausted as she tried to corral what appeared to be twin boys about the age of seven as they ran between the sidewalk and the porch, hopping over the rail, and back around again and again. A daughter, maybe thirteen-years old, doing her best to appear bored and embarrassed all at the same time. She looked up, caught Charlie looking, and shyly waved in his direction. Charlie returned the wave with a friendly smile.

Without looking at his mom, he said, "I know. I'm sorry. Like I said last night, I just lost track of time," which proved to be the wrong thing to say.

With a huff that revealed her frustration, she said, "Charlie, that's simply not acceptable. I mean, Jesus, you have a cell phone which broadcasts the time. Better yet, set an alarm to ring fifteen minutes before you're supposed to be home. You need strategies to help you be successful."

There she goes, always working in the teacher talk, Charlie thought as he sipped from his glass of lemonade, his focus still cast upon on the family next door and the lack of progress they were making in their attempt to hit the beach. The daughter, now furiously texting or Snapping, kept stealing glances in Charlie's direction. Having an effective strategy was his mom's answer to just about everything from cleaning your room, to doing homework–two things Charlie despised.

Miriam continued, "You have a responsibility to uphold your end of your freedoms, Charlie. Otherwise, you're going to lose them. Okay?"

"Okay," Charlie echoed, flatly, "Sorry. I'll try to do better."

The mom across the street had managed to gain control of the twins and had pointed them in the boardwalk's direction. They gleefully skipped down the street, pint-sized Tommy Bahama chairs strapped to their backs, pails, and shovels in hand. Mom, close behind, lugging her own chair and a bag of towels. Just a step or two behind was the dad, who pulled the largest beach wagon Charlie had ever seen stuffed full with coolers, more chairs, an umbrella, a few boogie boards, and a skim board. Last was the daughter, who threw one more bashful wave in Charlie's direction before returning to her phone. Charlie smiled and tossed his head. It seems he had made a new friend.

"Try? You know what Yoda says about trying." Charlie registered the attempted humor as signaling the end of the lecture, which wasn't as bad as he had thought. Was she walking on eggshells with *him?* he wondered.

"Yes, I do," Charlie said, turning back to his mom.

Charlie and his mom shared a smile, and she patted him on his knee. "So, anyway," she continued, "what were you doing at the tennis courts with Madison at midnight?" Charlie closed his eyes. *Not so in the clear as I thought.* "I mean, you weren't playing tennis, were you?"

"No Mom, we were not playing tennis," was about all Charlie was going to offer.

"I was being facetious, Charlie. Of course, you weren't playing tennis, but you had to be doing something until twelve-fifteen."

Charlie, scratching at his head, said, "We were just, you know, hanging out… talking about stuff… nothing major."

Miriam was quiet for a minute or two, but Charlie knew this conversation was far from over. Miriam was using her prying tone, an almost sing-song cadence meant to mask the veiled innuendo. Reflexively, his right leg began to bounce, which did not go unnoticed by his mother.

"You and Madison seem to spend a good amount of time together lately, much more than usual." She paused and let the statement hang out like bait on the end of a hook, hoping Charlie would bite, but Charlie wasn't one to eat breakfast. He just slowly turned to look at his mom, smiled without teeth, and then looked back into the street. "So… are you guys, like dating or something?" She pressed.

"What would the 'something' be, Mom?" Charlie asked, feeling evasive.

Her exasperation building, but trying to stay tone-less, Miriam said, "I don't know. Your generation has so many different names for things. I thought maybe you all had a different word for it now."

Charlie shook his head. "Nah, we still call it dating." He turned his attention to his lemonade and took a long, purposeful sip. He was proud of himself for his cunning ability in this moment to provide no answer to the one question to which his mother was seeking an answer.

"Honestly, Charlie. It's a simple question. I already know the answer, or at least I think I do, but I'd rather not assume things. I just thought we could have an adult conversation about your relationship, and maybe talk about things that go hand in hand with relationships."

Oh God, Charlie thought, knowing full well what the things were that went hand in hand with relationships probably meant, *I am so not having this conversation with you, mom.* Reprieve came from behind, or so Charlie thought. The screen door pushed open and out stepped Carson, with Sarah a few steps behind. They sat down in the swing opposite from where Charlie and his mom were sitting.

"Hi," Sarah said. "What are you guys talking about?"

"Well," Miriam began, "I was trying to talk to your brother about the status of his relationship with Madison, with whom he seems to spend an awful lot of time, but he's being purposefully elusive."

"Oh," Carson said, "I can help out with that. If you want to know the status of his relationship with Madison, just check his backpack."

Charlie whipped his head around so fast that the nerves in his neck pinched. If looks could kill, Carson would have disappeared in a puff of ashes, vaporized where he sat. His scorch mark emblazoned on the back of the swing. Carson, knowing full well what he had just done, returned his brother's hateful glare with a villainous smile. Charlie mouthed, *"I'm going to fucking kill you."* He could feel himself simmer.

Intrigued, and somewhat confused, Charlie's mom pointed a question at him. "What's in your backpack, Charlie?" she asked in a more than a curious tone.

Still glaring at his younger brother, Charlie countered with, "I think the bigger question, mom, is why was Carson rummaging around in my backpack? Don't you think?" He could barely mask the venom in his question.

Still matching Charlie's gaze, Carson spoke, "Oh. I was looking for sunscreen. Don't want to get burned. Melanoma and all that deadly crap." Carson challenged Charlie with his eyes, never breaking his stare. Tauntingly, he offered, "So, go on, big bro, tell mom what's in your backpack."

"What's in your backpack, Charlie?" his mother asked again, trepidation coloring her tone.

There was no way Charlie was going to answer that question. By now, his simmer had turned into a rolling boil and had all but consumed him. All he wanted to do was rip his brother from the swing and pummel him into unconsciousness; bloody his face until it was an unrecognizable pulp. It flabbergasted him as to why Carson would say that; why Carson would so purposefully betray him. A voice quick flashed in Charlie's head. *You have been a bit of an ass to him lately,* it said. He shoved the thought aside. This was unforgivable. Charlie's fists were gripping the armrests of the rocker and his breaths were coming in short, shallow pulls.

Not yet receiving an answer, Miriam pressed again, more firmly, "Charlie, what's in your backpack?"

Jumping from the rocker, he looked at his mom and said, perhaps too loudly, "Fucking sunscreen, Mom. Move past it." Miriam's face registered more confusion as she tried to process her son's level ten over-reaction. Without another glance in his brother's direction, Charlie hopped over the porch rail and disappeared behind the house. A few seconds later, an internal door slammed shut.

"What the hell just happened?" she said aloud.

"Just another typical day with big-bro," Sarah offered. "Explosive. Dismissive. Rude. So much fun to be around."

Remembering that her two younger children were on the porch as well, she turned to them in the swing. Much to her surprise, her second-born son looked almost pleased with himself. He swung, grinning, as if he somehow had just let loose damning information that would bring down a mafia kingpin.

"Carson. What's in Charlie's backpack?" she asked, almost fearful of the answer.

"Yeah," Sarah said. "What's in Charlie's backpack?"

Carson raised one eyebrow at his mother and cocked his head as if to say, 'you want me to answer that?' In deference to her daughter's presence and age, Miriam said, "You know what, Carson? Never mind. I'll ask Charlie again, sometime." Miriam knew the answer to the question, or at least she thought she did. There was no other reason why Charlie would act so belligerently defensive, but like she said minutes before, she didn't like to assume; particularly this assumption, as it added a whole new level of worry where Charlie was concerned. She quietly sipped her now lukewarm coffee as she processed everything that had just occurred.

▪   ▪   ▪

Charlie entered his room like a run-away locomotive. He threw the door shut with a force that rattled the windows and caused the pictures on the walls to jostle where they hung. His combined state of fury and worry, mixed with his feelings of betrayal, were so great that his hands were shaking. After pacing the short length of his room five times, he snatched the iPhone off of his bedside table and feverishly sent out a text.

You around?

Within seconds, the appearance of ellipses heralded a reply.

At Joey's hanging. What's up?

Damn-it, Charlie thought. Of course.

Nothing. Forget it.

You sure? You okay?

Yeah. Nvm.

Okay. See you at the beach later, and then Kelsey's tonight?

Yeah. Probably.

Charlie tossed the phone onto his bed, not even waiting to see if there was more from Jackson and took to pacing the floor again. The fire burning inside him was stoking itself and he grew concerned that he was going to lose control of the inferno this time, allowing it to incinerate everything in its path. He snatched his phone off of his bed and fired off another text.

Hey. You busy? Want to meet up?

He stood cradling the phone, staring at it as if his very life depended on a response. His body clocked another six laps back and forth across his bedroom before the response came.

Hey Charlie. Helping Kelsey right now with last minute stuff for tonight. What's up?

Nothing. Just needed to get out of the house. Beach later?

Of course. Text ya when I'm done.

Needing to be anywhere else but where he was, Charlie changed out of his basketball shorts and into a bathing suit. He grabbed his backpack and did a quick rummage to ensure that the evidence which spoke volumes towards his relationship status with Madison remained tucked away in the small pocket on the side. The pocket, he noted, was far too small to house any bottle of sunscreen, no matter how diminutive. Much to his relief, the contents of the pocket remained. Carson was just being meddlesome, which only fed his fury more.

Charlie tugged on a T-shirt. Then he crammed into his backpack everything he needed to get through the day without returning to his house for an extended period. Still fuming, he sat down on the edge of his bed and began to take deep breaths, trying to get some sense of control. He could hear his brother and sister laughing on the front porch, as if nothing had just happened, making him madder. *How could Carson say such a thing in front of his mother and Sarah? And why the hell was he poking around in my backpack?* Just another reason why he wanted his own room. There was no privacy at all when they were at the beach house. It was an old situation that grew more tiresome daily. His heart was still racing, and he felt like a squirrel inside a burlap bag. Both knees were bouncing frantically.

Without thinking, almost as if in a trance, Charlie stood and crossed the short distance over to his brother's immaculate side of the room. He stood staring at the meticulous nature of Carson's effects. Everything was in place, smoothed neatly, and buttoned down. It was like an IKEA showroom.

What was intended only as a childish act of vengeance, maybe knocking a pillow or two out of place, culminated in a full-blown, room shredding frenzy. Charlie couldn't stop himself. In less than a minute, he had managed to rip the covers off of Carson's bed, hurling them across the room, up-end his mattress against the wall, and empty the contents of his bureau onto the floor. Charlie stood for a minute amidst the chaos, panting; taking in his handy work. Satisfied, he casually hoisted on his backpack, intent on leaving. As he made his way to the threshold, Carson's beloved, framed one-thousand-piece puzzle of the boardwalk caught his eye, hanging on the wall above his brother's headboard. In a last act of fury, or stupidity, Charlie punched the picture. A spider web of cracked glass spread out in a circular pattern from where his knuckles impacted the glass. He made his way into the hallway and out the back door. Yanking his bike out of the garage, he hopped on and rode around to the front of the house. He passed the front porch where his family remained, without saying a word or casting a glance.

"Where are you going?" his mother called out.

Without turning, Charlie yelled back, "Crazy."

He steered his bike towards Ocean Avenue. He needed to be alone. The Beanery was the perfect place for that. As he made his way along the street in the already broiling heat, his only regret was that he wouldn't see the look on Carson's face when he walked into their room.

TEN

About five minutes after Charlie sat down with his iced coffee, his phone started to explode. The onslaught of text messages from Carson and phone calls from his mother must have taxed the surrounding cell towers, slowing down service for most everyone else in the vicinity. The all-caps SMS from his mom asking WHERE ARE YOU? prompted Charlie to turn off his phone. He didn't want to risk a tracking attempt. A small part of him regretted the maniacal redecorating of Carson's side of the room. It was a bit over-the-top and bordered on the behavior of a madman. The larger part of himself, however, didn't actually care. That part of him insisted Carson deserved it, being the meddling little twerp that he was. That part of him told him not to worry about the impeding confrontation with Miriam, and the likely grounding until he was twenty-one. That part of him whispered things to Charlie, sowed thoughts in his mind, thoughts that caused his heart to ache. Charlie was concerned about both parts of himself right about then.

He took a pull of the cold beverage as he stared out the window. The street was fairly empty, being the Fourth of July. Most people had already staked their small claim of sand at the beach or were gathering inside the cool comfort of their air-conditioned homes. There were only a handful of people in The Beanery enjoying their doses of caffeinated goodness amongst the company of friends.

Charlie was glad. He needed a little solitude right about now. He wasn't in the mood for anything or anyone, maybe not even himself. His mind wandered to the conversation Jackson had had with him about his dad leaving and sandcastles in the tide. Jackson was right, of course. He pretty much always was. Charlie would be lying to himself if he didn't admit to being jealous of Jackson's insightfulness. He always seemed to know the right thing to say, or just how Charlie was feeling. This was no exception. At some point, Charlie knew he had to just move on, and to stop trying to deflect the onslaught of his grief with propped up boogie boards. But like most words, those particular ones were easier said than done.

His stream of consciousness, now much like a seed pod on the breeze, continued its meandering and led him to where his head went when Madison had asked what he wanted most for his birthday last night. That darker part of him whispered again, *Sad, and somewhat pathetic, for a soon to be seventeen-year-old to ache over wanting a phone call from his dad.* But it would be more than just a call. Charlie struggled to put his feelings into a box and label them. It wasn't the physical act of calling that Charlie longed for, or even to hear his father's voice. In all honesty, Charlie struggled to talk to his dad, to come up with conversation beyond *How was school? How're the grades?* and other day-to-day banality that passes for conversation. This ache was more of a desire to know that he mattered. That there was some part of his dad, no matter how small, that missed him, and wanted to hear his voice and know how he was. The pain that Charlie could not purge, that festered like a glass splinter under his skin, was that he felt so immaterial, so forgotten. That's what he struggled to move past, to get over. How does a kid? Charlie wiped at the tears that slipped down his face and took another long pull from his iced coffee.

The quiet, gentle voice of Pops shook Charlie loose from his head. "Hi Charlie. I hate to rush you out, but I'm closing the shop early today for the holiday. Is there anything else I can get you?"

Charlie looked up and smiled a fake smile that he hoped passed for real. "Sure Pops. No, thank you. I'm good."

Pops nodded and then, much to Charlie's wonder, sat down across from him. "Are you good, Charlie? It's the Fourth of July, and you're in here all alone."

Nodding, Charlie stammered, "Yeah, Pops. I, um… I just needed to, I don't know," he said shrugging, "be alone for a bit, is all."

Pops smiled and drummed his fingers on the table. He looked like he was weighing whether to speak. Finally, he did, "Charlie, I've known you for a long time and I've owned this coffee shop for much longer. In all those years, from time to time, I've seen people look the way you look right now. Generally, one of two things causes it. But this time, I'm pretty certain you look the way you do because of just one. That being the loss of someone special, someone meaningful. When people lose someone, a hole opens up in their life that's hard to plug, and sometimes they're not sure how to close that hole." Charlie could feel his throat tightening, so he just nodded. Pops continued, "The thing with holes is, they're an aberration. They're meant to be closed. Whether it's a hole in a screen, or a hole in the side of a boat, or a hole in the wall. Holes exist, only as long as we allow them to. It might take a while to get around to closing the hole, to fixing it, and that's okay. But eventually, you realize that the only thing required to close the hole is a little effort. Otherwise, you're just left with a hole, feeling bad about not fixing it. Know what I mean?" Pops patted Charlie on the hand and stood. "Go find your friends, Charlie. Okay?"

Charlie nodded, feeling a bit like a little kid. "Okay, Pops. Thanks. And thanks for the iced coffee. It always hits the spot." The older man turned and walked away, when Charlie called out, "Hey, Pops. You said there were two things. What's the other?"

Pops chuckled, "The second is a choice that needs to be made, but the person just can't bring themselves to make the choice. Even though, in their hearts, they know exactly what they need to do." Pops chuckled again, "Seems I was wrong with you, Charlie."

Charlie cocked his head, confused. "Wrong about what, Pops?"

With a warm smile Pops said, "It seems that both apply to you." Turning away, he said, "Enjoy the Fourth, Charlie. Say hello to Jackson," with a wave of his hand.

Charlie reached for his phone and powered it up. He dumped his cup on the way out the front door and scooped up his bike. He knew there was hell to pay when he and his mother crossed paths. Truthfully, he knew he deserved it. However deserved, Charlie was going to put it off for as long as he could. He opened his phone and looked through the overload of information present until he found the one he was looking for. The text from Jackson simply said 'St. Charles'. It was all he needed to know just where his friend was. He pedaled away from The Beanery and headed for the beach to meet up with his friend. He hoped it was just Jackson, but knew the odds were not in his favor. There was a weight tugging on Charlie's shoulders that wasn't his backpack.

ELEVEN

Charlie steered his bike up the on-ramp to the boardwalk at St. Charles Place. He dodged a couple of people and pulled it up against the railing on the beach side. Hopping off, he rummaged in his backpack for his bike chain and lashed his cruiser to the fence. Looking out onto the beach, he scanned to see if he could spot Jackson in the distance, but the beach was packed, and he was just too far away.

Moving along the dune flanked entrance to the beach, Charlie motioned with his thumb to the strap of his backpack when he got to the young kid checking tags. Satisfied that Charlie could be properly admitted to the beach, he nodded as Charlie moved past him, out onto the sand. The beach was alive with colorful umbrella tops and kites. People, young and old, crammed together in the sand soaking up the sun. The surf was crowded, as people stood, swam, or boogie boarded, to escape the scorching midday heat from the sun. July at the shore could be brutal, and that day was no exception.

Threading himself between people and campsites, Charlie made his way over to Jackson, whom he had spotted along the high-tide line in the sand. As best he could tell, Jackson was alone, and Charlie was thankful for that. In his haste to escape the scene of the crime he created at home, Charlie had forgotten to grab a beach chair. He dropped his backpack in the sand beside Jackson and pulled out his towel.

"Hey," he said as he spread it out and plopped down into it.

Looking up, Jackson cheerfully returned the greeting. "Hey, Charlie. Where've you been? I texted you, like, an hour ago."

Charlie pulled a spray can of sunscreen out of a pocket on his backpack and covered himself in a chemical that, he often mused, was probably worse for him than the actual rays of the sun.

"Yeah. Sorry about that. Uhm… my phone was off," Charlie offered as an explanation. "Where is everyone? I figured by now everyone would be here."

"Yeah, well, Madison is still with Kelsey. They thought they'd be here around two-thirty, three o'clock. Joey needed a nap. He was, uhm…, a bit worn out. Don't know when he'll be getting here. That boy sleeps a lot," Jackson said, looking out across the ocean. Turning to Charlie, he said, "Where've you been?"

Charlie drew his knees up to his chest. He hooked his elbows over his knees and clasped his hands together. "Shit, Jackson. I screwed up big time."

Jackson could tell by the tone of Charlie's voice that he was serious. He sat up in his chair and twisted his body to face his friend. "What? What happened?" his friend asked, concerned. Charlie took the next few minutes relaying to Jackson the events that began at the tennis courts the night before, leading to the remarks made on his front porch, and culminated in the trashing of his brother's things. He explained how once he started, he just couldn't stop, and that it was almost like he wasn't present during the frenzied destruction, like he was somehow outside his body.

When he finished, Jackson sat quietly for a minute, thinking. The shredding of the room concerned him more than just a little. He had been worried for a good amount of time that Charlie was going to lose it, and it seemed that he had. He'd address that at a different time.

Scratching his head, Jackson said, "Son. You are screwed. Miriam is going to ground you until you are like thirty! What the hell were you thinking?"

"I guess I wasn't."

"You guess?" Jackson countered. "Yeah, buddy, you most assuredly were not thinking." Jackson took in his friend's pained expression, and his heart went out to him. "How can I help?"

Charlie looked out across the sand toward the ocean. The waves were barely rolling over, and the ocean was like smooth green glass. "Can you fly me to Tahiti, never to return?"

Jackson laughed, "Would if I could, my friend. I'd have to come with you though, 'cause I'd miss you. We'd fuck shit up."

Charlie turned back to face Jackson and smiled, "Yeah we would. Anyway, it's gotten to the point where I don't even want to be in that house anymore." Charlie's stomach was balling up, and he could feel himself sinking deeper into the darkness. He desperately did not want to go home. *If I could get on my bike and just ride away from everything*, he thought to himself, *everything.* "Anyway…"

Jackson, sensing Charlie's sinking disposition, tried a subject change to steer him away from himself. "So. What were you and Madison doing at the tennis courts until twelve-fifteen?" he said with a tone dripping with innuendo and casual allegation.

"Nothing, mom," Charlie said sarcastically.

Jackson smiled wryly, "Nothing? Is that what we're calling it these days?" he prodded.

Charlie laughed and shook his head. "Seriously, Jackson. Give me some credit. Do you honestly think I would do that at the tennis courts?"

Shrugging, Jackson said, "Hey, when the urge hits, it's hard to control, is all I'm saying."

Remembering the conversation he had with Madison about Jackson, and his discomfort when confronted with Jackson's relationship with Joey, Charlie thought this was a good time to perhaps get used to Jackson's sexuality.

"What about you?" he asked.

Jackson played coy. "What about me?"

Not exactly sure what to say, or what words to use, Charlie said, "What about you and Joey? Have you guys… you know?" Either out of awkwardness or uneasiness with the topic, Charlie couldn't quite bring himself to say the word. Instead, he said again, and this time with hand gestures for emphasis, "You know?"

Jackson laughed out loud at Charlie's clumsiness. Shaking his head in mock offense, he said, "Why Charles McIntyre, I do not believe that is any of your business."

Disbelievingly, Charlie said, "Seriously?"

Jackson laughed, "Nah, messing with ya." He paused for a second or two, "Um, Charlie, I appreciate what you're doing. I do. I'm kinda touched by it and all. But…" he trailed off, shaking his head.

"What?" Charlie asked, shrugging his shoulders.

Exhaling, Jackson said, "Are you sure you want to talk about this? I mean, my sex life with another guy? With Joey?"

Charlie wasn't sure. His anxiety was spiking as the conversation grew. He was angry with himself for being anxious, talking to his best friend about something that almost every teenager in the world talked about. It would be so effortless if Jackson was talking about a girl. No, he wasn't sure he wanted to have the conversation, but he was sure that he needed to try.

"Yeah. Absolutely, Jackson."

"Alright," Jackson said with a shy smile. "Then yeah. I have. Joey and I have, I mean. Yeah," Jackson's cheeks flushed pink as a smile spread across his face. Charlie couldn't help but see the genuine happiness in his friend's eyes.

Charlie, his stomach folding and kneading like dough in a mixer, smiled back. "Well, looks like we both became men this summer." The flash of a beach ball caught his eye, and he looked away. A realization flashed in his head and he spun back to his friend. "Hey. Wait a minute! You didn't tell me? When did this happen? I can't believe you didn't tell me!"

Jackson laughed again, "Charlie. I just did," he said with a smile that suggested there was more to his words than Charlie was picking up on. Sensing Charlie's confusion, Jackson continued, "It was today, Charlie. This morning. When you texted. It happened this morning."

"Wait. You took my text while…"

"Well, no, not while, but close to."

"Why the hell would you do that?" Charlie asked incredulously.

Jackson shrugged. *You haven't exactly been stable lately, Charlie. I worry about you, you know?* was what he said in his head.

Charlie stared at his friend for a while. They were no longer boys. They were changed in a way that was irrevocable. There were so many questions he wanted to ask Jackson, but then he worried that the fact he had so many questions said something about his sexuality. *Why*, Charlie wondered, *would a straight guy have so many questions about gay sex?* But he did.

"So, um…" Charlie started, "is Joey, you know?" He held his hands apart from one another, like he was sizing something up.

Jackson chuckled, catching Charlie's drift. Nodding, he said, "Yeah. Joey has nothing to be embarrassed about, and neither do I, in case you're wondering that, too." He paused for effect and added, "Madison tells me neither do you."

Stunned by his admission, Charlie exclaimed, "What? Madison *told* you?"

The look on Charlie's face was priceless. Jackson chuckled. With a wave of his hand, he said, "Nah. She didn't say that. Just messing with ya, again."

"Frickin, aye. Honestly, Jackson. You can be such an ass sometimes," Charlie said, feigning anger.

"Well?" Jackson asked coyly.

Charlie furrowed his brow at his best friend. "Really?"

"Hey, you brought up the subject."

Caught in a trap by his own curiosity, Charlie acquiesced, "I am confident that I have nothing to be embarrassed about in that area, Jackson."

Smiling, Jackson said, "Yeah. I didn't think you would. I mean, big hands and all."

"Wait. You think about me?" Charlie asked.

"You think about Joey?" Jackson said.

Touché, Charlie thought, "I think we better stop talking about this," Charlie said, suddenly feeling very embarrassed.

"I think you might be right," Jackson agreed.

A seagull, circling the group of people sitting immediately in front of Charlie and Jackson, dove and grabbed half of a sandwich from an unsuspecting toddler's hand. The sudden loss of lunch and startling nature of the seagull's precise sneak attack caused a scream, closely followed by tears. The gull, now in a battle with half a dozen other birds for the tasty tid-bit, flew off over the ocean. Both boys shook their heads disapprovingly. From behind them they heard a familiar voice saying, "Shoeb move".

Joey arrived on the scene, snapped open his chair and dropped it beside Jackson. Leaning over, he planted a greeting on Jackson's lips, shrugged off his backpack, climbed out of his t-shirt, and dropped into the Tommy Bahama.

Tossing his head in Charlie's direction, he said, "What's up, Charlie?" Jackson placed his hand on Joey's leg and affectionately dragged his fingers along the side of Joey's knee cap.

"Hey Joey," Charlie returned, looking away. He could feel himself grow uneasy. His shoulders tensed and his back stiffened. He shifted in the sand, hoping to push off his sudden restlessness. Seeing Joey now, his mind jumped back to the conversation he and Jackson were having just moments before. He could feel himself flush.

"Hey, Charlie? Is that sunburn, or are you blushing?" Joey asked from across the sand. Jackson looked at his friend and smirked.

Charlie, looking even more uncomfortable than before, caught Jackson's eye quickly, smiled awkwardly, and then looked away, shaking his head. Joey, picking up on the message that was silently communicated between Charlie and Jackson, said, "What did I miss? What were you two talking about?"

To Charlie's horror, Jackson seemed like he was actually going to answer Joey's question. "Oh. We were just talking about your…"

Charlie was quick to jump in, throwing a what-the-hell-are-you-doing-look at Jackson, "… your awesome surfing ability, Joey. You're getting good," Charlie said, perhaps too loudly.

Joey looked at Jackson for confirmation. Jackson, grinning wider than the Cheshire Cat, simply nodded. Joey, realizing what Charlie said was most likely a lie, looked back and forth between his two friends before sighing and saying, "okay".

Looking at Joey and Jackson sitting together and being privy to the intimate status of their relationship, Charlie felt a bit like a third-wheel. He wondered if Jackson felt the same on the occasions that he was hanging with Charlie and Madison. Funny, he thought. At the beginning of the summer, he wouldn't feel at all awkward or intrusive if he was sitting on the beach with just Jackson and Joey, the way he did now. Taking in his best friend, watching him talking quietly with Joey, laughing and smiling, and touching each other furtively, Charlie had just one thought - *this is weird*. A sudden wave of melancholy swept over Charlie, causing him to inhale sharply.

Looking back across the sea of people gathered in the sand, Charlie happened upon Kelsey walking towards them with Logan in tow. Stepping out from behind his older brother, Asher appeared as well, clutching the ever-present soccer ball.

"Fuck," Charlie said aloud at the sight of him. Jackson did a quick turn towards his friend, then traced off of Charlie's line of sight, seeing what caused the crass outburst. "What the hell is he doing here?" Charlie asked in a tone that did little to hide his disgust.

"Charles, my friend," Jackson offered, "I'm afraid that as long as our beloved Kelsey is shacking up with Logan, Asher will be an unfortunate annotation to that story."

Shaking his head at Jackson's wordiness, Joey offered a simpler statement, "Charlie, like it or not, the kid is a part of the group now. Get used to it."

Great, Charlie thought, *something else I need to get used to.* The trio arrived, set up camp, and exchanged social pleasantries. Charlie tight smiled back at everyone without saying a word. To Charlie, Logan wasn't too bad. He was pleasant enough, funny, even engaging, but Asher just rubbed Charlie the wrong way. That boy could give Charlie a million dollars, and Charlie would find fault with the way Asher handed it to him. Asher just being six feet away from him caused Charlie's tension to jack up. Charlie closed his eyes and took a few deep breaths. Unfortunately, his attempt to calm himself didn't go unnoticed.

"Hey Chuck, you alright there? You look a little pale," Asher launched.

Jackson noted Charlie's knee bouncing as he sat cross-legged on his towel. Running a hand through his hair, Charlie said, "Yep. All good," without even looking at Asher. Turning to Kelsey, he asked, "Where's Madison? She said earlier she was doing stuff with you, and then would come to the beach."

Asher jumped in, "Yeah, Kelsey. Where is Madison? Haven't seen her yet today. I miss that girl."

Joey piped up, "Don't you have anything better to do than to be your big brother's little tag-along, Asher?" Asher didn't even acknowledge Joey, being too deeply invested in his game of Let's-Set-Charlie-Off.

"Yeah. She said she had to take care of some things at home, and she would be down later. Honestly, I'm surprised she isn't here yet," Kelsey offered.

Asher chummed the waters, "Well, it looked like she took a shower and washed her hair. You know how that goes, but that was like half-hour ago."

Jackson, sensing the tension rising off of Charlie like heat vapors from a radiator, tried to take the conversation in a new direction. "Hey, Logan. Noah was wondering if you were up for some pool later on. He asked me to mention it if I saw you today. I think he might be at Sixth Street surfing right now, though there are probably half-a-million other people trying to do the same thing." Logan was about to answer, but Charlie's voice took control.

"How do you know Madison took a shower, Asser?" Charlie asked through gritted teeth. *There's the smirk*, Charlie thought.

"Oh. I can see into her room from my room. Not a lot, of course, but enough. I just happened to see her walk in wrapped in a towel. She had one wrapped around her head as well. You know, like a turban."

"So, you just, what? Stare into Madison's room… waiting," Charlie spoke deliberately.

Asher laughed it off. "Nah, Chuck. It's not like that. It was just my dumb luck, I guess, to be in my room at the exact moment your girlfriend appeared in her room wrapped in a towel."

"Asher," Logan began, "enough. Nobody cares."

Laughing, Asher said, "I think Chuck cares."

Jackson turned towards his best friend. Catching Charlie's eye, he simply shook his head 'no'. Silently telegraphing, 'don't let this idiot get to you.' Charlie nodded back at Jackson.

"I'm going to text her," Charlie said, digging into his backpack. "Was hoping she'd grab some lunch on the boardwalk today." Charlie twisted away from the group, rummaging in his backpack.

Asher, seeing an opportunity to hook an already agitated fish, threw a bit more chum into the water. In a voice that was purposefully too loud and directed more at Charlie's back than at Kelsey, Asher said, "Speaking of lunch, Kelsey. That was a lot of fun the other day. We should do that again. Me, you, Logan, Madison. It'd be cool. I mean, she seemed to enjoy it."

A single word flashed into Jackson's mind. A single four-letter word that is grammatically versatile and conforms to most every given situation and part of speech. This one included. He watched, somewhat fearfully, as Asher's words registered in Charlie's brain. His friend stiffened, straightening his back. Slowly turning back around to face the group, he looked directly at Asher. Asher, in turn, was smiling, confident that the hook had sunk in. Jackson held his breath.

"What did you say?" Charlie asked.

"We all had lunch the other day at that little place right on the beach." Asher paused for effect. He raised a hand, placing it in the middle of his chest in feigned surprise. "Oh. Wait. You didn't know that Madison and I had lunch? I'm sorry, Chuck. Hope I didn't spill the beans."

Charlie's heart pounded in his chest. The anger he felt was taking control. It had him in a headlock. His mind raced.

Turning to Kelsey, Charlie said, "She said she was with you. I texted her that day, and she said she was with you, having lunch." Charlie's stomach heaved and dropped. "She lied to me."

Kelsey tried to ease Charlie's concern. "Yes and no, Charlie. She was with me. It was just a friendly lunch. Nothing more, honestly. It's just that… well, Madison knows that you…"

"What? That I hate this guy's fucking guts?" Charlie cut in, pointing at Asher.

Kelsey stopped talking and shrugged. Jackson reached out and put his hand on Charlie's arm.

"Charlie," he said. Charlie yanked his arm away and shot Jackson a withering look. For a minute, Charlie was unsure what to do. He was so angry, but he couldn't figure out with who. Certainly Asher. His mere presence angered Charlie. Maybe Madison? Knowing how crazy Asher makes Charlie, was she just trying to spare him the rage? Still, she lied. She lied. Maybe he was mad at himself for so willingly throwing himself on Asher's spear. The only thing Charlie knew for certain was that he couldn't be there. The urge to pounce on Asher and pummel him was growing by the second. After the morning's display of crazy, Charlie was afraid he would lose it.

Standing abruptly, he grabbed at his towel, raining sand on just about everyone present. He shoved it into his backpack and took off for the boardwalk. Jackson popped up and took off after him. Hearing Jackson calling his name, Charlie finally stopped up on the boardwalk. Here he was, yet again, toe to toe with his best friend, struggling to hold on to his composure.

"What?" he said, venom dripping from every letter.

"Where are you going Charlie?" Jackson asked

"I don't know, Jackson. Anywhere but here. That kid, he just... she lied to me, Jackson. She lied to me. You know, I thought I saw them jogging together that morning, but I told myself, convinced myself, that I made a mistake. That there would be no way she would jog with such an asshole." Jackson could see the anger on Charlie's face morph into sadness. "Guess I was wrong."

"Charlie. Asher is just an ass, you know that. He's trying to get a rise out of you, and you're giving it to him."

"Please, Jackson, do not give me the, *he who angers you, controls you* line right now, okay? I am not in the fucking mood."

Jackson half-smiled, aware of his own ability to be annoying. "Okay, fair enough, but you have to know that Madison is not messing around with Asher behind your back. She wouldn't do that to you, Charlie. You have to know that," Jackson offered in an assuring tone.

Charlie started laughing, "Do I, Jackson? Do I really know anything, anymore, about anyone?" Charlie said, gesturing to his friend with both hands.

Jackson tilted his head, unsure of the drift Charlie was throwing down. "What the hell is that supposed to mean?" he asked, a bit defensively.

Blowing it off with a wave of his hand, Charlie said, "Nothing. Look, just let me go. I gotta go, Jackson. Just let me blow off some steam. It's been a hard day. Okay?" Charlie was pleading with his eyes.

He nodded and watched as Charlie hopped on his bike and sped away. Jackson was witness to the slow unraveling of his best friend and was hard pressed for a way to stop it. He stood there on the boardwalk feeling just about as helpless as a newborn.

■   ■   ■

Charlie wound up on the beach over by the Longport Bridge. He sat by himself in the shade of a pocked and scarred bridge abutment. His phone was an epic novel of missed calls and text messages from Jackson, Madison, and his mother. Surprisingly, and somewhat touchingly, there was even one from Joey asking if Charlie was okay. Weird. He fought the urge to just hurl the device into the ocean. He was sick of its incessant need for attention. The perpetual buzzing and chirping demanding he pay it heed. He was sick of being able to be found, of never being alone, so he turned it off again. He still felt angry, though he wondered why he used the word *still* when thinking about his anger. Still implied a supposed end. Is it *still* raining? Is the water *still* hot? His anger seemed constant, never ending. He was simply angry.

He hadn't yet been home to deal with the fallout from the manifestation of that anger earlier in the day, to face the deserved wrath of Miriam. He could only imagine what Romanesque torture would befall him for the epic destruction he rained down on Carson. He worried that there was something wrong with him because the more distance he got from the event, the less he cared about it. He should have felt bad, but he felt nothing at all. If he could be honest with himself, he didn't ever want to go back there, to go home. It seemed that the pleasantries of the porch days before were the exception to the norm. These days, the suffocating resentment that enveloped him when he was there was the norm. Realizing this just made him sadder. His heart hurt in his chest. *This place used to bring so much happiness. And now…* He poked at the sand with his finger. Well, now, he barely recognized it. Charlie ached for the carefree atmosphere of summers past. Long days spent hanging out with his circle of friends, doing little more than laughing and enjoying each other's company. While his friends were still his friends, things were changed. They stopped being just friends. They were no longer individuals, but couples romantically entwined. He and Madison, Jackson and Joey, Kelsey and the interloper, Logan. His mind returned to the recurring thought that maybe, just maybe, it was a mistake to date Madison, to allow that relationship to be anything more. Maybe they were better off being just friends? That was their history together. Friends. He thought that maybe what they did that muggy night not too long ago was also a misstep. One made way too fast and without thought of consequences. *But isn't that what teenagers do? Live way too fast without thought of consequence?* Now, because of that one act, things between him and Madison could never be the same. They shared a knowledge of each other that was theirs, and only theirs.

Then there was Jackson. He missed his friend even when he was in his company, which Charlie knew was crazy, but he couldn't help but feel that way. Jackson, too, was forever changed for Charlie. It was as if their history together was all erased and Charlie was meeting this kid for the first time. The feeling that things would never be the same again between him and Jackson troubled him so much it made his stomach hurt. He hated himself for feeling that way. He hated himself for how he felt when Joey and Jackson were together. He hated himself for thinking Madison was cheating on him. He hated himself for allowing Asher to get the best of him, always. He hated himself for the way he treated Carson. He hated himself for the way he treated his mother, but he just couldn't seem to stop. He hated himself for that, too. For not being able to stop.

Charlie hated himself. He was sick of himself, and if he was sick of himself, then weren't others too?

His heart lodged in his throat, choking off his air supply. Feeling lightheaded and confused, he realized with sudden clarity that he was in a fight for his life and he was losing. Charlie turned his head and looked up at the high point of the Longport Bridge, now curvy and blurred because of the tears in his eyes. Sitting there in the sand, drowning in his own depression, Charlie's mind traced out thoughts, like finger tracks in the sand. Whispers that had never before echoed around in his head. *What it would be like?* They teased. *Would it hurt when you hit the water? Would the impact knock me unconscious? Would it be like falling asleep?*

He hated himself, too, for thinking those thoughts. Hands shaking, Charlie stretched out on his back. He closed his eyes against the day.

TWELVE

Waking with a start, Charlie was very much confused by his whereabouts, and panic set in. Looking around frantically, it didn't take more than a second or two to recognize his surroundings. He had fallen asleep on his towel, and while he had dozed at the beach before, it surprised him at just how deeply and soundly he had slept. He quick checked his backpack to see if his belongings were still there. Much to his delight, everything was still inside. The long shadows stretching across the beach in the shapes of houses gave him an idea as to the time He powered up his phone to check the time: six twenty-one

"Shit," he said aloud to the few gulls that meandered about. He had been asleep for almost three hours. He hadn't been home all day. *Miriam must be ballistic*, he thought. He allowed himself a few more minutes to shake the last remnants of sleep from his body before standing to pack up his things. Making his way back to the street, he turned and took in the Longport Bridge, stretching over the channel. With great vigor, Charlie threw his middle finger at the span, turned his back to it, and continued on his way.

Once on the sidewalk, he fired off a text to his mom.

Sorry. Fell asleep. I'm fine. Sorry. For everything.

Then, without waiting for a reply, he punched up Jackson's number and hit the little telephone icon. It barely rang.

"Charlie?" Jackson's soft, concerned voice began.

"Hey Jackson…" but that was all Charlie could get out.

"For fuck's sake," Jackson's voice boomed so loudly that Charlie pulled the phone away from his ear. "Where the hell have you been? I have been trying to reach you all afternoon. Jesus Christ, Charlie, I thought you drowned or got hit by a car or something. What the hell?"

Jackson's emotion laced outburst made Charlie smile, which, he thought, was odd. *Maybe things hadn't changed between them.*

"Yeah. I'm sorry. I fell asleep on the beach. Pretty soundly, which is weird. But yeah. Sorry."

Jackson's sigh carried over the airwaves. "Okay. I'm glad you're not dead or kidnapped." Sighing again, he fired off three quick questions. "What happened today, Charlie? Why'd you disappear? What's going on?"

Where to begin? Do I start with my thoughts about the bridge or end with that? Maybe my loathing of myself? Or my apparent daddy issues? Do I touch briefly upon my concern that dating Madison is a mistake, and that I'm afraid all of us will never be the same? That in becoming more than friends we've ruined something so good and so perfect? Do I selfishly mention your being gay and the effect that has had on me? Where to begin? Charlie didn't want to get into any of that, not over the phone, and certainly not now.

Instead, Charlie chose honesty. "Soon, Jackson, I promise, but I kinda don't want to talk about that now. I don't know… I just wanted you to know that I wasn't dead, I guess." Charlie paused, remembering the dark whispers still echoing in his mind, "That I'm still here."

Silence filled the airwaves to the point where Charlie thought that maybe the connection had dropped. He thought he could hear a sniffle and an exhale, but it was so soft he couldn't be certain.

Finally, Jackson said with a thick voice, "Okay. I'm glad you're not dead."

Jackson sounded emotional, which wasn't helping Charlie's emotional state, so he pivoted the subject. "So, uhm… Kelsey's. You still planning ongoing?" Charlie inquired.

"Yeah, about that," Jackson said. He drew out his words and proceeded cautiously. "You should know that in the course of conversation today, it came out that Asher is going to be there. And, well, knowing that, are you sure you want to be there too?"

Charlie's jaw muscles flexed. He needed to just get a grip. Charlie had been on this island his whole life. Asher was the newcomer. These were Charlie's friends, and he needed to stop letting Asher interfere with that.

"Like Joey said, like it or not, the kid is a part of the group now. Guess I gotta get used to it," Charlie said.

"Okay. But we need a code word for when you're getting all worked up. You say it, and I'll find an excuse to get you away. You know, like maybe, raspberries."

Charlie laughed, "Sounds like a plan, Jackson. Thanks."

"Kelsey said to head over any time after eight. I was thinking eight-thirty. Joey's gonna meet me there."

That kid is a part of Jackson now. Guess I gotta get used to that, too. "Okay. I got some stuff I need to do, shower being first. I guess I'll see you there."

More silence from the other end of the phone. He knew the connection was still live because this time Charlie could hear Noah was talking in the background.

"You good, Charlie?" Jackson finally asked. The level of concern in his voice was apparent.

"Yeah. I am," Charlie lied. "We'll talk. I promise, okay?"

"Okay. And, hey. Good luck at home."

Charlie had completely forgotten about the room. It all came crashing back in an avalanche of worry.

"Shit. Yeah, I forgot about that. Thanks. I think I'm gonna need it. I'll see ya Jackson."

"See ya Charlie."

Charlie thumbed the hang-up button and shoved the phone into the pocket of his bathing suit. He hopped on his bike and steered it towards home.

■   ■   ■

If the Fourth of July was good for anything, Charlie thought, it was the well-cemented traditions enacted without fail every three-hundred and sixty-five days. By this time of the day, every adult he knew would already be at the beach having staked out their encampment for the night's pyrotechnic display. The wine and beer would flow freely, the finger food ample in its supply, and the casual conversation in full flow as they waited patiently for darkness to blanket the sky. Charlie's mom would be amidst her friends–all of his friends' parents and then some, gleefully knocking back some chilled chardonnay in an attempt to escape the day-to-day pressure of adulting. He wondered, briefly, if Dan was with her.

From across the street, the McIntyre residence appeared empty, though it was hard to be certain. There was no warm glow of the idiot box dancing off of window panes, the porch was deserted, and the front door closed. However, this didn't preclude Carson or Sarah from being in their rooms. The likelihood of that was nil, being this was the Fourth, and his siblings were most likely at the beach with their friends and the other adults. Still, Charlie couldn't be sure.

Hesitantly, like a mouse poking its head out from beneath a cupboard, Charlie cautiously walked his bike across the street and up the space between the two houses. He stowed it in the garage and tiptoed up the back steps. The backdoor was unlocked, but that wasn't anything out of the ordinary. He paused, listening, but the guts of the house were silent. Confident that no one was home, he pushed open the door and walked in. The house was dim, save for the small light over the stove, and an ancient lamp in the living room. Obviously, people weren't planning on being home before dark. Alone in the semi-darkness, Charlie scanned his surroundings. It certainly couldn't compare to Jackson's or Kelsey's house, but maybe for the first time, Charlie realized how quaint his family's home was. Awash with sentiment, he paused for a second to take it all in.

He shook the feeling and headed into the bathroom. He wanted to be in and out without running into any member of his family, particularly his mom. Stripping, he showered the sand and the grime of the day away. Wrapped in a towel, he padded across the hall to his room. What he saw there, beyond the threshold, stopped him dead in his tracks and pulled forth a gasp. Carson's side of the room looked as it always did. Gone was any trace of the mayhem he unleashed that morning. His bed was made, his clothes stuffed back into the drawers of his dresser, and the puzzle hung back on the wall, minus the glass. That scene didn't surprise him, nor was it the image that caused him to gasp in surprise. That image belonged to his side of the room. To Charlie's astonishment, his side of the room was the mirror image of Carson's side of the room. Someone had neatly made his bed. Clothes that once littered the floor were folded neatly and stacked at the foot of his bed. The drawers of his bureau were closed, no article of clothing hanging haphazardly out of the tops. His bathing suit and towel were hanging on his pegs. The top of his bureau, once an apocalyptic landscape of deodorant, cologne, hairbrushes, product, and widowed socks, was tidy. Not a bottle was out of place or laying on its side. He was at a loss for words as he observed a living space radically different from when he left in the morning.

Charlie walked over to his bed and ran his hand along it. He struggled to remember the last time it was made, most likely the day he and his family arrived back in June. He touched the piles of folded clothes and then laid a hand on the tidy bureau. He was so overcome with emotion that he dropped onto the edge of his bed, trying to process it all. He sat there, flabbergasted, still wrapped in his towel, trying to understand why Carson, or his mom, or anyone for that matter, would take the time to clean his side of the room after the childish, rage fueled, destruction he wreaked not eight hours beforehand. His inner voice used some very descriptive, terribly inappropriate words and phrases to describe himself.

Something on his nightstand that wasn't there before caught his eye. It was a picture frame, simple and wooden, the color of sand. Around the edge, in laid mahogany traced the frame's perimeter. Inside was the picture of him and his dad that he kept under his mattress. Charlie sat motionless, staring at the smiling faces staring back at him. Without knowing why, he reached out and grabbed the frame. He stared at it for a moment, remembering the day captured in time. Numbly, he returned the frame face down to the tabletop next to the head of his bed. He dressed, gathered the things he needed for the night, and left the house. The image of his dad's smiling face made his skin crawl.

THIRTEEN

To call Kelsey's pool parties a party was a bit of a stretch. The idea of a pool party conjures loud music, strung lights, a pool crammed with swimmers, more people congregating around the pool deck laughing and talking, food spread across tables, and drinks being hoisted in copious amounts.

Kelsey's pool parties were more of a gathering, subdued and intimate. The guest list usually involved her inner circle of friends, and the circle of friends that were just outside them. Charlie wasn't surprised then to see a few older kids there–Noah, Brooke, Kelsey's older siblings, of course, and the handful of friends that accompanied them. Nor was he surprised to see Logan and Asher hanging at the far end of the pool deck, chatting with the hostess. Mac DeMarco was spilling from the Bose speaker on the picnic table, mixing with the conversation of those in attendance, to set a comfortable, inviting atmosphere in the yard.

On his way to Kelsey's, Charlie did some damage control with his mom, and with Madison, texting explanations to smooth things over with both. Miriam was not happy about the room, but Charlie deflected by owning it, apologizing and saying, 'that he was going through some stuff, and would talk to her about it later'. That seemed to suffice–though not before an SMS tongue lashing. He was stunned that she did not demand he return home to be placed under house arrest for an undetermined amount of time because of his egregious act, and he was thankful for it. Maybe she was cutting him a break. Maybe she was hoping he'd let his guard down and then later ambush him when he wasn't expecting it. For whatever reason his mother showed leniency, he decided to enjoy the stay of execution, no matter how brief, and deal with it later.

Madison was not so easily deflected. Charlie could pick up on her anger, as well as anyone can pick up on anger through reading a text. He sided with her, validating her being pissed. There was no excuse, he said, and he was sorry. He suggested they talk at Kelsey's and confirmed that she was still going. She'd be there, she texted, and that made him smile.

Charlie walked into Kelsey's backyard and did a quick scan. He had one more person with whom he needed to make amends. He spotted Jackson alone and reclined in a lounge chair on the pool deck, looking as relaxed and at ease as anyone can at someone else's house. Another envy Charlie had about Jackson was that he was perfectly comfortable being alone in a gathering. Whereas Charlie would feel self-conscious and awkward, Jackson could not care less.

Charlie made his way over to the vacant chair beside Jackson, exchanging chin tosses and 'what's ups' with the few people he passed. Flopping down beside Jackson, Charlie smiled sheepishly. He still felt badly about his disappearing act that afternoon and he hoped his shamefaced grin projected that.

"Hey. Uhm… again, sorry about today, Jackson. I'm sorry if you were worried. I didn't mean for that to happen."

Jackson dismissed the statement with a wave of his hand. "Water under the bridge, Charles. It is best not to dwell on those things we cannot change, but instead, to endeavor to change those things that we can," he said in true Jacksonian form.

After a few seconds of pondering, Charlie pulled his eyebrows together, shook his head and raised both hands palms up as if to say, 'huh?'

"Change the way you communicate, asshole," Jackson clarified.

"Why couldn't you just say that? Always too many words with you."

"I was going to go with '*Things without all remedy, should be without regard, what's done is done*', but thought better about it," Jackson continued. Again, Charlie shook his head in perplexity. "Lady Macbeth?" Jackson said. Charlie just shrugged. "Do you not read anything that is assigned to you in school?" Jackson asked.

Charlie said with a laugh, "I try my best not to. Especially Shakespeare. Jesus God, talk about a slow, painful death. That's one medieval torture that still exists."

"And yet, you can quote an obscure line from The Dharma Bums."

"Go figure, Jackson. Like I said, that line resonated with me." Lately, Charlie thought to himself, most every one of his days ended in tears, or at the very least, the verge of tears. "Where's Joey? Is he coming?" Charlie asked, starting a new subject.

Jackson lifted his phone to check the time: eight forty-five.

"He should be here soon. If I've learned one thing during these past few weeks about Joey is that punctuality is not his strong suit. Unabashed cockiness and a shameless love of himself, definitely, but he's not one to be held captive by a clock." Jackson took a pause and with two quick taps of his finger on Charlie's knee said, "And where, might I ask, is your paramour?"

Smirking at Jackson's choice of words, Charlie responded, "Well, if by paramour you mean Madison, then she, too, should arrive shortly. I'm kinda glad she isn't here yet, what with Asser being here already."

"Raspberries, Charlie. Raspberries," Jackson said, and both boys laughed. That feeling of familiarity being with Jackson returned to Charlie, causing him to smile. This is what he longed for, just being with his best friend, hanging out, sharing inside jokes and making each other laugh. These moments seemed to evade Charlie all summer, and it was precisely what he needed right then. Charlie could feel himself relaxing. His tension and anxiety slipping away like soapsuds in a shower. He wasn't sure how long it would last. Instead, he allowed himself to enjoy it while it was present.

"So, hey, how are things with you and Joey? I mean, you guys getting along and stuff?"

"Yeah. Things are good. I mean, it was a little awkward at first, but now... I don't know. It's more comfortable. How about you and Madison?" Jackson inquired.

Charlie ran a hand through his hair and thought for a second or two, "We're good, I guess."

"You guess? What's that mean?" Jackson asked from behind questioning eyes.

"Yeah. I don't know. It was awkward at first, like you said, but it's not anymore. Lord knows we've gotten quite comfortable with each other, and we do get along well, but we always have, you know. It's just that..." Charlie trailed off, not wanting to vocalize the thought that had haunted him for quite some time.

Jackson, however, pressed for him to finish his sentence. "It's just that what, Charlie?"

Charlie, looking across the pool, wrestled with whether or not he should say it. As if saying it aloud would somehow conjure it into existence, like Bloody Mary or Beetlejuice. He returned his gaze to Jackson and said, "Do you ever think that maybe getting together with Joey was a mistake? Well, not a mistake," he corrected, "but more something that should have been left alone?"

Shaking his head, Jackson said, "Honestly, no. It's been good with Joey. I don't know how long it will last, or what will happen come the end of August, but I'm glad it happened. Do you feel that way about Madison?"

"Yeah," Charlie said, perhaps a bit too quickly. "Sometimes I do. Sometimes I just feel like maybe we ruined a good thing, just being friends. That maybe we should have left things as they were, just friends. You know? Like you said, what's going to happen come the end of August? We can't go back to being just friends. We've all been changed by the choices we've made and the things we have done this summer," Charlie ended his sentence with a shrug of his shoulders.

Jackson stared at his friend, allowing his words to sink in. He tried to craft some sort of response that would assuage Charlie's worry, but he never got the chance. Like perfectly crafted stage blocking, Madison and Joey arrived on scene, putting an end to the conversation. Looking up and seeing Madison, Charlie could feel himself blush, as if he'd been caught with his hand in the cookie jar. Jackson and Charlie sat up in the recliners, throwing their legs over the sides of the seat to make room for their respective partners. Madison ran a hand through Charlie's hair and, kissing him, she said hello. To the right of him, he could see Joey almost mirror Madison's actions. Again, the ease with which Jackson comported himself impressed Charlie.

"You two looked deep in conversation," Madison began. "What were you talking about?"

Joey picked up the ball. "I'm pretty sure you two were talking about my awesome good looks and rocking body, right?"

Charlie chortled, "Damn, Joey. You guessed it. I mean, how could you fault us, right? Look at you. Perfection in every way." Jackson listened for any hint of sarcasm or facetiousness, but didn't pick up on any. He smiled inwardly. He suspected Charlie was still uneasy over his and Joey's coupling. A little sliver of worry faded, erased by Charlie's genuine friendly banter with the boy Jackson had grown to care about.

"Well, I do believe you have seen the light, McIntyre," Joey shot back with a broad, affable smile, one Charlie returned.

Madison rolled her eyes exaggeratedly, showing that she, too, was playing along. "Anyway, Joseph, I hate to admit it, but puberty has been kind to you. You definitely glowed up." She raised her hand and Joey met it with a high-five.

"Oh great," Charlie said. "Someone else for me to worry about." He cringed when he heard the words slide out of his mouth and hoped to high Jesus that they went unnoticed. Jackson shook his head as if to say, 'you stupid, stupid boy'. Joey cocked an eyebrow.

Turning, Madison asked, "What is that supposed to mean, Charlie?"

Laughing it off, Charlie brushed it aside. "Nothing. I was just playing, you know? Caught in the magic of being with good friends, on the Fourth of July, at the shore." He held his breath and hoped his fast talking had the desired effect. Fortunately, the distraction came from elsewhere.

"Mads. It's about time you got here. I was starting to think you were avoiding me," Asher said, as he reached down and gave Madison a hug. All the while looking at Charlie. "What's up, Chuck?" he said in mid squeeze. Charlie couldn't be sure, but it seemed Madison cringed a bit. A good sign.

Charlie simply responded, "Asser."

Jackson chimed in, "Hey, you know what would be great right about now? Some fresh raspberries. Don't you think?" Smiling, Charlie looked at his friend and flashed him a peace sign, signaling all was well.

"Missed you on our jog this morning. It was lonely without you," Asher continued after releasing Madison from his arms. "Did I wear you out?"

In his head, Charlie heard Jackson's voice saying *he's just trying to get a rise out of you.* He didn't bite.

"Hey, Madison," Charlie interjected, "it's kinda hot. Let's grab something to drink and hop into the pool. What do you say?" Charlie pushed up out of his seated position and put his hand out, into which Madison placed hers. He helped her up out of the lounger and the two of them walked away. Charlie could feel Asher's glare burning a hole in the back of his head. He was proud of himself for not getting caught up in that sinkhole.

"Give it up, Asser," Joey said with a laugh. "She is *so* not into you."

Still watching the object of his desire walk away with the object of his umbrage, Asher simply said, "We'll see." Turning his back to the boys, he walked away, rejoining his brother and Kelsey who were now engaged in conversation with Noah.

■   ■   ■

The night had finally become dark enough for the annual display of pyrotechnic amazement in the form of colorful sparks raining down onto the Atlantic. The party goers had all made their way up to Kelsey's second floor deck to get a better view and were thoroughly engaged in the technicolor show. Immense explosions of color lit up the sky, illuminating the pool deck in red, green, blue, and yellow, like a dance floor in a nightclub. Echoes of blasts reverberated off of the houses, bouncing back and forth along the walls before fading away into the night.

Charlie and Madison stood waist deep, chest to chest, along the shallow end of the pool, taking in the spectacle from ground level. It was the first time all night that they were alone, and Charlie was itching to get something off of his mind. He was hesitant. The night had been going well, and he was feeling light. However, the question gnawed away at him. Not wanting to ruin the evening, but also not wanting to remain doubtful, he thought best to throw caution to the wind and take his chances. He was thinking about a way to begin the conversation when, as if reading his mind, Madison provided one for him.

"Everything okay? You seem a little preoccupied right now," she began. "I mean, beautiful night, amazing fireworks, hands on the waist of your girlfriend, skin to skin. This pretty much has 'make-out session' written all over it." As she finished, Madison ran her hand through Charlie's hair, down his neck, and across his chest, resting it right above his stomach. A pleasant sensation traipsed through Charlie.

Seeing the door open, Charlie walked in. "Actually, there has been something on my mind that I've been meaning to ask you. I just, I don't know. I don't want it to ruin the night."

Madison dropped her hand to his waist and took a slight step backwards, increasing the distance between the two. Cocking her head, she said half in jest, but somewhat seriously, "Should I be worried? Is this a break-up conversation?"

Charlie chortled and shook his head. "No. Gosh no." Madison smiled. In a slow, exaggerated way, she dragged her hand across her forehead, and flicked off the imaginary sweat. Charlie smiled and pressed on. *Here goes nothing*, he thought to himself. "The other day, when I was texting you, you said you were having lunch with Kelsey," he could feel Madison tense, which caused his stomach to roll a bit, "but Asher was there too, at least that's what he said today at the beach before you arrived. So, I was just wondering, why you didn't tell me? Why did you lie about that?"

Around them, the cacophony increased. Rapid fire explosions and overlaid bursts of light flooded the yard, signaling the beginning of the end of the display. Looking at Charlie, his face reflecting the light raining down on them, Madison's first thought was how handsome he looked right now; his hair windblown and falling perfectly about his face, eye's catching the lights from the sky; skin, tight and rippled with goose bumps from the chill in the air. She hoped the firework finale was not a projection of things to come for them.

"Yeah. That..." she started. "I'm sorry, Charlie. I have been meaning to say something..."

"But you didn't," Charlie cut in, maybe too forcefully. "And that was him I saw you jogging with that morning on the beach, wasn't it?" Madison dropped her eyes to the pool water and just nodded. "So..." Charlie had to pause before going on as his stomach leaped up into his throat. He let go of Madison and took a step backwards, away from her. Swallowing hard, he said, "... so, are you seeing him?" He had gotten it out. As much as he hated hearing those words spill out of his mouth, he felt better for it. Charlie braced himself for the answer he had already subscribed himself to.

Madison let go of his waist and raised her hand, palms up, "Wait? What?" she said, obviously confused, and a bit offended. "You think I am secretly dating Asher? For real?" Madison's voice raised a bit. Charlie could hear the annoyance in her tone, blended so subtly with hurt. "Why would you think that, Charlie?"

Charlie, never one to be overly in-tune with picking up a mood, could sense that things would not go smoothly from this point forward. Madison hopped up onto the side of the pool and took a seat, legs dangling in the water. He took a step towards her, but she put out a hand, signaling him to stop. "Well?" she asked.

Charlie, still waist deep in the water, did his best to explain himself. "Well," he began, "you lied to me about who you were with at lunch. And you are meeting up with him early in the morning to jog, so I just thought…"

"You just thought what, Charlie? That I was cheating on you? That's where your head goes?" Madison's voice grew louder, and her words came faster. "First of all, I can jog with whomever I want. Jogging does not mean I am dating anyone, for Christ's sake. It means I'm jogging with that person. He saw me return home from a jog one morning. He said he jogs as well and asked if we could do it together. I said sure. He texted me that morning while he was out jogging, and I said I'd meet him over by Fourth Street. End of that story." Charlie, feeling a bit dressed down, cast his eyes to the pool water. "You're right. I didn't tell you I was with Asher at lunch, I felt badly about that, I did. Not to put my mistake on you, but honestly, Charlie, you lose your shit every time Asher is around. It was wrong of me to not tell you, but I just didn't want to upset you. No good deed, huh?" She paused and took a deep breath. Shaking her head, she said, "Do you honestly think I would cheat on you, Charlie?"

"I just thought…"

Madison chopped off his words. "No, Charlie. You didn't think. That's the problem." Placing her palms flat on the pool deck, she pushed up into a stand and walked away.

"Madison. Wait…" But her back was turned. Charlie's stomach dropped.

By now, the fireworks had ended, and people were returning to the yard. Of course, Asher was one of the first people back. Of course, Asher had a front-row seat to witness Madison storming off, and of course, Asher had a comment.

"Looks like a little trouble in paradise," he said as he walked past Charlie, still standing in the pool, somewhat dumbfounded by the quick downturn that conversation took. Under his breath, Charlie threw a 'fuck-off' back at Asher. Upon hearing, Asher just smiled.

Charlie climbed out of the pool, dejected. He sought a seat at the far side of the yard and dropped himself down into it. *Well, that sure as hell didn't go as I planned,* he thought to himself. He replayed the events that had just unfolded, attempting to figure out where he went wrong, why he had upset Madison so. Was it that he had asked if she was seeing Asher? Or was it because he had assumed she was cheating on him with Asher? Or was it because he essentially called her a liar? Maybe all of the above?

"I seriously suck at dating," he said to himself out loud. He propped an elbow onto an armrest and dropped his chin into his hand. *On the bright side*, Charlie's mind continued, *at least you know she isn't dating Asser.* Just as quickly, his mind pivoted. *Wait a minute,* it said, *she never actually said she wasn't dating Asser*, it thought. *All she said was whether you thought she* would *cheat on you;* expertly, Charlie's mind messed with him. It had years of practice.

Standing up, Charlie wove around the pool deck, looking for Jackson. He saw Madison sitting at the picnic table. She was talking to Noah and Brooke. The look she shot him when they made eye-contact confirmed for Charlie the notion that he should stay out of

Madison's range for a bit. Jackson was chatting up Joey and Kelsey. Charlie walked up behind them and half-heartedly joined the conversation.

■   ■   ■

As all things must, the night at Kelsey's drew to a close just before eleven-thirty. A few kids had departed about thirty minutes before, but there were still a good portion of people now making their way out onto the street and home. Scanning the yard, Charlie saw Madison on the other side of the pool. She was making her way around. He walked towards her and met her at the midway point.

"Hey," he said a bit sheepishly.

"Hey," Madison returned uncomfortably. Charlie couldn't be sure if she felt that way because she was annoyed with him still, or because they hadn't spoken a word to each other for the rest of the night.

"I'll walk you home, if you like." He shrugged. *Please say yes,* his mind willed.

Madison looked around before she answered. "Uhm…, that's okay. Your house is in the opposite direction. Don't want to miss curfew," she said in a failed attempt at humor. Charlie's worried expression did not change. "Anyway, I got Logan and Asher to walk home with. I'll be okay."

Charlie bristled at the mention of Asher's name, but fought to conceal it. Madison smiled at him weakly. Side stepping him, she continued on her path toward the gate. Charlie reached down and slipped his hand into hers. Closing his fingers, he gently pulled her to a stop. Madison turned her head, but not her body.

"Are we okay?" Charlie asked nervously.

Madison could read the worry in Charlie's eyes like a book. "We will be, Charlie," she said sympathetically, throwing him a weak smile.

Not the answer Charlie was hoping for, and he tried not to look disappointed, but was certain he had failed. Madison let Charlie's hand drop away and walked across the yard. At the gate, she joined up with Asher and Logan and disappeared onto the street. Asher turned over his shoulder and threw a look back at Charlie. Charlie couldn't help but notice the smirk.

"Well, this night sucked," he said aloud to himself. "Just add it to the Why-I-Hate-the-Fourth-of-July list."

.   ▪   ▪

The night had turned humid and settled heavily on everything. The moisture in the air captured as a greenish haze around the heads of the streetlights. Madison walked next to Asher at a friendly distance, both trailing behind Logan as they closed the short distance from Kelsey's house to First Street. The conversation consisted mostly of small talk, the type of casual conversation two people who know each other, but don't know each other, might have. Weather. Netflix. A recap of the evening. Plans for tomorrow. As they rounded the corner onto their street, Asher brought up a particular event from the night, one Madison couldn't put out of her mind, yet was hoping to avoid.

"So. Everything okay with you and Chuck?" Asher asked, hoping it wasn't.

Asher's use of the nickname caused Madison to prickle. "You know he hates when you call him that, right? Which, I suppose, is why you call him that," Madison answered.

Asher just smirked and nodded his head, "So. You guys in a fight or something? I saw you walk away from him after fireworks. You two didn't seem to talk the rest of the night."

Are we in a fight? Madison thought to herself. She wasn't sure. She was more annoyed than angry. Boys can be so stupid sometimes. They're always jockeying with one another for some ridiculous sense of perceived dominance, always in competition, and always flexing. She was more offended by Charlie's doubt than by his accusation. It troubled her that he would question her fidelity, especially after what they had shared.

Shaking off the feelings, she said, "I don't know. I wouldn't call it a fight. It was more like an argument, a misunderstanding." She stopped and wondered how many details she should share. Hoping to turn the subject away from her and Charlie, she tacked the boat. "And anyway, what is it with you and him? You're always digging at him. Making some snide little comment meant to piss him off or flirting with me openly right in front of him. I swear you go out of your way to upset him. It's like you're looking for some boundary with him or seeing how far you can push before he pushes back. It's not cool, Asher. Charlie's a nice guy. I like him. A lot. You should try to get to know him better, rather than always looking for ways to upset him. Jesus."

While just barely seventeen years old, Asher had learned at an early age that there were times you spoke up and stated your case. Then, there were times, you fell silent and allowed yourself to be culpable, taking the accusations with quiet dignity. Asher knew the second of the two scenarios applied here. He just nodded in agreement, which is what he felt Madison needed right about then, not a counterargument or a plea to defend himself. Certainly not an honest explanation of his intent.

They walked quietly for a bit before he followed up, bringing the conversation back to the track he wanted. "So. What happened with Charlie, anyway?"

So much for steering the conversation in a different direction, Madison thought. What harm could there be in telling him? Maybe, she mused, just maybe Asher would understand why he needed to lighten up a bit around Charlie if she told him. Then again, maybe telling him would just provide Asher with a whole new clip of ammunition.

Sighing, she said, "He just accused me of doing something that I'm not, is all. He pissed me off."

Asher stopped walking; they were at the foot of Madison's stairs. Logan called good night from ahead and bounded up onto the porch, disappearing inside the house.

Turning back to Madison, Asher said, "Does he think we're dating or something?"

Madison, stunned slightly by Asher's hitting the proverbial nail on the head with his guess, just nodded. "Yes, Asher, he does. Honestly, with the way you act around me, I can see why."

Asher laughed quietly, almost under his breath. Madison tried to determine if the laugh was because Asher thought the situation was funny or because the situation was going as planned. Briefly, she wondered if she was being manipulated by the stunningly good-looking teenager standing before her.

"Us? Dating?" Asher said through another quiet laugh. "That's just crazy talk, isn't it?" he said cocking his head. Before Madison could answer, Asher leaned in and kissed her lightly on the cheek. Turning towards his house, he said, "Good night, Mads. It was a fun night. Maybe we can do it again?"

It wasn't a question, so much as a statement. He ducked down the side yard and vanished into the darkness. Madison was left standing on the sidewalk, hand to her cheek where Asher had just landed his lips, wondering just what the hell she had gotten herself into.

FOURTEEN

Miriam had been sitting on the front porch nursing a sweating glass of chardonnay since she returned from the beach after the fireworks. The citronella lantern burned brightly on the side table. The light from its flame danced across the porch ceiling, showering it with a welcoming warmness. The street was quiet. The house behind her was silent. Carson and Sarah had gone to bed about thirty minutes ago, and the porch was all hers. Miriam closed her eyes and bathed in the calm. She could feel the knot in her shoulders that had been present since the morning finally untie itself.

It had taken her quite some time to settle herself after Carson discovered his trashed room. She was absolutely livid upon finding the frenzied chaos Charlie had left behind when he left the house that morning. Her first impulse was to hunt Charlie down and drag him home. But her first duty, she realized, was to Carson, who was so obviously hurt and angry. Tensions ran high in the McIntyre residence for most of the morning. It didn't help that Sarah ran a derogatory commentary about her oldest brother like a monolog for a late-night TV show. For most of the day, Miriam was furious with Charlie, angry in a way she had never been with him before. She struggled to come to terms with how Charlie could do something so hateful to Carson, to his brother. It wasn't just the horror of the act itself, but also the violence. The room appeared as if a madman tore through it. A hurricane of crazy anger that was unstoppable. It scared her, Carson, and Sarah. She struggled to understand the level of fury that lived and grew inside her oldest child right now, and why it had taken root in the first place? He hadn't been right since his father left; she knew that, but this? It was the viciousness of the act that worried her most. What was going on inside Charlie that would cause him to commit such an atrocity, such a hateful display, she wondered.

Absent-mindedly, she punched the home button on her phone to get the time: eleven-forty. *Late again,* she thought of her firstborn, but let it go. She took another sip of her now warm wine. Before she could return the glass to the table, she could hear footfalls on the sidewalk. Charlie's shadow stretched down the concrete a few steps ahead of him as he grew nearer to the front porch. Upon seeing his mom, Charlie smiled weakly and sheepishly climbed the front steps. Remembering that he and she had yet to confront each other over his redecorating project, he cautiously approached the empty rocker. Gesturing to the seat, he silently asked permission to sit down. Miriam nodded approval, and he sank down next to her.

Charlie had heard the expression *the silence was deafening* before, but he never understood what it meant until that moment. The quiet on the porch screamed in his ears. It made itself known in a way he did not realize silence could make itself known. It was roaring in such a disconcerting way that Charlie wanted to hold his hands up to his ears to block it out.

Finally, his mother spoke, but it wasn't the tongue-lashing Charlie expected. "Can we talk about this morning without getting into a fight, Charlie?" his mother asked. She sounded weary, like all the life had drained out of her.

Charlie nodded yes, then spoke himself, "Mom. I am so sorry about trashing Carson's side of the room. I am. It's kinda made me sick all day."

Something about the tone of Charlie's voice told Miriam that he was being sincere and not just paying lip-service.

"You should be, Charlie," Miriam said sternly, but compassionately. "What you did was inexcusable behavior. You have no idea how hurt Carson was. Charlie, you crushed him. You may be unaware of this, as lately you pay very little attention to him except to insult him or tell him to fuck-off, but he adores you, Charlie. With him, you walk on water. You always have. You're his older brother. Trashing his stuff like that, well… it was devastating for him." His mother's words hit home, hard. Charlie didn't stop to think at all about Carson, not once today, not once for a while now. His throat tightened a bit at his selfish realization.

His mom continued, "I guess I'm just left wondering how you could do that? What could make you do that? What is happening inside you that would make you do something so violent?" His mother trailed off, leaving her questions floating on the night breeze.

Charlie pondered an answer, though he wasn't sure if he was actually supposed to provide one. Was his mother's query rhetorical? "I don't know. It was weird," Charlie explained. "One minute I was sitting on the edge of my bed. I was angry with him. Furious. I could feel my pulse in my temples, and my hands were shaking. The next thing I knew, I was standing in the middle of it."

Miriam's concern grew. "Charlie, are you saying you don't remember doing it? That you have no recollection of destroying Carson's side of the room?" Her voice projected her worry.

Charlie shook his head, "No, Mom. I remember doing it."

"Then what are you saying, Charlie?"

Charlie thought for a bit, trying to figure it all out himself. "I guess what I'm saying is, I remember doing it, but I also remember not being able to stop. Like, I couldn't keep myself from doing it until it was done, and while I was doing it, it was like watching a movie of me. I was there, in the room, but I wasn't." Charlie took a few slow, deep breaths as the feelings from the morning flooded back.

Miriam could see Charlie's jaw flexing as she tried to process what he had just told her. She was worried about this young man who sat across from her, this teenage boy who seven months ago was a different person. Carefree. Happy. Light. She felt a failure for not being able to help Charlie through whatever it was he was going through, but she couldn't force him to open up to her. She couldn't coax him out from behind the wall he was building. The best she could do was keep asking questions, keep reaching out.

After a moment, she said, "I've been thinking about this morning, and just where things went south with you. When Carson brought up your backpack, when he said that I should look inside, that's when you got angry, Charlie. It was like someone flipped a switch in you. All of a sudden, you were this ball of white-hot fury. That's when you went in the house, Charlie. We could all hear your bedroom door slam. It rattled the windows." Charlie braced himself against the question he knew was coming. "So, what *is* in your backpack, Charlie? Is it something bad?" Being a parent, and living in these times, her first thought was that it was a gun. Her second thought was that it was drugs.

Jesus, we've come full circle, Charlie thought to himself. "No, Mom. It's nothing bad. Nothing like that at all."

Scared she should ask, but also knowing there was no way she wasn't going to ask, Miriam posed her next round of questions.

"Is it a gun? It is drugs?" She winced at the sheer anxiety in her tone. Then she realized that neither of those things had anything to do with his relationship with Madison and felt a little foolish for asking.

"Jesus, Mom. No. It's not a gun, or drugs," Charlie balked. "And both of those things are bad," he offered hoping the humor would put a crack in the tension, "and what would those things have to do with my relationship with Madison?" he said incredulously.

Inwardly, his mother smiled as the teacher in her said in her head *'brain-match.'* "Then, what is in your backpack, Charlie, that would cause you to get so upset with Carson?" his mother pushed.

Seeing no way out of this conversation, Charlie had to come up with a way to answer the question without answering the question. He knew at this point his mother would not let this go until she had an answer.

Cleverly, Charlie offered one, "Something private. Something to keep me safe, mom. That's what's in my backpack. Something to keep me, and Madison, safe."

Miriam's brow furrowed in confusion as she tried to understand Charlie's cryptic answer. Then, as if cracking a Fibonacci sequence, her eyes lit up with sudden understanding. She had thought this earlier in the day, but just wasn't ready then to allow herself to admit it. She raised a hand to her open mouth and held it there for a second before returning it to the table. Reaching for her glass, she took a sip of wine, a long sip of her wine.

Returning her gaze to Charlie, she said, "Are you saying that you and Madison are…"

"All I'm saying is, I'm safe, Mom. Okay?" Charlie's tone implied a genuine desire for his mother not to seek a further answer. To his surprise, Miriam nodded, and so too did Charlie. There was something right in that moment of mutual understanding, almost like they had struck an armistice. Thinking it best to end on a high note, Charlie rose from the chair. "Goodnight Mom," Charlie said. "Oh, and thanks for tidying up my side of the room. It looks nice."

His mom shook her head. It was her turn to balk. "I didn't do that. There was no way I was going to clean your side of the room up, young man. Not after what you pulled. That was Carson. You need to thank *him*."

"What?" Charlie asked, blown away.

"Yup. Carson. You're lucky I didn't hunt you down and drag you home, mister."

"Yeah. I guess I am. Thanks for that... for giving me some space."

Charlie marveled at Carson's generosity. It was more than Charlie would ever have done. Guilt blew all over him like sand kicked up in a sudden gust of wind. He needed to make things right with his brother. He smiled at his mom and headed into the house.

Miriam just sat watching from the chair, wondering when Charlie had gotten so tall. She tried to remember just when his voice grew so deep and his shoulders so wide. She worried that maybe he was growing up a bit too hurriedly.

■   ■   ■

The room was dark when Charlie entered. In the small light that seeped in from the hallway and from around the shades, he could see that his side was still pristine. He made his way over to his bed, picked up the folded clothes at the foot, and placed them on the top of his bureau, intent on placing them in drawers in the morning. He could see the outline of Carson in the bed across from his. His face was to the wall with the sheet pulled up around his shoulders. Charlie stepped out of his shorts and peeled off his shirt. Pulling back the top sheet, he slid into bed. Settling on his back, one arm behind his head, he stared at the ceiling, wrestling with his conscience.

He sighed heavily and murmured into the darkness. "I know you're not asleep, Carson. I've been sharing a room with you long enough to know when you are. You tend to sleep mostly on your back or stomach, and right now you're facing the wall. When you do sleep on your side, it's your left side, not your right side, and you pull your legs up to your chest, which they're not right now, and your breathing isn't right either. When you sleep, you make this little wheezing sound, almost like a squeak."

Across the room, unseen by Charlie, Carson smiled. Somehow, knowing that his brother knew his sleeping habits in such detail comforted him. It meant that Charlie paid attention to him.

"Anyway, like I said, I know you're awake right now," Charlie continued, "so I know you can hear me. So…" Charlie hesitated, not sure what to say. Drawing in a breath, he continued, "So. I'm sorry about trashing your stuff. I don't know why I did that; it wasn't right. Shit, it was so far from right. It was just mean and hateful." Charlie paused again, searching for a direction to continue. "I'm sorry I hurt you," he went on, his voice catching. "I know I've been a real shit to you lately, to everyone. I don't know why, but I know you don't deserve it, and I'm going to do better. At least I'm going to try. So, anyway. That's what I wanted to say. So… there." Charlie spun to face the wall, kicking the sheet down around his waist. There was one last thing he wanted to say. Words he hadn't thought to utter to his brother for quite some time. Lifting his head, he added, "Good night, Carson."

The silence that filled the room at that moment seemed, at least to Charlie, to stretch on for a millennium. He lay there in the darkness, holding his breath. He wasn't sure why he wanted to hear something from the other side of the room. He only knew that he needed to. His body yearned for it, as if the sound itself was redemption, absolution, in a way, from the heartless insensitivity he had rained down on his brother that morning, these past months. He had just about given up, closing his eyes to welcome the emptiness of sleep, but then, faintly, almost unperceptively, it came.

"Good night, Charlie," Carson softly breathed into the darkness.

Charlie's breath caught. For a moment, one scary moment, Charlie thought his heart might explode.

FIFTEEN

Charlie's birthday arrived the way it always did, with Charlie sitting up in bed wondering why each July eighteenth came with such pomp and circumstance. He grew up hearing that his birthday, or anyone's birthday for that matter, was his special day, as if July eighteenth belonged solely to him and no one else. One birthday year, he did a quick Google search and discovered that approximately twenty-one million other people worldwide shared his exact birthdate. When taken into consideration, a fact like that makes the eighteenth day of July just a little less special. As his mom was fond of saying, special doesn't always mean good, and while Charlie's birthdays were always good, the attention he received invariably made him uncomfortable.

Jackson could never understand Charlie's indifference to his own birthday, but recognized his friend's uneasiness with being in the spotlight for the day, and respected that. His usual birthday message to Charlie was a text that read something like *Hey. It's July 18th. Hope it's a day.* Each year, Jackson's texts managed to wish Charlie a happy birthday without wishing Charlie a happy birthday, and Charlie always marveled at Jackson's creativity. Charlie referred to them as the Eighteenth Texts, because in Charlie's mind, it was just a day. One more revolution around the sun. One more number added to his age. Seventeen.

Rising that morning, Charlie didn't feel any differently than he did the day, the week, or the month before. He remembered what Joey had said back in June about being seventeen. As he stared at himself in the bathroom mirror, he understood. Same face, same hair, some fledgling stubble trying it's hardest to sprout into a beard, but more resembling some settled dust than actual hair. New day, same old, but there was one thing different this year. *This is my first birthday without my dad, but who gives a flying one, right?*

Pushing down the melancholy, he showered, dressed, and headed down the hall into the living room. His brother and sister sat beneath a Happy Birthday banner that was hung on the wall behind the couch. It was the same banner that had hung there for as long as he could remember. The only thing that changed was the number of siblings sitting beneath it. Upon seeing him, each wished him the obligatory Happy Birthday. Carson threw him an air-high-five, which Charlie reciprocated. Sarah got up, walked over to where he stood and gave him a hug–which, much to Charlie's astonishment, didn't come with a dig about how he smelled. Miriam came in from the kitchen and kissed him on the cheek, then warmly hugged him for what seemed an eternity.

As she rubbed her hand up and down his back, she said, "My little boy, all grown up." She handed him a glass of orange juice and said, with a wink and a smile, "Breakfast is almost ready. Your favorite, of course."

After the traditional chocolate chip pancake breakfast, presents were opened: a few T-shirts, a pair of tortoiseshell Ray-Ban Classic Wayfarers, and a new traction-pad for his surfboard. Charlie looked across the table, over the empty plates, and discarded gift wrap, at his family. While feeling content in the moment, he couldn't quite ignore the fact that there was one person missing, one empty chair pulled up to the oval table. As if remembering something, he pulled his phone out of his pocket to check the screen. Nothing, at least nothing from the one person from which he wished to hear. He hated himself for wanting to hear from him.

He shoved it back into his pocket with a frown. A sense of dread overtook him, threatening to squelch any happiness that he might be experiencing in the moment.

Between the remaining bites of her pancake, Sarah inquired about Charlie's day. "So, birthday boy. Any big plans for the day? Will you be seeing Madison?" she asked in a sing-song voice meant to imply something more than the words intended.

"Not that it's any of your business," Charlie began, "but, yeah. I am. We're having lunch."

Jeeringly, Sarah said, "Is *that* what they're calling it now?" Carson's pancake caught in his throat, and he half-choked, half-laughed at Sarah's innuendo. Charlie shot him a look, and Carson just shrugged.

Raising a hand as if taking an oath, Carson said, "I didn't say anything, I swear."

Missing the beat, Charlie's mom spoke up, "Is that what they're calling, what?" she asked, looking at Sarah, and then said to Carson, "What didn't you say?"

Shaking his head at his precocious little sister, who smiled smugly at him from across the kitchen table, Charlie said, "Nothing, Mom. Let's just move on, okay?" Miriam tossed quick glances at all three of her children, well aware that she definitely missed the inside joke.

Breakfast ended with Sarah and Carson heading out to meet friends. Charlie, now alone with his mother, helped clean up the mess, much to her delight. As he was loading the last of the plates into the dishwasher, he struck up a conversation.

"Thanks for everything, Mom. Especially the sunglasses. I've been looking at those for a while now," he said.

Draining the last of the coffee from the pot into her cup, Miriam looked over at Charlie and smiled. "You're welcome, Charlie. Happy birthday. And thank you for helping clear away the mess."

She crossed behind him and tousled his thick hair. Ordinarily, Charlie would cringe at his mom's display of affection more fitting for a six-year-old than a freshly minted seventeen-year-old, but something just felt right about it that morning.

Charlie closed the dishwasher door and followed his mother out onto the porch. The day was breaking nicely. Blue sky peaked out from behind billowing white clouds that lazily wafted about. The humidity was low for July, and the temperature was perfect. Charlie and his mom sat down in the rockers, listening to the island come alive around them. A thought rapidly occurred to Charlie, and he popped up from where he sat. He crossed the short porch distance and made his way over to the mailbox affixed to the wall by the front door. He lifted its worn lid to peek inside. Frowning, almost imperceptibly, he let the lid fall and returned to his place in the rocker.

Puzzled by his uncharacteristic action, his mom queried, "Looking for something in the mail?"

"Huh?" Charlie said, snapping back from the place his mind went to. "Oh. Um… no, nothing. Just, uh, I've never looked inside before, is all," he offered weakly.

Miriam's brow wrinkled. Surely, he didn't expect her to buy that one, did he? "Oh, okay. Well, mail usually doesn't come until the afternoon," she offered from behind her coffee cup. While Miriam may have missed the joke that bounced around the breakfast table a few minutes earlier, she wasn't as clueless this time. A dull ache grew in her heart. She knew exactly why Charlie looked in the mailbox. She hoped to high heaven that a card or something from his father would be there later in the day. She wasn't holding her breath. Her only wish was that the fallout from the impending disappointment was not on a scale equal to the Room Wrecking.

"So, what are your plans for your special day?" she asked, attempting to draw her son's attention away from the empty mailbox.

Upon hearing the term, he smiled inwardly, "Meeting up with Madison for lunch. Then some surfing with Jackson. Hanging on the beach later with friends, I guess. Is it all right if I don't come home for dinner?"

Miriam pondered the question for a few heartbeats. After all, it was Charlie's birthday, and she had a few plans saved for later in the day, but then remembered how important friends are at Charlie's age and thought differently.

With feigned hurt, she said, "Sure, I guess. I had planned a wonderful dinner and there was going to be cake, but…"

Charlie's groan interrupted her sentence. "God. Please, Mom. No cake. You know I don't even like cake, and you know how I feel about my birthday, so can we please…"

"Okay, okay," Miriam said laughing, "I was just kidding, anyway. There is no cake."

Charlie's voice shot up, shocked at his mother's statement. "What? You didn't get me a cake?"

His mother laughed out loud at her son's annoyance. "Ah-ha," she said, pointing a finger at him. "You do care about cake, got ya."

Picking up on his entanglement in the ruse, Charlie laughed along with his mother. It was the liveliest moment he had spent with her in a while, and it felt good to be laughing together instead of fighting or being embroiled in some tense conversation.

"Well," he said in his defense, "I like the idea of a cake, not necessarily the cake itself."

Miriam took a sip of her coffee and returned the cup to the table. "Well, no worries about dinner. Have fun with your friends today. Just remember to check in now and again so we don't have a repeat of the last time, okay? Honestly. I thought you were dead. Mind you, I wanted to kill you for what you pulled, but…"

Nodding in agreement, Charlie answered with an, "okay". The two of them sat for a while longer out on the porch, rocking quietly as the clouds crept by and the sun grew higher in the sky. Miriam was stuck on the image of Charlie opening the mailbox to look inside. She kept replaying it in her mind. After a bit, Charlie rose,

"Alright. Guess I'm gonna gather up my stuff and head over to Madison's. I'll look for you on the beach later, okay?"

His mother nodded approvingly at her son. She watched him as he stood and headed to the front door.

Before he stepped inside, she said, "Hey Charlie". He paused and twisted his torso towards her. "All good?" she asked thoughtfully. Charlie smiled and nodded, then continued on his way to his room. As the door clapped shut behind him, Miriam's gaze fell upon the oxidized green mailbox clinging to the wall. Goose bumps leaped up on her arms just then as a chill breeze skittered across the porch. Startled, she passed it off as coincidence, rather than some harbinger of doom, but even she couldn't convince herself of that.

Aloud, she said, "Miriam, you of all people know what Owen Meany would say about coincidence." An uneasiness settled over her. She had half a mind to perk a fresh pot of coffee, fill her cup, and wait on the porch for the mailman to arrive. Then thought that maybe a glass of wine would be better served. She tilted her wrist to look at her smartwatch. "It's Happy Hour somewhere," she mumbled to herself.

■   ■   ■

Madison lifted her phone, setting off whatever magic happened inside to cause the phone to display the time. It was nearing noon, and she knew Charlie would be by soon. Asher had occupied the chair across from her for the last twenty minutes or so. Seeing her sitting behind the railing, beneath the welcoming shade of the roof, he made his way up the steps and joined her in conversation. Isn't that what friends do? Madison remembered thinking as he so casually and comfortably slid into the chair across from her. She also remembered thinking to herself how incredibly hot Asher was sitting there, glistening with sweat. His five inch in-seam bathing suit clinging to his muscled thighs, and his form fitting sleeveless t-shirt didn't help to distract her from that fact. She remembered thinking how beautiful his eyes were. Currently, however, she was thinking about Charlie, and the fact that he would be standing there on the sidewalk, in-front of her porch, at any second. Distracted by her tilting of the phone, Asher asked jokingly if there was some place she needed to be.

"Um, no. There isn't," she said, laying the phone back down. "Charlie will be stopping by at any second. It's his birthday today, we're grabbing lunch. And..." she trailed off, gesturing to Asher with her right hand, as if pointing out the white elephant in the room.

Asher smirked and nodded, completing her sentence. "And you'd rather I not be sitting here when he does, right?" Guiltily, Madison shrugged once and bobbed her head. "Seriously, if I was dating someone that got so angry when one of my friends was around me, or was so threatened by the friendship, I think I'd have to end that relationship," Asher said, hoping it sounded as passive-aggressive as he intended it to be. "It's not like we're secretly dating or something." He counted a few beats before he dropped, "At least, not yet anyway." He smirked, throwing a confident look at Madison that fell just a few millimeters short of crossing over to bravado.

With an exaggerated laugh, Madison replied lightheartedly, "In your dreams, buddy."

Smiling back, Asher pushed up out of the chair, "Then I guess I'll see you tonight, Mads," he said and jogged gracefully down the steps. "Tell Chuck I said, 'happy birthday,'" he called as he walked back to his house.

Madison called after him, "You know he hates when you call him that!" Asher, walking away, raised his hand over his head and gave a thumbs-up. She found her eyes following him home, caught up in his confident, almost swaggered, gait. She admired how perfectly his clothes hung on his body, noticing the detail of his strong shoulders beneath his t-shirt and his well-defined calves.

Her eyes returned to and lingered on his ass. As much as she hated to admit it to herself, Madison found she was growing rather fond of the boy she once thought was an arrogant elitist, which, she remembered, he was. There was something about him she couldn't quite put her finger on. He had a certain mystery about him, a dangerous liaison, so to speak, like a loaded gun on a table. You know you shouldn't pick it up, but for whatever reason you're drawn to it, almost pained not to touch it. But there was also a softer side to Asher that she had come to know. A more vulnerable boy that seeped out of the hard, smug shell only when the two of them were alone. Madison likened Asher's dichotomy to the jock football player that secretly knit sweaters for pound dogs; always posturing with the boys, but unguarded when the boys weren't around. He could be engaging, charming, even. He could also be an undeniable ass. It was just that mixture of salty and sweet that Madison found so palatable. Were they becoming real friends? she wondered.

Asher stopped by his front door and looked across the porch. It was as if he knew Madison would still be watching, following him with her eyes. Flashing an award-winning smile, he tossed a goodbye with his chin in Madison's direction. Blushing, Madison waved, returning the farewell. Suddenly, she felt very hot, and the humidity was not to blame.

SIXTEEN

"Yo. Wait up, bro." Charlie didn't even need to turn around to see who was calling out to him as he made his way down the street in route to Madison's house. Even if he didn't recognize the baritone of the voice, the 'yo' and the 'bro' were telltale calling signs. Charlie halted his stride and turned just as Joey hopped the curb with his bike and came to a stop next to him. Joey straddled the bike between his legs. He was sweaty, and his skin shone in the bright sunlight. Charlie caught himself admiring the well-muscled arms gripping the handlebars.

"Happy birthday, Charlie. Where you off to?"

Charlie was confounded by Joey's acknowledgment of his birthday and voiced his surprise. "Thanks, Joey. Don't mean to offend, but I'm kind of surprised you know it's my birthday today. And Madison's, for lunch."

Joey's face registered his own bewilderment at Charlie's comment. "Jesus, Charlie. I've known you for more than a decade. We even go to school together. Give me some F'n credit." Charlie wasn't sure if Joey was offended or not. His tone didn't indicate any sign of hurt feelings, more annoyance than anything else.

"Touché." Joey was right. They had known each other for the better part of their whole lives, but the knowledge of one another did not run very deep. While Charlie would hesitate to say he wasn't Joey's friend, he would find it somewhat of a stretch to say that they were friends, more acquaintances. Their shared history seemed to span the weeks between the end of school and the start of the next school year. Though they spent most everyday together at the beach, once school resumed, they resorted to quick hellos as they passed one another in the hallways of high school, or from across a classroom they shared. Charlie wondered how you could spend so much time with a person in one situation, and then barely interact with them when the situation changed. His mind drifted to thoughts of his dad, which he quickly shook away.

"So, anyway, um, thanks for the birthday wishes. Did you stop just for that?" Joey was casually sliding his bike forward and backward. Charlie could tell there was something else on his mind. Truthfully, Charlie was feeling uncomfortable. He struggled to remember the last time he was one on one with Joey. An awkward silence settling over like a rain cloud was what he feared most in the moment.

"No. I mean, yeah, I saw you and wanted to wish you a happy birthday, but there is something I wanted to ask you about, and well, I mean, the two of us are rarely alone together, if ever, so when I saw you walking, I thought now would be a good time, if that's okay?" Joey held Charlie's gaze, continuing to roll his bike forward and backward under his wide stance.

For some reason, Charlie's mind rushed to the old west. The image of two gunslingers facing off flashed in his mind. He never viewed Joey as an enemy, but the mind sees what the mind sees. Not knowing what else to say or do, Charlie just shrugged his approval.

Joey nodded, but didn't speak immediately. He continued to stare at Charlie, but something about his gaze changed. His look became softer, more caring. He seemed vulnerable, sincere, which caused some concern in Charlie, as Charlie had never seen Joey as anything other than a cocky, over-confident jock.

"So, listen. I know you and Jackson are tight. I've kind of always admired that about the two of you, how at ease you are with one another, how close you guys are."

What the what? Charlie thought. *Is Joey about to open up?* He darted his eyes about the street, half expecting to be Punk'd.

Joey continued, "And I guess the two of us seeing each other came as a surprise…"

"To say the least," Charlie broke in, trying to deflect with some humor. To his surprise, though, Joey's expression softened even further. His eyes reflecting empathy.

Nodding, Joey went on, "Yeah. Sorry about that. I mean, sorry that you had to find out that way, not sorry about what you saw us doing. Anyway," Joey broke off and took a deep breath. "Anyway, I need to know that you're okay. That me and Jackson being together is okay…" He trailed off again, this time looking away, out across the street.

Charlie wasn't sure what was actually happening. The conversation abruptly took a turn towards the odd.

"Are you asking if I approve, Joey? Because I'm not too clear about what's going on here. You guys are free to see each other, I mean. It is what it is, right?"

Turning back to face Charlie, Joey's eyes filled, which surprised Charlie. "That's not what I'm asking Charlie. I'm not asking for your permission. I don't need it. I'm asking if you're okay with Jackson and me as a couple. I'm asking if you're alright with us being together as boyfriends, for lack of a better term, and with everything that goes along with that." Joey stopped and ran a hand through his hair. When he continued, there was something in his voice Charlie did not recognize, a heaviness not heard before, "Because like I said, I know how important you are to him, and I know how important he is to you, and I don't want to come between that friendship. So, if you're not okay with us…" Joey broke off, but he held Charlie's gaze. He took a few breaths, as if to compose himself. "If you're not okay with us, I'll step out."

There it was. Charlie could feel his stomach drop. Joey, and maybe even Jackson, must have picked up on Charlie's feelings of discomfort when he was around them. All this time, Charlie thought his uneasiness was subtle, hidden from the eye. Come to find out, maybe not so much. Like a rabbit that stands still in the middle of a field in the hopes of not being seen, maybe Charlie's disdain was just as obvious to those looking. Instantly, he felt horrible about himself, and scrambled to say something, anything.

"Jesus, Joey. No, no. You don't have to do that," Charlie took a deep breath, and let it out. "Look, I'd be lying if I said it wasn't, I don't know, weird... not you guys, but the situation, I guess. And not you or Jackson being gay, though I never would have seen that coming from either of you. It's weird in that... Jesus, I don't know what the fuck I'm trying to say."

Unexpectedly, and perhaps with perfect timing, Joey laughed, lightening the mood. "Take a second, Charlie. This is unfamiliar territory for all of us."

Charlie nodded and gathered his thoughts before he continued. Joey *wasn't* just some hyped up jock, Charlie mused. Suddenly, Joey was *human*.

"What I'm trying to say, Joey, is I don't want you to stop seeing Jackson. You make him happy, and that makes me happy. It is weird... you two, being together... weird, and sometimes I may seem uncomfortable, because... well, because I am. But it's because I'm just not used to thinking of either of you as gay and I'm not uncomfortable because you guys are a couple. I'm coming to terms with that. It's not always easy. When you guys are together, it sometimes feels like I'm meeting you both for the first time, and it's like I'm trying to figure out who you guys are all over again. But I'm trying, Joey, because you're right. Jackson is important to me and you are important to Jackson, so I guess, by default, that makes you sort of important to me as well." Charlie exhaled, as if he were holding his breath. It felt good to say what he had been thinking for weeks now. He felt lighter. Maybe he should try to purge the other thing that was weighing him down so much. Maybe it was time to talk about that as well?

Joey stood for a second or two, nodding his head, as if he were processing what they had said. Pensively, he spoke, "Okay. Thanks for that, Charlie. I appreciate your honesty, I do. You know, you sort of hit the nail on the head, there."

"How so?" Charlie asked.

"You said that it's like you're trying to figure out who we are all over again."

Puzzled, Charlie said, "Yeah, it is, but I'm not following."

Joey laughed and shook his head, but not in a critical, condescending way. "It's the same for us, Charlie. For Jackson and me. We're trying to figure out who we are all over again. I can't fully speak for Jackson, but for me, I've known I was gay since about fifth grade, and it scared the shit out of me. I didn't want to be gay. I wanted to be like every other guy I knew, like you, Charlie. So, I hid. All these years I've crafted a fake me, the me everyone sees. The jock. The guy's guy. The lady's man. Joe Hetero. I'd gotten used to that version of myself, almost believing, hell *wanting* to believe that's who I was. But it isn't. Now that I'm being honest with myself and others, it's like I'm a brand-new person. I suspect it's the same for Jackson and we're getting used to us because, for the first time, we're openly being who we really are, you know?"

When the hell did Joey become so deep thinking and perceptive? Charlie thought, startled by Joey's self-awareness. Could it be that he always was those things, but Charlie never bothered to notice? Maybe all these years he had allowed his preconceived notions to hamper his vision? Probably.

"I guess I never thought of it that way."

"Maybe it's time that you do. Anyway, thanks for stopping and listening. Happy birthday, Charlie. Guess I'll see you later on."

Joey hoisted himself onto the seat and maneuvered the bike back over the curb.

He was just about ready to pedal off when Charlie called out impulsively and for reasons he didn't fully understand, "Don't hurt him, Joey."

Joey turned to face Charlie and looked at him, deeply, and earnestly, "That's a two-way street, Charlie." He cycled away, leaving Charlie standing on the sidewalk wrapped in the honesty of those five words.

■   ■   ■

Asher had barely cleared his porch when Charlie arrived on the scene. Briefly, Madison hoped that Asher's departure wasn't witnessed by Charlie. A wave of guilt chased that thought, washing over her. The feeling surprised her, and she wondered why it mattered if Charlie had seen Asher on her porch? They were neighbors, after all. She and Asher weren't seeing each other, secretly or otherwise. They were friends, and only friends. So why did she feel like she was sneaking around behind Charlie's back?

She shook the remorse away and smiled affectionately as Charlie made his way up the steps and onto the porch.

"Hey. You look flushed. You feeling all right?" Charlie inquired.

Unconsciously, she raised a hand to her cheeks, as if trying to determine its color through touch.

"Must be the heat," she offered. She allowed herself to take him in as he stood there before her. He was handsome, she thought to herself. The last year had been good to him, filling him out, broadening him. More so, Charlie was a good person. He was kind and feeling, which only bolstered his attractiveness. There wasn't a duality to Charlie, like there was to Asher. He projected exactly who he was. Almost like a puppy, he was both adorable and charming. Though lately, there was a brooding, darker side to him that didn't exist before. A murkier version of Charlie that reared its head from time to time, more frequently of late. Don't we all have a side that we keep from others? Madison wondered. A part of our personality that we may not necessarily be proud of, or comfortable with, but exists nonetheless? Two sides to the same coin? Asher certainly did. Everyone does, right? Why would it be different for Charlie?

"Happy birthday, beautiful," Madison said as Charlie leaned in and kissed her. It was a quick kiss on the lips, little more than a touch and go. As he went to straighten up, Madison reached up and cupped the back of his head, keeping him locked in place. She kissed him back. Holding him there in her grasp for a moment long enough to be considered impassioned but not so long as to embarrass should anyone see them.

Madison broke her hold and smiled warmly. Charlie, somewhat taken aback by the fervent nature of the kiss, raised an eyebrow and said, "Wow, what was that for?"

Leaning back in her chair, Madison feigned insult. "Does a girl need a reason to passionately kiss her boyfriend?" she asked.

"I guess not." That term still struck Charlie as odd. Despite all they had been through together in the last weeks, all they had done, he still struggled to reconcile the fact that he and Madison were seeing each other, and that she was, indeed, his girlfriend. He didn't bristle at the term. It just didn't register as exact.

"It is, after all, your birthday. Consider it a part of your gift."

"Why, thank you. That's mighty kind of you," Charlie said in an exaggerated southern drawl. "I certainly don't mean to sound greedy, or anything, but is there more?" Charlie leaned across the space between them and returned Madison's kiss. His heart rate increased a tick, and his body resonated in a warmth unrelated to the heat of the day. This part of the relationship most certainly did not strike Charlie as odd.

"Wow. What was that for?" Madison asked, smiling.

Charlie just shrugged and plopped down in the chair next to her. "I would have been here sooner, but I ran into Joey. Well, actually, he ran into me, and we had the strangest conversation."

Silently, Madison thanked Joey, realizing that if the two hadn't stopped to talk, Charlie would most definitely have run into Asher either on the porch or on his way home. Who knows how that would have ended up? That feeling of guilt made another quick appearance, skating happily through Madison's conscience.

"Joey? What did he want?"

"Of all things, he asked if I was okay with him and Jackson seeing each other. He said that if I wasn't, he'd break it off. Crazy, right?"

"I don't know," Madison began. "Are you okay with Joey and Jackson seeing each other?"

Charlie could feel himself bristle at the question, "Jesus, not this conversation again," he said, maybe too critically. His cell phone buzzed in his pocket, and he dug in and anxiously pulled it out. Scanning the screen, he flipped it over and placed it face down on the arm of the chair.

Madison picked up on Charlie's tone and posture. Cautiously she offered, "Well, I'm just not sure that you were being honest with me, or yourself."

"What the hell is that supposed to mean, Madison? What? I'm lying to myself about my best friend?" Charlie offered, sitting up slightly in his chair. "Do you think I have issues with those two?" Charlie knew the fact that he absolutely did have issues caused his defensiveness, but his magazine was loaded and locked. *Nothing quite like the truth to set you off.*

Madison, sensing that perhaps she had touched a live wire, proceeded gingerly, "I'm just asking Charlie." Madison knew that a choice existed in the moment. She could change the subject, which would be the easier thing to do and would spare Charlie taking a hard look at himself. Being his birthday, that would be the best path.

The other choice was to explore the conversation and get at some truth. This path, she knew, could get rough, but not all paths in life are without risk. Never being one to shy away from risk, she chose the path with slightly more peril.

"Being honest, I have picked up on some uncomfortable vibes wafting off of you when Joey and Jackson are together, especially if they're being affectionate. More so recently than before. You seem to stiffen, and your mood and expression changes. It's as if you happened upon a terrible smell, or you see something that makes you prickly. I would imagine that, as Jackson's best friend, and knowing him as long as, and as well as you have, that seeing him being affectionate with another guy may make you uneasy, is all. It's a lot to get used to, right?" She threw out the question in an attempt at validation, hoping it would dial Charlie back a bit. She held her breath.

Charlie relaxed back into his chair. His phone buzzed again. He snatched it up and turned the screen to his face, but just as quickly put it back down. It was as if he was expecting a call or a text from someone.

"Yeah, Madison," he said in a much softer tone. "It is a lot to get used to, but like I said to Joey, I'm trying."

Guardedly, the way one might step onto a frozen lake to see if the ice will support your weight, Madison pressed on. Inwardly, she knew it was a bit of a hazard. These days, Charlie was fragile and hot-tempered, and she worried about changing his mood for the worse. But she also knew that Charlie needed to talk about this, and other things. Madison hoped that allowing himself to confront his feelings might ease the burden of carrying them alone.

"So, if I understand your response correctly," Madison began cautiously, "which I think I do, Jackson being gay, does sometimes make you uncomfortable. Yes?"

Charlie started bouncing his knee, and Madison noticed his left hand had curled into a fist. He didn't respond at first. Instead, he sat staring at the porch floor as if he were counting the number of nail heads in the old wood. He ran his right hand through his hair, then popped up out of his chair so unexpectedly that Madison startled.

"Yes, I guess. I mean, no. No. I don't know." Charlie's nervous energy manifested itself and he began to pace the porch. His words came faster now, more harried. "It's not that Jackson being gay makes me uncomfortable. It doesn't. I know people back home who are gay, and it doesn't bother me or make me uncomfortable when I see them or when I'm around them. So, no, it isn't Jackson's homosexuality that makes me uncomfortable, but for whatever reason, when I see him with Joey, it's just... it's just." Charlie stopped talking and pacing simultaneously. He was at the far side of the porch. Taking a deep breath, he placed both hands on the porch rail and leaned forward. Madison watched from her chair. She could see his back rise and fall with his breaths, as he tried to reign in his emotions. She wondered if maybe she had pushed too far and felt badly. Charlie straitened, turned and walked back over to where Madison was sitting. She rose to meet him and took him in her arms. Charlie buried his head in her neck, breathing in her smell; shampoo and sunscreen. He felt safe, protected. Softly, barely above a whisper, he finished his sentence.

"It's just that when I see them together, when I see Jackson kissing Joey, or holding Joey's hand, there's a bit of me that feels betrayed, and there's a bit of me that feels like I'm losing my best friend, and there's a bit of me that feels angry because I feel that way. And I don't know how to stop feeling that way." Charlie exhaled sharply, as if he had been holding his breath.

Madison gently took his face in both her hands and kissed him. She let her arms drop to his shoulders and then slowly ran her hands down his back to his waist and up again. Smiling affectionately, she conveyed her understanding of all he had said with a nod and another kiss.

"Stupid, huh? Definitely selfish."

"Not at all, Charlie. Your feelings are never stupid. They're your feelings. Embrace them. They are a part of who you are. But if you're unhappy with the way you feel, you can work to change that. Have you talked to Jackson?"

Charlie chortled, "No."

"Well, maybe it's time you do? I mean, if Joey has noticed, and I've noticed, it stands to reason that Jackson has noticed too. Maybe you guys just need to sit down and talk through it."

Charlie pulled away from Madison, taking a couple of steps backwards. He could feel himself beginning to boil and desperately tried to damp it down.

"And say what, Madison? 'Oh, hey Jackson, sorry if you've picked up on my uncomfortable vibes, it's just that, well, you know, it's relatively new to me that you like to suck face with guys, and what not, and it weirds me out just a bit, sorry, working on it. Hope to get it under control before it ruins our lifetime of friendship'. Something like that, Madison?" Charlie knew he was way over the edge with his tone, and immediately felt badly. He knew Madison was only trying to help. Reeling himself in, he said, "Shit. Sorry. You didn't deserve that." He unclenched his fists and forced himself to relax.

Ever gracious, which was another quality Charlie admired about the young woman standing in front of him, Madison shook her head and smiled.

"No need. I pushed you. It's okay." Madison walked over to Charlie and took his hand. Again, she tried to erase any guilt he may have felt at that moment. "It's okay."

Sighing, Charlie changed the subject, "How about we grab those burgers now, huh?"

Titling her head up to meet his lips, Madison kissed Charlie softly. Charlie's internal brawl was almost palpable. She wanted to just hug him, to fold him into the embrace of her arms and make his struggle just disappear, but she knew only he could do that. In time, she thought; she hoped.

"Burgers can wait," she said in his ear, running her hands up the outside of his thighs. The warmth of her breath and the weight of her touch caused lightning to course through Charlie's body.

"I don't have my backpack."

"That's okay. I got you covered; no pun intended." Charlie felt his knees buckle slightly. Turning, Madison led Charlie by the hand into the house and up the stairs.

■　　■　　■

It was the flicker of motion just above his field of vision that distracted Asher from endlessly scrolling through his phone as he sat on his bed, reclined against the headboard. Looking up, he was just in time to see Madison enter her room with Charlie in tow. Asher watched as Madison closed the door, and as they kissed, clinging to each other in an embrace. He watched as Madison peeled off Charlie's shirt. He watched as Charlie returned the action. Asher watched until they moved out of his line of sight. His imagination took over then, and yes, it ran wild. In that moment, Asher's jealously made itself known in his stomach. Waves of envy swelled up in him, threatening to drown him in his bed. Anger prickled at his skin like so many ants crawling on him. It was all he could do not to hurl his phone at the wall. Instead, he began to plot.

SEVENTEEN

With his legs spread across the width of his surfboard, Jackson bobbed gently with the motion of the water as he waited for a swell. It was the type of summer day you see in the movies, and the kind poets write about. He reveled in the sky's blueness, the warmness of the water, the heat of the air, and the peace of the moment. *I could do this all day, every day*, he thought to himself, as the ocean lapped against his board, spilling onto the tops of his thighs. To Jackson, little was more tranquil than being on his surfboard, feeling the pulse of the sea.

About ten feet off to his left and slightly in front of him, Charlie sat perched on his board, waiting. At the moment, his eyes were closed, head tilted back slightly, raised to the waning afternoon sun, as it arced on its trajectory towards the bay. His hands were on his thighs, palms down. As he rose and fell with the waves, to Jackson, it appeared as if his friend was meditating. Now and again, Charlie's abdominals flexed as he worked his core to keep his balance. In the late-afternoon sun, with its rays bouncing off of the water and ricocheting off of Charlie's slick, bare torso, Charlie could have been a still shot in CARVE magazine.

The boys had been out in the water for about an hour now, and while the waves weren't the best, Jackson was happy to have this time with just his friend. They hadn't talked much in all the time they were in the water; they didn't need to. Each other's company and the waves were enough. Jackson flashed to when they were younger; to a time when, from sun up to sun down, they barely parted company. Each summer day bleeding into the next, with sleep being the only real time they were apart. It seemed lately, though, the two of them had had some difficulty finding time to hang out. Sure, they saw each other most every day, but their significant others and circle of friends were usually in tow. One casualty of relationships, Jackson surmised, was time spent with just your best friend. Noting the distance between them now out on the ocean, Jackson wondered if perhaps there was also a metaphor somewhere adrift on the waves.

The boys had ridden their bikes down to Morningside Beach around three in the afternoon. After a text from Charlie, Jackson had swung over to meet him at Madison's house. When he arrived, Charlie and Madison were on the steps, practically entwined. They were sitting shoulder to shoulder, thigh to thigh, hands entangled in each other's. Smiling, the two were talking to one another quietly. Upon his arrival, Jackson immediately felt like he was intruding, as if he had walked in on a very private moment. For a flash, he felt embarrassed for dropping by, despite the invitation. Charlie and Madison said hello simultaneously and then broke out in laughter. Puzzled by their merriment, Jackson felt like the tail end of an inside joke. As if he weren't privy to information that both Charlie and Madison shared. Another flash of emotion, only this time, jealousy? Shaking it loose, Jackson noted the grin on his friend's face and immediately surmised why they might be so full of mirth. He could feel himself blush. *Was he intruding?* he wondered to himself. *That's just stupid, Jackson,* his mind answered back.

After parting Madison's company with a kiss, Charlie hopped on Jackson's handlebars. It had been a while since Jackson had pedaled Charlie along in this fashion, and Charlie's growth spurt was evident. By the time they rode the few blocks to Charlie's house, Jackson's thighs were burning. Hopping off, Charlie ran around to the back of his house to grab his bike and board. Jackson rolled his bike back and forth between his legs while he waited. On the breeze, Jackson thought he caught wisps of Charlie's mom's voice, high-pitched, but it wafted off before he could be certain.

Without warning, the gate flew open, and Charlie burst through. He struggled to get the bike through the opening as he wrestled with his surfboard clutched under his free arm. His backpack hung haphazardly across one shoulder. His face was red, and it was obvious to Jackson that his mood had soured hard and fast.

"Let's get the fuck out of here," Charlie muttered as he brushed past Jackson, intent on the curb. Shoving his other arm through his loose backpack strap, he dropped his board into the side rack, hopped on his bike and took off toward North Street and the beach.

Flustered, Jackson was hot at his heels, catching Charlie's pace and arriving at his side a block away.

"Hey. What's going on?" Without response, Charlie dropped his head and shoulders and pedaled on faster, as if he were fleeing. Again, matching his friend's pace, Jackson tried a second time. "Charlie, come on man, slow down. What happened?"

This time, Charlie sat up and let go of his handlebars, allowing the bike to coast for a bit.

"So, I walk in the yard, and my mom and that dude, Dan, were sitting at the picnic table."

"Okay. So. Not the first time they've been together. I mean, you know they're friends."

The bike warbled, so Charlie pumped a few times to give it momentum, but remained upright. "Yeah. Friends," he said, barely hiding his contempt. "Friends my ass, Jackson. Guess they weren't expecting me to pop in. It was a bit of a surprise for the both of them."

"I'm not following you, Charlie. Gotta help me out here."

Abruptly, Charlie leaned forward and squeezed the brakes on either side of his handlebars. The bike fishtailed, leaving a stretch of burned rubber like a scar running down the face of the street.

The rear wheel broke contact with the tar, pitching the bike forward before the bike came to a stop. Not expecting such a rapid deceleration, Jackson shot past Charlie and he had to turn around and bike back to him.

"Dude?" Jackson launched in baffled frustration.

Charlie looked troubled, confused, and angry all at once. "I walked in on them. They were there, sitting on the same side of the picnic table. They were making out, Jackson. I walked in on them making out. My mom was all over him. Fuck, I've never even seen her kiss my dad that way. Just friends, huh, mom? Well, friends don't have their tongues in other friend's throats. I mean, Jesus Christ, what the hell? And then... and then, because, you know, I caught them off guard, *Dan,* jumps up, which I definitely wished he hadn't, because when he stood up, I could tell just how into the little make-out session he was. Who the hell wants to see that? And the whole thing was just so fucked up. I mean, Jesus. What the fuck?" Charlie's eyes pleaded with Jackson to offer some pearl of wisdom or a tiny phrase that would help make sense of what he had just bore witness to. For all the angst Jackson could see in his friend's eyes, in his face, the best thing Jackson could offer was a shrug of his shoulders.

Sighing and shaking his head, Charlie started back on his way to the beach. "Exactly, there's nothing to say. Let's go."

They spent the rest of the ride in silence, Charlie just ahead of Jackson. When they got to the beach, they chained their bikes to the split-rail fence and headed down to the sand. Right before the high tide mark, Charlie shrugged out of his backpack, peeled off his shirt, and walked out into the ocean, surfboard in tow. Jackson, uncertain how to make things right, or what even to say, hung back and just gave Charlie some space. He hoped the waves and rides would wash off the sour, but here he was, straddling his board, watching his friend off in the distance, still seemingly under the same cloud he was when he arrived.

As if sensing he was being watched, Charlie opened his eyes and turned towards Jackson. Charlie always had an uncanny ability to do that; to know when Jackson was watching him or thinking about him. Sometimes, it weirded Jackson out. Sometimes he thought it was pretty cool, like maybe Charlie could read his mind. Maybe after all these years, they shared a connection at a deeper level, similar to the rumored connection twins share.

Making eye contact, Charlie tossed a peace sign in Jackson's direction and smiled weakly. Jackson blushed like a kid who got caught stealing cookies. He tossed his chin in Charlie's direction and smiled back. A swell rolled in at that moment. Catching it out of the corner of his eye, Charlie dropped forward onto his board. Attention behind him, watching the wave, he paddled to meet the rise of the water. His board caught, and he popped up, gracefully and without effort. Jackson watched his friend as he took the wave backside, then hitting a perfect cut-back to pick up some speed. Charlie carved, turning back into the path of the wave, and launched off the lip, catching some serious air. He landed it and rode toward the shore before bailing in the shallows. Jackson's grin spread from ear to ear as he marveled at Charlie's skill.

On the beach, Charlie turned to Jackson. He raised his arm towards the sky and, with his index finger pointing to the clouds, he made three quick circles. Jackson nodded and began paddling for shore. He caught a small swell, and rode it in, hopping off before his fins bottomed out in the sand. Unfastening the leash around his ankle, he walked the short distance to Charlie and dropped onto the sand beside him.

"Damn, son. That was quite the ride. Perfect way to end a mediocre day of surfing."

Charlie smiled and nodded his head silently. His gaze never left the ocean.

As if speaking to the waves, he said, "Hey. You mind if I shower at your house? And maybe borrow some clothes? Including underwear if that isn't too weird. And uhm... I guess, would it be okay if I just crashed with you tonight? I, uhm… I don't want to go home, Jackson."

"Yeah. Of course. No worries." Jackson held his friend in his gaze. The worry for him, that was never too far from his mind, returned and roosted in his heart.

Charlie nodded again, still not looking at Jackson. He was hard to read at the moment. Jackson could tell he definitely wasn't mad by his tone and the calmness that seemed to settle over him. But he wasn't okay, either. As Charlie sat in the sand, hunched over, grabbing his ankles with his hands, to Jackson, he seemed almost defeated. He looked like he had just given up. As if the weight of whatever he had been carrying with him finally broke him.

"You want to talk about it, Charlie?"

Turning to Jackson, Charlie shrugged, "I don't know," he said with a palpable sadness. "I mean, what's there to say? At least I didn't walk in on them smashing, you know? Jesus, how would you ever move past that?" Jackson chuckled softly in agreement. Solemnly, Charlie watched the waves roll in. Turning to his friend, he breathed, "She's moved on, Jackson. I guess that means…" but Charlie broke off and looked away. Grabbing at his backpack, he pulled out his phone and took in the screen. He shook his head slightly and tossed the phone haphazardly back into the bag.

"I guess that means what, Charlie?"

Charlie let his head fall back so that he could take in the sky as a sigh escaped him, "I guess that means they're not getting back together, and, yeah, I know how stupid and pathetic that sounds."

There it is, Jackson thought. It's about time. "Nah. It's not stupid or pathetic," he said, shaking his head.

"Yeah, it is, Jackson," Charlie returned, but his tone wasn't sharp. It was more dejected than angry. "I'm seventeen years old, and I've been pining away these last months like some fucking dumbass third grader hoping that my divorced parents would somehow get back together and magically, everything would go back to the way things were. One big happy family, that maybe, wasn't ever happy at all. I mean, how fucking pitiful does that make me?" Charlie asked. "This isn't some movie, or sappy Hulu show. It's life. Real life. And real life just blows. It just fucking blows." He turned back to the ocean. "And it's my birthday. Jesus, not the best timing of dear old mom to get caught practically dry humping another guy. Happy fucking birthday, Charlie. Meet your new dad. And where the hell has *he* been? I haven't heard from my dad in…" Charlie's voice caught, and he drew in his breath sharply.

Jackson swallowed hard, trying to dislodge the stone in his throat. He had absolutely no idea what to say in that moment, which was a situation unfamiliar to him. He always had some witticism, or some trinket of advice to offer in any setting. But, there, in the sand, beside his best friend, watching as the last remnants of his hope shriveled up and blew away on the wind, he drew a blank. His first inclination was to give him a hug, but it's not in the Bro Code to give anything more than a bro hug, and somehow, this situation wasn't right for that. Given Charlie's state of mind, he was uncertain about how his friend would perceive a hug. He'd never hugged Charlie before, not meaningfully anyway. They high fived, and chest bumped, sure, but never a hug. *Guys don't do that, right?*

Instead, and not knowing what else to do, Jackson just placed a hand on Charlie's shoulder and squeezed lightly. He hoped that the gesture conveyed more than its simplicity to Charlie. He hoped that somehow Charlie could pick up the depth of Jackson's empathy for him right now, how much his heart hurt for him. He hoped it telegraphed that Jackson was there for him whenever and always.

Upon feeling the slight weight of Jackson's touch, Charlie turned. He first looked at Jackson's hand. For a brief second Jackson worried that there was a hint of contempt in Charlie's gaze, as if Charlie perceived his hand upon his shoulder as some untoward advance, something more than just support. Then Charlie raised his eyes to meet Jackson's, and there was a sincerity, a warmth, in them.

"Thanks for surfing with me today, Jackson," Charlie said. "It means a lot to me that we do this together. It always has. Being out there, on the water, with just you… well… it's like… perfect, you know?"

Jackson nodded, "Yeah, it is."

"Yeah. It is." Charlie's inner voice continued on, silently saying how happy he was to have Jackson as his friend; how he didn't know what he would do without Jackson; how he wasn't sure he would survive all this, if not for him. Those things he could never say out loud to another guy. He paused and allowed himself to bask in the company of his best friend, and the warm feeling of comfort that came with it.

"Now, what do you say we get out of here before we do something stupid, like hug?"

Nodding, Jackson dropped his hand and stood up. As they gathered up the loose ends of their day, Charlie pulled his phone out of his backpack once again. In life, little things often go unnoticed; the small oil stain on the driveway under the engine; just a whisper of sarcasm in a compliment; an inside joke. However, as slight an action as it was, Charlie's small drop of his shoulders upon looking at his phone did not go unnoticed by his friend. Jackson knew what he was looking for, just as surely as he knew that what he was looking for wouldn't be there.

EIGHTEEN

"Well, well, well," Asher said in a light-hearted tone as he came upon Madison perched on a picnic table bench outside of Bennie's bakery. She cradled an iced-coffee drink of some sort in one hand and was picking at what looked to be an orange-cranberry muffin top with the other. Startled by the sudden voice, she looked up, recognized the handsome face staring down at her, rolled her eyes jokingly and smiled.

"A young lady, all by herself, in this dangerous part of town. Lord knows what terrible mishap could befall her as she innocently nibbled her pastry." Asher slid himself onto the bench opposite her. "A mugging? A curbside abduction?" He glanced at her iPhone perched on the edge of the table. "An unattended phone pilfered by some pre-teen skateboard rat? Nefarious deeds of all sorts."

"Oh, yes. Fourth and Ocean, quite the perilous section of the neighborhood. In fact, there's talk going around that some family from Boston just moved in down around First and Atlantic. Rumor has it the dad is mafia and is spearheading some shady dealings over in Atlantic City. There goes the neighborhood." Madison raised an eyebrow and popped a piece of muffin into her mouth, chewing unhurriedly behind her slight smile.

Asher laughed, "Yeah, can't trust those Bostonians. Especially the ones that lived in Beacon Hill brownstones and summered on

Martha's Vineyard. Frickin, trust-fund babies. Spoiled little rich kids, always up to no good."

Madison raised her iced coffee. "I'll drink to that," she said, and pulled some liquid up through the straw. She placed the cup back on the table and returned to eating her muffin. She could feel her guard go up as soon as Asher sat down and felt guilty about it. They were friends, weren't they? If Jackson or Joey dropped in or her, she'd be relaxed, happy to see them. Instead, she couldn't quite shake the feeling that Asher was up to something.

Looking around, as if taking in the total surroundings, Asher continued, "Not your usual coffee spot, Bennie's. Thought you were a Berenato's fan?"

How would he know that?

"Well, yes, and no. Berenato's is my morning go-to, because it's so close to my house. And then there's The Beanery, which is Jackson's favorite place for anything coffee. But The Beanery is a bike ride. Bennie's, here, for me anyway, is the place for anything iced. And the muffins are the best. Not to mention the raspberry shortbread cookies, if you can get them." She broke a piece off the bottom of her muffin and held it out for Asher to try. He reached across and grabbed, making sure his fingers slid against her hand as he did. He popped it into his mouth.

"Not too shabby," he said with a smile.

Madison slid the rest of the muffin bottom across the tabletop. "Please, feel free. I only like the top."

She eye-balled Asher suspiciously as he took the muffin, thanked her, and popped a piece into his mouth. *This is damn peculiar.* She suddenly felt like she was in a game of chess, and she was waiting for Asher to make his next move. She arched her eyebrow again and smiled, as if to say, let's play this game out. As she waited for the next scene to begin, she took another sip of her drink.

"So, where's the birthday boy? Thought you two had plans for lunch, or… something."

Madison caught the way Asher paused and then drew out the word *something.* There was an accusation or perhaps an understanding in the way he said it, like he knew something he wasn't necessarily supposed to know, or he was fishing for information. Feeling uncomfortable, she shifted her position on the hard-wooden bench.

"We spent some time together, did some things. He's surfing right now with Jackson, down around Morningside."

Asher found an avenue to explore and pivoted down it. "Wait. He left you to go hang out with his friend? Thought you guys were spending the day together, getting lunch and doing stuff," *there was the pause and drawn-out word, again,* Madison noticed, "and all that. What kind of boyfriend bails on his girlfriend to go hang with his friend? I mean, aren't those two together like day and night, anyway? Seems weird that they hang around so much. And isn't Jackson gay?" Asher let the thinly veiled suggestion hang in the air between them.

Madison, picking up on what Asher was dropping, cocked her head and rolled her eyes. "You're an idiot, Asher. Yeah, Jackson is gay, but Charlie and Jackson's relationship isn't like that. They've been friends forever. They always go surfing on his birthday. Hell, they go surfing together all the time. Early in the morning, later at night, middle of the day. Maybe if you spent some time trying to get to know Charlie, rather than constantly trying to piss him off, you might have realized that," Madison's dander was up.

Asher shrugged. "Still, he bailed on you. Just saying. If you were my girlfriend, and it was my birthday, I'd want to spend the day with you. Hanging out, maybe some Netflix and chill. My hands all up in your hair. Not go surfing with my bestie. Especially if, as you say, my bestie and I went surfing together all the time."

The *Netflix and chill* comment riled Madison. While she tried not to let on how pissed she was, because that was absolutely Asher's intent right now, she could feel her face reddening, and her voice had a quiver to it.

"You know, Asher, you are the rain cloud in an otherwise blue sky."

"Wow. Didn't know you were a poet, Mads. You should write that down."

Shaking her head, Madison replied, "Not a poet. U2."

"Me too, what Mads?"

"Never mind, Asher."

With a shrug, Asher said, "What-evs, Mads."

He again reached across the table and placed his hand on top of hers in an action that was way too presumptuous and way too familiar for Madison's liking. The weight of his hand set her nerves on edge, as if her skin was just touched by the stripped end of a live wire.

"Back to Chuck," Asher continued. "Maybe he and Jackson are doing more than just surfing together. Maybe, just maybe, they're like besties with benefits. They seem to spend an inordinate amount of time together. An outsider might think they were dating or something. Maybe Jackson has something that good old Chuck can't get with you, if you know what I mean…" Asher let the innuendo hang out there.

Madison slid her hand from beneath Asher's larger one, the way one might if they had reached into a dark hole and touched something wet, something slimy.

Meeting him with steely eyes, she said, "You know, Asher, for someone so handsome, and so privileged, you can be a real asshole sometimes. It's a shame that your inner beauty doesn't match what's on the outside," she said contemptuously. She pulled some of her drink through the straw, then added, "What do you want, anyway? Why are you here?"

Asher turned on the award-winning smile, "I don't want anything, Mads," he breathed. "I'm here because I saw a beautiful young lady, who happens to be my friend, sitting by herself at a picnic table on the sidewalk. Thought you could use some company, is all." He reached across the table and placed his hand on top of hers again. "Sorry if I upset you. Wasn't my intent. Just can't help but wonder why Charlie would choose Jackson over you. Seems a stupid choice to me."

She looked at him up and down with her eyes, trying to contain her anger and maintain her composure. He was not going to get in her head, the way he has gotten in Charlie's.

"There was no choice, Asher," she said evenly. "Charlie is surfing with his friend. That's all there is to it."

Shrugging, Asher politely, if not facetiously, agreed, "If you say so, Mads." He stood up, readying himself to leave, "Guess I'll head home. If you're ready, we could walk together, if you'd like."

At the moment, there was little less that Madison wanted to do than to walk home with Asher. His brazenness astounded her. She thought back to earlier in the day when the two of them were on her porch, just chatting like friends. It was casual. This experience was the exact opposite of that. This felt more calculated and dangerous.

"Um, thanks. I'm good. Gonna pop over to Kelsey's and see what's up there. Maybe hang by the pool for a bit."

"Okay. If Logan is there, tell him I said 'hey'."

"Yeah, sure. No problem."

"Alright, Mads. Guess I'll see you later tonight on the beach."

"Huh? What do you mean?"

"What do you mean, what do I mean? We're all hanging later on the beach, you know, for Chuck's birthday. Isn't that the routine?"

"Yeah, it is, and we are. But how do you know about it?"

Asher laughed, "Kelsey. That girl keeps me in the loop. I'll see ya," Asher turned and made his way down Ocean toward First. He was feeling rather pleased with himself for the groundwork he laid with Madison, and there was a spring in his step. If all went accordingly, by the end of the night, Charlie and Madison would be no more.

Madison sat watching Asher grow smaller as he made his way further and further down the street. *What the hell had just happened?* Was Asher actually trying to suggest that Charlie and Jackson were some secret item? Did he actually think that he and she could be in a relationship together? And just what loop was Kelsey keeping him in? She quickly gathered up her phone and coffee and began the walk over to her friend's house. As she walked, she fired off a text:

You home?

Yeppers

I'm on my way.

Everything okay?

Not sure, I think. Logan with you?

Just left.

Good. Be there in a few.

Okay. I'm by the pool. See ya gurl.

Madison shoved the phone in her pocket. She had an uneasy feeling about what had just transpired, but couldn't quite figure out why.

■   ■   ■

Jackson's bed just feels so much more comfortable than mine, Charlie thought to himself as he lay on it, tracking the circuitous path of the ceiling fan with his eyes. Of course, it was definitely bigger than Charlie's bed. As if to manifest the thought, Charlie stretched out his arms and legs, spread eagle style, across the length of the mattress. Not having to share a room with his brother, Jackson's space could accommodate a larger bed. In this instance, a queen. Since Charlie had to share an already smaller room with Carson, he was relegated to a twin. While it wasn't so bad in years past-the bed, not having to share his room with his brother-Charlie's growing length and width challenged the dimensions of his tiny bed. As it was, when fully stretched out, his feet hung over the edge. The one, and possibly the only thing Charlie missed about being back home, was his larger bed and his personal space.

Charlie looked around the room. It was as familiar to him as was his very own. He had been hanging with Jackson in this room for years, playing video games, talking, laughing, and sneaking beer. They grew up in this room, together. Taking in his surroundings, he smiled at how very little Jackson's room had changed. Sure, the wall decorations came and went, but Jackson's orange and white surfboard still stood in the corner next to the closet, where it lived since he out-grew it and needed a bigger one. The electric guitar he got for his eighth birthday hung on the wall, having never been played. A collection of skateboards scattered about and sticking out from under the bureau, the same white bureau that always graced the wall. The paint on the drawer pulls worn in places from years of being touched. The antique lava lamp he picked up at a summer yard sale when they were both ten was still on his bedside table. Charlie felt safe here, wrapped in the comfort of the familiar. In all the change the past months had brought, Charlie was happy to be in a place where time seemed to have stood still.

His phone buzzed in his pocket. Digging it out, it annoyed him to find yet another text from his mother. He dropped the phone onto his chest.

Jackson stepped into his room at that moment, wearing nothing but a towel wrapped around his waist, his hair still dripping from the shower. He disappeared into his closet, emerging seconds later in shorts and holding a T-shirt. He rolled on some deodorant, slid into the tee, and sat down on the edge of the mattress and toweled his hair. Charlie's phone went off again.

"You've been checking your phone a lot since we got out of the water. Even when it doesn't go off. You looking for something in particular? Or are you just bored with my company?" Jackson knew what Charlie was looking for, hoping for. He hoped that his broaching the subject would lead Charlie into a discussion of what he would do if, or when, he didn't hear from his father today.

"Huh?" Charlie asked coyly. "What are you talking about? I'm not looking for anything. Honestly. You know these things," Charlie said with a wave of his iPhone, "they're designed to distract."

"So… you're not maybe hoping there's a text from anyone in particular, then? Maybe someone you might not have heard from yet?" Jackson charged the key and took the shot. "Like, maybe your dad?"

Jackson stared at Charlie, questioning him with his eyes. Daring him to begin the conversation that Jackson had wanted to have all summer. Charlie stared at Jackson in defiant silence. His eyes clearly telegraphing that perhaps, just perhaps, Jackson went a bit too far. It was as if they were both kids again and stuck in a battle of '*who's going to blink first.*' It was Charlie.

"I love your bed. It's so freaking comfortable," he said, taking the conversation away from him, away from his pain. "I'm never leaving it. Sure as hell beats the tiny hard slab of concrete I sleep on at my house."

Okay, Charlie. If this is the way you want to play it, Jackson thought, *I'll play.*

"Yeah. It is comfortable, but you ain't staying, 'cause I ain't sharing my sleeping space with you, friend. Feel free to crash on the floor. Or on the couch out in the TV room."

With a playful smirk, Charlie said, "Oh. What's the matter? Don't trust yourself with me in the same bed as you?"

Jackson cocked his head as if to say 'Seriously?'

"Kidding." Charlie's phone went off rapidly, three times.

"You gonna get that?" Jackson said with a toss of his head in the phone's direction.

Charlie sat up and pushed back against Jackson's headboard. "Nah. It's just Miriam. She's been pinging me since the beach. Her abundance of texts run the gambit from apologizing, rationalizing, explaining, and inquiring as to if I'm okay."

"You're not going to answer her?"

"My friend, silence *is* an answer."

Darth Vader's theme filled Jackson's room. Both boys looked at each other and laughed.

"She knows you're talking about her," Jackson said, and then paused for a second or so while the digitized musical notes floated about. "You should get that. She's probably worried or something. Maybe she just wants to know where you are."

Charlie shook his head. He swung his legs over the side of the bed, stood up, and paced the room. Jackson swore he could see the faint peach-fuzz hair on his arm's stand up on their ends. He watched as the muscles in Charlie's neck tensed. He rolled his shoulders twice, as if trying to dislodge a knot.

"I know. I know I should respond to her; I fucking know. But what do I say, Jackson? What... what words could I possibly offer? Maybe something like *Hey mom, no worries. It's okay you were making out with that guy in the yard, and he was rubbing his junk all over you. No problem. Looked like you were having fun. I know he was. And hey, by the way, I'm gonna hang at Jackson's house tonight, so feel free to tear up the sheets. I got some spare wrappers buried in the bottom of my sock drawer if you need them. Just be careful not to wake the kids.* Something like that?" He stopped pacing and turned to look at his friend. Nervously, he ran a hand through his hair a couple of times.

"Uhm, no. I wouldn't recommend that, Charlie."

"No shit, Sherlock." Charlie could hear the edge in his voice, as clearly as he could see the hurt register on Jackson's face. He was also acutely aware of the fist his hand had balled itself into. He drew in a deep breath and let it out. "Sorry. I am… it's just that I don't honestly know what to say to her right now, you know?" Charlie shrugged his shoulders.

Jackson nodded, "You okay?"

Charlie laughed, but not in the way you would at a joke. It was more of a maniacal laugh, like a crazy clown or a madman laughing at the wall in an asylum. The sound actually scared Jackson a little.

"Jackson, I haven't fucking been okay since January. Not one fucking day."

Another crack in the wall, Jackson thought, "I know, Charlie," he said. "I know, and it worries me. You're holding a lot of shit in, and you won't let it out. Which is just so… so you, you know?" Charlie nodded but said nothing. "Look. You want to just, I don't know, hang here, tonight? Stay in, play some video games, order a pizza, drink some beers? Talk? Like we used to?"

Charlie stood silently for a while, as if weighing the invitation against what lay ahead for the evening. Honestly, the idea of spending the rest of the night with just Jackson came with a certain appeal. It would be nice to hang the way they used to, in his room, being goofy, but he knew if he stayed in, Jackson would find a way to make him talk, and he wasn't quite ready for that. Charlie's mind flashed to Madison and all they shared. When he left her earlier in the day, the plan was to meet up at the beach later on and see where the night took them. It wouldn't be fair to her to back out of that, was it?

Charlie pulled his phone out and fired off a text to his mom to assuage her concern. When finished, he turned to Jackson. "That would be great, and I appreciate the offer. Let's go meet up with everyone and see where the night goes. It's a nice night."

"Yeah, it is, and it's your birthday."

"Yeah, that too."

"Was that text to your mom? Let her know you were okay, and that you were with me?" Jackson asked.

"Yes, mom, it was. Are you happy?" Charlie said sarcastically.

"I am. Let's go."

The boys exited Jackson's room into the small living room that Jackson and his brother shared. Simultaneously, Noah walked through the back door with Brooke. They were hand in hand, looking perfect together, as always.

Upon seeing his brother and Charlie, Noah said, "Hey Charlie, happy birthday."

"Thanks, man. Appreciate it."

"It's your birthday, today?" Brooke queried with a smile. She always looked at Charlie as if he were a teddy bear she wanted to just cuddle, and that was okay with Charlie.

Charlie just nodded.

"Well then, Happy Birthday," Brooke said and pulled him into a hug, rocking him gently from side to side.

Damn, why does she always smell so good? Charlie thought as he raised his arms to return the hug. She ran her hands up and down his back, causing Charlie to have to think of baseball. Brooke released him and rubbed his upper arms, smiling warmly at him. Charlie took a couple of steps towards the door.

"What are you two lovebirds going to do tonight?" Noah questioned.

"Fuck shit up," Charlie replied, as he and Jackson pushed open the back door and emerged into the yard like a couple of gangsta rappers, sans the simulated rain and smoke machine. It wouldn't be for a few hours yet, but Charlie would come to realize just how prophetic his three words were.

NINETEEN

What sets summer days and nights at the shore apart from the ordinary days and nights that occurred from the beginning of September through the beginning of June was the total and complete uncertainty of them.

Once on the island for the summer, the structure and scheduling that was married to all the other days took a vacation itself. There were no practices to get to and no games to show up for. There was no homework that needed to be done, or reports that needed to be written. There was no alarm clock waking you up, and certainly no ten-p.m. deadline to be home and in bed. Then, trying to turn your brain off so you could begin the next day of mundane, routine, stuck-in-a-rut existence.

At the shore, life's monotonous cycle of lather, rinse, and repeat, exited. Once on the island, life seemed to just pause. You could finally exhale and allow your body to relax into the leisure of the beach, the casualness of the day, and cleanse yourself of the everyday toxins that seeped into your skin during the school year. Each rising sun was a blank slate, and what was written upon it was determined by what time you got up, the weather report, the size of the waves, your mood, or the company you kept. That was what Charlie loved so much about being at the beach house, about being in Ocean City–the freewheeling, easy-going nature of his existence. Granted, he struggled to find that peace this season, that calmness that generally swept over him the second the car crossed from the mainland, over the Ninth Street bridge, and onto the island. There were moments of it, to be sure, spread out across these past many weeks. They seemed, though, to be blackened by his own mood, by the shadow he so willingly cast upon himself, by the cancer he readily refused to excise, knowing full well that it was gradually consuming him.

The last couple of hours with his friends harkened back to the simpler days on the island, the ones he loved the most. He and Jackson had met up with Madison at her house. The plan was for everyone to rendezvous on the Boardwalk at Park Place and just see where the road led them.

Kelsey showed up with Logan in tow, and a box of birthday cupcakes she made that day. Joey arrived seconds after and the six of them devoured the treats walking along the well-traveled planks towards Wonderland. The idea of stopping in the ancient amusement park for old times' sake was briefly tossed about. The group of friends, with one newcomer in tow, even strolled through reminiscing about days gone by when they would spend hours there purchasing tickets and reveling in the thrills of the rides. Kelsey tried to explain the magic of the Wonderland to Logan, but not having grown up there, and not experiencing the cramped, crowded, tired old place as a child, he was apathetic, at best.

As most nights spent on the boardwalk went, one-foot step followed another in an uncharted, accidental route, that wandered aimlessly from T-shirt shops, to candy stores, to fast food windows, to mini-golf, and back again, until eventually the friends found themselves sitting in the sand on Third Street, talking, laughing, and replaying the highlights of the night.

For Charlie, he wouldn't have wanted to spend his birthday any other way. At some point, the storm cloud that was momentarily dissipated by the levity of the night crept back over his head and settled in. Earlier, he had wondered briefly when it would return, as no matter how distracted he ever was, it always did. This time, oddly enough, the growing lateness of the hour, and the silence of his cellphone, hastened it. He felt the uneasiness of it rolling in like an ocean fog that crept upon the shore. He quietly wandered off to see if he could shake it without anyone noticing.

As with all feelings, even pain, Charlie had gotten used to the sensation, how it weighed on him. He'd gotten adept at judging the severity of the tempest based upon the knot in his stomach, or the ache in his chest. As he walked quietly away from his friends, the bundle of bricks that settled in his abdomen laden his steps, and he knew this one was going to be hard to endure.

The tide was low, and the ocean was calm, calmer than he had seen it in quite some time, almost like glass. If he didn't know any better, Charlie would have sworn he was sitting on the edge of a lake. He made his way out to the furthest point of the breaker, and was now sitting with his back to the sand, looking out across the darkening water. From time to time, he could hear Joey laughing or Kelsey talking. At times, the jumble of their conversation blended together to create a tangled murmur of words. The sound of his friends' voices floating on the air was soothing, but simultaneously turned up his melancholy. The grip on his cell phone tightened. He was so lost in himself that when Madison sat down beside him, he startled.

"Hey. I didn't even see you wander off. How long have you been sitting here?" She ran her hand through the hair on the back of his head, playing with the locks, twisting them between her fingers. Her touch was still like electricity running through him.

"I don't know. Not long. A while, can't be certain."

"Things okay?"

"Yeah. Sure," Charlie answered in the way you answer when you are feeling the exact opposite of the words coming out of your mouth. Madison didn't miss it, but didn't comment on it either. Charlie continued talking, but more to the sea than to her.

"I like sitting out here, at the end of the jetty, with the entire ocean stretched out before you. As far as you can see, it's just water, and you know that thousands of miles out there is Europe, but that doesn't matter, because all you can see is water." He paused, as if uncertain what to say next, or where to take the conversation. Madison dropped her hand from his head to his knee. She absentmindedly twirled the small hairs there on the inside of Charlie's thigh.

"And in all that open space, there is so much uncertainty. You don't know what's out there, or what you might encounter, or what might even happen to you. It's all just unknown, sort of like tomorrow, in a way. No one knows what tomorrow will bring. You just have to wait for it and hope it's good.

"Behind me, well, behind me, is everything that I know. Everything that has already happened leading up to where I am right now, at this moment in time. All the bullshit, all the stress, all the hurt. It's all there, behind me, and it's like, if I don't turn around, if I don't move from this spot, I don't have to acknowledge any of it. I can just keep looking out over the ocean, looking at tomorrow."

Charlie's metaphor set off a dull ache in Madison's heart. She was silent for a while, trying to find words to help, uncertain as to what to say, or where to even start.

When she finally spoke, her words were deliberate, and calculated. "At some point, the tide is going to come back in. The ocean is going to rise, and wipe away everything that is here right now, submerging all of these rocks and everything on them. In a sense, the rising tide is like tomorrow, because it clears away what's left from today. It smooths the sand. It wipes the slate clean. It gives a fresh start, like tomorrow." She paused, turning to look at Charlie, to gauge his expression, but he just sat, staring blankly across the Atlantic.

"Problem is, Charlie, if you don't move from this spot, if you don't yield to the tide, the water gets higher and higher. Swallowing you. You got to move with the tide, Charlie, move towards what's behind you, getting closer and closer to it. If you don't, if you choose to stay fixed to this spot, you drown. The world, my world, would be a darker place if that happened. What's behind you, good or bad, is a part of you, a part of your history, but it doesn't define you, or your tomorrow, you know?"

Charlie turned to face Madison. His eyes were red and damp.

When he spoke, his voice was thick, his words stunted. Barely above a whisper, he said, "He didn't call. It's my birthday, Madison, and he didn't call me or text. I mean, who the fuck does that to their kid? What kind of parent forgets their kid's birthday?"

Charlie looked away and continued to stare out beyond the sea, beyond tomorrow. Madison drew closer to Charlie, inching across the boulder they found themselves upon. Lost for words, she gently placed her left hand on Charlie's right shoulder and drew him in to her, cradling him. She half expected him to pull away, to put up that wall that boys do to barricade in any emotional response, stave off even the slightest perception of weakness, and to keep out even their closest allies. Much to her surprise, and perhaps pleasure, Charlie collapsed into her. He wrapped his arms around her back and clung to her as if he were floundering amid a cold, dark sea, and she was his life preserver.

Madison knew Charlie had been struggling since the first day she saw him way back in June. She knew he was carrying baggage that he, for whatever reason, simply would not put down, baggage that he slugged around with him every day no matter how unbearable it became to hold. For the first time that summer, Madison could feel Charlie's pain. She felt the weight of that burden. She understood his anguish. It overwhelmed her in that moment, and she marveled at how he had managed to not yet be completely broken by it. All she could do was hold him as tightly as he was holding her.

TWENTY

The sun was dipping well behind the Ferris wheel, throwing long shadows across the boardwalk. By the time Charlie and Madison rejoined the small group of friends gathered in the sand, the sky was melting from blue to purple. To Jackson, Charlie seemed dimmer than he had been just a few hours earlier when the two of them were in his room. His eyes were red, and he moved sluggishly. With a worried expression, Jackson tracked Charlie as he dropped into the sand across from him and offered up a weak smile when their eyes met. Madison, still standing, ran her hand through Charlie's hair as she made her way across the semi-circle of friends to Jackson.

In a voice lost on the wind for anyone other than the intended recipient, she said to Jackson, "His dad hasn't called or texted yet. He's upset, Jackson. He'll never let you know it, but he is. It's crushing him."

"Shit. I was afraid this would happen. Thanks, Madison." Madison smiled and nodded

Jackson dug his phone out of his pocket and fired off a quick text.

Hey. You okay?

Madison moved past Jackson and dropped into the sand next to Kelsey, who was in a lighthearted conversation with Logan. It was then that Madison noticed Asher sitting next to his brother and swore under her breath. An uneasiness passed over her like a breeze. She spun to look at Charlie and then back to Asher, who smiled and tossed his head at her.

Charlie, jostled by the phone pinging in his pocket, pulled it out and looked at the screen. Looking up and over at Jackson, he just nodded and stuffed the phone back into his pocket.

Charlie wasn't okay. He sat in a fog. The fact that he hadn't heard from his dad all day was like an itch inside his brain. He couldn't scratch it, and as such, he couldn't get rid of it. It was his sole focus, and while he was aware of his surroundings, he didn't seem to actually be a part of them. Conversation drifted past like mist. He registered words, laughter, but couldn't tell you what his friends were talking about. What he could hear loudly was emanating from inside, repeating over and over: *He didn't call. He doesn't care.* He was aware of Asher being there, as surely as he was aware that Asher moved closer to Madison in the sand, but he couldn't tell you when Asher arrived, or if he had been there the whole time. Charlie couldn't say for certain what they were saying. He could pick up pieces: *Bennie's, how soft her hands were...* but was lost as to the gist of the conversation. His heart drummed, loudly, violently almost, but not quite loud enough to drown out the voices in his head. His breathing came quicker, his lungs expanding and collapsing to match his pulse. Images flashed in his eyes like PowerPoint slides advancing too rapidly: *Asher smiling, his hand on Madison's knee, him brushing hair away from her face.*

Charlie quickly became aware of being on top of Asher in the sand. He watched his left hand connecting over and over with Asher's face. He was aware of his own bloody knuckles, and the blood flowing from Asher's nose, from his mouth. While Asher had Charlie by about five pounds and two inches, he lacked the one thing that had taken Charlie over, that had finally consumed him.

Charlie had his rage, and that rage powered every punch he threw, one after another, repeatedly jack-hammering down.

Abruptly, two arms seized Charlie around his torso, and yanked him upward, off of Asher, into a standing position. Charlie cocked his left arm as he struggled to shake loose from the vice-like grip that held him in place. He kept swinging, connecting mostly with air, but try as he might, he couldn't shake free.

"Charlie, stop! Knock it the fuck off! Do you hear me, Charlie? Stop!" Jackson's voice broke the spell, and the world snapped back into focus. Charlie ceased struggling and became acutely aware of all eyes on him. Madison stood with her hand to her mouth. Kelsey crouched next to Asher, holding a sweatshirt to his nose. Joey was holding Logan back.

Charlie struggled to manage his breathing, to slow down his racing heart, to quiet his pulse that was thrumming in his ears. He wrenched his shoulders back and forth, struggling to get free. Finally, he growled, "Fucking let me go, Jackson."

Jackson let his arms fall away. Charlie turned to face him, chest heaving as he tried to catch his breath. Hatred played out behind his eyes.

"Jesus Christ, Charlie?" Jackson cried. "What the fuck is wrong with you? What was that? Who was that? Honestly, Charlie, it's like I don't even fucking know who you are anymore."

Charlie stood in the sand, fists clenched, and took in Jackson. His friend's last few words played again and again in his head. They bounced around in his skull, echoing off of the sides. Charlie heard his own words forming in his head, angry, hateful words.

People react to different situations in different ways. Nervousness might trigger excessive talking. Social anxiety may manifest as an aloofness. People sometimes laugh at funerals. In this instance, the more Charlie perseverated on what Jackson said, the more hilarious it became, and Charlie started to laugh heartily, unable to catch his breath. The sound emanating from Charlie was frightening. Jackson had heard it earlier that day, when he had asked Charlie if he was okay. Jackson's worry fast became fear, not for himself, but for his friend.

When the fit passed, Charlie re-leveled his gaze at Jackson and spat venom, "Oh, Jackson. That is fucking hysterical, coming from you. Absolutely fucking hysterical. You don't know who I am anymore? You don't know *me*? Really? Who the fuck are *you* these days, Jackson? I mean, after all this time, after all these years, suddenly you're a goddamned faggot. And you don't know me? *Who the fuck are you, Jackson*?" he screamed.

Jackson staggered backwards as if Charlie's words were bullets, and he took two to the chest. His eyebrows narrowed as he shook his head in disbelief.

"Charlie," was all he said in a voice that sounded like a dying breath.

The punch came out of nowhere. It connected squarely with Charlie's face, somewhere between his left eye and his nose. The force of the impact sent bright white light coursing through his brain, blinding him temporarily, and knocked him onto his ass into the sand. Immediately, he could taste the coppery brine of his own blood as it flowed past his lips and into his mouth. When his vision cleared, Joey was standing over him, straddling his torso. Anger, and offense, played out across his face.

"Don't you ever use that word again. Do you hear me, asshole? Especially when you are talking about him, because he cares about you, more than he cares about himself, or anyone. Don't you ever."

Joey stood for a second, scowling at Charlie splayed out in the sand. Charlie had never seen Joey so angry and for a second he half expected another punch, or a kick to the rib cage, but Joey turned away and walked over to Jackson and placed his hands on his shoulders. Bending his head to look into Jackson's downcast eyes, he said something that Charlie couldn't hear. Jackson nodded, and the two of them walked away in the opposite direction from Charlie. By now, Asher was standing up, his brother Logan beside him. Asher's nose had stopped bleeding but was starting to swell.

Madison made her way to where Charlie was sitting in the sand, still bleeding, "Charlie, what is wrong with you?" she gasped, disgust and astonishment heavy in her voice. "What you said to Jackson, what you just called him. How could you? He's your best friend. What is wrong with you?"

Shaking her head as if Charlie was now something to pity, or maybe scorn, she walked away from him, heading for the boardwalk. Kelsey and Logan moved away as well, with Asher in tow. As he grew smaller with distance, Asher turned and looked back at Charlie. The sun had sunken lower into the sky, casting a dimness across the sand. Charlie couldn't be sure, but it looked to him like Asher smiled, a cold, dark smile. Charlie knew then that he had done just what Asher had hoped he would do. Sabotage himself.

Charlie sat in the sand. His blood pooled on his shirt. The pain in his face, his nose, and his eye thrummed with his heartbeat. He sat there alone, his stupidity his only company. The look on Jackson's face burned into his memory. He couldn't un-see the hurt. Charlie's eyes brimmed as the realization of what he had just done cuddled up next to him, wrapped him in a bear hug, and slowly squeezed off his air supply.

TWENTY-ONE

Miriam had poured a glass of chardonnay and settled into the recliner opposite the TV. The sun was down below the rooftops and the dimness of the early evening threw shadows about the room like lingering ghosts. She clicked on the lamp, scaring them away. Dan had left some hours ago, apologetic and somewhat sheepish after the sudden appearance of Charlie. Try as she might to dispel any feelings of fault, Dan insisted on bearing the weight of responsibility. She struggled to determine if that was chivalrous of him, or just Dan being a bullheaded man. As a grown woman, she handled her own decisions. She didn't need some man to take the blame, accepted or projected. She could have turned the events of the day and dodged his advances. Truth was, she didn't want to. She was just as much at fault as he was, both guilty of only a horrible sense of time.

The timing was bad, as it was the middle of the day, in the backyard. She just wasn't thinking. Charlie's face when he rounded the corner and stumbled into their display projected such pain, such betrayal. She could still see his eyes every time she closed hers. He looked so broken. She should have leveled with him the first day he stumbled upon her and Dan sitting on the porch. She should have made it known then that she did have feelings for Dan, and that he had feelings for her. Charlie wasn't a kid anymore, and maybe, she thought, just maybe he didn't need as much shielding as did his siblings. She hadn't heard from Charlie since, save for a brief text saying he was spending the night with Jackson, and that was a couple of hours ago. Charlie's ghosting her had become commonplace the past few weeks. While that fact weighed heavily on her heart, she had become somewhat accustomed to the long periods of silence. Charlie had started to change months ago, she knew. She just wasn't certain when the transformation would end, or who would exist in her son's place when it did.

As she tried to figure out how to pick up the pieces of the shattered afternoon, she took a gulp of her wine. She was thankful for the buttery flavor, the quiet house, and the time to think. She could feel herself melt into the chair as the cool liquid washed over her taste buds. As most parents know, serenity in a household doesn't last long, and the quaint bungalow at the beach was no exception. As if proving the point, the front door flew open with such force that it banged off of the wall and slammed back into the person charging into the house. It startled Miriam so, that she leaped up from the chair and crashed into Charlie as he entered the living room. For a brief instance, she didn't even recognize him because of the blood on his face and shirt, and his now swelling nose and blackening eyes. She clutched at his shoulders, trying to hold him in place. Recognition washed across her face first, followed closely by panic.

"Charlie! Oh my God, Charlie. Are you alright? What happened to you?"

Wrenching himself free from her grasp, Charlie retreated to the far end of the living room. "I'm fine, Mom! Jesus!" But his face betrayed his words and his tone suggested anything but being okay.

Miriam moved over to him and fired off rapid questions, giving no time between for Charlie to even answer.

"Charlie. This is not fine! Who did this to you? What happened? Where's Jackson?" she asked, looking past Charlie towards the front door to see if perhaps he was standing in the threshold. "Is he okay?" She reached out and took her son by the shoulders.

Charlie swallowed hard at the mention of Jackson's name. His brow furrowed, and he began to gulp air. Miriam watched as his eyes brimmed. Her mind leaped immediately to her son's best friend and imagined the horrific catastrophes that may have befallen him.

"Oh my God, Charlie. Is Jackson okay?"

With a voice that sounded like someone had their hands wrapped around his throat, crushing his larynx, Charlie said, "I fucked up, Mom. I fucked up so bad, and I don't think I can fix it."

In that moment, another crack appeared in the wall Charlie had been building these past months. It was a small crack, but small cracks topple dams. Overcome, Charlie dropped his head onto his mother's shoulders, gave into his grief and cried. Deep, gut-wrenching sobs poured forth from Charlie, filling his mother with worry, and bringing tears to her eyes as well. She clutched him tightly as he shook in her arms.

In yet another round of bad timing, the screen door clicked closed. Miriam turned to see Carson stopped dead in his tracks, startled by his brother's meltdown. Charlie heard the door too and pulled away from his mother's embrace. He turned his back to Carson and tried to swallow the raw emotion that remained, but struggled to do so. He hurriedly wiped away any tears that remained, but the streaks in his bloody face were telltale signs.

"Mom?" Carson said in a worried tone.

"Hi, Carson, honey. Everything is okay. It's okay. Why don't you head down to your room? Alright? I'll be down soon." She turned her attention to Charlie and then back to Carson and forced a smile. "Go on, honey."

Carson nodded and began walking towards his room at the other end of the hall. As he passed his mom, he said, "Is Charlie okay? What happened to his face?"

"Charlie is fine, babe. Do you know where Sarah is?"

Carson nodded; eyes still fixed on his older brother, he said, "Emily's." Carson took a few steps towards Charlie, but stopped when Charlie stepped away from his approach.

"Head on down, Carson. It's okay. Everything is okay."

Miriam watched as her middle child made his way down to his room. Convinced he was out of sight, she walked back over to Charlie and placed a hand on his shoulder. Charlie shrugged it off, moving away from her.

Gently, as if she was touching someone wrapped in barbed wire, Miriam placed her hands on Charlie's arms and gently spun him around so he was facing her. Charlie's face was a mess. His eyes blackened, his nose was bloody and swollen. Blood covered his shirt and shorts.

She touched his cheek, haltingly, "Charlie, what happened tonight? You need to tell me what happened to you."

Charlie shrugged free of his mother's grasp again and began to pace the living room. He could feel the months of anger and resentment bubbling inside him again. His stomach felt like it had folded in on itself. The raw emotion that gurgled and churned inside him was nauseating, and he fought off the urge to throw up. The tidal wave of despair that had been building in Charlie since January finally crashed onto the shore.

Charlie spun to face his mom. He started speaking. His voice was furious and clipped. "This happened, Mom," he said, gesturing wildly with his arms to the entire room. "This happened. You and dad breaking up. Him leaving. Him leaving all of us. This happened!" he screamed.

Startled by Charlie's fury, she took a few steps backwards, away from him. Unrelenting, Charlie matched her distance by taking the same number of steps towards her. She could see the rage in his eyes, and it scared her.

"My whole fucking world collapsed back in January," Charlie screamed. "It just fell down on top of me and buried me. Every day, every fucking day, I crawl through the rubble trying to find some light, struggling to find the air, and I can't. I can't get out from under it. It's always there, it's always fucking there, mom. Pressing down and pressing down and pressing down. Crushing me. There are days I can't breathe because the weight is so heavy. It's killing me. Every fucking day, it kills me a little more." Abruptly, he paused as if to catch his breath, or perhaps figure out what to say next, or maybe because he was spent, but in that moment, Miriam could see the anger drain away. His shoulders sagged and his eyes filled with tears. Softer now, almost a whisper, Charlie continued, "And I'm just… I'm just so tired, Mom. I'm just so tired of dying a little bit. Every day."

Miriam's throat closed. Charlie's torment filled the room, devouring all the air. She could feel it on her skin. Quickly, she wiped away a tear that slipped down her cheek.

Charlie stood in the middle of the living room sucking in breath, as if he had just finished a race. Miriam, motionless, was watching her son from across the room. She wasn't sure if she should give him his space or embrace him in a hug. The mom part of her wanted to scoop him up and rock him in her arms. The teacher part of her told her to give him some space right now, let him decide the outcome, and what he needed. Let him make the next move. Time seemed to stand still. When Charlie spoke again, it was quiet, almost quizzical.

Slowly, shaking his head, he said, "You two chose each other. You were in love. You made a promise. You made us. *He* made us. Me, and Carson, and Sarah. And now," Charlie's voice stuck in his throat, and he inhaled sharply, "and now, we're like some old toy that he got bored with and doesn't want anymore. Just cast us aside, forgotten. How does that happen, Mom?"

The mom part of Miriam kicked into gear. She closed the small distance in the room that separated her from her son and wrapped him up in her arms.

Through his tears, he said, "He didn't even call me today. Why doesn't he want us anymore, Mom? Why doesn't he want me? What did I do, Mom? What did I do to make him just forget me?"

Charlie's last few words smacked his mother hard. It all made sense at that moment. Charlie's distancing himself, his brooding nature, his mood swings, all fell into place like pieces of a puzzle. For months now, he had been searching for some responsibility for his father's departure, some culpability in the ghosting of his family. Her stomach knotted. That weight would crush anyone. She pulled back from her embrace so she could look her son in the eye.

With hands resting gently on his shoulders, she said softly, "Oh, Charlie, you didn't do anything. Not a thing. Do you understand that?"

Lifting his head from her shoulder, tears still on his cheeks, Charlie said, "Then why, Mom? What happened?"

Miriam exhaled. That was a question she had asked herself many a day and night. She asked it over morning coffee. She asked it in the middle of teaching a lesson. She asked it as she sat on the couch late at night with the television as her only companion. What happened? She rubbed her son's shoulders softly and took a step back from him.

"I don't know, Charlie," she said with a shrug. "Sometimes, things just fall apart through no-one's fault. Relationships can be a lot like shoelaces. No matter how tightly you think they're tied, sometimes they come undone for no apparent reason. Our knot... your dad's and mine, it just unraveled." She paused for a second, again looking Charlie square in the eyes. "This wasn't your fault, Charlie. Do you understand?"

Charlie nodded and wiped at his tears.

A terrible sadness settled over her. It was hard enough to be sixteen, to navigate the murky, choppy waters of adolescence, let alone be carrying around the weight of feeling forgotten by a parent; the weight of thinking that perhaps somehow you were to blame. In her sadness, however, came some relief. She was happy that Charlie had finally conveyed what he was feeling, that he finally let out what he was keeping inside—well, exploded all over her was more like it. *A zit doesn't go away until it's popped.* Maybe this would be the beginning of Charlie's healing?

A new frustration regarding her ex-husband rose in her—*add it to the list*, she thought. She knew he had all but shut the kids off, as surely as she knew that his silence and complete lack of acknowledgement would be the hardest on Charlie. For months, she had fruitlessly tried to express this to her ex-husband, imploring him to reach out to the kids, to reach out to Charlie, but her pleading fell on deaf ears. She pushed her building anger towards her ex-husband aside. That could wait. Right then, she needed to be there for Charlie.

"Okay. I'm glad you finally let that out, Charlie. My God, why didn't you say something? I feel absolutely terrible that you've been carrying that around all these months. And we can talk more about that, shit, we're going to talk more about that, but, Charlie, honey," she continued, cupping her son's face gently in her hands, "none of that explains your face, the bloody nose, your blackening eyes. Your blood-soaked shirt," she paused and looked over his face, mentally wincing at the mess that was standing before her. "So, what happened out there tonight, Charlie? Who did this to you?"

Charlie blew out some air and jerked his face out of his mother's hands. His throat was tightening again, and he didn't want to break down in front of his mother for a second time that evening. Purposely, he moved away and into the dining room, taking a seat at the table so that his back was to his mother, who was still standing in the living room. Running a hand through his hair, he swallowed the emotions that were yet again threatening a Mount Vesuvius level eruption.

Miriam followed and took a seat at the small table across from him. She watched silently as Charlie's eyes glistened. He kept running his hand across his jawline, as if massaging some imaginary beard.

Finally, she fired a gentle coax across his bow. "Charlie?"

Charlie swiveled his head, making eye contact with his mom. Miriam arced her eyebrows and cocked her head. Universal mom language for *Well...?*

"Joey punched me, Mom. That's what happened to my face."

Miriam sat up in her chair. "Joey?" she asked incredulously, "Joey Mastromani? I thought you guys were friends?"

"Yeah, we are, I guess. Though maybe not so much anymore."

Miriam leaned forward, placing her hands onto the tabletop, "Honey, why would Joey punch you in the face?" she asked, confusion clear in her tone. "And, well, I don't mean to sound mocking, but are you sure it was only one punch?"

Charlie snorted and shook his head, "Yeah, Mom. It was one punch. He's been working out."

"Okay. Okay, sometimes friends get into fights... I guess. But what did you do to him?" Miriam's brows had furrowed, trying to understand what had happened. *Sometimes, it's easier pulling a tooth out with a pair of tweezers than it is trying to get information out of a teenage boy.*

Charlie shook his head, "I didn't do anything to him, mom," but before he could finish, his mother jumped in.

"So then, why did he punch you?" Her motherly instinct took over inexplicably at that moment. Abruptly, she pushed back her chair and made her way into the kitchen. She grabbed the dish towel from where it hung on the oven handle and headed over to the freezer. Placing some ice cubes in it, she knotted the end and walked back into the dining room.

"Here. Put this on your face, your nose is ballooning. God, I hope it isn't broken." She reached out to touch it, but Charlie yanked his head away.

"It's not broken, Mom." He took the towel and rested it against the side of his nose. Though painful, the ice was oddly satisfying.

Miriam sat down in the chair next to him. "Charlie, I feel like we're playing twenty questions. Cut to the chase, babe. What the hell happened out there tonight?"

Charlie knew he wasn't getting out of the dining room until he told his mother everything. He also knew it would be mere minutes before Sarah walked through the door. Last thing he wanted was to be sitting at the table, bloody, with an ice compress on his face when that happened. He was also concerned that reliving it again would bring forth another wave of tears. No little sister should ever see her oldest brother blubbering like some toddler who just dropped his ice-cream cone on the sidewalk. *Who was it that said, 'the truth shall set you free'? he wondered.*

"Joey hit me because I called Jackson a goddamned faggot. Okay? I called my best friend…" Charlie's voice stuck, and he turned away for a second as the gravity of what he had done pressed heavy against his chest. He took a deep breath to center himself. "I called my best friend a goddamned faggot and I can't take that back." Charlie dropped the dish towel full of ice onto the table. Turning to look at his mom, he said, "I fucked up, Mom. My words were so hateful… to Jackson. I can't take it back, and I don't think I can fix this, and I don't know what to do now."

Miriam placed her hand on top of her son's and patted it gently, still confused about what had exactly happened. *Why would Jackson care if Charlie called him that word, beyond maybe being pissed off about it? And why would Joey punch Charlie for using the word? Boys*–she thought with mild frustration.

"Well, Charlie. That's an ugly word and you shouldn't be using it, even in jest, but that doesn't explain why Joey would punch you. Especially if you didn't call Joey that word. I still don't understand."

Charlie laughed a small laugh. *Parents*, he thought. *They think they know what's going on in their kid's lives, based upon the tiny little bits of information we let them know, or they see on social media, but they have no idea.*

"Mom, Jackson is gay. He came out in June, and so is Joey." He paused briefly, giving them both sometime to process the information that still didn't fully register with Charlie. "And they're a couple."

For the second time that night, the words coming out of her son's mouth caused her to sit up in her chair.

"Wait. What? Jackson is gay? Jackson and Joey are gay? And they're a couple? Like, a dating couple?" She shook her head a couple of times. "Like you and Madison are a couple?"

Charlie nodded his head. "Surprise."

TWENTY-TWO

For what seemed like the hundredth time that summer, Charlie found himself awake in bed and staring at the ceiling. It had taken another twenty minutes at the dining room table catching his mother up on everything that had happened since arriving back on the island in mid-June with him and his friends, well, almost everything. He strategically avoided any details about him and Madison, and he was thankful that those details had remained off of his mother's radar. He wasn't sure if he was ready to candidly discuss the fact that he was no longer a virgin. Those conversations were best saved for your best friend, though Charlie wondered if he still had one; he doubted he did.

His phone was strangely silent that evening, though, given the circumstances and his absolute stupidity, he wasn't surprised. He had repeatedly texted Jackson, Face Timed, and Snapped him. His last text, about an hour ago, simply read:

Jackson? Please?

But nothing came back. The silence from his phone filled his room. Charlie wasn't sure what was keeping him awake, the pit in his stomach, or the overwhelming remorse for his actions, for what he said. Every time he closed his eyes, he could see Jackson's face reflecting the pain from the verbal knife that Charlie plunged deep into his chest. Whatever the reason, the fact was, sleep eluded him.

On the other side of the room, Carson was wheezing, having nodded off quite some time ago. When Charlie came to bed–maybe an hour ago? Maybe more? - Carson apologized for overhearing the conversation that took place in the dining room. He asked Charlie if he wanted to talk, but Charlie shrugged it off with a quipped 'nope', climbed into his bed and faced the wall. Yet another action he now regretted. As he lay there, staring at the same crack in the ceiling, the little voice in his head said, *what the fuck is wrong with you?*

Sitting up, Charlie kicked off the sheet. He reached for his cell phone. As he lifted it to his face, the screen lit up: eleven forty-five. Quietly, he climbed out of bed and slipped into a pair of shorts and a hoodie. He needed to get out of the room and out of the house. He needed to just get away from himself, but unfortunately, he was wherever he went. Sliding into a pair of flip-flops, he made his way towards the bedroom door. He pulled it open gingerly to not wake his brother. Escaping noiselessly into the hall, he made his way out the back door.

He stood for a second in the yard and took in the surroundings. The night was cool and clear, and the freshness washed over him. That was the thing about the beach. No matter how stifling the day was, the night always offered some relief. He needed to talk to someone. On any other night, he'd make his way over to Jackson's house, but this night was unique in that Charlie knew Jackson did not want to see or hear from him. Madison came to mind, though he wasn't sure if she wanted to see him either. He had not received a message from her since leaving the beach earlier in the night, bloody and broken. Feeling anxious as he was, he'd just have to take a chance and hope she'd welcome him.

As he set off for her house, he thought about how he would get in touch with her. He could text, but if she was asleep, she probably wouldn't hear the phone. He could call, but that risked waking up the entire house. He could toss gravel at her bedroom window like some love-struck Romeo in some hackneyed Rom-Com, but with the way his day was going, he'd probably break the glass.

When he rounded the corner onto First Street, he was relieved to see the small glow of a candle burning on Madison's front porch. Between that and the light of the distant streetlight, he could make out Madison sitting in an Adirondack, alone. Though surprised that she was still awake, Charlie was glad. As he got closer, an uneasiness spread through him. His footfalls on the sidewalk gave him away, and Madison turned to meet his gaze. She held it for a second, then turned away.

Not a good sign. Normally, he would just walk up onto the porch and sit next to her. This evening, though, was not their normal. Instead, he stopped on the sidewalk, at the foot of the porch steps.

Hands in his pockets, elbows locked, he simply said, "Hey."

"Hey," she returned without looking at him.

"Didn't expect to see you, you know? At this time of night."

"Then why did you walk over here, Charlie?"

Charlie noted her tone, not sharp, but not welcoming either. He shrugged, "Don't know. Couldn't sleep. Was hoping that maybe we could talk? Can I come up?"

She eye-balled him from above. He looked helpless, penitent, and beautiful in his remorse. Her inner voice told her to *tell him to go to hell,* but there was another voice that said *He's had a rough time. Cut him some slack.* Though his behavior that night was frightening and inexcusable. He was like a wild man, a crazed person. The look in his eyes when he was pummeling Asher scared her. Charlie was gone, replaced by some rage filled maniac. *Tell him to go home,* the first voice said again, but the other voice said, *It's Charlie.*

Shrugging, Madison said, "Your face is a mess," then gestured with her hand to the empty seat next to her. Charlie sheepishly made his way up the steps and sat down.

For a while, perhaps a long while, the only conversation was that of the crickets chirping to one another in the darkness. An occasional car intruded on the symphony. Charlie's stomach was churning, and he was just about to suffocate from the quiet when Madison spoke up.

"What the hell happened tonight, Charlie? Who was that?"

That was me, Madison. That was everything I've been keeping stuffed down inside since January, finally breaking free of the chain. That was all my pain, all my anxiety, all my rage set loose. That was me. "I don't know, Madison. I'm sorry. I am. I don't know who that person was. It's just that, for whatever reason, Asher gets to me and when he pushed your hair back from your face, I just lost it."

"Lost it, Charlie? That was way beyond losing it. You were frightening. I didn't know you. You didn't even look like you. The way your face was… you scared me, Charlie. You scared all of us, and then what you said to Jackson, Charlie. What you called him…" Madison broke off. Her words shook loose a shard of a memory. Jackson's words flashed through Charlie's head; *It's like I don't even know who you are anymore.* His gut contorted.

"And what is it about Asher that sets you off? Do you think that he and I are sleeping together or something? Do you think he's my little side piece?"

Hearing it out loud, from another person, from her, made Charlie realize how dumb it actually sounded. He shook his head, "No. Not really."

Madison was quick. "Not really, Charlie? So, a part of you thinks that?"

Charlie back pedaled, "No. No, that's not what I meant." This conversation was not going the way he had hoped. "It's just that…"

"Look, Charlie. Asher was way out of line tonight, not just tonight. He's way out of line a lot, and I've already had that conversation with him. But, like it or not, Asher is my neighbor. Shit, he lives *right there*," she pointed sharply to the structure lying in the shadows next door. "His family bought the house, so for the foreseeable future he is now a part of summers at the Shore. So, what? Are you going to beat the shit out of him every time he talks to me? Every time you might think that something is going on? Is that your plan?"

"No. Of course not. It's just that..." Charlie broke off his sentence and looked away.

Madison shrugged with her hands. "It's just what, Charlie?"

"You know he looks in your bedroom window, right?" Charlie fired, hoping to cast some blame in another direction.

Madison smirked and shook her head. "Yeah. I know. Maybe I look in his too, Charlie." Charlie looked like he had just been slapped in the face, and she immediately regretted saying what she did. It was spiteful, said solely for the sake of injuring.

A silence settled over them, with Charlie being lost for what to say. It was good to hear Madison say that Asher was out of line, but Charlie's retort did not have the effect for which he had hoped. Now, it seemed, that Madison watched through her darkened window as Asher moved about his bedroom. He could feel himself getting angry about her comment and tried to douse the fire that was smoldering, always so close to the surface. He looked down at his feet, hoping that some words of wisdom or comfort miraculously made their way into his head. In one deep breath, he pulled in some air.

"Look, Charlie. I like you. Maybe a lot. Probably more than I should at this age, but this person you've become, this new skin you've slipped into, it worries me. It worries all of us." *Oh, great. Now my friends are talking about me when I'm not around. Poor Charlie, what's wrong with Charlie? Charlie is a hot mess.* The smolder was igniting.

Madison stopped talking and exhaled. She turned to look out over the darkened street, taking a sip of whatever beverage was in the plastic cup that sat on the side table.

She began talking without looking at Charlie. "Jackson was right when he said that he doesn't recognize you anymore. I don't recognize you anymore, Charlie. You used to be so, I don't know, light, and silly, and cheerful, and charming, and sweet."

She turned her attention back to him. *He is beautiful*, she thought, *even with that car-wreck of a face.* Her chest swelled a bit with that now too familiar feeling of just wanting to be with him, to hold him, to touch him. She pushed it aside, and instead faced the hard decision she knew she had to make, for him, and for her.

"But lately, it's like you've taken all the things that made you, you, and buried them away somewhere. I don't think you know who you are anymore, Charlie, or who you want to be." In the dim light, Charlie could see Madison's eyes glisten. "And I think… and I think you need to figure you out. God, I hope you figure you out, because I miss you, Charlie. We all miss *you*." Madison's voice was becoming thick, which caused Charlie's stomach to churl and his throat to tighten. "And I think… I think the best way for you to figure you out, to sort out whatever you're going through, this pain you have over your dad leaving, is to focus on you. You need to find you, and what you need, without any distractions from others. From me." With a quick jerk, Madison swiped away a tear that had spilled out and slid down her cheek.

Across from her, Charlie sat blinking, his brow furrowed and creased. It was as if what she was saying was being broadcast live, but on a three second time delay. The sudden realization impacted Charlie's head with the force of a brick, causing him to actually shake it.

"Wait. Wait a minute," he mumbled disbelievingly. "Are you… are you breaking up with me?"

Silently, tears spilled freely down Madison's cheeks. She struggled to get the words out. "Yeah, Charlie. I think I am. At least for a bit, anyway. I can't be with you like this. Worrying whether or not you're going to explode every time Asher is around, or because you see me talking with some other guy, or not knowing what inner turmoil is consuming you."

Charlie rose to his feet. "Look, Madison," he implored, "tonight was wrong. I was wrong about so many things. I was wrong. But we don't need to do this, you don't need to do this. I'll make things right, Madison. I promise." He reached out and wiped the tears away with his thumb as they rolled down Madison's face, his own threatening to spill over at any second, "Please…"

Madison gently took his hand in hers. Sadly, she said, "We need a break, Charlie. You need a break, some time to figure you out. You need to focus on you. I mean, look…" She stopped talking and pointed down at Charlie's arm. His left hand was curled into a fist, his arm trembling slightly. "You're always making a fist, Charlie. I hate that you feel this way, that, for whatever reason, you're carrying around all this anger and pain. It hurts me to see you like this," she said, "but I can't make it all go away. I can't fix you, only you can do that." She paused briefly, taking him in with her eyes, wondering what tomorrow would bring for them. "Go home, Charlie. It's getting late." She rose from her chair and made her way to the front door, leaving Charlie standing where he was on the porch. Before heading in, Madison paused. Looking back at Charlie, she said, "I am glad we took our driver's test together, Charlie. I'm glad it was you. I'll always be glad it was you." She smiled warmly at him, wiping away another tear. While she knew this wasn't the last time she would see him, the moment felt very much like a goodbye. "Good night, Charlie," she said and disappeared into the house.

"Madison, please don't walk away, not tonight," Charlie said. But the door closed behind her, drowning out any chance of her hearing. The latch catching was louder than a gunshot and hurt ten times as much. Charlie slumped back against the porch railing and sucked in some air as his stomach pushed its way up into his throat. Around him, the darkness of the night came crashing in, wrapping itself around him like a smothering blanket. Pushing off of the railing, he vaulted down the front steps and ran because he just didn't know what else to do. He ran past houses and cars, past people having late-night conversations on their porches. He ran on autopilot, head down, legs pumping, until he found himself in front of the only place he knew to go. Chest heaving, he dug deep into his pocket and wrenched out his phone.

You up?

He waited, holding the phone and praying as if the three tiny ellipses that signaled a text back were the key to saving his life right now. In a preternatural way, he knew they were.

Jackson? You up?

Nothing.

Come on, man. Text back.
Jackson, please?

Charlie stood in the dark, his face illuminated by the LED glow of his phone screen, and waited. He waited for what seemed a years' worth of time, and then just a sliver more, before putting the silent phone back into his pocket. In one night's time, he managed to lose his best friend, and his girlfriend. He obliterated seventeen years' worth of friendship with just two words and alienated himself from everyone. This sudden realization that he was alone, that he had lost yet more people from his life, exploded in his head. He inhaled sharply, trying to catch his breath, trying to swallow the churning emotions that battled within him. He struggled to keep everything at arm's length, just on the other side of his wall. Desperate, he tried one last time. He pulled up his friend's contact info on his phone and stabbed at the camera icon. The chirpy FaceTime tone filled the quiet night, momentarily drowning out the crickets, ironically happy against an otherwise dire situation. *Come on-Jackson. Answer the fucking call. Please answer the call.* But he didn't. At that moment, Charlie's anxiety crushed him. Devastated, he stumbled slightly and dropped onto the front steps of Jackson's house. He was lost.

Charlie wasn't sure just how long he sat in the dark on Jackson's front steps. His mind was blank, as if everything that had happened was so overwhelming, it just crashed. Then, a thought appeared in his darkness. Rising, he walked around to the back of Jackson's house, and found his bike, still chained to the fence where he had left it earlier in the day; earlier, when things were so different; earlier, when the night held so much promise. The voices in his head were back. One whispered, mockingly, *Funny, isn't it? You said you were going to fuck shit up... looks like you did.* Crouching, Charlie unlocked his bike. Standing, he hopped on and pedaled off. He was going on autopilot again, riding without thinking about direction or route. He'd been riding these streets all his life. Each one held a memory. They were so comfortable to him.

Around him, people slept behind dark windows as the night crept quietly into the early morning hours. His travels occasionally caught a rabbit off guard, causing the animal to scamper across a lawn or to dart under a car. He startled a racoon, rummaging for a late-night snack. He passed a twenty-something couple making out against a parked car -maybe the end to a serendipitous beach hook-up earlier in the day; maybe the beginnings of a far greater adventure that was about to unfold. He rode on, illuminated briefly by the wash of the streetlights, before exiting the cone into darkness as he drove out from beneath. He pushed forward through the night, riding.

When he finally stopped, he found himself at the zenith of the Longport Bridge. Coasting to the curb, Charlie let the bike slip from his hands. He grabbed the railing and hoisted himself up onto it, and sat down. His legs dangled above the sloshing water, dozens of feet below. One of his flip-flops slipped off, falling down into the blackness, but he didn't care. He shook the other loose from his foot and watched as it too floated down, disappearing into the dark sea. The night sky was still clear, and the light from the moon bounced and played off of the whitecaps below, scattering light across the surface. He sat there, taking in the evening's beauty, the dazzling display of the stars, the whispering of the waves as they lapped the bridge footings and collided with one another. For everything that had occurred in the past few hours, now Charlie was numb. He wasn't angry. He wasn't sad. He didn't feel like crying. *In fact, right now, I don't feel anything at all.* His attention fell to the water so far beneath him. *Will it hurt when I hit the water? Will the impact knock me unconscious? Will it be like falling asleep?*

His hands gripped the railing tightly, holding on, white-knuckled clinging, and then he just let go.

■   ■   ■

Usually a heavy sleeper, his brother's rummaging around quietly in the dark of their room awakened Carson. It's funny how you can recognize sounds in the dark, shorts being pulled on, hair sliding through the top of a sweatshirt, the muffled clap of flip-flops. When the catch on the door clicked shut, Carson sat up and looked at the clock: eleven forty-five. Ordinarily, he wouldn't give a second thought to his brother sneaking out in the middle of the night. Ordinarily, Carson would assume that he was meeting up with Jackson for some late night/early morning carousing; or meeting up with Madison for a tryst in a now dark and empty lifeguard stand, but this wasn't an ordinary night. When he walked into the living room earlier in the night, what he saw knocked the breath out of him. He had never seen his brother that way before. It wasn't the condition of his face that startled Carson so much as the condition of his brother. He was sobbing, guttural cries that frightened Carson. Charlie seemed so broken, so destroyed, and Carson had never seen him as anything but strong and confident. After being shushed away to his room, Carson tried to catch the gist of what was going on, but the door was closed, and he could only pick up bits and pieces of conversation. When Charlie finally arrived, he didn't want to talk. There was an uneasiness that spread through Carson's gut like slow-moving poison. Nevertheless, he laid back down and fell into a fitful sleep.

When he woke again, he immediately looked towards his brother's side of the room. In the darkness, he could see that the bed was empty. The small digital clock on his bed-side table displaying the time, five after one. Carson reached for his phone. His uneasiness grew quickly into panic. For a second, he didn't know what to do, but then instinct took over. He jumped out of bed and threw on some clothes. With stealth abilities he inherited from his older brother, he made his way out of the house and into the yard. Grabbing his bike, he charged off into the dark, pedaling faster than he had ever in his life.

It wasn't long before he reached his destination. In the harsh illumination of the bridge light, he could make out his brother sitting on the railing. He closed the distance between them in an instant and called out, "Charlie?"

Up ahead, hearing his name in the otherwise silent night, startled Charlie, causing him to jump a bit. His hands latched back onto the railing to stabilize himself as he lurched ever so slightly forward. He turned in the sound's direction and saw Carson coasting up on his bike.

Hopping off as he came to a stop, his eyes were round with worry. "Charlie? What are you doing? Why are you up there?" Looking around nervously at their surroundings, he added, "Up here?"

Charlie looked back out across the ocean and shrugged. "It's been a shitty day, Carson. Fuck, it's been a shitty couple of months." *What am I doing up here?* "Guess I just needed someplace quiet to think." *Was that it? You just wanted to think? Nothing more?*

Carson took a hesitant step towards his older brother, his hands raised and outstretched, as if not to startle Charlie into reacting. "Are you... are you alright?" Charlie could hear the concern in his brother's voice.

Was he alright? Would he ever be alright? He hadn't been alright in so long; he'd forgotten what alright felt like. Would he even recognize feeling alright at this point in his life? Charlie just shrugged his answer.

Then turning back to face his brother he said, "Bigger question I guess is what are you doing here? How did you know where I was?"

Carson smiled a weak smile that tried to project calm, but only accomplished alarm, and pulled his phone out of his pocket, waving it at his brother. Taking another small step towards his brother, he added quietly, his voice trembling, "Charlie, can you please get down from there? Please?"

"Yeah, sure," Charlie responded nonchalantly. He swung his legs back to the street side of the railing and jumped down onto the pavement. His bare feet hit the cool cement, and he remembered that his flip-flops now belonged to the ocean.

He had barely connected with the ground when Carson rushed over and grabbed him in a bear hug; the force of which caused Charlie to stumble back into the railing. Charlie caught his brother in his arms.

"Don't you ever do that, Charlie. Don't you ever do that, do you hear me? Ever!" Carson's voice broke, and he squeezed Charlie even tighter, burying his face into his brother's chest. It suddenly occurred to Charlie what the scene must have looked like when Carson pulled up on his bike; middle of the night, sitting on the railing of a bridge, staring down into the water.

A wave of empathy swept over him as Charlie understood where Carson's thoughts traveled. "Jesus, Carson, no. No. I wasn't thinking about... I would never do that, Carson. Never."

"Promise me, Charlie. You have to promise me that you will never do that. I lost dad. I can't lose you too. I just can't." His brother was crying now, and much in the same way a yawn spreads, Charlie could feel himself well. Tears filled his eyes and spilled out, rolling down his cheeks.

"I promise, Carson. I'm not going anywhere. Okay? I promise." Charlie felt his brother's head nod.

"You can't ever do that, Charlie. You can't ever," Carson's voice was muffled, his breath warm against Charlie's chest.

Charlie held tightly onto his younger brother for a bit, pulling him in closer, rubbing his back. Carson reciprocated by tightening his grip. He struggled to remember the last time he had hugged Carson, if ever he had. He struggled to remember the last time he had actually been nice to Carson, a time when he hadn't been a stand-off-ish, condescending little prick. It certainly had been a while, yet here Carson was, in the middle of the night, on the Longport Bridge, come to rescue him. Earlier in the night, Charlie couldn't even be bothered to talk to him. *You're a dick, Charlie.*

Breaking the hug, Charlie looked into his brother's face. Carson wiped at the tears that clung to his cheeks.

Charlie offered a closed lip smile, then said, "It's late. Let's go home, okay? If mom decides to run a bed-check, she'll freak out, and hey, don't tell her about the location service on our phones, alright?" He gave his brother's shoulders a reassuring rub, Carson nodded in agreement.

"You know you can turn that off, right?" Carson inquired.

"Yeah. I know. Just forgot to do it, I guess." Though he didn't forget. Truth of the matter was, it was on so Jackson could always find him, as was Jackson's, so Charlie could always find him.

The two boys picked up their bicycles and pointed them toward their street, their house. "Hey Carson," Charlie called quietly to his brother as he threw a leg over the crossbar, "if you tell anyone I was crying, I'll smother you in your sleep, okay?" he said with a smile.

Carson laughed, "Okay. Same"

It was Charlie's turn to laugh. "I'd like to see you try that, little man."

They set off for home with the early morning stars as their only companions, pedaling at a leisurely pace, side by side, in silence. The quiet was strangely comforting to Charlie, not awkward or uncomfortable. He looked over at his brother, perhaps noticing him for the first time in months. Nostalgia suddenly popped up in his throat like some burp that catches you off guard. He and Carson had, at one time, been close, as close as siblings separated by four years can be, friends, even. Maybe puberty got in the way of that? Maybe conceit?

As the bikes quietly glided through the night, a new appreciation for Carson sprang up in Charlie, and perhaps, a better understanding of how selfishly he had been acting these past months.

TWENTY-THREE

The day dawned gloomy, with billowing dark clouds threatening rain. Miriam had risen early, troubled all night by the emotional scene that played out with Charlie. When she was asleep, it was fitful, and plagued by dreams that were not quite nightmares, but not quite pleasant either. She had lain awake in bed since the sky was turning purple, running through all the scenarios in which she exacted revenge on her ex-husband for the part he played, or perhaps for the lack of a part he played, in everything that led up to Charlie's break hours before.

It was just after seven a.m. when she gave up any hope of falling back to sleep and decided to greet the day on the porch with a cup of coffee. Before doing so, she quietly opened the door to the boys' room. Both of them lay comfortably in their beds, their breath coming slow and deep. Seeing them asleep, stretched out in their beds, she struggled to believe that at one time she could hold them between her hand and elbow, resting comfortably on her forearm. Charlie towered over her now, and she and Carson were eye level. She wished she could freeze Sarah in time, all of them actually, but the joy of being a parent is watching your children grow into adults, grow into their lives. That joy, however, also doubles as pangs of melancholy for the children they leave behind–the double-edged sword.

Though cloudy and dark, the temperature was comfortable, and the slight breeze coming off of the ocean was soft and cooling. As Miriam cradled the cup of coffee in her hands, she pondered how she was going to get Charlie to talk about what he was going through these past months. She wondered how she would get him to face his demons, and to understand that he wasn't alone in all of this. She understood teenage boys were not very forthcoming with their feelings, and often buttoned up tighter when pushed to talk. In the end, she guessed she would play off of him and make it up as it unfolded.

The opportunity came sooner than she had expected. Much to her surprise, seeing how barely twenty minutes had passed since she sat down in the swing, the screen door pushed open. Charlie emerged wearing just a faded pair of cotton gym shorts, holding his own cup of steaming coffee. Making his way over to the swing, he sat down next to his mom with just a quiet "morning" and pulled from the cup. He propped his heels against the porch floor and began to gently rock in the swing. Miriam noticed his leg wasn't bouncing, Charlie's tell when he was anxious or uncomfortable. She placed her hand lightly on his knee and gave a squeeze, then returned it to her coffee cup.

"Hot coffee?" Miriam inquired, surprised at her eldest's choice.

Charlie looked down at the steaming cup in his hand and offered a shrug. "Thought maybe I'd branch out... you know, try on some new shoes, so to speak. Besides, isn't it the required beverage to gain entrance into the Coffee Club here on the porch?"

Miriam chuckled, "Oh, we're open to all kinds of beverages here on the porch."

Charlie nodded and took a sip from the cup. It was pungent, strong, but not entirely unpleasant. He took another sip, allowing silence to take up residence between them for a bit.

"So," Charlie said, and Miriam couldn't help but smile.

"So," she returned, "your face doesn't look nearly as bad as I thought it would this morning. You're almost recognizable as my son."

Charlie turned to look at his mom. Smiling with just half his mouth, he nodded and said, "Thanks. I was expecting worse, myself. Joey can pack a punch. I'd hate to actually be on his bad side. Well, I don't know. Maybe I am." He paused and then shrugged, "It must have been the ice."

Miriam nodded, "Does it hurt?"

"What? My face? No."

Barely containing her snort, she chortled, "Well, it's killing me."

"Nice one, Mom," Charlie said, shaking his head and rolling his eyes.

Miriam patted him again on the knee, and the two returned their attention to their coffees and the gloomy day that was breaking around them. A rainy day at the beach was sometimes a welcomed respite from the routine of the everyday. Rain was an excuse to hole up in your room and just be with yourself. Charlie looked out across the porch rail at the dark clouds encroaching on the island from the bay. His mind flashed to The Half-Blood Prince and the ominous specter that appears in the sky after Dumbledore's death. He hoped his day went better than that, but somehow doubted it would.

After another brief silence, Miriam tested the waters. "So. You okay this morning? Is there anything you want to talk about?"

Where do I start? Charlie wondered. *Sneaking out of the house? Madison dumping him? Jackson not taking his call or responding to his texts? Carson thinking he was going to throw himself off of the Longport Bridge? Him thinking maybe he should throw himself off of the Longport Bridge? His feeling worthless in his father's eyes? Wondering if he's destroyed a few valued friendships? Him beginning to realize what an ass he's been? Where to start?* His stomach lurched.

Charlie just shook his head as a response, then added, "Thanks. I'm okay. Or at least, I think I will be."

Miriam smiled and nodded. "Okay." Perhaps against her better judgment, or maybe despite it, she decided to push just a little. "Charlie, I know that your dad leaving has been hard. I know it's been weighing on you heavily, evidently heavier than I thought. We're all still here for you–Carson, and even Sarah–when she's not criticizing everyone or condemning what you're wearing. I'm still here for you. Should you... you know, need to talk. Okay?"

"Thanks, Mom. ... I, uhm. I know I've been a jerk..."

Miriam put up a hand and cut him off. Shaking her head, she said, "No, Charlie. No. You've just been a teenager trying to come to terms with the world that he knew being swept away in an afternoon. You don't have to apologize for that."

"Yeah, Mom. I do," Charlie pushed on, "I have been a jerk. I've been an ass to you for no real reason. A part of me blamed you for dad leaving, as if you weren't good enough at being a wife or a partner, or somehow caused him to leave. I know that isn't true, but it's what I was clinging to. And dad's ignoring me..." Charlie trailed off, shaking his head. He took another sip of his coffee, swallowed, and continued. "I've all but shut out Carson and Sarah. Shit, look at the mess I made last night. Jackson won't talk to me. He's never not talked to me. I'm scared that he never will again, and Madison, well she dumped me, said I need to figure myself out, figure out the type of person I want to be." He paused again, mapping out in his head what to say next. "If yesterday showed me anything, it showed me the kind of person I don't want to be anymore. Angry. Hateful. Resentful. Alienating. Self-pitying. Stupid, so stupid. So, I *am* sorry, Mom, I am. Because you're right. You're still here, and he isn't. So, I'm going to try to be better to the people who are still in my life. I just hope it's not too late."

Miriam blinked away the few tears that sprang up. She took a minute to make sure her voice wouldn't crack when she spoke. She had a host of things she wanted to say to him right then; a myriad of suggestions and advice and life-lessons she had learned navigating the streets of her own growing up, but that was for another time. Charlie needed to steep in his own revelations about himself for a bit.

So, she defaulted, "Do. Or do not. There is no try," she said with a small smile.

Half smiling again, Charlie said, "Jesus, Mom. Don't try to be cool."

"I'll *try*," she said. And they both shared a chuckle.

When the laugh faded on the breeze, Miriam gently patted her son's knee. "Promise me we'll talk more about this, about how you're feeling, about how you've felt, when you're ready."

"I promise, Mom."

"Good. Now, how about a warmup on that coffee?"

"Sure, thanks."

Miriam ruffled her son's hair as she stood and made her way back inside for the pot of coffee. Though not the extensive conversation she had hoped would come, she was pleased with how the day began. *Baby steps,* she thought to herself. While she knew there was much more baggage to unpack with Charlie, she was happy that he at least unlocked the suitcase. *Now,* she thought to herself playfully, *if I can just get him to clean up his side of the room.*

TWENTY-FOUR

"Well, there you are. It's about time you showed up." Pops was cleaning a small cafe table closest to the door when Charlie pushed it open and stepped inside. Pops straightened and turned, standing in front of Charlie, who propped the door open with his left hand. The confusion of the odd greeting must have registered on Charlie's face.

Damp rag in one hand, clean silverware in the other, Pop's jerked his head to the front bay window of the coffee shop. "He's been sitting there for the last few hours looking like he's lost his best friend, and here you are. Not so lost after all."

Charlie swiveled his head, tracking the line Pops had indicated. There, at his favorite table, sitting with his back to the front door, was the one-person Charlie had been looking for since mid-morning. His stomach rolled ever so slightly. Charlie was thankful that Jackson's back was to the door. He wasn't entirely certain that Jackson wouldn't stand up and leave the second he saw him.

"Yeah. Thanks, Pops. Been looking for him. Though, I'm not so sure about the best-friend part right now." Charlie let go of the door and it softly slid shut behind him.

"Pisshaw," Pops said. "Friends fight. Friends make up. It happens."

Charlie cocked his head. "How did you know we were fighting? Though I don't think the word 'fight' captures what's happened."

He looked warmly at Charlie, the way a grandfather may gaze upon a favored grandchild. He tapped his temple with his index finger. "Intuition, son." He patted Charlie softly on the shoulder in a reassuring way. Then, motioning again to the corner with his head, he said, "Now, go. Make things right." Pops stuffed the rag into his apron and moved away, taking up his usual station behind the counter. He made eye contact with Charlie one more time and nodded.

Drawing in a deep breath, Charlie walked over to where Jackson was sitting. Though not overly crowded, Charlie wished there were fewer people in the café- none at all would be perfect. He didn't know how this was going to play out with Jackson. Last thing he wanted was to be a part of an uncomfortable, perhaps angry scene that unfolded in front of total strangers enjoying various forms of caffeine on this cloudy, July day.

Jackson sat semi-hunched over, the palms of his hands against his forehead propping him up. Charlie stepped around from Jackson's left to the other side of the table and stood for a second or two, not knowing what to say. What was perfectly clear was that he was so incredibly nervous, and that flustered him. His mouth was like a desert and his heart pounded in his chest. Ordinarily, he would have just sat down, not giving the simple action a second thought. Ordinarily, he would have been so relaxed and at ease. But things between the two young men, at the moment, were the furthest from ordinary as things had ever been.

"Can I sit down?" Charlie asked in a voice that did not project confidence.

Jackson looked up. A small chuckle escaped him, but not an amused one. It was the type of chuckle that is little more than air being forced from your lungs out through your nose. The kind you might invoke when confronted with the absurd. The kind that screams, *are you fucking kidding me?* Jackson sat back in his chair and motioned to the empty side of the table with his hand.

Charlie didn't think it possible, but as he slid back the chair and dropped into it, his mouth dried up further. He quick scanned the café for a portable defibrillator as his heart raced in his chest. He dropped his eyes to the tabletop, not able to bring himself to look at his friend of a lifetime. Uncomfortably, he scratched at the back of his neck.

"You keep bouncing that knee so fiercely on this old rickety floor, and the vibrations are going to knock the table over."

Charlie's eyes shot up to meet Jackson's gaze, thinking that maybe his comment was a white flag, but Jackson's expression was steely and cold. He took another deep breath, slowly.

"What do you want, Charlie?" Jackson fired off. If you could assign a temperature to Jackson's tone, Charlie guessed it would be roughly the same as mid-winter in Antarctica.

Charlie arced his eyebrows, "To talk, I guess."

Jackson chuckled that chuckle again, chilling the blood in Charlie's veins. "Haven't you already said enough, Charlie? I mean, Jesus? Do you have another knife you want to bury in me? What more can you possibly have to say?"

Shit, Charlie thought. *Shit.* He exhaled, the way one might do when trying to muster the courage to face the inevitable. "Yeah. I do have more to say, Jackson. A lot more."

Jackson looked out the window. A group of people walking by caught his eye. They were laughing and carrying shopping bags. The cloudy day forcing them from the beach into the stores. When they walked beyond the view of the glass, Jackson turned back to Charlie, absent-mindedly clicking the nail on his ring finger with the nail of his thumb. His expression was blank, almost vapid, staring through Charlie as if he simply wasn't there.

Charlie had never seen his friend look so dejected, so dismal. He seemed so utterly broken, and Charlie knew he was to blame. *Look at him* the voice in Charlie's head said, *you did this.* That old Chinese proverb *A journey of 1,000 miles begins with the first step* popped into Charlie's head. He suspected that there would be many, many steps over the even many more miles before he could make things right with Jackson again. He knew where he had to start, what needed to be said first. Beyond that, he was unsure. So, cautiously, he took that first step.

"Jackson. I am so sorry for what I said, for what I called you. I didn't mean that, honestly. I was angry, out of control angry, and I was lashing out, and you didn't deserve that... you don't deserve that, and I feel terrible about it, and... well... I'm so sorry. I wish I could take it back, but I know I can't. I can't make you un-hear it."

Charlie paused, perhaps to give Jackson a chance to reply, or maybe because he needed to work up the courage to say what he was going to say next. The level of honesty he was about to lay out on the table was something that scared him, because boys just didn't say out loud the things he was about to say to Jackson. His friend's expression hadn't changed, and that made Charlie's stomach drop.

He drew in a deep breath and continued, "That day my dad walked out on me, on us, was devastating. It was like coming home and seeing your house burning to the ground, and I didn't know what to do or where to go. I didn't know if I wanted to run or curl up in a ball in my room. I could barely think straight. The one thing that was clear, though, the one impulse I had, that I knew in my heart was right, was to call you." Charlie sat back and ran a hand through his hair. "I called you, Jackson, because I had to talk to you. I *needed* to talk to you. Not my mom, not my siblings, not even my asshole father. *You."* Charlie could feel himself becoming emotional, so he stopped to quell the rise. He looked across the café, at the people sitting at tables, ordering at the counter, going about their day. Suddenly, it didn't matter that they were there. It didn't matter to him what they might hear, or what they might see. What mattered was what he was about to do.

Turning back to his friend, who still sat emotionless across from him, he continued, "You're my best friend, more than my best friend. You are a part of me, a part of who I am. I don't think about me without thinking about you, Jackson." Charlie could feel his cheeks flush. His vision blurred from the tears coming on. He worried, briefly, that the cork was going to pop on his bottle of squelched feelings.

"The past six months have been a real shit show for me. It was too much change way too fast, out of nowhere, for me to handle. Every morning, that change punched me in the gut when I woke up, every day when I got home from school, and every night before I fell asleep. It pummeled me every time I walked past my driveway and his car was missing, every time I walked by his empty home office, every time I faced his empty space at the table. Every day that passed without a word from him was like I took another beating. The hole he left just kept pummeling me, and pummeling me, and pummeling me, and I couldn't get away from it. Fuck, I can't get away from it." Charlie's voice was thick, but he pressed on.

"All winter and into the spring, all I kept thinking about was that I just need to get to summer. I just need to be at the beach with Jackson, because I knew once I got here, once I made it out of my house back home, and got to the beach, everything would be the same. You and I would hang out, and do stupid shit, and laugh, and surf, and I could forget about the giant hole in my life, because I'd be with..." Charlie's voice caught in his throat, and he let his sentence end, unfinished. He glanced away, trying to mask the emotion he knew his eyes would reveal.

For the first time since sitting down, Jackson's expression softened. He stopped looking through Charlie and looked right at him, saw his pain, and for a moment, Jackson felt sorry for him. But then, he remembered what his best friend called him in a fit of anger. He remembered the pain those words caused. He remembered feeling like his heart had been carved out with a kitchen knife and stomped upon. Quickly, any sympathy Jackson might have been feeling for Charlie washed away.

In a voice devoid of any sentiment or emotion whatsoever, Jackson asked, "What's your point, Charlie? Do you even have one? Or are you hoping that maybe I'll just feel sorry for you and let this all go?" Jackson could see the impact his words register on Charlie's face. *Good,* he thought to himself.

Charlie dropped his eyes to the table, deflated. Jackson's words stung, cut into him, and he knew then how Jackson felt last night. He continued without looking at Jackson, his gaze fixed on the world beyond the windows. "I wanted to make it to summer, Jackson, because I'd be with you. I needed to be with you. Then I got here, and suddenly everything started to change. My relationship with Madison. Our circle of friends. Things with Joey... and things with you. You changed, and I just couldn't wrap my head around it, because all I wanted was for things to be the same. I just needed everything to be the same, and they're not, and I know that what I said, what I called you, has changed us too, maybe forever..." Charlie had to stop again to catch his breath. Even so, he struggled to continue, "... and that makes me physically ill. Because of all the things in my life that have changed, you not talking to me, you not being my friend, my best friend, is the one change I think that will be the most devastating, the one I don't think I'll ever move past. I can't imagine my life without you being my friend Jackson."

Charlie sat in silence for a second or two, breathing deeply to slow his heart rate, to regain some semblance of composure, "Anyway, Jackson. I just hope that you can forgive me, is all, I guess, because I am sorry, more than my bumbling words can ever convey." Charlie stopped. Returning his gaze to Jackson, he waited for him to say something, anything, that would show a path towards some sort of reconciliation, no matter how small.

The air between the two boys was stolid, the tension palpable. It occurred to Jackson that they were like magnets right then, each facing one another with the same poles. The force building up between them served only to push the other away. He knew that right now, he was the magnet that needed to flip poles, to switch sides, so the space between them was no longer a barrier. But he just couldn't bring himself to do it, because he wasn't ready. He wasn't sure he would ever be ready. *That word… how could he call me that word?*

Charlie had been honest with him, spilling more heartfelt words than Jackson could ever remember coming out of Charlie's mouth. Jackson owed Charlie the same courtesy, the same honesty, no matter how difficult that honesty was. He knew what he needed to say, but the words stuck in his throat. This was Charlie, after all, his best friend of a lifetime. He grew up with Charlie, cared deeply for Charlie, and could never have imagined that Charlie would say what he did. But he had said it, nonetheless. That was the fly in the ointment. Charlie said it.

"I can forgive you, Charlie. In time, forgive those words. I know, at least I like to think that I know, that you didn't mean them." Jackson looked up at the ceiling, sighing heavily, "I know I can forgive you for saying them because of us, because of our history, because you are my very best friend. You really are…" Jackson paused. The next part was what he had been thinking about all night and all morning. It stuck with him, clung to him like a bad reputation, and no matter how hard he tried, Jackson couldn't shake loose this thought, this feeling. The next part, he knew, would be hard to say.

"The problem, Charlie, is that while I can forgive you saying them, I don't know if I can ever forget those words. Forget that *you* said them, Charlie. You," Jackson exhaled. "And I'm afraid that for a while, anyway, or maybe forever, I don't know, but I'm afraid that every time I see you, every time you see me, every time we're together, my fear is that I'm going to wonder if that's all you see when you look at me. If the only thing you see now, when you see me, is a goddamned faggot." Jackson's voiced cracked, and he glanced away. Charlie's eyes welled. He noticed Jackson's hands on the table, balled into fists. "That, Charlie, cuts me to the bone."

"You're right about one thing," Jackson continued. "What you said to me, those words, they have changed us. They set us on a path, a course, from which I'm not sure how we recover. I'm not sure that I want…" Jackson allowed his voice to trail off, uncertain he could finish the sentence out loud. Instead, he pivoted. "A lot has changed in your life this year, Charlie. I get it, I do. But you are wrong about something. I haven't changed. I'm just finally allowing myself to be the person I am." Jackson's Adam's Apple bobbed up and down a few times. His voice fell to a whisper, laced with pain, "Of all the people in my life, Charlie, of all the people who matter to me, I thought you would understand that most of all." Jackson shook his head sadly, "And it seems that my fear about telling you I was gay turned out to be correct. I've lost you, Charlie. I lost you."

Charlie's stomach was roiling. Jackson's last words hit home with such a force. He fought to stay in control of the surging sadness that was coursing through him at the moment. He swallowed hard to keep from throwing up. He really had fucked things up, perhaps irrevocably.

His friendship with Jackson was disappearing before him like cotton candy in a puddle, his brain simply refusing to accept it, "Jackson, please…"

Jackson shook his head again, "I gotta go, Charlie," he said, and rose from his seat. "I need to move on from this place. Been sitting here way too long." Without another word, Jackson started for the door.

"Jackson, please don't walk away, not you too…"

Like a sliver of sunshine breaking through a dark cloud, Jackson stopped. He didn't turn around right away. It seemed as if he was mulling over a thought. He half turned, twisting slightly so his shoulders angled back to the table, but then he righted himself and took a step towards the door. Charlie's heart sank.

Then Jackson stopped again. This time, he spun with conviction and walked back to where Charlie was still sitting, but he didn't sit down. The color had drained from his face, as if what he was about to say turned his stomach.

"You know, Charlie. It seems to me that you've spent the better part of this summer pushing people away. People who care about you. Your mom. Your brother. Madison. Me. It's as if you're trying to clear space in your life for someone who obviously doesn't have space in his life for you." He paused, letting his words sink in, before adding, "How's that working out for you, McIntyre? We're still here, *I'm* still here, and he isn't." He lingered a moment longer, staring Charlie down. Then turned and headed for The Beanery's front door.

"Jackson," Charlie whispered as he watched the door close behind his friend. Charlie dropped his head into his hands and stuffed down the urge to cry, again stifling the urge to throw up. *How was he going to fix this?* Lingering in the shadows of his mind like some nefarious character in a dark alley was a more painful thought. *This isn't fixable, is it?*

A light touch on his shoulder caused him to look. As if materializing out of thin air, Pops stood next to him, looking reassuring. "Charlie?"

Charlie just shook his head. "I messed up, Pops. My stupid mouth. My anger about my dad. I hurt Jackson. I hurt him real bad. Pops, I killed our friendship. Obliterated it. I don't think Jackson is ever going to speak to me again, and I can't say that I blame him."

Pop's nodded understandingly. He looked to the front door, as if tracking some residual image of Jackson leaving, then back to Charlie. "Jackson didn't tell me what actually happened, just that words were said. Unforgivable words, as he put it. The thing with words, though, is no matter how hard they were, with some distance, and some time, they soften. He needs time to think. You need time to think. And time? Well, they say time heals all wounds, Charlie."

Nodding sadly, Charlie said, "Funny, I've heard it said that time is a fire in which we all burn, and Pops, last night, those words, *my words*, they scorched our friendship."

Pops patted Charlie on the shoulder and offered a warm, reassuring smile that did little to reassure Charlie. As he moved away, he allowed his hand to drag across Charlie's shoulders, giving a small squeeze before he let go. Charlie was wondering what had just happened. He had no idea what his next step should be; what he should do to mend the chasm between him and Jackson that just opened up before his eyes. He wondered if he should go after him. Maybe, he thought, he should give him space and time—as Pops suggested. He worried he would never see him again, that this was the end. The only thing that was certain to Charlie in that horrible moment was that try as he might, there was no keeping change at bay. It was ubiquitous and constant, touching everything and everyone. Much like the tide, the best one could do with change was to move with it.

"Fuck," was all Charlie said as he sat paralyzed in the middle of this strange, barren landscape in which he had abruptly found himself.

AUGUST

"Summer will end soon enough, and childhood as well."
– George R.R. Martin

ONE

Charlie's own voice calling out startled him from a deep sleep. For a panic filled second or three, he couldn't place himself within his surroundings, and he bolted upright to gather his bearings. The soft light of the range hood seeping in from the kitchen threw just enough brightness, allowing Charlie's brain to register that he was, in fact, in his own living room. He sank back down into the recliner where he found himself, as the last remnants of his dream faded from his mind. His heart was still racing, and he drew in slow, deep breaths to settle himself. Someone had thrown a light blanket over him at some point in the evening to keep away the chill. The last thing he could remember was watching some dumb series on Netflix that Carson and Sarah were into, both dialoguing over the dialogue the entire time. Obviously, he had nodded off at some point, although for the life of him he could not remember when that was. Evidently, his slumber was such that he remained unstirred as his family readied themselves for bed. Of late, he often found himself quite weary, though certainly not from an over exertion.

These last few weeks spent without his friends, without Jackson, he had come to the realization that the life his siblings led at the beach was decidedly different from the life he led. Carson and Sarah had an earlier curfew than he did, so they spent the bulk of their night inside. Most evenings for them happened in the living room, staring at the glow box, talking about whatever inane show graced the flat screen mounted to the wall. Occasionally, Miriam extended their curfew, and they remained out and about with their friends, roaming the neighborhood, skirting the edge of being in trouble, making memories they would talk about for years, but never past ten p.m.

Charlie was never home much before eleven-thirty, nor was he around during the day. His summers took place outside, from street to street, beach to beach, and back again. To Charlie, the house was more of a re-staging zone; shower, change of clothes, a grab of needed accessories, refueling, and a spot to rest his head when the adventure was complete; only to repeat the pattern the next day. The idea of hanging with his family had never once skated across his mind as a thought, nor a consideration. They were people he saw in passing; figures that existed on his periphery with whom he occasionally interacted, but more often than not, caused him annoyance.

In the myriad of days since he last saw Jackson as he walked out of The Beanery, all that had changed. His family, his house, the room he found himself in, had become his mainstay. Early on, Charlie avoided his friends, choosing to remain apart from them because of his own embarrassment, his own stupidity. As the days wore on, and his phone remained silent, he had to come to terms with the fact that the damage he had caused was ostensibly irreparable. Understandably, he was devastated. There were days he barely got out of bed, spending them facing the wall, soaking in a puddle of his own self-pity, and rebuffing every attempt made by his mom, or his brother, to engage in some, any, activity. It took his sister, in her ever correct and condescending way, to pull him from the cement like grip of his funk.

"Dumbass. You fucked up. Welcome to life. Get over yourself."

It overjoyed Charlie when, in the last few days of July, one afternoon, his phone lit up with a text from Madison. It was a short, simple text:

Been thinking about you. You okay?

To Charlie, it was a lifeline that he grasped with both hands. He and Madison began to see each other not long after that, not much, and certainly not in the way they once had. Charlie was grateful for every second, no matter how few he spent with her, talking. Their first meeting, on a bench outside the beach patrol station, was awkward. To Charlie, it felt almost like two strangers forced to share a table at a coffee shop, trying to make small talk. Choppy, disjointed conversation with long periods of dead air. But it didn't matter to Charlie how uncomfortable it was. He was just thankful to be in the presence of a friend.

As the weeks passed, Charlie and Madison gradually settled back into each other. While they weren't quite back to the place they left off before they began dating, Charlie knew that level of comfort would eventually return.

Madison was the only friend he had seen. He didn't count the morning a week, or so back when he pulled open the door at Hooked on Breakfast just as Joey was walking out. Both came to an immediate halt, standing inches apart, chest to chest. Charlie could feel his face flush, as Joey's gaze lasered through him, searing right into his skull and out the back of his head. Feebly, Charlie lifted his chin and offered a shamefaced, 'hey,' that fell yards short. Joey returned the greeting icily without looking at Charlie. As he left, Joey bumped Charlie's shoulder as he pushed past him and continued down Asbury Ave. The interaction was brief, but formidable, and it remained with Charlie for days after.

While Charlie missed his friends, the one absence that was like a blast crater was Jackson's. There were no words that could describe that sizeable loss. It hung around Charlie's neck as he slogged through each day. He tried contacting Jackson for a good many days after they last saw each other, but Charlie's attempts at connecting with Jackson went unanswered. Finally, he just gave up.

Sighing, Charlie pushed down on the recliner's footrest, forcing it into its upright position. Kicking his legs and feet free of the blanket, he stood up and leisurely wandered into the kitchen. He snatched an empty glass off of the countertop and pressed it against the refrigerator door, waiting as it filled with cool water. There, at eye level, the calendar screamed the month at him. Immediately, his eyes were drawn to the red circle ringing the twentieth, indicting their last day at the beach. His mother would return to her classroom the following Monday, having to set up for the new school year and sit through the mindless district in-services meant to invigorate, but serving only to dull—according to his mother. In years past, his dad would schedule vacation from the firm to cover the following week, so Charlie's and his siblings' summer wasn't cut too short. But that was then, and this was now. They'd all be heading back to their home, lamenting the end of summer, and gearing up for another school year—Charlie's Junior year in high school.

Though this year, Charlie mused to himself, was different. This August didn't bring with it the customary melancholy that attached itself to the waning days of summer and followed Charlie around like some annoying toddler that wouldn't leave him alone. A constant reminder that his days of leisure were numbered; an unspoken foreboding heralding the tedious days to come.

No, standing there, in the kitchen, looking around in the dim light cast by the range hood, Charlie felt almost relieved that the summer was ending, which in and of itself, was a feeling both strange and unnerving to him. He wasn't quite looking forward to school, but neither was he morose about leaving the beach, this house, this time. He'd come to realize that while he loved the beach, and all that summer brought with it, it was being with Jackson, and his friends, that made everything... well, perfect. Without them, without Jackson, everything came up short.

He tried to explain this to his mother one sunny afternoon when she stumbled across him sitting once again in the middle of the garage floor, in a beach chair, sipping a beer disguised as a Coke. He tried to explain to her that without Jackson to share the adventure; it wasn't an adventure. It was just a day, and that the boring days were piling up, one after another. He tried to convey that, much like a tree falling in the forest with no one to hear, doing things by yourself: surfing, biking, hanging out, is still just being by yourself, and no fun at all. No matter what you are doing. If he was going to be by himself, not having fun, he might as well just do it at home. It was less sad–he didn't add that being at home kept him in proximity to the beer fridge.

Shaking her head in a very parental sort of way, his mother suggested that he was in charge of his own adventure and his own fun. No one should depend on someone else to validate them, or determine the course of their life, or to bring happiness to them. Happiness wasn't something to be found. Instead, it was something from within. It was a way of thinking, of being. She went on to say that he certainly didn't need anyone other than himself to make the most of his day, because the day belonged to him, and no one else. To Charlie it sounded like some sort of post-divorce -take charge-of-your-own-life, empowerment TED Talk, but being a couple of beers into the afternoon, he thought it best not to annunciate much. Instead, he simply nodded and continued to stare out through the door and into the yard.

Leaving the beach this August couldn't come fast enough as far as Charlie was concerned. Downing the remaining water in his glass, he placed it in the sink and got on with his night. Charlie headed down the hallway to his room. He passed Sarah's on the left, and the bathroom on his right, before the sorry train in which he was a passenger arrived at its final destination. His room was dark, but that mattered not. He knew the path to his bed on the far side by heart. With his eyes closed, he could walk it. He'd managed to keep his half relatively tidy since that infamous day in July when he completely melted down, so the worry of tripping on scattered clothing and towels was minimal. As he stepped out of his shorts. Carson's voice in the dark startled him.

"Hey Charlie, you alright?"

"Hey. Sorry I woke you. Yeah. I'm alright. Why do you ask?"

Carson sat up and faced his brother, who was climbing beneath the sheet. "I could hear you in the living room. You were calling out. You sounded, I don't know, scared, I guess."

The dream came crashing back into Charlie's psyche in rich detail.

"You were calling Jackson. You kept saying his name."

Charlie settled into his pillow. "Yeah. Bad dream is all. It was nothing."

"You want to talk about it?"

What to say? Did Charlie want to tell his little brother about his dream? Would that make him seem vulnerable, or silly? Since that night on the bridge, Charlie had included his brother more, or at least excluded him less. Here was yet another opportunity for Charlie to let him in, if even just a bit. He took it.

"It was dumb. I um, was surfing, alone, and I got caught in a rip-tide, a bad one, and I was being pulled out... out far, and as hard as I tried, I couldn't get back in closer to the shore..." Charlie hesitated as the feeling of panic he experienced in his dream became all too real again, "And it was weird because the whole beach was empty. There was no one else around except for Jackson, and he was sitting in the sand, just above the waterline, just watching me. He was just sitting there, watching. I called out for help. I kept calling to him for help, but he wouldn't move. He just sat there, watching it happen, watching me get sucked away, and I kept getting pulled out further and further, until finally, he was just this dot, way off in the distance, and I was alone. All alone in the middle of the ocean, unable to get back to shore," Charlie shook the feeling away. "Stupid, I know."

Carson settled back onto his pillow and crossed both arms behind his head. He was quiet for a while, for such a time that Charlie had thought he had fallen back to sleep. But out of the darkness, a phrase floated across the divide between the beds.

Barely above a whisper, but loud, so incredibly loud, he said, "You miss him, don't you?"

Carson's words were powerful and poignant, causing Charlie to catch his breath. Mirroring his brother's position in bed, Charlie lay there in the dark before answering, pondering his next words because, 'yeah, I do,' just wasn't potent enough. You miss the sun after a stretch of cloudy days. You miss your shows as you wait for the new season to drop. You miss the weekend, come Monday morning during the school year. This was bigger, heavier.

Charlie began hesitantly. "Sometimes, when I wake up in the morning, there's a millisecond where my brain thinks '*I'm gonna call Jackson and see what he's up to*', and then I remember. Or, in the middle of the day, I see something, or I'm reminded of something, and I reach for my phone to text him, and then I remember. Or at night, when I'm sitting on the porch and I'm bored, and the thought pops '*I'll hit Jackson up*', and I remember. Then, in the next millisecond after remembering, it's all so real again, and it just comes crashing in. Like being knocked over by a wave, and it sweeps over you, and the pressure holds you down, but then just as quickly, it passes, and in its place, there's this overwhelming sense of loss, in that millisecond after, ya know? And I just can't figure it out. It's like..." Charlie paused, searching for an analogy that would come close to describing his feelings, a way, with words, he could get Carson to understand, "... it's like my arm was cut off, and I'm staring at it lying on the sidewalk, but it's just not registering in my head, that my arm is lying on the sidewalk, because I still feel it, attached to me. There's this disconnect, where you know it happened, but you can't fathom it happening, or understand that it happened, but then, suddenly, it all makes sense, and you're horrified." Charlie let out a breath. "It's like that, Carson."

In the darkness, Charlie could hear his younger brother shifting his position. The tired old box spring of his bed protesting under his slight weight. Charlie turned his head on his pillow to face his brother, but remained on his back. As his eyes adjusted, he could make out Carson facing him, his head propped up on one elbow.

"Like last winter, when I'd come downstairs and I was confused for a second as to why dad wasn't there? Or when it was like, later at night, and we're all sitting around the living room, and I caught myself wondering when dad was coming home. Or when you think 'I'll ask dad,' and then remember that he's gone, and the wind sorta goes out of you real quick, and your stomach feels like it does on the down drop of a roller coaster, but then just as quick, you're okay. Well, not okay, really. But okay, you know?"

Charlie was stunned by his brother's recounting. It was the first time Charlie had heard his brother talk about their dad's absence. He never once thought that either of siblings had moments like that, like he did, and he felt bad.

"Yeah, Carson. Just like that."

Silence settled over the brothers again as each thought about what the other had said. Carson's bed groaned and creaked spastically as he repositioned himself, settling into what would be a welcomed return to slumber. "So, you miss him."

Charlie wasn't sure if Carson meant his father this time or was still referencing Jackson. In all honesty, he did miss his dad, or at the very least, he missed the idea of his dad. But he missed Jackson exponentially more. Jackson was a part of Charlie's life in a way that no parent could ever be a part of their kid's life. In the dark, in the waning hours of the night, Charlie thought that whatever Carson's meaning, it was irrelevant. In either case, the answer to the question was the same. One just more powerfully than the other.

"Yeah. I do."

"Yeah. Me too. Good night, Charlie. Stay out of the ocean."

Charlie smiled in the dark at his brother's jest, "Good night, Carson."

TWO

Asher sat idly on one of the high back wooden rockers that graced one side of the enormous front porch. The ceiling fan was spinning lazily, pushing down a slight breeze. There was far more comfortable furniture opposite from where he sat, but he found the slow, gentle front-to-back rocking helped to pass the solitary hours. It was a gorgeous August day, unusual in the low humidity, and throngs of people moved up and down the block on their way too, or from the beach.

In all the passersby, there were three girls about his age, maybe a year or so younger, who had trekked past his porch about a half dozen times in the last forty-five minutes. Each time casting furtive glances in his direction, followed by a giggle or a shy, awkward wave. He hadn't seen them before, and so assumed they were renting somewhere on the block, or in the vicinity, for a week or so. On their last ramble by, the taller of the three suggested he should take his shirt off as it was so hot out. Asher, never one not to show off, smiled. Then, in a graceful, practiced manner, sat forward, reached behind his head with both hands and peeled off his shirt. The three young ladies stared at his now bare torso as they continued walking down the street. One, though Asher wasn't sure which, commented on his abs before disappearing down the street and out of Asher's view.

What surprised Asher wasn't the girls' attention or brazen approach. No, he was used to that. Hell, he didn't go anywhere where he wasn't complimented on his looks or felt people's eyes on him as he walked across a room or strolled down the street. He had been told too many times, for all of his life, just how striking he was for him not to believe it. For better or worse, though probably worse, Asher took advantage of his charm and his appearance. He used it the way one might wield power or influence to navigate his way through his life; to get what he wanted; to do what he wanted; when he wanted.

What surprised Asher was how little he was interested in pursuing the three girls. Despite their obvious fawning, he had no desire to follow up. As he sat there, alone on the porch, he knew the reason he was so disinterested in trying to get with one or all of those girls stemmed from the one person who all of his charm, stunning good looks, and obvious wealth failed to capture. Madison Walker.

The night of Charlie's birthday, that night where he purposefully sent Charlie into an apoplectic meltdown and allowed himself to take a beating, did not quite end the way Asher had planned. Charlie was predicable enough, to be sure: exploding all over the place like unstable TNT. But in the aftermath, Madison proved to be not as easily manipulated as Asher had believed.

About an hour or so after they all left the beach, and after Asher had cleaned himself up, he received a text from Madison asking him to meet her. She said she'd come to him, which, being right next door, was fine with Asher. That part went according to his plan—take a beating, show Madison what a loose cannon Charlie was, then make a move. It didn't matter to Asher where they met, as long as they ended the night in his room. He had never been so far off the mark in his life.

Asher went out and positioned himself on the front porch so that he could see Madison as she approached his house. She strolled out her front door, down the steps of her porch, and marched over to where Asher was sitting. She made her way up onto Asher's porch, but stopped by the front door, not moving any closer. What followed was the most profound dressing down that Asher had ever received in his life. Madison lit into him for a good fifteen minutes, not stopping to let Asher get a word in edge-wise. Madison's rebuke of him was honest and, at times, harsh. The gist mostly revolving around him being a spoiled, Machiavellian prick. Words like 'entitled', 'selfish', 'egotistical', 'disgraceful', and 'sophomoric' still stuck in Asher's head all these days later. Sure, he had been called those words many times. Although sophomoric and Machiavellian were new ones that he had to look up. But for whatever reason, they hurt coming from Madison. Though 'hurt' wasn't exactly the right word. They didn't hurt. No words ever hurt Asher. He brushed them off as being rooted in jealousy—of his wealth, of his status, of his good looks. Madison's words didn't hurt. Far worse, he realized. Madison's words mattered. That was unfamiliar territory for him. She went on to inform him that he owed Charlie an apology, insisting upon it, actually. Further stating that until that happened, there was little more she had to say to him, if anything at all.

At first, Asher cast it all aside. *Who the fuck is she to tell you what to do?* was the familiar song that played in Asher's head. He didn't need her, or anyone. He decided who he hung around with, and with whom he didn't. So, he took to hanging with his brother, who was always in the company of Kelsey, and as such Madison, but every time Asher showed up, Madison departed, staying true to her word.

Asher soon came to realize that being with his brother and Kelsey was practically being alone. They were constantly engaged in their own conversation, or would disappear completely, returning giggling, flushed and disheveled sometime later. Asher decided one day on the beach as Logan and Kelsey clung to each other like seaweed stuck to your legs, that being by himself was better than suffering through one more one-sided conversation or the constant display of carnal attraction.

As the solitary days wore on, he found the one thought that kept occupying his mind, the presence he missed the most, was Madison. He missed talking to her, seeing her, and just hanging with her. In a moment of self-actualization, Asher realized that maybe he never actually was interested in dating Madison, more so he was interested in pissing Charlie off—because he knew he could. Asher was more interested in Madison's company as a friend more than anything else. After all, she was the first person he had met in this new town, the first person to welcome him. She mattered to him, after all, just not in the way he had originally hoped for.

Which is why Asher didn't want to pursue those young ladies. Madison made him question himself, question how he treated people. He knew nothing would be right until things were right with Madison. He knew what he needed to do to mend that bridge. He was just loathed to do it. Asher never apologized for anything, ever. He never sought forgiveness. He just wrote people off and moved on. To him, having friends had always been like playing poker. You keep the cards you want, discard the ones you don't, and pull replacements from the deck. Yet, here he was, considering the unthinkable. *What the hell has she done to you? She's made you all soft.*

"Or maybe she's turning me into a person," he said quietly to himself.

He grabbed his T-shirt off of the adjacent rocker and slipped it over his head. Standing, he set off down First Street towards Ocean, then banked left. The girls were right; it was hot in the sun, and it wasn't too long before his armpits dampened, and his T-shirt clung to his back. But it wasn't a far walk, and he was grateful that there were some trees on the street for shade. On his way, he practiced what he would say, what words he could choose that would accomplish the desired effect, without making him seem weak or groveling. A host of soliloquies played out in Asher's head, but none seemed quite right. In the end, he decided to wing it.

He turned down his intended block and could see his destination off in the near distance. Mentally, he breathed a sigh of relief as the person he was heading to see was sitting on the front steps. He hadn't thought about a course of action when he arrived. Did he ring the bell? Knock on the door? Head around to the yard? He had never actually been to the house before, and didn't quite know what to expect. He was glad that at least that much was solved for him. As he closed the last few feet, he inhaled some courage.

"Hey. You got a minute?"

Charlie, sitting on his front steps, looked up from whatever TikTok video was playing on his cell phone screen. Asher could recognize the mash-up of disbelief, disgust, and curiosity that played across Charlie's face upon recognizing who it was standing before him. He waited for the 'fuck off' that was sure to come. Charlie stood up purposefully. He squared himself to Asher. Remembering the power of Charlie's left-hook, Asher steeled himself against the inevitable well-deserved punch, but neither the profanity, nor the left-hook, came.

"What do you want, Asher?"

Charlie's use of his real name registered with Asher and caused a twinge of guilt to run through him.

"Uhm… I'm here because… I guess I owe you an apology. And so… I… uhm… I guess that's why I'm here."

Charlie snorted and shook his head. "You guess?" he said a bit too acidly.

Picking up on his tone, Asher back-pedaled, "No. Not, I guess. I know." Asher looked down at the sidewalk, and then back to Charlie, "Uhm… look. That night, after you pummeled me–which I deserved, by the way - Madison came by my house, and, well, she lit into me. I mean, really lit into me, which I wasn't expecting…"

Charlie tried to stifle the smile that was spreading across his face, but to no avail. That Madison, she was one strong young woman.

"… and she said some things to me that just hit home, and got me to thinking… about stuff, about you, and about how I treat people, how I treated you, and I can't seem to get them out of my head. Madison said she wouldn't talk to me again until I apologized, and I kinda miss seeing her…"

Charlie cocked his head and knitted his eyebrows. A subtle action not lost on Asher.

Knowing exactly where Charlie's head went, Asher placed both hands, palms up in front of him and continued, "No. No. Not like that. I don't want to get with her. I just… I just miss talking to her, is all."

In the same second, Charlie both empathized with Asher and hated himself for doing so.

"So," Asher continued, "I apologize. And not just because Madison said I have to. I'm sorry because I am. I shouldn't have pushed you the way I did. I've been pretty much an ass to you for no real reason since the very first day we met. That was wrong. I was wrong." Asher shifted his weight from foot to foot, broadcasting the uncomfortable position he willingly placed himself in. Like most teenage boys who never know what to do with their hands, Asher shoved his deep into his pockets. Charlie just stood there, motionless.

"Anyway, I'm sorry. About everything, really, but mostly how I treated you and what I tried to do to you and Madison, and what all that caused. That was not cool, and I hope that maybe, maybe we could start again… as friends, even?" Asher pulled his right hand out of his pocket and stuck it out, a universal gesture of peace now hanging in the air between the two.

Charlie looked at it, not sure what to do. This was one of those moments that one never expects to happen. A moment so implausible that it's very existence would violate all rules of physics and nature. Yet, here it was—Asher—conceited, arrogant, stuck-up, obnoxious, Asher with his hand out, asking for forgiveness. *Forgiveness.* Charlie was no stranger to his position. Hesitantly, he wrapped his hand around Asher's hand and pumped it slowly.

"How about we start again as not enemies, and see where it goes?"

Asher laughed, a genuine laugh, and smiled a genuine smile. For the first time since coming to meet him, Charlie didn't want to punch him in the face.

"Okay, yeah. That'd be good. Thanks Chuck…" he cringed at the word, catching himself, "I mean, Charlie. Thanks, Charlie."

Using *his* real name did not go unnoticed, or unappreciated, by Charlie, either. "I'll see ya, Asher," Charlie said and turned to head into the house, leaving Asher on the sidewalk. The screen door barely clicked shut when Carson fired a question across Charlie's bow.

"What the hell did he want?" he asked.

"To apologize for being an absolute shit all summer."

Carson furrowed his brow and shook his head in disbelief. "And did you accept it?"

"Yeah. I did."

Stymied, Carson bolted over to the window on the far side of the living room, the one that wasn't under the porch roof. Pulling back the curtain, he craned his neck, peering up and out, prompting a quizzical look from his brother.

"What are you looking for?"

"Flying pigs," he responded in a manner that was dryer than the Sahara Desert.

THREE

The knock-on Jackson's door roused him from the midday nap he had slipped into, not because of being tired, but brought on by sheer boredom. He rolled over onto his back and called out, "Come in." Placing his arms behind his head, his own odor wrinkled his nose, and he decided a shower was long overdue. His bedroom door broke contact with the frame, revealing his brother Noah, bare chested.

"Surf's up. Wanna hit the beach with me?" His eyes were hopeful.

Jackson stretched and yawned, briefly weighing the offer before declining, "Nah. Think I'm just gonna lay here. Don't know, maybe take a shower." He shrugged.

Noah pushed the door open and walked into his room. "Mind if I sit down?" he asked, indicating with his hand to the edge of Jackson's bed closest to him. Jackson shook his head, then slid over to the opposite edge, making some room. He crossed his arms over his chest, not wanting to risk offending his brother with his somewhat pungent smell.

Noah sat down and looked around the room. "Man, this place hasn't changed in years. A few things here and there, but for the most part, this could be the ten-year-old you, or the sixteen-year-old, well, almost seventeen-year-old you."

Jackson pushed himself up against the headboard into a seated position. "Yeah. Some things are timeless."

Noah smirked and nodded. "Yeah, that's true, but some things aren't. Some things change." He paused, and repositioned himself to face his younger brother, "You've changed. A lot. Not just over the past few years, but even in these past few weeks. You rarely come out of this room, and when you do, I don't know, you're not Jackson. You're some version of Jackson. A version of Jackson with some pieces missing or something, making him not quite right."

Jackson ran a hand through his oily hair and shook his head. "I don't know what you're talking about, Noah. Last time I looked in the mirror, I was looking back at me. So… it's me," Jackson offered sarcastically. He knew full well what his brother was insinuating, but he wasn't going to make this easy for him, or willingly travel down that path. Truth be told, Jackson struggled most everyday now without Charlie in his life. He kept waiting for himself to get used to the absence, to move on to an existence that did not include his former friend, to a time when the loneliness he felt, even when in the company of Joey or others, would pass. He was fearful it never would. He sometimes caught himself wondering if this was how Charlie felt about his dad?

Undaunted, Noah pushed on. "I think you know what I mean, Jackson."

"Really? 'Cause, I'm not too sure. Enlighten me, big brother," Jackson popped up from the bed and paced the room. He could feel himself getting steamed.

Noah stood up, "Okay. You want it straight. You got it, little brother. The piece of you that's missing is Charlie. You haven't been the same since you cut ties with him. You hole up in this room, and lay in that bed, wallowing in your own stupid self-pity. You don't even bathe regularly. Maybe it's time you get on with it or get over it."

Noah's sternness stopped Jackson in his tracks. His last few words rested uncertainly in his head, "What do you mean, 'get on with it, or get over it'?"

Noah took a couple of steps in Jackson's direction. He began, a softer edge to his voice, "What I mean is, either get on with forgiving your best friend for being an incredibly dumb-fuck, and in case you haven't met Charlie, he can be rather skilled at being an incredibly dumb-fuck, or get on with your life without him in it. Either way, it's time for you to move your chair or drown in the high tide. You choose."

Noah's last words rang all too familiar in Jackson's head. These last few weeks without Charlie had been more difficult than Jackson imagined, and he imaged it would be difficult. He stifled the gurgling emotions churning and rolling within, corking that bottle again.

"Honestly, Noah? After what he said? I'm what, just supposed to forgive him? Have you forgotten what he called me? My so-called best friend? Because I haven't. I hear it every fucking day, Noah. Every. Fucking. Day."

Noah shook his head. "No, Jackson. I haven't forgotten. I don't suspect I ever will, nor will you, or he. I'm just worried about you, is all." He paused again, searching for the right words. As he did, he stepped closer to his brother. "Look, what he called you was dead wrong. If I was there, I would have punched him too, and whether or not you forgive him, well, that's up to you, but here's what I know. He was angry and out of control. He didn't mean it, and I know he regrets it, and wishes he could take it back. He's said so, a hundred fucking times he's said so. Jesus, it's a reoccurring theme with him."

"Wait," Jackson cut in. "How do you know? Are you talking with him?" he asked incredulously.

Noah shook his head. "Not actually talking. Jackson, Charlie texts me three or four times a week asking about you. He said you won't respond to him, but that didn't matter. He needed to know how you were, and that's what he asks, all the time. '*How's Jackson doing?*'" Noah exhaled. "He is genuinely sorry, Jackson. You're his best friend, and he cares about you. You know that. I know that. Hell, the whole fucking north side of the island knows that. So. The tide is coming in. What're you gonna do?"

Knowing that Charlie had been clandestinely inquiring about him for weeks warmed Jackson, but he didn't want to be warmed. He wanted to stay angry, to stay distant. He wanted Charlie to remain the bad guy.

Jackson struggled to keep the cork in place. "I don't know what the fuck to do, Noah? Okay? I miss him, I do, so much, so fucking much, but I keep hearing it in my head, and every time it feels like someone is pulling out my guts with their bare hands," Jackson's voice faltered. "I thought he was my friend."

Nodding, Noah took another step towards his brother, wanting to be in closer proximity should a break occur. Quietly, he said, "He is your friend. He always has been. Look. Change is hard, and Charlie has had a lot of change to deal with. That's not to say you haven't either. You both have, but people react differently to change. Some people accept it. Some people run from it. Some people try to hold it off, no matter the damage that causes. He's sorry, Jackson. Genuinely sorry, and if you can forgive and forget, then you should. You guys, you two stupid, goofy, moronic idiots are perfect together, and broken, apart. If you can't forgive him, if you can't forget what he called you, then you need to cut him loose and move on with your life. Because this change," he tapped his brother on the chest, "this change in you isn't one I like, or one I'm willing to accept, and neither should you. Okay?"

Jackson just nodded from fear that any words spoken in that moment would bring about tears.

Noah nodded as well and clapped his brother on the shoulder the way boys show affection to one another without risking that the actual action conducted be mistaken for heart-felt affection. "Good. Now, go take a shower and wash off this stink."

FOUR

The mint green envelope addressed to Charlie showed up in the copper mailbox roughly ten days or so after his birthday. It's arrival, really closer to August than to Charlie's birthday. No one was sure how long it had been in the mailbox, as checking the mail every day was an act that often went uncompleted at the beach. Checking the mail was something you did at home, something that was a part of the school-year normal. Once at the beach, no one wanted to be reminded of life back home. Instead, reveling in the fact that the mail didn't matter here, the day of the week didn't matter here, the time of day didn't matter here. Once at the beach, all that mattered was the weather report, and the time of high tide.

So, the envelope could have rested in the mailbox for days, or maybe just hours, but the damp, crinkled condition of the paper suggested it had been out in the humidity for a stretch. The only certainty, in Charlie's mind anyway, was that it wasn't there for his birthday, nor the immediate days that followed.

He recognized the writing, the characteristic slant of a left-handed person, the sloppy looping of letters together to form words. The penmanship was unmistakable. To the untrained eye, it could be mistaken for his own, but who the hell sends a card to themselves? No, Charlie knew who the card was from as he walked away from it and left it in the copper mailbox that was affixed tightly to the wall.

At some point, later that day, or maybe the next, the card wound up on the kitchen table. It was brought to Charlie's attention by his mom, a casual, '*Hey, Charlie. There's a card on the kitchen table addressed to you,*' as he stepped through the living room on his way to the porch, iced tea in hand.

"Yep," he said as he pushed open the screen door.

Then things got interesting. The innocuous mint green envelope began to move about the house after that, as if it came to life at night. It was almost like a game of 'Elf on the Shelf,' wherein the minty mailed greeting would need to be found in a different place from the day before. The envelope came to rest on end tables and perch on counter tops. It was magnetically affixed to the refrigerator door. It hung by tape to the bathroom mirror and even took a quick nap on his bed pillow. Some days it appeared under his cell phone. Wherever the Hallmark communication appeared, Charlie just ignored it.

His paying no mind to the correspondence must have driven his siblings crazy. They desperately wanted him to play along, to open it. One afternoon, a week or so, after the card arrived, Charlie was wasting the day away on the porch swing, when Sarah and Carson pushed open the screen door and stood boldly before him, intent on an intervention.

"You know there's a card for you, right?" Sarah began.

"Yep."

"You know it's from dad, right?" Carson interjected.

"Yep."

"Well, there's probably a check or money inside," Sarah continued, trying to coax an opening.

"Yep."

His siblings tossed frustrated glances at one another. Carson looked like he was going to slap Charlie. If Sarah was older, Charlie entertained, she probably would.

"Well, aren't you going to open it?" Carson asked, his irritation clear in his voice.

"Nope."

"Ugh. You are impossible, Charles McIntyre!" his sister said, before pivoting on her heels and storming off into the house.

Carson remained behind. After a bit, he took a seat next to his brother on the swing and the two just rocked back and forth for a while longer. Just as Charlie was beginning to feel uncomfortable sitting in silence, swinging with his younger brother in plain sight of anyone and everyone who walked by, Carson spoke up.

"Why won't you open it, Charlie?" he asked quietly.

Charlie pondered that question, which, on its face, was as innocuous as the mint green envelope, but much like the envelope, opening up that question held the risk of harm.

Turning to his brother, he said after a breath, "I have this idea, in my head, of what I want to be in that envelope. What I think should be in that envelope, and, well… I'm kinda afraid that when I do open it, and what I want to be in it, isn't, I'll…"

"Go back to that place, that dark place."

"Yeah."

Carson sat, rocking the swing with the ball of his foot. Patting his brother on the thigh, he stood up and said, "I get it." He continued across the porch to the front door. Pausing before going in, he turned back to Charlie. "You know you have to open it, right?"

"Yep."

Carson nodded and disappeared inside.

■   ■   ■

A good number of days later, Charlie opened the card. One night, in the small hours of the new morning, he crept quietly into the kitchen and plucked the card from its resting place up against the napkin holder to the right of the microwave. Just as quietly, he opened the front door and took up residence on the front porch. It was a muggy evening. The air was hanging thick and viscous. Even the crickets seemed to be put off by the dampness and heat as they half-heartedly called out to one another under the starlit sky.

He sat for a long time with the card in his lap, just staring at the lettering on the front. In a weird way, it was like staring at his dad. The chaotic penmanship was the only genuine connection to his father he had had for months. Charlie slid his index finger under the now loosened lip of the envelope and gingerly slid it across the length, freeing it's grasp on the rest of the protective cover. Delicately, he removed the card, a simple black card with *Happy Birthday* written in rainbow-colored letters. Taking a deep breath, he opened it up, reading the inside. While what he had hoped to be inside wasn't, what was there, etched in his dad's scratch, was regrettably just what he had actually expected.

Charlie cocked an eyebrow, closed the greeting and slid it back into the envelope. He chuckled to himself, shaking his head as he made his way back to bed.

■   ■   ■

The sun was already fairly high in the sky when Charlie awoke the next morning to find his sheets kicked off and wrapped around his ankles. He scratched lazily at his nether regions as he ran his itinerary for the day through his head.

"Yep, same as yesterday. Sit in the living room. Sit on the porch. Sit in the garage. Go to bed," he said to no one but himself.

Piercing the morning air, his text message chime brought him a glimmer of hope, and he turned to reach for it. A moment of confusion set in as the little black box was not on the table beside his bed. It chirped again and drew his attention to the floor. Charlie reached down and scooped it up from atop his crumpled t-shirt and checked the screen.

Hey? You awake?
Want to do something today?

He couldn't suppress the grin caused by the text from Madison. It spread across his face like flames running through a field of tall, dry grass. He fired back.

Yeah. Sure. Mind doing something with me first?

Sure. What's up?

Let me grab a shower. I'll hit you back in about 15?

Great.

Charlie popped out of bed and hit the bathroom. Suddenly, the day carried with it a feeling that he hadn't experienced in a good many weeks.

■   ■   ■

Carson was stepping out of the outdoor shower wrapped in a towel at the same time Charlie was wheeling his bike out of the garage. The sight of his brother, smile on his face, bike in hand, backpack in its familiar place, emerging from the garage took him by surprise, and caused him to balk at what he saw.

"Hey. Where are you going? And why…" he pointed at Charlie and made a couple of circular motions like he was stirring an iced drink with his finger, "… so cheerful? What is this? What's happening? What's going on?"

"Hey Carson. Meeting up with Madison."

Carson smiled and arced his eyebrows, "Oh? You two back…"

But Charlie cut him off. "No. Nothing like that. Just hanging out."

Carson nodded and made his way to the back door, clutching the top of the towel folded at his waist with one hand. He paused, one foot on the first step, and turned back. "You open that card yet?" he inquired.

Charlie stopped wheeling, "Yeah. I did."

Carson eyed his brother, looking for some clue as to his emotional state. "Was it what you expected?"

"It wasn't what I had hoped for, but, yeah, it was exactly what I expected."

"You okay?" Carson asked with compassion tinting his words.

"Yeah. I am Carson. Thanks." He smiled at his brother, then added, "Gotta go"

■   ■   ■

The ride to Madison's house was brief, and as expected, she was waiting on the sidewalk, holding on to her bike. Charlie pulled up, smiled, and said hello. It was astonishing to him how just seeing her improved his day.

"Let's go," he said and pedaled towards the Gardens.

"Where are we going?" Madison called after him, pumping hard to catch up.

"Just follow me," Charlie called back.

The two wove through streets and around corners, passing cars and kids alike. As with any bike ride on the north side of the island, it wasn't long before the two arrived at their destination. Charlie hopped off his bike, allowing it to fall to the ground. As Madison pulled in behind him, she hopped off and made her way over to where Charlie was standing.

"Okay, Charlie. Mind telling me why we are standing at the rail on the Longport Bridge?"

"Told you. I have something to do." He shrugged his backpack off his shoulder and pulled it around in front of him so the straps were facing the ocean. He unzipped one of the side pockets and pulled out the card.

Madison tilted her head. "Is that a birthday card?"

"It sure is. From my dad. Want to read it?"

"Charlie. I uhm… I don't know. Isn't that private, between you and your dad?" Madison's discomfort with the idea reflected in her voice.

"You would think. Go ahead." Charlie held out the card, "Honestly. It's okay."

Hesitantly, Madison reached across the distance and took the card from Charlie. She made a quizzical face, to which Charlie nodded. She opened the card and dropped her eyes to read what was written inside. When she was done, she closed the card and handed it back to her friend, "Oh Charlie…"

"Wow, right?" Charlie said with feigned gratification. "What a great message. *Happy birthday, Charlie. Dad.* I mean, the friggin card says Happy Birthday on the cover. So really, all he had to come up with was my name, and his. Maybe added 'love' before his signature? Stellar effort, on Mr. McIntyre's behalf, don't you think?"

"I'm sorry, Charlie."

Charlie brushed it off. "Nah. Don't be. I'm not." He looked out across the ocean from a place he had spent way too much time that summer. "Crazy thing is, Madison, the last time I saw Jackson, he nailed this, this stupid thing I've been doing. He told me I was pushing people away, like I was trying to clear space in my life for someone who had no space in his life for me, and he nailed it. He absolutely fucking nailed it.

"I mean, look at the card. *Happy Birthday, Charlie.* He hasn't spoken to me since February, hasn't even texted, and all he could manage was Happy Birthday? No, *how've you been?* No, *how's life treating you?* No, *how you holding up?* No… *nothing.* It has taken eight months of me burying my head in my own misfortune, and that card, to make me realize that *nothing* is exactly what I need to expect from my dad. So, should I get a text message, or a phone call, or even a card with just a fucking ounce, one fucking ounce of sentiment in it, I'll be pleasantly surprised, because that would be more than I expected. I mean, why the hell should I care? He doesn't."

Madison looked at him thoughtfully, "You care, because he's your dad, and no matter how distant or unavailable he is, he's still your dad." She paused for a second and looked past him, across the inlet, "I guess having parents is like having a spouse; for better or worse, through sickness and health, 'til death do you part." She looked back at Charlie.

"Well, I certainly don't wish him dead," Charlie said, his voice laced with melancholy, "but maybe it's just time for us to part."

What happened next certainly fell into the category of things Charlie didn't expect–which if this summer was a category on Jeopardy, the entire summer sure as hell would fall into the *Things You Didn't Expect* category. Madison stepped in closer, pulling him into a hug, drawing him into her tightly. At first, Charlie didn't know how to respond, because this hug was more than a 'friend' hug, and they were decidedly *only* friends these days. Then, reflexively, his arms closed around the small of her back and he exhaled, breathing out what little poison was left that still coursed through him. He swiftly remembered how safe this simple act felt, how it blocked out the entire world around him, how wonderful, and breathtaking, and intimate it was in its simplicity. Charlie sank into her embrace, clinging to the feeling, not wanting it to end, but if the summer taught him one thing, it was that all things end.

Breaking the embrace, Madison asked, "You sure you're okay? I mean, your dad's absence has weighed on you for so long now."

"Yeah, Madison. I think I am okay. Finally."

Madison saw the honesty in Charlie's eyes. "Okay. Good, but why are we on the bridge, Charlie?"

"To do this." Charlie turned to the railing and flung the card out across the ocean, causing Madison to gasp. They both watched as it arced and banked, cutting swarths through the air, before gravity took control, tugging it down into the rippling water.

"Why did you do that?"

"It needed to be done. *I* need to be done. Holding onto my anger about my dad has cost me so much this summer. Our relationship. My friendship with Jackson, with everyone. But Jackson… that's been the toughest. Earlier in the summer, he told me that with my dad, I was trying to hold back the tide, as impossible as that is, and he was right. I kept thinking that… well, it doesn't matter what I was thinking, because I was wrong. Now, I need to turn the page, end this chapter of my life, and move on. That's what Jackson was telling me. That's what you were telling me that night on the jetty. Let the tide smooth the sand, in a sense."

Madison knew in her heart that Charlie was right. He had clung to the idea of his dad coming back, or even being a part of his life for far too long. That notion had just about consumed him, and Charlie had suffered the ill effect, but there was one frayed thread he needed to tighten up. She knew that if he didn't, he'd suffer the ill effects of that for months, maybe years, to come.

She pressed. "Have you ironed out the wrinkles with Jackson?"

Charlie just shook his head. "He won't take my calls or respond to my texts. So… no."

Madison stepped backwards, treading pretty close to exasperation. "You need to tell him how you feel, Charlie."

Madison's remarks were confusing to Charlie. Did she think he hadn't?

"I have. I've told him I'm sorry a hundred times. He won't have it."

Madison shook her head. "Honestly, boys can be so stupid," she said. "Charlie, sorry is what you *are*. You need to tell him how you *feel*. How you feel about him, and your friendship. You need to tell him that you love him, that he lives right here." She placed her hand palm up on Charlie's chest, right over his heart.

It was Charlie's turn to take a step back. Only he threw in a scoff as added punctuation. In his mind, Madison's suggestion was beyond the pale. "What? I'm not telling him that. Don't be ridiculous."

Madison allowed the exasperation she was keeping at bay to wash over her. "What is so ridiculous about telling your best friend that you love him? You do love him, don't you?" Madison pushed.

Charlie shoved his hands into his pockets, obviously uncomfortable with the question just presented to him. "Well… I mean… yeah. I guess, but I can't tell him that."

"Well, why the hell not?" Madison asked, exasperated.

"Because Madison," Charlie's tone suggesting his own exasperation, "guys don't go around telling their friends, no matter how good a friend they are, that they love them. It's just not what we do, and besides," Charlie looked out across the water again, "I'm not too sure Jackson and I are friends anymore. That's another thing I need to come to terms with and just accept." Charlie let his words disappear on the breeze. Then, with a bit of decisiveness in his tone, he added, "Jackson and I are not friends anymore. There. I said it out loud."

Madison's frustration played out all over her face as if it were ice cream dripping down a toddler's chin. Shaking her head in annoyance, she said, "Boys. I don't get you. You're all freakin morons."

"Yep. We are," Charlie agreed. He moved closer to the railing. Madison sidled up beside him and draped an arm around his shoulder in a gesture that wasn't quite intimate, but a tad bit more than just a friendly squeeze. They both watched as the mint green envelope wafted lazily along the current toward the bay until it disappeared from sight beneath the bridge. As it did, Charlie said, "End of chapter. Turn the page."

CHAPTER LAST

The sun danced and bounced off of the rippling water, sending thousands of diamonds glinting across the surface of the ocean. It was another beautiful day. A cloudless blue sky stretched unendingly on to the horizon, spotted here and there by a seagull, or a small plane trailing a banner advertising something meant for the Shoebies. Around him, vacationers, islanders, and day-trippers alike were sucking the day out of the day.

Charlie sat on his towel, alone, digging his feet into the warm sand, the sun radiating on his back. His surfboard lay fins up next to him, heating in the late afternoon sun. Against his better judgment, and perhaps because he just couldn't bear to listen anymore, he took his mother's advice about finding his own adventure and set out for Morningside Beach to catch some waves. He thought Morningside best, as his friends—ex-friends? Friends-on-hiatus?-wouldn't be there; sticking instead to the more familiar territory further down the island closer to home. He was right. There wasn't a soul in sight that he recognized.

Though the surf was kicking, when he got to the point where he was to head out, the water washing over his feet, soaking his ankles, he stopped. He looked out across the water at the few surfers who were already in the lineup, hoping. Not seeing the one person he truly wished to be there, he turned around and headed back up the slope. Lately, surfing didn't hold the same thrill as it once did. Even when he had surfed alone in the past, there was always a story to recount for Jackson, or an incredible ride he couldn't wait to share. Surfing these days simply reminded him of things he was so desperately trying to forget.

That was about an hour ago. The sun was creeping to the bay side of the island, taking groups of people with it. The crowd was thinning, and the shadows stretching, but Charlie just wasn't ready to head back to the house. There was about a week left before he and his family called the summer a wrap and headed back home. While he was looking forward to putting this summer behind him, he just couldn't bring himself to leave the beach that day. So, he sat, looking out across the vast blueness of the sea, getting used to his new solitary existence, or at least making a gallant effort.

Unlike solid surfaces, which echo footfalls, sand has a way of muffling sound with its yielding, soft nature. Because of this, Charlie was completely unaware that someone was approaching him from behind, nor was he aware that this person had been watching him for quite some time from the edge of the spit-rail fence. Running through his head all the reasons why he should just turn around and head home, as well as all the reasons why he shouldn't; the pros eventually outweighed the cons.

"Dining on ashes?"

Charlie wasn't sure what startled him more, the voice out of nowhere, or the surfboard dropping into the sand beside him, which he immediately recognized. He sprang from a seated position as if the sand he was sitting on ignited. Spinning around in the sound's direction, his breath caught. Charlie was so flummoxed that words escaped him. He stood in the sand, in the late afternoon sun, mouth agape. Still staring in disbelief, he realized he had stopped breathing and took a quick breath. His heart swelled in his chest.

"Hey," Jackson said, tossing his chin in Charlie's direction, his eyes never leaving Charlie's face.

Charlie fought hard to stave off the urge to rush forward, wrap him in a bear hug and swing him around. He struggled to contain the mixture of fear, mingling with unbridled excitement that swirled up from deep within him, causing him to be suddenly nauseous.

He took a couple of deep breaths. "Hey."

The two boys faced each other, on either side of this fresh territory between them that was recognizable, but somehow so strange. It had been weeks since they were in such proximity to one another, let alone in each other's presence at all. There was an awkwardness in the air, arcing like so much electricity from a downed wire, that neither was familiar with, nor knew how to navigate.

Charlie wondered if Jackson's stomach was lurching as violently as his was. He wasn't sure whether this was a final showdown, or first steps towards amends. Either way, in that moment, Charlie knew with all certainty the answer to the question Madison asked him a few days before. *It is so good to see you. I am so sorry I was such a fucking moron. I hope to Christ that you can forgive me and forget that I ever said those awful words because my life without you in it has been absolutely unbearable. I miss you,* was what Charlie wanted to say. Though, what teenage boys want to say, especially when those words convey the depth of feeling they can have for one another, is often a far cry from what they actually do say.

"So, how'd you know I was here?" Charlie asked.

Jackson dug his phone out of the pocket of his bathing suit and shook it at him in a manner that was strangely identical to the way Carson had done that night so many weeks before on the Longport Bridge. "Your location service is still active."

Charlie shifted his weight from one leg to the other. "You came looking for me?"

Jackson bounced his weight from leg to leg as well, but never took his eyes off of Charlie. Nodding, he said, "Yeah. I guess I did.

Um, I saw the surf was up, I checked the app and the report was great, and so I, well, I thought maybe, maybe you and I could catch some waves."

Charlie glanced at the ocean, and then back to Jackson. He could feel his throat tightening, and was worried that if he spoke, he would break. Instead, he used his head to show his agreement.

"Okay. Good." For the first time since arriving, Jackson broke his gaze, glancing away, then back at his friend. "Yeah. Good," he said, bobbing his head.

There was an uncomfortable moment where neither boy knew what to do next, but then Jackson pulled out of his backpack, peeled off his shirt, picked up his board and began walking towards the shoreline. Charlie went to pick up his board, but stopped, leaving it lying in the sand. His heartbeat picked up.

He jogged after his friend and called out, "Jackson, wait. Hold up a sec." His voice was already unsteady. Jackson halted and turned back towards Charlie. He let his board drop into the sand. They closed the small distance between them.

Charlie's throat was tight. He took a few more steps towards Jackson. Charlie was worried that with his throat constricted as it was, he would only be able to manage a whisper. He needed to make sure that Jackson heard what he was about to say. Charlie blew out some air, struggling with his own emotions.

"I see you, Jackson," he said, hoping that Jackson would believe him; *needing* him to believe him. "Right now, standing here in front of me. I see *you.*" A single tear slipped over Charlie's lid, but Charlie wasn't embarrassed by it. He allowed it to slide down his cheek without wiping it away. "And every time we're together, every single time, I'll only see you, Jackson. Just. You. I swear. You have to believe me. Please, believe me."

Jackson stood motionless, which surprised him because inwardly, Charlie's words bowled him over. His eyes brimmed slightly, recognizing the meaning behind what Charlie had said.

Those words were the best apology Jackson could have hoped for. He bobbed his head slowly and said, "I believe you, Charlie. I do."

Charlie blew out the breath he was holding, but he wasn't finished. There was more he had to say, "We've known each other a long time, Jackson. Shit, our whole lives, and you have to know that I..." He exhaled sharply but went on, "Jackson... I hope you know that I... you know..." Charlie looked around self-consciously, running the back of his fingers of one hand over the stubble on his cheek, "I, um, guess, what I'm trying to tell you is that... you know..." he stammered, knowing how profoundly he felt for the kid standing before him, but just not being able to vocalize those emotions into words, because those three words that he had every intention of saying, just couldn't capture the depth of feeling Charlie had for Jackson. Those three words, so hackneyed, so overused, fell incredibly short of expressing how interwoven Jackson was into Charlie's very own being. How greatly Charlie needed Jackson in his life. Those three words could never convey that, could they?

Jackson saved him, "Yeah," he said, "I know." Uncomfortably, Jackson scratched at the back of his head, "Me too, Charlie." Jackson nodded his head a couple of times. "Me too."

Charlie nodded and smiled slightly. "I know."

Once again, Charlie found himself, as he frequently had that summer, squared off with his best friend–shoulder to shoulder, toe to toe. Though this time, the space between them wasn't thick, it wasn't tense; it wasn't hostile. Charlie pulled in his surroundings. The sun glowed orange over the houses, tendrils of light caressing their rooftops. A light breeze rippled over the sand and across his chest, prickling his skin. The waves spilled onto the shoreline, murmuring softly as they broke, speaking to him in a language he held so dear. He was with his best friend, a minor miracle in Charlie's mind. He knew they were forever changed by this summer, by the events of the last few months that had placed them on this new path. A path along which there would need to be strides taken, and time given, until they both once again fell into step with one another, regaining the familiarity and comfort they once shared before June faded into July, which then melted into August. A time before the rising tide of adulthood swept away the few remnants of their childhoods. But this was a start.

For the first time in a very long time, things felt right with Charlie.

In Charlie's head, it seemed an eternity had passed as the two of them stood staring at one another, there in the sand, in the place he loved the most. Or maybe it was just a millisecond. When moments are perfect, they tend to get lost in time.

Jackson broke the quiet, "Now," he said softly, tossing his head towards the ocean, "what do you say we get in the water before we do something stupid, like hug?"

Jackson's words struck a chord, causing a chuckle to escape Charlie. "I've been doing stupid things all summer," Charlie said as he took a step forward and pulled his friend into an embrace. It was another moment, one scary moment, wherein Charlie thought his heart might explode.

ACKNOWLEDGMENTS

I have to first thank Karin, my wonderfully patient and uber supportive better half. From the onset of the first chapter through the final edit, she has read, reread, and reread again every one of the roughly 130,000 plus words that make up this novel. Her never-ending encouragement saw me through countless months of writing, and bolstered me through the struggle and self-doubt. I also must thank my two children, Joshua and Emma. Their enthusiasm for this novel and their confidence in its quality gave me the conviction to push through the rejections and keep trying until *Holding Back the Tide* found its home. Without the support of my family, you wouldn't have just read this book.

It would be remiss of me if I didn't mention others who were instrumental in this novel's success. Dana Klein, and Noreen Fantasia, two of the earliest readers of my manuscript. The feedback they provided was invaluable. Conversations about dialogue, situations, and just how kids would or wouldn't react were most helpful, and gave truth to the characters born within these pages.

I owe thanks to Tim Smyth, fellow teacher and author of the outstanding educational book *Teaching with Comics and Graphic Novels*. I am convinced that his guidance and advice during the arduous query stage on the road to publication was instrumental in me getting my foot in Black Rose Writing's door.

Speaking of which, I must thank Reagan Rothe and the team at Black Rose Writing for publishing this novel and giving it the chance to be read. It is somewhat fitting that I was sitting on the beach in Ocean City when I read Reagan's email offering me a book deal. From the beginning, the publishing process was cordial, efficient, and a pleasure. Reagan was quick to answer my many questions, no matter what time of day I fired off an email. I often wondered when, or if, the man slept. I would also like to thank David King and his team. They did a remarkable job designing the cover, and were most helpful with the myriad of further edits and revisions that took place before publication. Publishing with Black Rose Writing has simply been superb.

My editor, Brianna DePerro, is owed great kudos for the hours of dedicated work and her skilled eye. Thank you for coming along on this adventure and making *Holding Back the Tide* the very best book it could be. From typos, and grammatical errors, to narration that went on perhaps a bit too long, and untying knotted up sentences, Brianna's help was instrumental in getting this book to publication.

Of course, I owed a debt of gratitude to the Wahl/Kunzier family: Liz, Mary, Jonathan, Tina, Jack, Claire, Libby, William, and Brendan. Decades ago, this wonderful, crazy, remarkable clan introduced this Shoebie and my family to Ocean City, New Jersey, bestowed upon us honorary islander status, and turned us into lovers of Third Street Beach. Thank you for always opening up 712 to us; especially the use of the outdoor shower!

My last nod goes to Dave and Sue Brown. Thank you for every invitation to OCNJ, and making 233 a home away from home for us.

ABOUT THE AUTHOR

Frank DeRuosi grew up in East Boston, Massachusetts. He currently lives in Ambler, Pennsylvania, with his wife, Karin. He has two grown children, Joshua, a carpenter and an Antarctic explorer, and Emma, a graphic designer.

Frank's favorite place to write is the worn, leather recliner in the sun room, accompanied by a cup of coffee that he never really finishes. When he isn't writing, Frank and Karin can often be found on their patio enjoying the pleasant ambiance of a wood fire, and the company of good friends and family.

By day, Frank is a teacher at Blue Bell Elementary with 20 years of experience. Presently, he teaches second grade.

Holding Back the Tide is his first novel. You can follow Frank on Facebook at Frank DeRuosi, Author, and on Instagram at frank_deruosi_author.

NOTE FROM THE AUTHOR

Word-of-mouth is crucial for any author to succeed. If you enjoyed *Holding Back the Tide*, please leave a review online—anywhere you are able. Even if it's just a sentence or two. It would make all the difference and would be very much appreciated.

Thanks!
Frank J. DeRuosi

We hope you enjoyed reading this title from:

BLACK ROSE
writing™

www.blackrosewriting.com

Subscribe to our mailing list – *The Rosevine* – and receive **FREE** books, daily deals, and stay current with news about upcoming
releases and our hottest authors.
Scan the QR code below to sign up.

Already a subscriber? Please accept a sincere thank you for being a fan of Black Rose Writing authors.

View other Black Rose Writing titles at
www.blackrosewriting.com/books and use promo code
PRINT to receive a **20% discount** when purchasing.

CPSIA information can be obtained
at www.ICGtesting.com
Printed in the USA
JSHW021955260723
45458JS00001B/22